# JOSEPH CONRAD

# LORD JIM

## A TALE

First included in the Premier Classics Series, 2008

Chronology © 1992 by Knopf Publishing Group

ISBN-13: 978-0-307-29153-0
ISBN-10: 0-307-29153-7

Printed in the United States

This Premier Classics Paperback edition printed in 2008

# CONTENTS

---

# LORD JIM

# CHRONOLOGY

| DATE | AUTHOR'S LIFE | LITERARY CONTEXT |
|------|---------------|------------------|
| 1853 | | Charlotte Brontë: *Villette.* |
| 1856 | Marriage of Apollo Korzeniowski to Ewelina Bobrowska in Oratów. | Bernard Shaw born. |
| 1857 | December 3: birth of their son, Józef Teodor Konrad Korzeniowski (later to be known as Joseph Conrad). | Flaubert: *Madame Bovary.* Baudelaire: *Fleurs du mal.* |
| 1859 | Family moves to Żytomierz. | Dickens: *A Tale of Two Cities.* |
| 1861 | Apollo Korzeniowski arrested in Warsaw for patriotic conspiracy. | Dickens: *Great Expectations.* |
| 1862 | Conrad's parents exiled to Vologda, Russia: he accompanies them. | Turgenev: *Fathers and Sons.* Ruskin: *Unto This Last.* |
| 1863 | Family moved to Chernikhov. | Thackeray dies. |
| 1865 | Death of Conrad's mother. | Birth of Kipling and Yeats. |
| 1866 | Stays with uncle at Nowochwastów. | Dostoevsky: *Crime and Punishment.* |
| 1869 | Death of Apollo Korzeniowski; Conrad becomes ward of relatives. | Tolstoy: *War and Peace.* |
| 1870 | Taught by Adam Pulman in Kraków. | Charles Dickens dies. |
| 1871 | Also taught by Isydor Kopernicki. | Dostoevsky: *The Devils.* |
| 1872 | Resolves to go to sea. | George Eliot: *Middlemarch.* |
| 1874 | Leaves Poland for Marseille to join French merchant navy. | Hardy: *Far from the Madding Crowd.* |
| 1875 | Sails Atlantic on *Mont-Blanc.* | Thomas Mann born. |
| 1876 | Serves as steward on *Saint-Antoine.* | Death of George Sand. |
| 1877 | Possibly involved in smuggling arms to Spanish royalists. | Tolstoy: *Anna Karenina.* |
| 1878 | Shoots himself in chest, recovers, and joins British ship *Mavis.* | Hardy: *The Return of the Native.* |
| 1879 | Serves on clipper *Duke of Sutherland.* | Ibsen: *A Doll's House.* |
| 1880 | Sails to Australia on *Loch Etive.* | Dostoevsky: *The Brothers Karamazov.* |
| 1881 | Second mate of *Palestine.* | Death of Dostoevsky and Carlyle. |

## HISTORICAL EVENTS

Crimean War begins.
Crimean War ends. Freud born.


Indian Mutiny.


Darwin's *Origin of Species*.
Emancipation of Russian serfs.
American Civil War begins.
Bismarck gains power in Prussia.


American slaves freed. Polish uprising.
American Civil War ends.


Gandhi born. Suez Canal opens.


Franco-Prussian War. Lenin born.

Paris Commune.

Mazzini dies. Bertrand Russell born.
Winston Churchill born.


Bakunin dies.

Russia declares war on Turkey.

Afghan War. Congress of Berlin.

Zulu War. Einstein and Stalin born.


Tsar Alexander II assassinated.

| DATE | AUTHOR'S LIFE | LITERARY CONTEXT |
|---|---|---|
| 1882 | Storm-damaged *Palestine* repaired. | Birth of Virginia Woolf and James Joyce. |
| 1883 | Shipwrecked when *Palestine* sinks. | Nietzsche: *Thus Spake Zarathustra*. |
| 1885 | Sails to Calcutta on *Tilkhurst*. | Birth of D. H. Lawrence. |
| 1886 | Takes British nationality; qualifies as captain. | Stevenson: *Dr Jekyll and Mr Hyde*. |
| 1887 | Sails to Java on *Highland Forest*. | Birth of Marianne Moore. |
| 1888 | Master of the ship *Otago*. | Birth of T. S. Eliot. |
| 1889 | Resigns from *Otago* and settles in London, writing *Almayer's Folly*. | Death of Robert Browning. |
| 1890 | Works in Belgian Congo. | Ibsen: *Hedda Gabler*. |
| 1891 | Officer of *Torrens* until 1893. | Hardy: *Tess of the D'Urbervilles*. |
| 1894 | *Almayer's Folly* accepted by Unwin. Meets Edward Garnett and Jessie George. | R. L. Stevenson dies; Aldous Huxley born. Kipling: *The Jungle Book*. |
| 1895 | *Almayer's Folly* published. | Crane: *The Red Badge of Courage*. Hardy: *Jude the Obscure*. |
| 1896 | *An Outcast of the Islands*. Marries Jessie George. Meets H. G. Wells. | William Morris dies; Scott Fitzgerald born. |
| 1897 | Corresponds with Cunninghame Graham. *The Nigger of the 'Narcissus'*. | Kipling: *Captains Courageous*. |
| 1898 | *Tales of Unrest*. Enters collaboration with Ford Madox Hueffer (later known as Ford Madox Ford). First son, Borys, born. | Wilde: 'Ballad of Reading Gaol'. Wells: *War of the Worlds*. Rilke: *Advent*. |
| 1899 | *Heart of Darkness* serialized. Serialization of *Lord Jim* begins. | Birth of Hemingway. |
| 1900 | *Lord Jim* (book). J. B. Pinker becomes Conrad's agent. | Death of Ruskin, Nietzsche, Oscar Wilde and Stephen Crane. |
| 1901 | *The Inheritors* (co-author Hueffer). | Kipling: *Kim*. |
| 1902 | *Youth* volume. | Gorky: *The Lower Depths*. |
| 1903 | *Typhoon* volume. *Romance* (co-author Hueffer). | James: *The Ambassadors*. Birth of George Orwell. |
| 1904 | *Nostromo*. | Chekhov: *The Cherry Orchard*. |
| 1905 | *One Day More* (play) fails. | Wells: *Kipps*. |
| 1906 | *The Mirror of the Sea* (with Hueffer). Second son, John, born. | Samuel Beckett born. Ibsen dies. |
| 1907 | *The Secret Agent*. | Birth of W. H. Auden. |
| 1908 | *A Set of Six* (tales). | Bennett: *The Old Wives' Tale*. |

HISTORICAL EVENTS

Death of Garibaldi and Darwin.

Marx dies. Mussolini born.


Cunninghame Graham becomes MP.

'Bloody Sunday': Graham arrested.
Wilhelm II becomes Kaiser.
London Dock Strike
Hitler born.
Bismarck resigns.

Nicholas II becomes Tsar.
Greenwich bomb outrage.

Engels dies.


McKinley elected President.


Queen Victoria's Diamond Jubilee.


War between Spain and USA.
Death of Bismarck and Gladstone.
Curies discover radium.


Boer War (until 1902).
First Hague Conference.
Russia occupies Manchuria.


Queen Victoria dies.

Panama secedes from Colombia.
First aircraft flight.
Russo-Japanese War (until 1905).
Russian Revolution: Duma founded.
Anglo-Russian Entente.
San Francisco earthquake.

Second Hague conference.
Austria annexes Bosnia and Herzegovina.

| DATE | AUTHOR'S LIFE | LITERARY CONTEXT |
|------|---------------|------------------|
| 1909 | Quarrels with Hueffer. | Death of Swinburne. |
| 1910 | Moves to Capel House, near Ashford. | Yeats: *The Green Helmet.* |
| 1911 | *Under Western Eyes.* | William Golding born. |
| 1912 | *A Personal Record. 'Twixt Land and Sea* (tales). *Chance* serialized in *New York Herald.* | Patrick White born. Pound: *Ripostes.* |
| 1913 | Meets Bertrand Russell. | Lawrence: *Sons and Lovers.* |
| 1914 | Book of *Chance* has large sales. Conrad becomes prosperous at last. | Joyce: *Dubliners.* Birth of Dylan Thomas. |
| 1915 | *Within the Tides* (tales); *Victory.* | Lawrence: *The Rainbow.* |
| 1916 | *The Shadow-Line* serialized. | Henry James dies. |
| 1917 | *The Shadow-Line* (book). | Anthony Burgess born. |
| 1918 | Borys Conrad wounded in war. | Death of Wilfred Owen. |
| 1919 | *The Arrow of Gold.* | Woolf: *Night and Day.* |
| 1920 | *The Rescue.* | Lawrence: *Women in Love.* Katherine Mansfield: *Bliss.* |
| 1921 | *Notes on Life and Letters.* | Huxley: *Crome Yellow.* |
| 1922 | *The Secret Agent* (play) fails. | Eliot: *The Waste Land.* Joyce: *Ulysses.* |
| 1923 | Visits USA to acclamation. *The Rover.* | Yeats wins Nobel Prize. Huxley: *Antic Hay.* |
| 1924 | Declines knighthood. Dies of heart attack; buried at Canterbury. | Forster: *A Passage to India.* Shaw: *Saint Joan.* |
| 1925 | Publication of *Tales of Hearsay* and the unfinished *Suspense.* | Eliot: *Poems 1909–25.* Shaw wins Nobel Prize. |
| 1926 | *Last Essays.* | Kafka: *The Castle.* |
| 1927 | *Joseph Conrad: Life & Letters,* written and edited by G. Jean-Aubry. | Woolf: *To the Lighthouse.* |

# CHRONOLOGY

---

When this novel first appeared in book form a notion got about that I had been bolted away with. Some reviewers maintained that the work starting as a short story had got beyond the writer's control. One or two discovered internal evidence of the fact, which seemed to amuse them. They pointed out the limitations of the narrative form. They argued that no man could have been expected to talk all that time, and other men to listen so long. It was not, they said, very credible.

After thinking it over for something like sixteen years I am not so sure about that. Men have been known, both in the tropics and the temperate zone, to sit up half the night 'swapping yarns'. This, however, is but one yarn, yet with interruptions affording some measure of relief; and in regard to the listeners' endurance, the postulate must be accepted that the story *was* interesting. It is the necessary preliminary assumption. If I hadn't believed that it *was* interesting I could never have begun to write it. As to the mere physical possibility we all know that some speeches in Parliament have taken nearer six than three hours in delivery; whereas all that part of the book which is Marlow's narrative can be read through aloud, I should say, in less than three hours. Besides – though I have kept strictly all such insignificant details out of the tale – we may presume that there must have been refreshments on that night, a glass of mineral water of some sort to help the narrator on.

But, seriously, the truth of the matter is, that my first thought was of a short story, concerned only with the pilgrim ship episode; nothing more. And that was a legitimate conception. After writing a few pages, however, I became for some reason discontented and I laid them aside for a time. I didn't take them out of the drawer till the late Mr William Blackwood suggested I should give something again to his magazine.

It was only then that I perceived that the pilgrim ship episode was a good starting-point for a free and wandering tale; that it was an event, too, which could conceivably colour the whole 'sentiment of existence' in a simple and sensitive character. But all these preliminary moods and stirrings of spirit were rather obscure at the time, and they do not appear clearer to me now after the lapse of so many years.

The few pages I had laid aside were not without their weight in the choice of subject. But the whole was re-written deliberately. When I sat down to it I knew it would be a long book, though I didn't foresee that it would spread itself over thirteen numbers of 'Maga'.

I have been asked at times whether this was not the book of mine I liked best. I am a great foe to favouritism in public life, in private life, and even in the delicate relationship of an author to his works. As a matter of principle I will have no favourites; but I don't go so far as to feel grieved and annoyed by the preference some people give to my Lord Jim. I won't even say that I 'fail to understand . . .' No! But once I had occasion to be puzzled and surprised.

A friend of mine returning from Italy had talked with a lady there who did not like the book. I regretted that, of course, but what surprised me was the ground of her dislike. 'You know,' she said, 'it is all so morbid.'

The pronouncement gave me food for an hour's anxious thought. Finally I arrived at the conclusion that, making due allowances for the subject itself being rather foreign to women's normal sensibilities, the lady could not have been an Italian. I wonder whether she was European at all? In any case, no Latin temperament would have perceived anything morbid in the acute consciousness of lost honour. Such a consciousness may be wrong, or it may be right, or it may be condemned as artificial; and, perhaps, my Jim is not a type of wide commoness. But I can safely assure my readers that he is not the product of coldly perverted thinking. He's not a figure of Northern Mists either. One sunny morning in the commonplace surroundings of an Eastern roadstead, I saw his form pass by – appealing – significant – under a cloud – perfectly silent. Which is as it should be. It was for me, with all the sympathy of which I was capable, to seek fit words for his meaning. He was 'one of us'.

*June, 1917.*                                                    J.C.

# LORD JIM

To
Mr and Mrs G. F. W. Hope
with grateful affection
after many years
of friendship

'It is certain
my conviction gains infinitely
the moment another soul
will believe in it'

*Novalis*

# CHAPTER ONE

HE WAS an inch, perhaps two, under six feet, powerfully built, and he advanced straight at you with a slight stoop of the shoulders, head forward, and a fixed from-under stare which made you think of a charging bull. His voice was deep, loud, and his manner displayed a kind of dogged self-assertion which had nothing aggressive in it. It seemed a necessity, and it was directed apparently as much at himself as at anybody else. He was spotlessly neat, apparelled in immaculate white from shoes to hat, and in the various Eastern ports where he got his living as ship-chandler's water-clerk he was very popular.

A water-clerk need not pass an examination in anything under the sun, but he must have Ability in the abstract and demonstrate it practically. His work consists in racing under sail, steam, or oars against other water-clerks for any ship about to anchor, greeting her captain cheerily, forcing upon him a card – the business card of the ship-chandler – and on his first visit on shore piloting him firmly but without ostentation to a vast, cavern-like shop which is full of things that are eaten and drunk on board ship; where you can get everything to make her seaworthy and beautiful, from a set of chain-hooks for her cable to a book of gold-leaf for the carvings of her stern; and where her commander is received like a brother by a ship-chandler he has never seen before. There is a cool parlour, easy-chairs, bottles, cigars, writing implements, a copy of harbour regulations, and a warmth of welcome that melts the salt of a three months' passage out of a seaman's heart. The connection thus begun is kept up, as long as the ship remains in harbour, by the daily visits of the water-clerk. To the captain he is faithful like a friend and attentive like a son, with the patience of Job, the unselfish devotion of a woman, and the jollity of a boon companion. Later on the bill is sent in. It is a beautiful and humane occupation. Therefore good water-clerks are scarce. When a water-clerk who possesses Ability in the abstract has also the advantage of having been brought up to the sea, he is worth to his employer a lot of money and some humouring. Jim had always good wages and as much humouring as would have bought the fidelity of a fiend. Nevertheless, with black ingratitude he would throw up the job suddenly and depart. To his employers the reasons he gave were obviously inadequate. They said 'Confounded fool!' as soon as his back was turned. This was their criticism on his exquisite sensibility.

To the white men in the waterside business and to the captains of ships he was just Jim — nothing more. He had, of course, another name, but he was anxious that it should not be pronounced. His incognito, which had as many holes as a sieve, was not meant to hide a personality but a fact. When the fact broke through the incognito he would leave suddenly the seaport where he happened to be at the time and go to another — generally farther east. He kept to seaports because he was a seaman in exile from the sea, and had Ability in the abstract, which is good for no other work but that of a water-clerk. He retreated in good order towards the rising sun, and the fact followed him casually but inevitably. Thus in the course of years he was known successively in Bombay, in Calcutta, in Rangoon, in Penang, in Batavia — and in each of these halting-places was just Jim the water-clerk. Afterwards, when his keen perception of the Intolerable drove him away for good from seaports and white men, even into the virgin forest, the Malays of the jungle village, where he had elected to conceal his deplorable faculty, added a word to the monosyllable of his incognito. They called him Tuan Jim: as one might say — Lord Jim.

Originally he came from a parsonage. Many comman-
ders of fine merchant-ships come from these abodes of
piety and peace. Jim's father possessed such certain knowledge of the Unknowable as made for the righteousness of
people in cottages without disturbing the ease of mind
of those whom an unerring Providence enables to live in
mansions. The little church on a hill had the mossy greyness of a rock seen through a ragged screen of leaves. It had
stood there for centuries, but the trees around probably
remembered the laying of the first stone. Below, the red
front of the rectory gleamed with a warm tint in the midst
of grass-plots, flower-beds, and fir-trees, with an orchard
at the back, a paved stable-yard to the left, and the sloping
glass of green-houses tacked along a wall of bricks. The
living had belonged to the family for generations; but Jim
was one of five sons, and when after a course of light
holiday literature his vocation for the sea had declared
itself, he was sent at once to a 'training-ship for officers of
the mercantile marine.'

He learned there a little trigonometry and how to cross
top-gallant yards. He was generally liked. He had the third
place in navigation and pulled stroke in the first cutter.
Having a steady head with an excellent physique, he was
very smart aloft. His station was in the fore-top, and often
from there he looked down, with the contempt of a man
destined to shine in the midst of dangers, at the peaceful
multitude of roofs cut in two by the brown tide of the
stream, while scattered on the outskirts of the surrounding
plain the factory chimneys rose perpendicular against a
grimy sky, each slender like a pencil, and belching out
smoke like a volcano. He could see the big ships departing,
the broad-beamed ferries constantly on the move, the little
boats floating far below his feet, with the hazy splendour of
the sea in the distance, and the hope of a stirring life in the
world of adventure.

On the lower deck in the babel of two hundred voices he
would forget himself, and beforehand live in his mind the

sea-life of light literature. He saw himself saving people
from sinking ships, cutting away masts in a hurricane,
swimming through a surf with a line; or as a lonely cast-
away, barefooted and half naked, walking on uncovered
reefs in search of shellfish to stave off starvation. He confronted savages on tropical shores, quelled mutinies on the
high seas, and in a small boat upon the ocean kept up the
hearts of despairing men – always an example of devotion
to duty, and as unflinching as a hero in a book.

'Something's up. Come along.'

He leaped to his feet. The boys were streaming up the
ladders. Above could be heard a great scurrying about and
shouting, and when he got through the hatchway he stood
still – as if confounded.

It was the dusk of a winter's day. The gale had freshened
since noon, stopping the traffic on the river and now blew
with the strength of a hurricane in fitful bursts that boomed
like salvoes of great guns firing over the ocean. The rain
slanted in sheets that flicked and subsided, and between
whiles Jim had threatening glimpses of the tumbling tide,
the small craft jumbled and tossing along the shore, the
motionless buildings in the driving mist, the broad ferry-
boats pitching ponderously at anchor, the vast landing-
stages heaving up and down and smothered in sprays.
The next gust seemed to blow all this away. The air was
full of flying water. There was a fierce purpose in the gale, a
furious earnestness in the screech of the wind, in the brutal
tumult of earth and sky, that seemed directed at him, and
made him hold his breath in awe. He stood still. It seemed
to him he was whirled around.

He was jostled. 'Man the cutter!' Boys rushed past him.
A coaster running in for shelter had crashed through a
schooner at anchor, and one of the ship's instructors had
seen the accident. A mob of boys clambered on the rails,
clustered round the davits. 'Collision. Just ahead of us.
Mr Symons saw it.' A push made him stagger against
the mizzen-mast, and he caught hold of a rope. The old

training-ship chained to her moorings quivered all over, bowing gently head to wind, and with her scanty rigging humming in a deep bass the breathless song of her youth at sea. 'Lower away!' He saw the boat, manned, drop swiftly below the rail, and rushed after her. He heard a splash. 'Let go; clear the falls!' He leaned over. The river alongside seethed in frothy streaks. The cutter could be seen in the falling darkness under the spell of tide and wind, that for a moment held her bound, and tossing abreast of the ship. A yelling voice in her reached him faintly: 'Keep stroke, you young whelps, if you want to save anybody! Keep stroke!' And suddenly she lifted high her bow, and, leaping with raised oars over a wave, broke the spell cast upon her by the wind and tide.

Jim felt his shoulder gripped firmly. 'Too late, young-ster.' The captain of the ship laid a restraining hand on that boy, who seemed on the point of leaping overboard, and Jim looked up with the pain of conscious defeat in his eyes. The captain smiled sympathetically. 'Better luck next time. This will teach you to be smart.'

A shrill cheer greeted the cutter. She came dancing back half full of water, and with two exhausted men washing about on her bottom boards. The tumult and the menace of wind and sea now appeared very contemptible to Jim, increasing the regret of his awe at their inefficient menace. Now he knew what to think of it. It seemed to him he cared nothing for the gale. He could affront greater perils. He would do so – better than anybody. Not a particle of fear was left. Nevertheless he brooded apart that evening while the bowman of the cutter – a boy with a face like a girl's and big grey eyes – was the hero of the lower deck. Eager questioners crowded round him. He narrated: 'I just saw his head bobbing, and I dashed my boat-hook in the water. It caught in his breeches and I nearly went overboard, as I thought I would, only old Symons let go the tiller and grabbed my legs – the boat nearly swamped. Old Symons is a fine old chap. I don't mind a bit him being grumpy with us. He swore at me all the time he held my leg, but that was only his way of telling me to stick to the boat-hook. Old Symons is awfully excitable – isn't he? No – not the little fair chap – the other, the big one with a beard. When we pulled him in he groaned, "Oh, my leg! oh, my leg!" and turned up his eyes. Fancy such a big chap fainting like a girl. Would any of you fellows faint for a jab with a boat-hook? – I wouldn't. It went into his leg so far.' He showed the boat-hook, which he had carried below for the purpose, and produced a sensation. 'No, silly! It was not his flesh that held him – his breeches did. Lots of blood, of course.'

Jim thought it a pitiful display of vanity. The gale had ministered to a heroism as spurious as its own pretence of terror. He felt angry with the brutal tumult of earth and sky for taking him unawares and checking unfairly a generous readiness for narrow escapes. Otherwise he was rather glad he had not gone into the cutter, since a lower achievement had served the turn. He had enlarged his knowledge more than those who had done the work. When all men flinched, then – he felt sure – he alone would know how to deal with the spurious menace of wind and seas. He knew what to think of it. Seen dispassionately, it seemed contemptible. He could detect no trace of emotion in himself, and the final effect of a staggering event was that, unnoticed and apart from the noisy crowd of boys, he exulted with fresh certitude in his avidity for adventure, and in a sense of many-sided courage.

# CHAPTER TWO

AFTER two years of training he went to sea, and entering the regions so well known to his imagination, found them strangely barren of adventure. He made many voyages. He knew the magic monotony of existence between sky and water: he had to bear the criticism of men, the exactions of the sea, and the prosaic severity of the daily task that gives bread – but whose only reward is in the perfect love of the work. This reward eluded him. Yet he could not go back, because there is nothing more enticing, disenchanting, and enslaving than the life at sea. Besides, his prospects were good. He was gentlemanly, steady, tractable, with a thorough knowledge of his duties; and in time, when yet very young, he became chief mate of a fine ship, without ever having been tested by those events of the sea that show in the light of day the inner worth of a man, the edge of his temper, and the fibre of his stuff; that reveal the quality of his resistance and the secret truth of his pretences, not only to others but also to himself.

Only once in all that time he had again the glimpse of the earnestness in the anger of the sea. That truth is not so often made apparent as people might think. There are many shades in the danger of adventures and gales, and it is only now and then that there appears on the face of facts a sinister violence of intention – that indefinable something which forces it upon the mind and the heart of a man, that this complication of accidents or these elemental furies are coming at him with a purpose of malice, with a strength beyond control, with an unbridled cruelty that means to tear out of him his hope and his fear, the pain of his fatigue and his longing for rest: which means to smash, to destroy, to annihilate all he had seen, known, loved, enjoyed, or hated; all that is priceless and necessary – the sunshine, the memories, the future, – which means to sweep the whole precious world utterly away from his sight by the simple and appalling act of taking his life.

Jim, disabled by a falling spar at the beginning of a week of which his Scottish captain used to say afterwards, 'Man! it's a pairfect meeracle to me how she lived through it!' spent many days stretched on his back, dazed, battered, hopeless, and tormented as if at the bottom of an abyss of unrest. He did not care what the end would be, and in his lucid moments overvalued his indifference. The danger, when not seen, has the imperfect vagueness of human thought. The fear grows shadowy; and Imagination, the enemy of men, the father of all terrors, unstimulated, sinks to rest in the dulness of exhausted emotion. Jim saw nothing but the disorder of his tossed cabin. He lay there battened down in the midst of a small devastation, and felt secretly glad he had not to go on deck. But now and again an uncontrollable rush of anguish would grip him bodily, make him gasp and writhe under the blankets, and then the unintelligent brutality of an existence liable to the agony of such sensations filled him with a despairing desire to escape at any cost. Then fine weather returned, and he thought no more about it.

His lameness, however, persisted, and when the ship arrived at an Eastern port he had to go to the hospital. His recovery was slow, and he was left behind.

There were only two other patients in the white men's ward: the purser of a gunboat, who had broken his leg falling down a hatchway; and a kind of railway contractor from a neighbouring province, afflicted by some mysterious tropical disease, who held the doctor for an ass, and indulged in secret debaucheries of patent medicine which his Tamil servant used to smuggle in with unwearied devotion. They told each other the story of their lives, played cards a little, or, yawning and in pyjamas, lounged through

the day in easy-chairs without saying a word. The hospital
stood on a hill, and a gentle breeze entering through the
windows, always flung wide open, brought into the bare
room the softness of the sky, the languor of the earth, the
bewitching breath of the Eastern waters. There were per-
fumes in it, suggestions of infinite repose, the gift of endless dreams. Jim looked every day over the thickets of
gardens, beyond the roofs of the town, over the fronds of
palms growing on the shore, at that roadstead which is a
thoroughfare to the East, – at the roadstead dotted by
garlanded islets, lighted by festal sunshine, its ships like
toys, its brilliant activity resembling a holiday pageant,
with the eternal serenity of the Eastern sky overhead and
the smiling peace of the Eastern seas possessing the space
as far as the horizon.

Directly he could walk without a stick, he descended
into the town to look for some opportunity to get home.
Nothing offered just then, and, while waiting, he associated naturally with the men of his calling in the port.
These were of two kinds. Some, very few and seen there but
seldom, led mysterious lives, had preserved an undefaced
energy with the temper of buccaneers and the eyes of
dreamers. They appeared to live in a crazy maze of plans,
hopes, dangers, enterprises, ahead of civilisation, in the
dark places of the sea; and their death was the only event
of their fantastic existence that seemed to have a reasonable
certitude of achievement. The majority were men who,
like himself, thrown there by some accident, had remained
as officers of country ships. They had now a horror of
the home service, with its harder conditions, severer
view of duty, and the hazard of stormy oceans. They
were attuned to the eternal peace of Eastern sky and
sea. They loved short passages, good deck-chairs,
large native crews, and the distinction of being white.
They shuddered at the thought of hard work, and led
precariously easy lives, always on the verge of dismissal,
always on the verge of engagement, serving Chinamen,

Arabs, half-castes – would have served the devil himself had he made it easy enough. They talked everlastingly of turns of luck: how So-and-so got charge of a boat on the coast of China – a soft thing; how this one had an easy billet in Japan somewhere, and that one was doing well in the Siamese navy; and in all they said – in their actions, in their looks, in their persons – could be detected the soft spot, the place of decay, the determination to lounge safely through existence.

To Jim that gossiping crowd, viewed as seamen, seemed at first more unsubstantial than so many shadows. But at length he found a fascination in the sight of those men, in their appearance of doing so well on such a small allowance of danger and toil. In time, beside the original disdain there grew up slowly another sentiment; and suddenly, giving up the idea of going home, he took a berth as chief mate of the *Patna*.

The *Patna* was a local steamer as old as the hills, lean like a greyhound, and eaten up with rust worse than a condemned water-tank. She was owned by a Chinaman, chartered by an Arab, and commanded by a sort of renegade New South Wales German, very anxious to curse publicly his native country, but who, apparently on the strength of Bismarck's victorious policy, brutalised all those he was not afraid of, and wore a 'blood-and-iron' air, combined with a purple nose and a red moustache. After she had been painted outside and whitewashed inside, eight hundred pilgrims (more or less) were driven on board of her as she lay with steam up alongside a wooden jetty.

They streamed aboard over three gangways, they streamed in urged by faith and the hope of paradise, they streamed in with a continuous tramp and shuffle of bare feet, without a word, a murmur, or a look back; and when clear of confining rails spread on all sides over the deck, flowed forward and aft, overflowed down the yawning hatchways, filled the inner recesses of the ship – like water filling a cistern, like water flowing into crevices and crannies, like water rising silently even with the rim. Eight hundred men and women with faith and hopes, with affections and memories, they had collected there, coming from north and south and from the outskirts of the East, after treading the jungle paths, descending the rivers, coasting in praus along the shallows, crossing in small canoes from island to island, passing through suffering, meeting strange sights, beset by strange fears, upheld by one desire. They came from solitary huts in the wilderness, from populous campongs, from villages by the sea. At the call of an idea they had left their forests, their clearings, the protection of their rulers, their prosperity, their poverty, the surroundings of their youth and the graves of their fathers. They came covered with dust, with sweat, with grime, with rags – the strong men at the head of family parties, the lean old men pressing forward without hope of return; young boys with fearless eyes glancing curiously, shy little girls with tumbled long hair; the timid women muffled up and clasping to their breasts, wrapped in loose ends of soiled headcloths, their sleeping babies, the unconscious pilgrims of an exacting belief.

'Look at dese cattle,' said the German skipper to his new chief mate.

An Arab, the leader of that pious voyage, came last. He walked slowly aboard, handsome and grave in his white gown and large turban. A string of servants followed, loaded with his luggage; the *Patna* cast off and backed away from the wharf.

She was headed between two small islets, crossed obliquely the anchoring-ground of sailing-ships, swung through half a circle in the shadow of a hill, then ranged close to a ledge of foaming reefs. The Arab standing up aft, recited aloud the prayer of travellers by sea. He invoked the favour of the Most High upon that journey, implored His blessing on men's toil and on the secret purposes of their hearts; the steamer pounded in the dusk the calm water of the Strait; and far astern of the pilgrim ship a screw-pile lighthouse, planted by unbelievers on a treacherous shoal, seemed to wink at her its eye of flame, as if in derision of her errand of faith.

She cleared the Strait, crossed the bay, continued on her way through the 'One-degree' passage. She held on straight for the Red Sea under a serene sky, under a sky scorching and unclouded, enveloped in a fulgor of sunshine that killed all thought, oppressed the heart, withered all impulses of strength and energy. And under the sinister splendour of that sky the sea, blue and profound, remained still, without a stir, without a ripple, without a wrinkle – viscous, stagnant, dead. The *Patna*, with a slight hiss, passed over that plain luminous and smooth, unrolled a black ribbon of smoke across the sky, left behind her on the water a white ribbon of foam that vanished at once, like the phantom of a track drawn upon a lifeless sea by the phantom of a steamer.

Every morning the sun, as if keeping pace in his revolutions with the progress of the pilgrimage, emerged with a silent burst of light exactly at the same distance astern of the ship, caught up with her at noon, pouring the concentrated fire of his rays on the pious purposes of the men, glided past on his descent, and sank mysteriously into the sea evening after evening, preserving the same distance ahead of her advancing bows. The five whites on board lived amidships, isolated from the human cargo. The awnings covered the deck with a white roof from stem to stern, and a faint hum, a low murmur of sad voices, alone revealed the presence of a crowd of people upon the great blaze of the ocean. Such were the days, still, hot, heavy, disappearing one by one into the past, as if falling into an abyss for ever open in the wake of the ship; and the ship, lonely under a wisp of smoke, held on her steadfast way black and smouldering in a luminous immensity, as if scorched by a flame flicked at her from a heaven without pity.

The nights descended on her like a benediction.

# CHAPTER THREE

A MARVELLOUS stillness pervaded the world, and the stars, together with the serenity of their rays, seemed to shed upon the earth the assurance of everlasting security. The young moon recurved, and shining low in the west, was like a slender shaving thrown up from a bar of gold, and the Arabian Sea, smooth and cool to the eye like a sheet of ice, extended its perfect level to the perfect circle of a dark horizon. The propeller turned without a check, as though its beat had been part of the scheme of a safe universe; and on each side of the *Patna* two deep folds of water, permanent and sombre on the unwrinkled shimmer, enclosed within their straight and diverging ridges a few white swirls of foam bursting in a low hiss, a few wavelets, a few ripples, a few undulations that, left behind, agitated the surface of the sea for an instant after the passage of the ship, subsided splashing gently, calmed down at last into the circular stillness of water and sky with the black speck of the moving hull remaining everlastingly in its centre.

Jim on the bridge was penetrated by the great certitude of unbounded safety and peace that could be read on the silent aspect of nature like the certitude of fostering love upon the placid tenderness of a mother's face. Below the roof of awnings, surrendered to the wisdom of white men and to their courage, trusting the power of their unbelief and the iron shell of their fire-ship, the pilgrims of an exacting faith slept on mats, on blankets, on bare planks, on every deck, in all the dark corners, wrapped in dyed cloths, muffled in soiled rags, with their heads resting on small bundles, with their faces pressed to bent forearms: the men, the women, the children; the old with the young, the decrepit with the lusty – all equal before sleep, death's brother.

A draught of air, fanned from forward by the speed of the ship, passed steadily through the long gloom between the high bulwarks, swept over the rows of prone bodies; a few dim flames in globe-lamps were hung short here and there under the ridge-poles, and in the blurred circles of light thrown down and trembling slightly to the unceasing vibration of the ship appeared a chin upturned, two closed eyelids, a dark hand with silver rings, a meagre limb draped in a torn covering, a head bent back, a naked foot, a throat bared and stretched as if offering itself to the knife. The well-to-do had made for their families shelters with heavy boxes and dusty mats; the poor reposed side by side with all they had on earth tied up in a rag under their heads; the lone old men slept, with drawn-up legs, upon their prayer-carpets, with their hands over their ears and one elbow on each side of the face; a father, his shoulders up and his knees under his forehead, dozed dejectedly by a boy who slept on his back with tousled hair and one arm commandingly extended; a woman covered from head to foot, like a corpse, with a piece of white sheeting, had a naked child in the hollow of each arm; the Arab's belongings, piled right aft, made a heavy mound of broken outlines, with a cargo-lamp swung above, and a great confusion of vague forms behind: gleams of paunchy brass pots, the foot-rest of a deck-chair, blades of spears, the straight scabbard of an old sword leaning against a heap of pillows, the spout of a tin coffee-pot. The patent log on the taffrail periodically rang a single tinkling stroke for every mile traversed on an errand of faith. Above the mass of sleepers a faint and patient sigh at times floated, the exhalation of a troubled dream; and short metallic clangs bursting out suddenly in the depths of the ship, the harsh scrape of a shovel, the violent slam of a furnace-door, exploded brutally, as if the men handling the mysterious things below had their breasts full of fierce anger: while the slim high hull of the

steamer went on evenly ahead, without a sway of her bare
masts, cleaving continuously the great calm of the waters
under the inaccessible serenity of the sky.

Jim paced athwart, and his footsteps in the vast silence
were loud to his own ears, as if echoed by the watchful stars:
his eyes roaming about the line of the horizon, seemed to
gaze hungrily into the unattainable, and did not see the
shadow of the coming event. The only shadow on the sea
was the shadow of the black smoke pouring heavily from
the funnel its immense streamer, whose end was constantly
dissolving in the air. Two Malays, silent and almost
motionless, steered, one on each side of the wheel, whose
brass rim shone fragmentarily in the oval of light thrown
out by the binnacle. Now and then a hand, with black
fingers alternately letting go and catching hold of revolving
spokes, appeared in the illumined part; the links of wheel-
chains ground heavily in the grooves of the barrel. Jim
would glance at the compass, would glance around the
unattainable horizon, would stretch himself till his joints
cracked with a leisurely twist of the body, in the very excess
of well-being; and, as if made audacious by the invincible
aspect of the peace, he felt he cared for nothing that could
happen to him to the end of his days. From time to time he
glanced idly at a chart pegged out with four drawing-pins
on a low three-legged table abaft the steering-gear case.
The sheet of paper portraying the depths of the sea presented a shiny surface under the light of a bull's-eye lamp
lashed to a stanchion, a surface as level and smooth as the
glimmering surface of the waters. Parallel rulers with a pair
of dividers reposed on it; the ship's position at last noon was
marked with a small black cross, and the straight pencil-
line drawn firmly as far as Perim figured the course of the
ship – the path of souls towards the holy place, the promise
of salvation, the reward of eternal life – while the pencil
with its sharp end touching the Somali coast lay round and
still like a naked ship's spar floating in the pool of a
sheltered dock. 'How steady she goes,' thought Jim with

wonder, with something like gratitude for this high peace
of sea and sky. At such times his thoughts would be full of
valorous deeds: he loved these dreams and the success of his
imaginary achievements. They were the best parts of life,
its secret truth, its hidden reality. They had a gorgeous
virility, the charm of vagueness, they passed before him
with a heroic tread; they carried his soul away with them
and made it drunk with the divine philtre of an unbounded
confidence in itself. There was nothing he could not face.
He was so pleased with the idea that he smiled, keeping
perfunctorily his eyes ahead; and when he happened to
glance back he saw the white streak of the wake drawn as
straight by the ship's keel upon the sea as the black line
drawn by the pencil upon the chart.

The ash-buckets racketed, clanking up and down the
stoke-hold ventilators, and this tin-pot clatter warned him
the end of his watch was near. He sighed with content, with
regret as well at having to part from that serenity which
fostered the adventurous freedom of his thoughts. He was
a little sleepy, too, and felt a pleasurable languor running
through every limb as though all the blood in his body had
turned to warm milk. His skipper had come up noiselessly,
in pyjamas and with his sleeping-jacket flung wide open.
Red of face, only half awake, the left eye partly closed, the
right staring stupid and glassy, he hung his big head over
the chart and scratched his ribs sleepily. There was something obscene in the sight of his naked flesh. His bared
breast glistened soft and greasy as though he had sweated
out his fat in his sleep. He pronounced a professional
remark in a voice harsh and dead, resembling the rasping
sound of a wood-file on the edge of a plank; the fold of his
double chin hung like a bag triced up close under the hinge
of his jaw. Jim started, and his answer was full of deference;
but the odious and fleshy figure, as though seen for the first
time in a revealing moment, fixed itself in his memory for
ever as the incarnation of everything vile and base that lurks
in the world we love: in our own hearts we trust for our

salvation in the men that surround us, in the sights that fill our eyes, in the sounds that fill our ears, and in the air that fills our lungs.

The thin gold shaving of the moon floating slowly downwards had lost itself on the darkened surface of the waters, and the eternity beyond the sky seemed to come down nearer to the earth, with the augmented glitter of the stars, with the more profound sombreness in the lustre of the half-transparent dome covering the flat disc of an opaque sea. The ship moved so smoothly that her onward motion was imperceptible to the senses of men, as though she had been a crowded planet speeding through the dark spaces of ether behind the swarm of suns, in the appalling and calm solitudes awaiting the breath of future creations. 'Hot is no name for it down below,' said a voice.

Jim smiled without looking round. The skipper presented an unmoved breadth of back: it was the renegade's trick to appear pointedly unaware of your existence unless it suited his purpose to turn at you with a devouring glare before he let loose a torrent of foamy, abusive jargon that came like a gush from a sewer. Now he emitted only a sulky grunt; the second engineer at the head of the bridge-ladder, kneading with damp palms a dirty sweat-rag, unabashed, continued the tale of his complaints. The sailors had a good time of it up here, and what was the use of them in the world he would be blowed if he could see. The poor devils of engineers had to get the ship along anyhow, and they could very well do the rest too; by gosh they— 'Shut up' growled the German stolidly. 'Oh yes! Shut up – and when anything goes wrong you fly to us, don't you?' went on the other. He was more than half cooked, he expected; but anyway, now, he did not mind how much he sinned, because these last three days he had passed through a fine course of training for the place where the bad boys go when they die – b'gosh, he had – besides being made jolly well deaf by the blasted racket below. The durned, compound, surface-condensing,

rotten scrap-heap rattled and banged down there like an
old deck-winch, only more so; and what made him risk his
life every night and day that God made amongst the refuse
of a breaking-up yard flying round at fifty-seven revolutions, was more than *he* could tell. He must have been born
reckless, b'gosh. He ... 'Where did you get drink?' inquired
the German, very savage, but motionless in the light of
the binnacle, like a clumsy effigy of a man cut out of a
block of fat. Jim went on smiling at the retreating horizon;
his heart was full of generous impulses, and his thought
was contemplating his own superiority. 'Drink!' repeated
the engineer with amiable scorn: he was hanging on with
both hands to the rail, a shadowy figure with flexible legs.
'Not from you, captain. You're far too mean, b'gosh. You
would let a good man die sooner than give him a drop of
shnaps. That's what you Germans call economy. Penny
wise, pound foolish.' He became sentimental. The chief
had given him a four-finger nip about ten o'clock – 'only
one, s'elp me!' – good old chief; but as to getting the old
fraud out of his bunk – a five-ton crane couldn't do it.
Not it. Not to-night anyhow. He was sleeping sweetly
like a little child, with a bottle of prime brandy under his
pillow. From the thick throat of the commander of
the *Patna* came a low rumble, on which the sound of the
word *schwein* fluttered high and low like a capricious
feather in a faint stir of air. He and the chief engineer had
been cronies for a good few years – serving the same jovial,
crafty, old Chinaman, with horn-rimmed goggles and
strings of red silk plaited into the venerable grey hairs of
his pigtail. The quay-side opinion in the *Patna's* home-port
was that these two in the way of brazen peculation 'had
done together pretty well everything you can think of.'
Outwardly they were badly matched: one dull-eyed,
malevolent, and of soft fleshy curves; the other lean, all
hollows, with a head long and bony like the head of an old
horse, with sunken cheeks, with sunken temples, with an
indifferent glazed glance of sunken eyes. He had been

stranded out East somewhere – in Canton, in Shanghai, or perhaps in Yokohama; he probably did not care to remember himself the exact locality, nor yet the cause of his shipwreck. He had been, in mercy to his youth, kicked quietly out of his ship twenty years ago or more, and it might have been so much worse for him that the memory of the episode had in it hardly a trace of misfortune. Then, steam navigation expanding in these seas and men of his craft being scarce at first, he had 'got on' after a sort. He was eager to let strangers know in a dismal mumble that he was 'an old stager out here.' When he moved a skeleton seemed to sway loose in his clothes; his walk was mere wandering, and he was given to wander thus around the engine-room skylight, smoking, without relish, doctored tobacco in a brass bowl at the end of a cherrywood stem four feet long, with the imbecile gravity of a thinker evolving a system of philosophy from the hazy glimpse of a truth. He was usually anything but free with his private store of liquor; but on that night he had departed from his principles, so that his second, a weak-headed child of Wapping, what with the unexpectedness of the treat and the strength of the stuff, had become very happy, cheeky, and talkative. The fury of the New South Wales German was extreme; he puffed like an exhaust-pipe, and Jim, faintly amused by the scene, was impatient for the time when he could get below: the last ten minutes of the watch were irritating like a gun that hangs fire; those men did not belong to the world of heroic adventure; they weren't bad chaps though. Even the skipper himself... His gorge rose at the mass of panting flesh from which issued gurgling mutters, a cloudy trickle of filthy expressions; but he was too pleasurably languid to dislike actively this or any other thing. The quality of these men did not matter; he rubbed shoulders with them, but they could not touch him; he shared the air they breathed, but he was different.... Would the skipper go for the engineer?... The life was easy and he was too sure of himself – too sure of himself to... The line dividing his meditation from a surreptitious doze on his feet was thinner than a thread in a spider's web.

The second engineer was coming by easy transitions to the consideration of his finances and of his courage.

'Who's drunk? I? No, no, captain! That won't do. You ought to know by this time the chief ain't free-hearted enough to make a sparrow drunk, b'gosh. I've never been the worse for liquor in my life; the stuff ain't made yet that would make *me* drunk. I could drink liquid fire against your whisky peg for peg, b'gosh, and keep as cool as a cucumber. If I thought I was drunk I would jump overboard – do away with myself, b'gosh. I would! Straight! And I won't go off the bridge. Where do you expect me to take the air on a night like this, eh? On deck amongst that vermin down there? Likely – ain't it! And I am not afraid of anything you can do.'

The German lifted two heavy fists to heaven and shook them a little without a word.

'I don't know what fear is,' pursued the engineer, with the enthusiasm of sincere conviction. 'I am not afraid of doing all the bloomin' work in this rotten hooker, b'gosh! And a jolly good thing for you that there are some of us about the world that aren't afraid of their lives, or where would you be – you and this old thing here with her plates like brown paper – brown paper, s'elp me? It's all very fine for you – you get a power of pieces out of her one way and another; but what about me – what do I get? A measly hundred and fifty dollars a month and find yourself. I wish to ask you respectfully – respectfully, mind – who wouldn't chuck a dratted job like this? 'Tain't safe, s'elp me, it ain't! Only I am one of them fearless fellows....'

He let go the rail and made ample gestures as if demonstrating in the air the shape and extent of his valour; his thin voice darted in prolonged squeaks upon the sea, he tiptoed back and forth for the better emphasis of utterance, and suddenly pitched down head-first as though he had been clubbed from behind. He said 'Damn!' as he tumbled;

an instant of silence followed upon his screeching: Jim and
the skipper staggered forward by common accord, and
catching themselves up, stood very stiff and still gazing,
amazed, at the undisturbed level of the sea. Then they
looked upwards at the stars.

What had happened? The wheezy thump of the engines
went on. Had the earth been checked in her course? They
could not understand; and suddenly the calm sea, the sky
without a cloud, appeared formidably insecure in their
immobility, as it poised on the brow of yawning destruction. The engineer rebounded vertically full length and
collapsed again into a vague heap. This heap said 'What's
that?' in the muffled accents of profound grief. A faint
noise as of thunder, of thunder infinitely remote, less
than a sound, hardly more than a vibration, passed slowly,
and the ship quivered in response, as if the thunder had
growled deep down in the water. The eyes of the two
Malays at the wheel glittered towards the white men, but
their dark hands remained closed on the spokes. The sharp
hull driving on its way seemed to rise a few inches in
succession through its whole length, as though it had
become pliable, and settled down again rigidly to its work
of cleaving the smooth surface of the sea. Its quivering
stopped, and the faint noise of thunder ceased all at once,
as though the ship had steamed across a narrow belt of
vibrating water and of humming air.

# CHAPTER FOUR

A MONTH or so afterwards, when Jim, in answer to pointed questions, tried to tell honestly the truth of this experience, he said, speaking of the ship: 'She went over whatever it was as easy as a snake crawling over a stick.' The illustration was good: the questions were aiming at facts, and the official Inquiry was being held in the police court of an Eastern port. He stood elevated in the witness-box, with burning cheeks in a cool lofty room: the big framework of punkahs moved gently to and fro high above his head, and from below many eyes were looking at him out of dark faces, out of white faces, out of red faces, out of faces attentive, spellbound, as if all these people sitting in orderly rows upon narrow benches had been enslaved by the fascination of his voice. It was very loud, it rang startling in his own ears, it was the only sound audible in the world, for the terribly distinct questions that extorted his answers seemed to shape themselves in anguish and pain within his breast, – came to him poignant and silent like the terrible questioning of one's conscience. Outside the court the sun blazed – within was the wind of great punkahs that made you shiver, the shame that made you burn, the attentive eyes whose glance stabbed. The face of the presiding magistrate, clean shaved and impassible, looked at him deadly pale between the red faces of the two nautical assessors. The light of a broad window under the ceiling fell from above on the heads and shoulders of the three men, and they were fiercely distinct in the half-light of the big court-room where the audience seemed composed of staring shadows. They wanted facts. Facts! They demanded facts from him, as if facts could explain anything!

'After you had concluded you had collided with something floating awash, say a water-logged wreck, you were ordered by your captain to go forward and ascertain if there was any damage done. Did you think it likely from the force of the blow?' asked the assessor sitting to the left. He had a thin horseshoe beard, salient cheek-bones and with both elbows on the desk clasped his rugged hands before his face, looking at Jim with thoughtful blue eyes; the other, a heavy, scornful man, thrown back in his seat, his left arm extended full length, drummed delicately with his finger-tips on a blotting-pad: in the middle the magistrate upright in the roomy arm-chair, his head inclined slightly on the shoulder, had his arms crossed on his breast and a few flowers in a glass vase by the side of his inkstand.

'I did not,' said Jim. 'I was told to call no one and to make no noise for fear of creating a panic. I thought the precaution reasonable. I took one of the lamps that were hung under the awnings and went forward. After opening the forepeak hatch I heard splashing in there. I lowered then the lamp the whole drift of its lanyard, and saw that the forepeak was more than half full of water already. I knew then there must be a big hole below the waterline.' He paused.

'Yes,' said the big assessor, with a dreamy smile at the blotting-pad; his fingers played incessantly, touching the paper without noise.

'I did not think of danger just then. I might have been a little startled: all this happened in such a quiet way and so very suddenly. I knew there was no other bulkhead in the ship but the collision bulkhead separating the forepeak from the forehold. I went back to tell the captain. I came upon the second engineer getting up at the foot of the bridge-ladder: he seemed dazed, and told me he thought his left arm was broken; he had slipped on the top step when getting down while I was forward. He exclaimed, "My God! That rotten bulkhead 'll give way in a minute, and the damned thing will go down under us like a lump of lead." He pushed me away with his right arm and ran before me up the ladder, shouting as he climbed. His left arm hung by his side. I followed up in time to see the captain rush at him and knock him down flat on his back. He did not strike him again: he stood bending over him and speaking angrily but quite low. I fancy he was asking him why the devil he didn't go and stop the engines, instead of making a row about it on deck. I heard him say, "Get up! Run! fly!" He swore also. The engineer slid down the starboard ladder and bolted round the skylight to the engineroom companion which was on the port-side. He moaned as he ran. . . .'

He spoke slowly; he remembered swiftly and with extreme vividness; he could have reproduced like an echo the moaning of the engineer for the better information of these men who wanted facts. After his first feeling of revolt he had come round to the view that only a meticulous precision of statement would bring out the true horror behind the appalling face of things. The facts those men were so eager to know had been visible, tangible, open to the senses, occupying their place in space and time, requiring for their existence a fourteen-hundred-ton steamer and twenty-seven minutes by the watch; they made a whole that had features, shades of expression, a complicated aspect that could be remembered by the eye, and something else besides, something invisible, a directing spirit of perdition that dwelt within, like a malevolent soul in a detestable body. He was anxious to make this clear. This had not been a common affair, everything in it had been of the utmost importance, and fortunately he remembered everything. He wanted to go on talking for truth's sake, perhaps for his own sake also; and while his utterance was deliberate, his mind positively flew round and round the serried circle of facts that had surged up all about him to cut him off from the rest of his kind: it was like a creature that, finding itself imprisoned within an enclosure of high stakes, dashes round and round, distracted in the night,

trying to find a weak spot, a crevice, a place to scale, some
opening through which it may squeeze itself and escape.
This awful activity of mind made him hesitate at times in
his speech. . . .

'The captain kept on moving here and there on the
bridge; he seemed calm enough, only he stumbled several
times; and once as I stood speaking to him he walked right
into me as though he had been stone-blind. He made no
definite answer to what I had to tell. He mumbled to
himself; all I heard of it were a few words that sounded
like "confounded steam!" and "infernal steam!" – something about steam. I thought. . .'

He was becoming irrelevant; a question to the point cut
short his speech, like a pang of pain, and he felt extremely
discouraged and weary. He was coming to that, he was
coming to that – and now, checked brutally, he had to
answer by yes or no. He answered truthfully by a curt
'Yes, I did;' and fair of face, big of frame, with young,
gloomy eyes, he held his shoulders upright above the box
while his soul writhed within him. He was made to answer
another question so much to the point and so useless, then
waited again. His mouth was tastelessly dry, as though he
had been eating dust, then salt and bitter as after a drink of
sea-water. He wiped his damp forehead, passed his tongue
over parched lips, felt a shiver run down his back. The big
assessor had dropped his eyelids, and drummed on without
a sound, careless and mournful; the eyes of the other above
the sunburnt, clasped fingers seemed to glow with kindli-
ness; the magistrate had swayed forward; his pale face
hovered near the flowers, and then dropping sideways
over the arm of his chair, he rested his temple in the palm
of his hand. The wind of the punkahs eddied down on the
heads, on the dark-faced natives wound about in voluminous draperies, on the Europeans sitting together very hot
and in drill suits that seemed to fit them as close as their
skins, and holding their round pith hats on their knees;
while gliding along the walls the court peons, buttoned

tight in long white coats, flitted rapidly to and fro, running on bare toes, red-sashed, red turban on head, as noiseless as ghosts, and on the alert like so many retrievers.

Jim's eyes, wandering in the intervals of his answers, rested upon a white man who sat apart from the others, with his face worn and clouded, but with quiet eyes that glanced straight, interested and clear. Jim answered another question and was tempted to cry out, 'What's the good of this! what's the good!' He tapped with his foot slightly, bit his lip, and looked away over the heads. He met the eyes of the white man. The glance directed at him was not the fascinated stare of the others. It was an act of intelligent volition. Jim between two questions forgot himself so far as to find leisure for a thought. This fellow – ran the thought – looks at me as though he could see somebody or something past my shoulder. He had come across that man before – in the street perhaps. He was positive he had never spoken to him. For days, for many days, he had spoken to no one, but had held silent, incoherent, and endless converse with himself, like a prisoner alone in his cell or like a wayfarer lost in a wilderness. At present he was answering questions that did not matter though they had a purpose, but he doubted whether he would ever again speak out as long as he lived. The sound of his own truthful statements confirmed his deliberate opinion that speech was of no use to him any longer. That man there seemed to be aware of his hopeless difficulty. Jim looked at him, then turned away resolutely, as after a final parting.

And later on, many times, in distant parts of the world, Marlow showed himself willing to remember Jim, to remember him at length, in detail and audibly.

Perhaps it would be after dinner, on a verandah draped in motionless foliage and crowned with flowers, in the deep dusk speckled by fiery cigar-ends. The elongated bulk of each cane-chair harboured a silent listener. Now and then a small red glow would move abruptly, and expanding light up the fingers of a languid hand, part of a face in profound repose, or flash a crimson gleam into a pair of pensive eyes overshadowed by a fragment of an unruffled forehead; and with the very first word uttered Marlow's body, extended at rest in the seat, would become very still, as though his spirit had winged its way back into the lapse of time and were speaking through his lips from the past.

# CHAPTER FIVE

'OH YES. I attended the inquiry,' he would say, 'and to this day I haven't left off wondering why I went. I am willing to believe each of us has a guardian angel, if you fellows will concede to me that each of us has a familiar devil as well. I want you to own up, because I don't like to feel exceptional in any way, and I know I have him – the devil, I mean. I haven't seen him, of course, but I go upon circumstantial evidence. He is there right enough, and, being malicious, he lets me in for that kind of thing. What kind of thing, you ask? Why, the inquiry thing, the yellow-dog thing – you wouldn't think a mangy, native tyke would be allowed to trip up people in the verandah of a magistrate's court, would you? – the kind of thing that by devious, unexpected, truly diabolical ways causes me to run up against men with soft spots, with hard spots, with hidden plague spots, by Jove! and loosens their tongues at the sight of me for their infernal confidences; as though, forsooth, I had no confidences to make to myself, as though – God help me! – I didn't have enough confidential information about myself to harrow my own soul till the end of my appointed time. And what I have done to be thus favoured I want to know. I declare I am as full of my own concerns as the next man, and I have as much memory as the average pilgrim in this valley, so you see I am not particularly fit to be a receptacle of confessions. Then why? Can't tell – unless it be to make time pass away after dinner. Charley, my dear chap, your dinner was extremely good, and in consequence these men here look upon a quiet rubber as a tumultuous occupation. They wallow in your good chairs and think to themselves, "Hang exertion. Let that Marlow talk."

'Talk! So be it. And it's easy enough to talk of Master Jim, after a good spread, two hundred feet above the sea-level, with a box of decent cigars handy, on a blessed evening of freshness and starlight that would make the best of us forget we are only on sufferance here and got to pick our way in cross lights, watching every precious minute and every irremediable step, trusting wc shall manage yet to go out decently in the end – but not so sure of it after all – and with dashed little help to expect from those we touch elbows with right and left. Of course there are men here and there to whom the whole of life is like an after-dinner hour with a cigar; easy, pleasant, empty, perhaps enlivened by some fable of strife to be forgotten before the end is told – before the end is told – even if there happens to be any end to it.

'My eyes met his for the first time at that inquiry. You must know that everybody connected in any way with the sea was there, because the affair had been notorious for days, ever since that mysterious cable message came from Aden to start us all cackling. I say mysterious, because it was so in a sense though it contained a naked fact, about as naked and ugly as a fact can well be. The whole waterside talked of nothing else. First thing in the morning as I was dressing in my state-room, I would hear through the bulk-head my Parsee Dubash jabbering about the *Patna* with the steward, while he drank a cup of tea, by favour, in the pantry. No sooner on shore I would meet some acquaintance, and the first remark would be, "Did you ever hear of anything to beat this?" and according to his kind the man would smile cynically, or look sad, or let out a swear or two. Complete strangers would accost each other familiarly, just for the sake of easing their minds on the subject: every confounded loafer in the town came in for a harvest of drinks over this affair: you heard of it in the harbour office, at every ship-broker's, at your agent's, from whites, from natives, from half-castes, from the very boatmen squatting half-naked on the stone steps as you went up – by Jove!

There was some indignation, not a few jokes, and no end of discussions as to what had become of them, you know. This went on for a couple of weeks or more, and the opinion that whatever was mysterious in this affair would turn out to be tragic as well, began to prevail, when one fine morning, as I was standing in the shade by the steps of the harbour office, I perceived four men walking towards me along the quay. I wondered for a while where that queer lot had sprung from, and suddenly, I may say, I shouted to myself, "Here they are!"

'There they were, sure enough, three of them as large as life, and one much larger of girth than any living man has a right to be, just landed with a good breakfast inside of them from an outward-bound Dale Line steamer that had come in about an hour after sunrise. There could be no mistake; I spotted the jolly skipper of the *Patna* at the first glance: the fattest man in the whole blessed tropical belt clear round that good old earth of ours. Moreover, nine months or so before, I had come across him in Samarang. His steamer was loading in the Roads, and he was abusing the tyrannical institutions of the German empire, and soaking himself in beer all day long and day after day in De Jongh's back-shop, till De Jongh, who charged a guilder for every bottle without as much as the quiver of an eyelid, would beckon me aside, and, with his little leathery face all puckered up, declare confidentially, "Business is business, but this man, captain, he make me very sick. Tfui!"

'I was looking at him from the shade. He was hurrying on a little in advance, and the sunlight beating on him brought out his bulk in a startling way. He made me think of a trained baby elephant walking on hind-legs. He was extravagantly gorgeous too – got up in a soiled sleeping-suit, bright green and deep orange vertical stripes, with a pair of ragged straw slippers on his bare feet, and somebody's cast-off pith hat, very dirty and two sizes too small for him, tied up with a manilla rope-yarn on the top of his big head. You understand a man like that hasn't the ghost of a chance when it comes to borrowing clothes. Very well. On he came in hot haste, without a look right or left, passed within three feet of me, and in the innocence of his heart went on pelting upstairs in the harbour office to make his deposition, or report, or whatever you like to call it.

'It appears he addressed himself in the first instance to the principal shipping-master. Archie Ruthvel had just come in, and, as his story goes, was about to begin his arduous day by giving a dressing-down to his chief clerk. Some of you might have known him – an obliging little Portuguese half-caste with a miserably skinny neck, and always on the hop to get something from the shipmasters in the way of eatables – a piece of salt pork, a bag of biscuits, a few potatoes, or what not. One voyage, I recollect, I tipped him a live sheep out of the remnant of my sea-stock: not that I wanted him to do anything for me – he couldn't, you know – but because his childlike belief in the sacred right to perquisites quite touched my heart. It was so strong as to be almost beautiful. The race – the two races rather – and the climate ... However, never mind. I know where I have a friend for life.

'Well, Ruthvel says he was giving him a severe lecture – on official morality, I suppose – when he heard a kind of subdued commotion at his back, and turning his head he saw, in his own words, something round and enormous, resembling a sixteen-hundred-weight sugar-hogshead wrapped in striped flannelette, up-ended in the middle of the large floor space in the office. He declares he was so taken aback that for quite an appreciable time he did not realise the thing was alive, and sat still wondering for what purpose and by what means that object had been transported in front of his desk. The archway from the ante-room was crowded with punkah-pullers, sweepers, police peons, the coxswain and crew of the harbour steam-launch, all craning their necks and almost climbing on each other's

backs. Quite a riot. By that time the fellow had managed to
tug and jerk his hat clear of his head, and advanced with
slight bows at Ruthvel, who told me the sight was so
discomposing that for some time he listened quite unable
to make out what that apparition wanted. It spoke in a
voice harsh and lugubrious but intrepid, and little by little it
dawned upon Archie that this was a development of the
*Patna* case. He says that as soon as he understood who it
was before him he felt quite unwell – Archie is so sympathetic and easily upset – but pulled himself together and
shouted "Stop! I can't listen to you. You must go to the
Master Attendant. I can't possibly listen to you. Captain
Elliot is the man you want to see. This way, this way." He
jumped up, ran round that long counter, pulled, shoved: the
other let him, surprised but obedient at first, and only at
the door of the private office some sort of animal instinct
made him hang back and snort like a frightened bullock.
"Look here! what's up? Let go! Look here!" Archie flung
open the door without knocking. "The master of the *Patna*,
sir," he shouts. "Go in, captain." He saw the old man lift his
head from some writing so sharp that his nose-nippers fell
off, banged the door to, and fled to his desk, where he had
some papers waiting for his signature: but he says the row
that burst out in there was so awful that he couldn't collect
his senses sufficiently to remember the spelling of his own
name. Archie's the most sensitive shipping-master in the
two hemispheres. He declares he felt as though he had
thrown a man to a hungry lion. No doubt the noise was
great. I heard it down below, and I have every reason to
believe it was heard clear across the Esplanade as far as the
band-stand. Old father Elliot had a great stock of words
and could shout – and didn't mind who he shouted at
either. He would have shouted at the Viceroy himself.
As he used to tell me: "I am as high as I can get; my pension
is safe. I've a few pounds laid by, and if they don't like
my notions of duty I would just as soon go home as
not. I am an old man, and I have always spoken my mind.

All I care for now is to see my girls married before I die."
He was a little crazy on that point. His three daughters
were awfully nice, though they resemble him amazingly,
and on the mornings he woke up with a gloomy view of
their matrimonial prospects the office would read it in his
eye and tremble, because, they said, he was sure to have
somebody for breakfast. However, that morning he did not
eat the renegade, but, if I may be allowed to carry on the
metaphor, chewed him up very small, so to speak, and – ah!
ejected him again.

'Thus in a very few moments I saw his monstrous bulk
descend in haste and stand still on the outer steps. He had
stopped close to me for the purpose of profound meditation: his large purple cheeks quivered. He was biting his
thumb, and after a while noticed me with a sidelong vexed
look. The other three chaps that had landed with him
made a little group waiting at some distance. There was a
sallow-faced, mean little chap with his arm in a sling, and a
long individual in a blue flannel coat, as dry as a chip and no
stouter than a broomstick, with drooping grey moustaches,
who looked about him with an air of jaunty imbecility. The
third was an upstanding, broad-shouldered youth, with his
hands in his pockets, turning his back on the other two who
appeared to be talking together earnestly. He stared across
the empty Esplanade. A ramshackle gharry, all dust and
venetian blinds, pulled up short opposite the group, and the
driver, throwing up his right foot over his knee, gave
himself up to the critical examination of his toes. The
young chap, making no movement, not even stirring his
head, just stared into the sunshine. This was my first view
of Jim. He looked as unconcerned and unapproachable as
only the young can look. There he stood, clean-limbed,
clean-faced, firm on his feet, as promising a boy as the sun
ever shone on; and, looking at him, knowing all he knew
and a little more too, I was as angry as though I had
detected him trying to get something out of me by false
pretences. He had no business to look so sound. I thought

to myself – well, if this sort can go wrong like that . . . and I felt as though I could fling down my hat and dance on it from sheer mortification, as I once saw the skipper of an Italian barque do because his duffer of a mate got into a mess with his anchors when making a flying moor in a roadstead full of ships. I asked myself, seeing him there apparently so much at ease – is he silly? is he callous? He seemed ready to start whistling a tune. And note, I did not care a rap about the behaviour of the other two. Their persons somehow fitted the tale that was public property, and was going to be the subject of an official inquiry. "That old mad rogue upstairs called me a hound," said the captain of the *Patna*. I can't tell whether he recognised me – I rather think he did; but at any rate our glances met. He glared – I smiled; hound was the very mildest epithet that had reached me through the open window. "Did he?" I said from some strange inability to hold my tongue. He nodded, bit his thumb again, swore under his breath: then lifting his head and looking at me with sullen and passionate impudence – "Bah! the Pacific is big, my friendt. You damned Englishmen can do your worst; I know where there's plenty room for a man like me: I am well aguaindt in Apia, in Honolulu, in . . ." He paused reflectively, while without effort I could depict to myself the sort of people he was "aguaindt" with in those places. I won't make a secret of it that I had been "aguaindt" with not a few of that sort myself. There are times when a man must act as though life were equally sweet in any company. I've known such a time, and, what's more, I shan't now pretend to pull a long face over my necessity, because a good many of that bad company from want of moral – moral – what shall I say? – posture, or from some other equally profound cause, were twice as instructive and twenty times more amusing than the usual respectable thief of commerce you fellows ask to sit at your table without any real necessity – from habit, from cowardice, from good-nature, from a hundred sneaking and inadequate reasons.

'"You Englishmen are all rogues," went on my patriotic
Flensborg or Stettin Australian. I really don't recollect now
what decent little port on the shores of the Baltic was
defiled by being the nest of that precious bird. "What are
you to shout? Eh? You tell me? You no better than other
people, and that old rogue he make Gottam fuss with me."
His thick carcass trembled on its legs that were like a pair of
pillars; it trembled from head to foot. "That's what you
English always make – make a tam' fuss – for any little
thing, because I was not born in your tam' country. Take
away my certificate. Take it. I don't want the certificate. A
man like me don't want your verfluchte certificate. I shpit
on it." He spat. "I vill an American citizen begome," he
cried, fretting and fuming and shuffling his feet as if to free
his ankles from some invisible and mysterious grasp that
would not let him get away from that spot. He made
himself so warm that the top of his bullet head positively
smoked. Nothing mysterious prevented me from going
away: curiosity is the most obvious of sentiments, and it
held me there to see the effect of a full information upon
that young fellow who, hands in pockets, and turning his
back upon the sidewalk, gazed across the grass-plots of the
Esplanade at the yellow portico of the Malabar Hotel with
the air of a man about to go for a walk as soon as his friend is
ready. That's how he looked, and it was odious. I waited to
see him overwhelmed, confounded, pierced through and
through, squirming like an impaled beetle – and I was half
afraid to see it too – if you understand what I mean.
Nothing more awful than to watch a man who has been
found out, not in a crime but in a more than criminal
weakness. The commonest sort of fortitude prevents us
from becoming criminals in a legal sense; it is from weakness unknown, but perhaps suspected, as in some parts of
the world you suspect a deadly snake in every bush – from
weakness that may lie hidden, watched or unwatched,
prayed against or manfully scorned, repressed or maybe
ignored more than half a lifetime, not one of us is safe.

We are snared into doing things for which we get called
names, and things for which we get hanged, and yet the
spirit may well survive – survive the condemnations, survive the halter, by Jove! And there are things – they look
small enough sometimes too – by which some of us are
totally and completely undone. I watched the youngster
there. I liked his appearance; I knew his appearance; he
came from the right place; he was one of us. He stood there
for all the parentage of his kind, for men and women by no
means clever or amusing, but whose very existence is based
upon honest faith, and upon the instinct of courage. I don't
mean military courage, or civil courage, or any special kind
of courage. I mean just that inborn ability to look tempta-
tions straight in the face – a readiness unintellectual
enough, goodness knows, but without pose – a power of
resistance, don't you see, ungracious if you like, but priceless – an unthinking and blessed stiffness before the outward and inward terrors, before the might of nature, and
the seductive corruption of men – backed by a faith invulnerable to the strength of facts, to the contagion of
example, to the solicitation of ideas. Hang ideas! They
are tramps, vagabonds, knocking at the back-door of your
mind, each taking a little of your substance, each carrying
away some crumb of that belief in a few simple notions you
must cling to if you want to live decently and would like to
die easy!

'This has nothing to do with Jim, directly; only he was
outwardly so typical of that good, stupid kind we like to feel
marching right and left of us in life, of the kind that is not
disturbed by the vagaries of intelligence and the perver-
sions of – of nerves, let us say. He was the kind of fellow you
would, on the strength of his looks, leave in charge of the
deck – figuratively and professionally speaking. I say
I would, and I ought to know. Haven't I turned out young-
sters enough in my time, for the service of the Red Rag, to
the craft of the sea, to the craft whose whole secret could be
expressed in one short sentence, and yet must be driven

afresh every day into young heads till it becomes the component part of every waking thought – till it is present in every dream of their young sleep! The sea has been good to me, but when I remember all these boys that passed through my hands, some grown up now and some drowned by this time, but all good stuff for the sea, I don't think I have done badly by it either. Were I to go home tomorrow, I bet that before two days passed over my head some sunburnt young chief mate would overtake me at some dock gateway or other, and a fresh deep voice speaking above my hat would ask: "Don't you remember me, sir? Why! little So-and-so. Such and such a ship. It was my first voyage." And I would remember a bewildered little shaver, no higher than the back of this chair, with a mother and perhaps a big sister on the quay, very quiet but too upset to wave their handkerchiefs at the ship that glides out gently between the pier-heads: or perhaps some decent middle-aged father who had come early with his boy to see him off, and stays all the morning because he is interested in the windlass apparently, and stays too long, and has got to scramble ashore at last with no time at all to say good-bye. The mud pilot on the poop sings out to me in a drawl, "Hold her with the check line for a moment, Mister Mate. There's a gentleman wants to get shore.... Up with you, sir. Nearly got carried off to Talcahuano, didn't you? Now's your time; easy does it.... All right. Slack away again forward there." The tugs, smoking like the pit of perdition, get hold and churn the old river into fury; the gentleman ashore is dusting his knees – the benevolent steward has shied his umbrella after him. All very proper. He has offered his bit of sacrifice to the sea, and now he may go home pretending he thinks nothing of it; and the little willing victim shall be very sea-sick before next morning. By-and-by, when he has learned all the little mysteries and the one great secret of the craft, he shall be fit to live or die as the sea may decree; and the man who had taken a hand in this fool game, in which the sea wins every toss, will be pleased to have his back slapped by a heavy young hand, and to hear a cheery sea-puppy voice: "Do you remember me, sir? The little So-and-so."

'I tell you this is good; it tells you that once in your life at least you had gone the right way to work. I have been thus slapped, and I have winced, for the slap was heavy, and I have glowed all day long and gone to bed feeling less lonely in the world by virtue of that hearty thump. Don't I remember the little So-and-so's! I tell you I ought to know the right kind of looks. I would have trusted the deck to that youngster on the strength of a single glance, and gone to sleep with both eyes – and, by Jove! it wouldn't have been safe. There are depths of horror in that thought. He looked as genuine as a new sovereign, but there was some infernal alloy in his metal. How much? The least thing – the least drop of something rare and accursed; the least drop! – but he made you – standing there with his don't-care-hang air – he made you wonder whether perchance he were nothing more rare than brass.

'I couldn't believe it. I tell you I wanted to see him squirm for the honour of the craft. The other two no-account chaps spotted their captain, and began to move slowly towards us. They chatted together as they strolled, and I did not care any more than if they had not been visible to the naked eye. They grinned at each other – might have been exchanging jokes, for all I know. I saw that with one of them it was the case of a broken arm; and as to the long individual with grey moustaches he was the chief engineer, and in various ways a pretty notorious personality. They were nobodies. They approached. The skipper gazed in an inanimate way between his feet: he seemed to be swollen to an unnatural size by some awful disease, by the mysterious action of an unknown poison. He lifted his head, saw the two before him waiting, opened his mouth with an extra-ordinary, sneering contortion of his puffed face – to speak to them, I suppose – and then a thought seemed to strike him. His thick, purplish lips came together without a

sound, he went off in a resolute waddle to the gharry and
began to jerk at the door-handle with such a blind brutality
of impatience that I expected to see the whole concern
overturned on its side, pony and all. The driver, shaken
out of his meditation over the sole of his foot, displayed at
once all the signs of intense terror, and held with both
hands, looking round from his box at this vast carcass
forcing its way into his conveyance. The little machine
shook and rocked tumultuously, and the crimson nape of
that lowered neck, the size of those straining thighs, the
immense heaving of that dingy, striped green-and-orange
back, the whole burrowing effort of that gaudy and sordid
mass troubled one's sense of probability with a droll and
fearsome effect, like one of those grotesque and distinct
visions that scare and fascinate one in a fever. He disappeared. I half expected the roof to split in two, the little
box on wheels to burst open in the manner of a ripe cotton-
pod – but it only sank with a click of flattened springs, and
suddenly one venetian blind rattled down. His shoulders
reappeared, jammed in the small opening; his head hung
out, distended and tossing like a captive balloon, perspir-
ing, furious, spluttering. He reached for the gharry-wallah
with vicious flourishes of a fist as dumpy and red as a lump
of raw meat. He roared at him to be off, to go on. Where?
Into the Pacific, perhaps. The driver lashed; the pony
snorted, reared once, and darted off at a gallop. Where?
To Apia? to Honolulu? He had 6,000 miles of tropical belt
to disport himself in, and I did not hear the precise address.
A snorting pony snatched him into "ewigkeit" in the
twinkling of an eye, and I never saw him again; and, what's
more, I don't know of anybody that ever had a glimpse of
him after he departed from my knowledge sitting inside a
ramshackle little gharry that fled round the corner in a
white smother of dust. He departed, disappeared, vanished, absconded; and absurdly enough it looked as though
he had taken that gharry with him, for never again did I
come across a sorrel pony with a slit ear and a lackadaisical

Tamil driver afflicted by a sore foot. The Pacific is indeed big; but whether he found a place for a display of his talents in it or not, the fact remains he had flown into space like a witch on a broomstick. The little chap with his arm in a sling started to run after the carriage, bleating, "Captain! I say, Captain! I sa-a-ay!" – but after a few steps stopped short, hung his head, and walked back slowly. At the sharp rattle of the wheels the young fellow spun round where he stood. He made no other movement, no gesture, no sign, and remained facing in the new direction after the gharry had swung out of sight.

'All this happened in much less time than it takes to tell, since I am trying to interpret for you into slow speech the instantaneous effect of visual impressions. Next moment the half-caste clerk, sent by Archie to look a little after the poor castaways of the *Patna*, came upon the scene. He ran out eager and bare-headed, looking right and left, and very full of his mission. It was doomed to be a failure as far as the principal person was concerned, but he approached the others with fussy importance, and, almost immediately, found himself involved in a violent altercation with the chap that carried his arm in a sling and who turned out to be extremely anxious for a row. He wasn't going to be ordered about – "not he, b'gosh." He wouldn't be terrified with a pack of lies by a cocky half-bred little quill-driver. He was not going to be bullied by "no object of that sort," if the story were true "ever so!" He bawled his wish, his desire, his determination to go to bed. "If you weren't a God-forsaken Portuguee," I heard him yell, "you would know that the hospital is the right place for me." He pushed the fist of his sound arm under the other's nose; a crowd began to collect; the half-caste, flustered, but doing his best to appear dignified, tried to explain his intentions. I went away without waiting to see the end.

'But it so happened that I had a man in the hospital at the time, and going there to see about him the day before the opening of the Inquiry, I saw in the white men's ward that little chap tossing on his back, with his arm in splints, and quite light-headed. To my great surprise the other one, the long individual with drooping white moustache, had also found his way there. I remembered I had seen him slinking away during the quarrel, in a half prance, half shuffle, and trying very hard not to look scared. He was no stranger to the port, it seems, and in his distress was able to make tracks straight for Mariani's billiard-room and grog-shop near the bazaar. That unspeakable vagabond, Mariani, who had known the man and had ministered to his vices in one or two other places, kissed the ground, in a manner of speaking, before him, and shut him up with a supply of bottles in an upstairs room of his infamous hovel. It appears he was under some hazy apprehension as to his personal safety, and wished to be concealed. However, Mariani told me a long time after (when he came on board one day to dun my steward for the price of some cigars) that he would have done more for him without asking any questions, from gratitude for some unholy favour received very many years ago – as far as I could make out. He thumped twice his brawny chest, rolled enormous black and white eyes glistening with tears: "Antonio never forget – Antonio never forget!" What was the precise nature of the immoral obligation I never learned, but be it what it may, he had every facility given him to remain under lock and key, with a chair, a table, a mattress in a corner, and a litter of fallen plaster on the floor, in an irrational state of funk, and keeping up his pecker with such tonics as Mariani dispensed. This lasted till the evening of the third day, when, after letting out a few horrible screams, he found himself compelled to seek safety in flight from a legion of centipedes. He burst the door open, made one leap for dear life down the crazy little stairway, landed bodily on Mariani's stomach, picked himself up, and bolted like a rabbit into the streets. The police plucked him off a garbage-heap in the early morning. At first he had a notion they were carrying him off to be hanged, and fought for liberty like a hero, but when I sat down by his bed he had been very quiet for two days. His lean bronzed head, with white moustaches, looked fine and calm on the pillow, like the head of a war-worn soldier with a child-like soul, had it not been for a hint of spectral alarm that lurked in the blank glitter of his glance, resembling a nondescript form of a terror crouching silently behind a pane of glass. He was so extremely calm, that I began to indulge in the eccentric hope of hearing something explanatory of the famous affair from his point of view. Why I longed to go grubbing into the deplorable details of an occurrence which, after all, concerned me no more than as a member of an obscure body of men held together by a community of inglorious toil and by fidelity to a certain standard of conduct, I can't explain. You may call it an unhealthy curiosity if you like; but I have a distinct notion I wished to find something. Perhaps, unconsciously, I hoped I would find that something, some profound and redeeming cause, some merciful explanation, some convincing shadow of an excuse. I see well enough now that I hoped for the impossible – for the laying of what is the most obstinate ghost of man's creation, of the uneasy doubt uprising like a mist, secret and gnawing like a worm, and more chilling than the certitude of death – the doubt of the sovereign power enthroned in a fixed standard of conduct. It is the hardest thing to stumble against; it is the thing that breeds yelling panics and good little quiet villainies; it's the true shadow of calamity. Did I believe in a miracle? and why did I desire it so ardently? Was it for my own sake that I wished to find some shadow of an excuse for that young fellow whom I had never seen before, but whose appearance alone added a touch of personal concern to the thoughts suggested by the knowledge of his weakness – made it a thing of mystery and terror – like a hint of a destructive fate ready for us all whose youth – in its day – had resembled his youth? I fear that such was the secret motive of my prying. I was, and no mistake, looking for a miracle. The only thing that at this distance of time strikes me as miraculous is the extent of my imbecility. I positively hoped to obtain from that battered and shady invalid some exorcism against the ghost of doubt. I must have been pretty desperate too, for, without a loss of time, after a few indifferent and friendly sentences which he answered with languid readiness, just as any decent sick man would do, I produced the word *Patna* wrapped up in a delicate question as in a wisp of floss silk. I was delicate selfishly; I did not want to startle him; I had no solicitude for him; I was not furious with him and sorry for him: his experience was of no importance, his redemption would have had no point for me. He had grown old in minor iniquities, and could no longer inspire aversion or pity. He repeated *Patna?* interrogatively, seemed to make a short effort of memory and said: "Quite right. I am an old stager out here. I saw her go down." I made ready to vent my indignation at such a stupid lie, when he added smoothly, "She was full of reptiles."

'This made me pause. What did he mean? The unsteady phantom of terror behind his glassy eyes seemed to stand still and look into mine wistfully. "They turned me out of my bunk in the middle watch to look at her sinking," he pursued in a reflective tone. His voice sounded alarmingly strong all at once. I was sorry for my folly. There was no snowy-winged coif of a nursing sister to be seen flitting in the perspective of the ward; but away in the middle of a long row of empty iron bedsteads an accident case from some ship in the Roads sat up brown and gaunt with a white bandage set rakishly on the forehead. Suddenly my interesting invalid shot out an arm thin like a tentacle and clawed my shoulder. "Only my eyes were good enough to see. I am famous for my eyesight. That's why they called me, I expect. None of them was quick enough to see her go, but they saw that she was gone right enough, and sang out together – like this." ... A wolfish howl searched the very recesses of my soul. "Oh! make 'im dry up," whined the

accident case irritably. "You don't believe me, I suppose,"
went on the other, with an air of ineffable conceit. "I tell
you there are no such eyes as mine this side of the Persian
Gulf. Look under the bed."

'Of course I stooped instantly. I defy anybody not to
have done so. "What can you see?" he asked. "Nothing," I
said, feeling awfully ashamed of myself. He scrutinised my
face with wild and withering contempt. "Just so," he said,
"but if I were to look I could see – there's no eyes like mine,
I tell you." Again he clawed, pulling at me downwards in
his eagerness to relieve himself by a confidential commun-
ication. "Millions of pink toads. There's no eyes like mine.
Millions of pink toads. It's worse than seeing a ship sink. I
could look at sinking ships and smoke my pipe all day long.
Why don't they give me back my pipe? I would get a smoke
while I watched these toads. The ship was full of them.
They've got to be watched, you know." He winked faceti-
ously. The perspiration dripped on him off my head, my
drill coat clung to my wet back: the afternoon breeze swept
impetuously over the row of bedsteads, the stiff folds of
curtains stirred perpendicularly, rattling on brass rods, the
covers of empty beds blew about noiselessly near the bare
floor all along the line, and I shivered to the very marrow.
The soft wind of the tropics played in that naked ward as
bleak as a winter's gale in an old barn at home. "Don't you
let him start his hollering, mister," hailed from afar the
accident case in a distressed angry shout that came ringing
between the walls like a quavering call down a tunnel. The
clawing hand hauled at my shoulder; he leered at me
knowingly. "The ship was full of them, you know, and we
had to clear out on the strict Q. T.," he whispered with
extreme rapidity. "All pink. All pink – as big as mastiffs,
with an eye on the top of the head and claws all round their
ugly mouths. Ough! Ough!" Quick jerks as of galvanic
shocks disclosed under the flat coverlet the outlines of
meagre and agitated legs; he let go my shoulder and
reached after something in the air; his body trembled

tensely like a released harp-string; and while I looked down, the spectral horror in him broke through his glassy gaze. Instantly his face of an old soldier, with its noble and calm outlines, became decomposed before my eyes by the corruption of stealthy cunning, of an abominable caution and of desperate fear. He restrained a cry – "Ssh! what are they doing now down there?" he asked, pointing to the floor with fantastic precautions of voice and gesture, whose meaning, borne upon my mind in a lurid flash, made me very sick of my cleverness. "They are all asleep," I answered, watching him narrowly. That was it. That's what he wanted to hear; these were the exact words that could calm him. He drew a long breath. "Ssh! Quiet, steady. I am an old stager out here. I know them brutes. Bash in the head of the first that stirs. There's too many of them, and she won't swim more than ten minutes." He panted again. "Hurry up," he yelled suddenly, and went on in a steady scream: "They are all awake – millions of them. They are trampling on me! Wait! Oh, wait! I'll smash them in heaps like flies. Wait for me! Help! H-e-elp!" An interminable and sustained howl completed my discomfiture. I saw in the distance the accident case raise deplorably both his hands to his bandaged head; a dresser, aproned to the chin, showed himself in the vista of the ward, as if seen in the small end of a telescope. I confessed myself fairly routed, and without more ado, stepping out through one of the long windows, escaped into the outside gallery. The howl pursued me like a vengeance. I turned into a deserted landing, and suddenly all became very still and quiet around me, and I descended the bare and shiny staircase in a silence that enabled me to compose my distracted thoughts. Down below I met one of the resident surgeons who was crossing the courtyard and stopped me. "Been to see your man, Captain? I think we may let him go to-morrow. These fools have no notion of taking care of themselves, though. I say, we've got the chief engineer of that pilgrim ship here. A curious case. D. T.'s of the worst kind. He has been drinking hard in that Greek's or Italian's grog-shop for three days. What can you expect? Four bottles of that kind of brandy a day, I am told. Wonderful, if true. Sheeted with boiler-iron inside, I should think. The head, ah! the head, of course, gone, but the curious part is there's some sort of method in his raving. I am trying to find out. Most unusual – that thread of logic in such a delirium. Traditionally he ought to see snakes, but he doesn't. Good old tradition's at a discount nowadays. Eh! His – er – visions are batrachian. Ha! ha! No, seriously, I never remember being so interested in a case of jim-jams before. He ought to be dead, don't you know, after such a festive experiment. Oh! he is a tough object. Four-and-twenty years of the tropics too. You ought really to take a peep at him. Noble-looking old boozer. Most extraordinary man I ever met – medically, of course. Won't you?"

'I had been all along exhibiting the usual polite signs of interest, but now assuming an air of regret I murmured of want of time, and shook hands in a hurry. "I say," he cried after me, "he can't attend that inquiry. Is his evidence material, you think?"

'"Not in the least," I called back from the gateway.'

# CHAPTER SIX

'THE authorities were evidently of the same opinion. The inquiry was not adjourned. It was held on the appointed day to satisfy the law, and it was well attended because of its human interest, no doubt. There was no incertitude as to facts – as to the one material fact, I mean. How the *Patna* came by her hurt it was impossible to find out; the court did not expect to find out; and in the whole audience there was not a man who cared. Yet, as I've told you, all the sailors in the port attended, and the waterside business was fully represented. Whether they knew it or not, the interest that drew them there was purely psychological – the expectation of some essential disclosure as to the strength, the power, the horror, of human emotions. Naturally nothing of the kind could be disclosed. The examination of the only man able and willing to face it was beating futilely round the well-known fact, and the play of questions upon it was as instructive as the tapping with a hammer on an iron box, were the object to find out what's inside. However, an official inquiry could not be any other thing. Its object was not the fundamental why, but the superficial how, of this affair.

'The young chap could have told them, and, though that very thing was the thing that interested the audience, the questions put to him necessarily led him away from what to me, for instance, would have been the only truth worth knowing. You can't expect the constituted authorities to inquire into the state of a man's soul – or is it only of his liver? Their business was to come down upon the consequences, and frankly, a casual police magistrate and two nautical assessors are not much good for anything else.

I don't mean to imply these fellows were stupid. The magistrate was very patient. One of the assessors was a sailing-ship skipper with a reddish beard, and of a pious disposition. Brierly was the other. Big Brierly. Some of you must have heard of Big Brierly – the captain of the crack ship of the Blue Star line. That's the man.

'He seemed consumedly bored by the honour thrust upon him. He had never in his life made a mistake, never had an accident, never a mishap, never a check in his steady rise, and he seemed to be one of those lucky fellows who know nothing of indecision, much less of self-mistrust. At thirty-two he had one of the best commands going in the Eastern trade – and, what's more, he thought a lot of what he had. There was nothing like it in the world, and I suppose if you had asked him point-blank he would have confessed that in his opinion there was not such another commander. The choice had fallen upon the right man. The rest of mankind that did not command the sixteen-knot steel steamer *Ossa* were rather poor creatures. He had saved lives at sea, had rescued ships in distress, had a gold chronometer presented to him by the underwriters, and a pair of binoculars with a suitable inscription from some foreign Government, in commemoration of these services. He was acutely aware of his merits and of his rewards. I liked him well enough, though some I know – meek, friendly men at that – couldn't stand him at any price. I haven't the slightest doubt he considered himself vastly my superior – indeed, had you been Emperor of East and West, you could not have ignored your inferiority in his presence – but I couldn't get up any real sentiment of offence. He did not despise me for anything I could help, for anything I was – don't you know? I was a negligible quantity simply because I was not *the* fortunate man of the earth, not Montague Brierly in command of the *Ossa*, not the owner of an inscribed gold chronometer and of silver-mounted binoculars testifying to the excellence of my sea-manship and to my indomitable pluck; not possessed of an

acute sense of my merits and of my rewards, besides the
love and worship of a black retriever, the most wonderful of
its kind – for never was such a man loved thus by such a
dog. No doubt, to have all this forced upon you was exasperating enough; but when I reflected that I was associated in these fatal disadvantages with twelve hundred
millions of other more or less human beings, I found I
could bear my share of his good-natured and contemptuous pity for the sake of something indefinite and attractive
in the man. I have never defined to myself this attraction,
but there were moments when I envied him. The sting of
life could do no more to his complacent soul than the
scratch of a pin to the smooth face of a rock. This
was enviable. As I looked at him flanking on one side the
unassuming pale-faced magistrate who presided at
the inquiry, his self-satisfaction presented to me and to
the world a surface as hard as granite. He committed
suicide very soon after.

'No wonder Jim's case bored him, and while I thought
with something akin to fear of the immensity of his contempt for the young man under examination, he was probably holding silent inquiry into his own case. The verdict
must have been of unmitigated guilt, and he took the secret
of the evidence with him in that leap into the sea. If
I understand anything of men, the matter was no doubt
of the gravest import, one of those trifles that awaken ideas
– start into life some thought with which a man unused to
such a companionship finds it impossible to live. I am in a
position to know that it wasn't money, and it wasn't drink,
and it wasn't woman. He jumped overboard at sea barely a
week after the end of the inquiry, and less than three days
after leaving port on his outward passage; as though on that
exact spot in the midst of waters he had suddenly perceived
the gates of the other world flung open wide for his reception.

'Yet it was not a sudden impulse. His grey-headed mate,
a first-rate sailor and a nice old chap with strangers, but in

his relations with his commander the surliest chief-officer I've ever seen, would tell the story with tears in his eyes. It appears that when he came on deck in the morning Brierly had been writing in the chart-room. "It was ten minutes to four," he said, "and the middle watch was not relieved yet of course. He heard my voice on the bridge speaking to the second mate, and called me in. I was loth to go, and that's the truth, Captain Marlow – I couldn't stand poor Captain Brierly, I tell you with shame; we never know what a man is made of. He had been promoted over too many heads, not counting my own, and he had a damnable trick of making you feel small, nothing but by the way he said 'Good morning.' I never addressed him, sir, but on matters of duty, and then it was as much as I could do to keep a civil tongue in my head." (He flattered himself there. I often wondered how Brierly could put up with his manners for more than half a voyage.) "I've a wife and children," he went on, "and I had been ten years in the Company, always expecting the next command – more fool I. Says he, just like this: 'Come in here, Mr Jones,' in that swagger voice of his – 'Come in here, Mr Jones.' In I went. 'We'll lay down her position,' says he, stooping over the chart, a pair of dividers in hand. By the standing orders, the officer going off duty would have done that at the end of his watch. However, I said nothing, and looked on while he marked off the ship's position with a tiny cross and wrote the date and the time. I can see him this moment writing his neat figures: seventeen, eight, four a.m. The year would be written in red ink at the top of the chart. He never used his charts more than a year, Captain Brierly didn't. I've the chart now. When he had done he stands looking down at the mark he had made and smiling to himself, then looks up at me. 'Thirty-two miles more as she goes,' says he, 'and then we shall be clear, and you may alter the course twenty degrees to the southward.'

'"We were passing to the north of the Hector Bank that voyage. I said, 'All right, sir,' wondering what he was fussing about, since I had to call him before altering the course anyhow. Just then eight bells were struck: we came out on the bridge, and the second mate before going off mentions in the usual way – 'Seventy-one on the log.' Captain Brierly looks at the compass and then all round. It was dark and clear, and all the stars were out as plain as on a frosty night in high latitudes. Suddenly he says with a sort of a little sigh: 'I am going aft, and shall set the log at zero for you myself, so that there can be no mistake. Thirty-two miles more on this course and then you are safe. Let's see – the correction on the log is six per cent, additive; say, then, thirty by the dial to run, and you may come twenty degrees to starboard at once. No use losing any distance – is there?' I had never heard him talk so much at a stretch, and to no purpose as it seemed to me. I said nothing. He went down the ladder, and the dog, that was always at his heels whenever he moved, night or day, followed, sliding nose first, after him. I heard his boot-heels tap, tap on the after-deck, then he stopped and spoke to the dog – 'Go back, Rover. On the bridge, boy! Go on – get.' Then he calls out to me from the dark, 'Shut that dog up in the chart-room, Mr Jones – will you?'

'"This was the last time I heard his voice, Captain Marlow. These are the last words he spoke in the hearing of any living human being, sir." At this point the old chap's voice got quite unsteady. "He was afraid the poor brute would jump after him, don't you see?" he pursued with a quaver. "Yes, Captain Marlow. He set the log for me; he – would you believe it? – he put a drop of oil in it too. There was the oil-feeder where he left it near by. The boatswain's mate got the hose along aft to wash down at half-past five; by-and-by he knocks off and runs up on the bridge – 'Will you please come aft, Mr Jones,' he says. 'There's a funny thing. I don't like to touch it.' It was Captain Brierly's gold chronometer watch carefully hung under the rail by its chain.

'"As soon as my eyes fell on it something struck me, and I knew, sir. My legs got soft under me. It was as if I had seen him go over; and I could tell how far behind he was left too. The taffrail-log marked eighteen miles and three-quarters, and four iron belaying-pins were missing round the main-mast. Put them in his pockets to help him down, I suppose; but, Lord! what's four iron pins to a powerful man like Captain Brierly. Maybe his confidence in himself was just shook a bit at the last. That's the only sign of fluster he gave in his whole life, I should think; but I am ready to answer for him, that once over he did not try to swim a stroke, the same as he would have had pluck enough to keep up all day long on the bare chance had he fallen overboard acciden-tally. Yes, sir. He was second to none – if he said so himself, as I heard him once. He had written two letters in the middle watch, one to the Company and the other to me. He gave me a lot of instructions as to the passage – I had been in the trade before he was out of his time – and no end of hints as to my conduct with our people in Shanghai, so that I should keep the command of the *Ossa*. He wrote like a father would to a favourite son, Captain Marlow, and I was five-and-twenty years his senior and had tasted salt water before he was fairly breeched. In his letter to the owners – it was left open for me to see – he said that he had always done his duty by them – up to that moment – and even now he was not betraying their confidence, since he was leaving the ship to as competent a seaman as could be found – meaning me, sir, meaning me! He told them that if the last act of his life didn't take away all his credit with them, they would give weight to my faithful service and to his warm recommendation, when about to fill the vacancy made by his death. And much more like this, sir. I couldn't believe my eyes. It made me feel queer all over," went on the old chap in great perturbation, and squashing something in the corner of his eye with the end of a thumb as broad as a spatula. "You would think, sir, he had jumped overboard only to give an unlucky man a last show to get on. What with the shock of him going in this awful rash way, and thinking myself a made man by that chance, I was nearly

off my chump for a week. But no fear. The captain of the
*Pelion* was shifted into the *Ossa* – came aboard in Shanghai
– a little popinjay, sir, in a grey check suit, with his hair
parted in the middle. 'Aw – I am – aw – your new captain,
Mister – mister – aw – Jones.' He was drowned in scent –
fairly stunk with it, Captain Marlow. I daresay it was the
look I gave him that made him stammer. He mumbled
something about my natural disappointment – I had better
know at once that his chief officer got the promotion to the
*Pelion* – he had nothing to do with it, of course – supposed
the office knew best – sorry. . . . Says I, 'Don't you mind old
Jones, sir; damn his soul, he's used to it.' I could see directly
I had shocked his delicate ear, and while we sat at our first
tiffin together he began to find fault in a nasty manner with
this and that in the ship. I never heard such a voice out of a
Punch and Judy show. I set my teeth hard, and glued my
eyes to my plate, and held my peace as long as I could; but at
last I had to say something: up he jumps tiptoeing, ruffling
all his pretty plumes, like a little fighting cock. 'You'll find
you have a different person to deal with than the late
Captain Brierly.' 'I've found it,' says I, very glum, but pretending to be mighty busy with my steak. 'You are an old
ruffian, Mr – aw – Jones; and what's more, you are known
for an old ruffian in the employ,' he squeaks at me. The
damned bottle-washers stood about listening with their
mouths stretched from ear to ear. 'I may be a hard case,'
answers I, 'but I ain't so far gone as to put up with the sight
of you sitting in Captain Brierly's chair.' With that I lay
down my knife and fork. 'You would like to sit in it yourself
– that's where the shoe pinches,' he sneers. I left the saloon,
got my rags together, and was on the quay with all my
dunnage about my feet before the stevedores had turned to
again. Yes. Adrift – on shore – after ten years' service – and
with a poor woman and four children six thousand miles
off depending on my half-pay for every mouthful they ate.
Yes, sir! I chucked it rather than hear Captain Brierly
abused. He left me his night-glasses – here they are; and

he wished me to take care of the dog – here he is. Hallo, Rover, poor boy. Where's the captain, Rover?" The dog looked up at us with mournful yellow eyes, gave one desolate bark, and crept under the table.

'All this was taking place, more than two years afterwards, on board that nautical ruin the *Fire-Queen* this Jones had got charge of – quite by a funny accident, too – from Matherson – mad Matherson they generally called him – the same who used to hang out in Haï-phong, you know, before the occupation days. The old chap snuffled on –

'"Ay, sir, Captain Brierly will be remembered here, if there's no other place on earth. I wrote fully to his father and did not get a word in reply – neither Thank you, nor Go to the devil! – nothing! Perhaps they did not want to know."

'The sight of that watery-eyed old Jones mopping his bald head with a red cotton handkerchief, the sorrowing yelp of the dog, the squalor of that fly-blown cuddy which was the only shrine of his memory, threw a veil of inexpressibly mean pathos over Brierly's remembered figure, the posthumous revenge of fate for that belief in his own splendour which had almost cheated his life of its legitimate terrors. Almost! Perhaps wholly. Who can tell what flattering view he had induced himself to take of his own suicide?

'"Why did he commit the rash act, Captain Marlow – can you think?" asked Jones, pressing his palms together. "Why? It beats me! Why?" He slapped his low and wrinkled forehead. "If he had been poor and old and in debt – and never a show – or else mad. But he wasn't of the kind that goes mad, not he. You trust me. What a mate don't know about his skipper isn't worth knowing. Young, healthy, well off, no cares. . . . I sit here sometimes thinking, thinking, till my head fairly begins to buzz. There was some reason."'

'"You may depend on it, Captain Jones," said I, "it wasn't anything that would have disturbed much either of us two,"

I said; and then, as if a light had been flashed into the muddle of his brain, poor old Jones found a last word of amazing profundity. He blew his nose, nodding at me dolefully: "Ay, ay! neither you nor I, sir, had ever thought so much of ourselves."

'Of course the recollection of my last conversation with Brierly is tinged with the knowledge of his end that followed so close upon it. I spoke with him for the last time during the progress of the inquiry. It was after the first adjournment, and he came up with me in the street. He was in a state of irritation, which I noticed with surprise, his usual behaviour when he condescended to converse being perfectly cool, with a trace of amused tolerance, as if the existence of his interlocutor had been a rather good joke. "They caught me for that inquiry, you see," he began, and for a while enlarged complainingly upon the inconveniences of daily attendance in court. "And goodness knows how long it will last. Three days, I suppose." I heard him out in silence; in my then opinion it was a way as good as another of putting on side. "What's the use of it? It is the stupidest set out you can imagine," he pursued, hotly. I remarked that there was no option. He interrupted me with a sort of pent-up violence. "I feel like a fool all the time." I looked up at him. This was going very far – for Brierly – when talking of Brierly. He stopped short, and seizing the lapel of my coat, gave it a slight tug. "Why are we tormenting that young chap?" he asked. This question chimed in so well to the tolling of a certain thought of mine that, with the image of the absconding renegade in my eye, I answered at once, "Hanged if I know, unless it be that he lets you." I was astonished to see him fall into line, so to speak, with that utterance, which ought to have been tolerably cryptic. He said angrily, "Why, yes. Can't he see that wretched skipper of his has cleared out? What does he expect to happen? Nothing can save him. He's done for." We walked on in silence a few steps. "Why eat all that dirt?" he exclaimed, with an oriental energy of expression – about the only sort of energy you can find a trace of east of the fiftieth meridian. I wondered greatly at the direction of his thoughts, but now I strongly suspect it was strictly in character; at bottom poor Brierly must have been thinking of himself. I pointed out to him that the skipper of the *Patna* was known to have feathered his nest pretty well, and could procure almost anywhere the means of getting away. With Jim it was otherwise: the Government was keeping him in the Sailors' Home for the time being, and probably he hadn't a penny in his pocket to bless himself with. It costs some money to run away. "Does it? Not always," he said, with a bitter laugh, and to some further remark of mine – "Well, then, let him creep twenty feet underground and stay there! By heavens! *I* would." I don't know why his tone provoked me, and I said, "There is a kind of courage in facing it out as he does, knowing very well that if he went away nobody would trouble to run after him." "Courage be hanged!" growled Brierly. "That sort of courage is of no use to keep a man straight, and I don't care a snap for such courage. If you were to say it was a kind of cowardice now – of softness. I tell you what, I will put up two hundred rupees if you put up another hundred and undertake to make the beggar clear out early to-morrow morning. The fellow's a gentleman if he ain't fit to be touched – he will understand. He must! This infernal publicity is too shocking: there he sits while all these confounded natives, serangs, lascars, quartermasters, are giving evidence that's enough to burn a man to ashes with shame. This is abominable. Why, Marlow, don't you think, don't you feel, that this is abominable; don't you now – come – as a seaman? If he went away all this would stop at once." Brierly said these words with a most unusual animation, and made as if to reach after his pocket-book. I restrained him, and declared coldly that the cowardice of these four men did not seem to me a matter of such great importance. "And you call yourself a seaman, I suppose," he pronounced, angrily. I said that's what I called myself, and I hoped I was too. He heard me out, and made a gesture with his big arm that seemed to deprive me of my individuality, to push me away into the crowd. "The worst of it," he said, "is that all you fellows have no sense of dignity; you don't think enough of what you are supposed to be."

'We had been walking slowly meantime, and now stopped opposite the harbour office, in sight of the very spot from which the immense captain of the *Patna* had vanished as utterly as a tiny feather blown away in a hurricane. I smiled. Brierly went on: "This is a disgrace. We've got all kinds amongst us – some anointed scoundrels in the lot; but, hang it, we must preserve professional decency or we become no better than so many tinkers going about loose. We are trusted. Do you understand? – trusted! Frankly, I don't care a snap for all the pilgrims that ever came out of Asia, but a decent man would not have behaved like this to a full cargo of old rags in bales. We aren't an organised body of men, and the only thing that holds us together is just the name for that kind of decency. Such an affair destroys one's confidence. A man may go pretty near through his whole sea-life without any call to show a stiff upper lip. But when the call comes ... Aha! ... If I ...:"

'He broke off, and in a changed tone, "I'll give you two hundred rupees now, Marlow, and you just talk to that chap. Confound him! I wish he had never come out here. Fact is, I rather think some of my people know his. The old man's a parson, and I remember now I met him once when staying with my cousin in Essex last year. If I am not mistaken, the old chap seemed rather to fancy his sailor son. Horrible. I can't do it myself – but you ..."

'Thus, apropos of Jim, I had a glimpse of the real Brierly a few days before he committed his reality and his sham together to the keeping of the sea. Of course I declined to meddle. The tone of this last "but you" (poor Brierly couldn't help it), that seemed to imply I was no more noticeable than an insect, caused me to look at the proposal with indignation, and on account of that provocation, or for some other reason, I became positive in my mind that the inquiry was a severe punishment to that Jim, and that his facing it – practically of his own free will – was a redeeming feature in his abominable case. I hadn't been so sure of it before. Brierly went off in a huff. At the time his state of mind was more of a mystery to me than it is now.

'Next day, coming into court late, I sat by myself. Of course I could not forget the conversation I had with Brierly, and now I had them both under my eyes. The demeanour of one suggested gloomy impudence and of the other a contemptuous boredom; yet one attitude might not have been truer than the other, and I was aware that one was not true. Brierly was not bored – he was exasperated; and if so, then Jim might not have been impudent. According to my theory he was not. I imagined he was hopeless. Then it was that our glances met. They met, and the look he gave me was discouraging of any intention I might have had to speak to him. Upon either hypothesis – insolence or despair – I felt I could be of no use to him. This was the second day of the proceedings. Very soon after that exchange of glances the inquiry was adjourned again to the next day. The white men began to troop out at once. Jim had been told to stand down some time before, and was able to leave amongst the first. I saw his broad shoulders and his head outlined in the light of the door, and while I made my way slowly out talking with some one – some stranger who had addressed me casually – I could see him from within the court-room resting both elbows on the balustrade of the verandah and turning his back on the small stream of people trickling down the few steps. There was a murmur of voices and a shuffle of boots.

'The next case was that of assault and battery committed upon a money-lender, I believe; and the defendant – a venerable villager with a straight white beard – sat on a mat just outside the door with his sons, daughters, sons-in-law, their wives, and, I should think, half the population of his village besides, squatting or standing around him. A

slim dark woman, with part of her back and one black
shoulder bared, and with a thin gold ring in her nose,
suddenly began to talk in a high-pitched, shrewish tone.
The man with me instinctively looked up at her. We were
then just through the door, passing behind Jim's burly back.

'Whether those villagers had brought the yellow dog
with them, I don't know. Anyhow, a dog was there, weaving
himself in and out amongst people's legs in that mute
stealthy way native dogs have and my companion stumbled
over him. The dog leaped away without a sound; the man,
raising his voice a little, said with a slow laugh, "Look at
that wretched cur," and directly afterwards we became
separated by a lot of people pushing in. I stood back for a
moment against the wall while the stranger managed to
get down the steps and disappeared. I saw Jim spin round.
He made a step forward and barred my way. We were alone;
he glared at me with an air of stubborn resolution. I became
aware I was being held up, so to speak, as if in a wood.
The verandah was empty by then, the noise and movement
in court had ceased: a great silence fell upon the building, in
which, somewhere far within, an oriental voice began to
whine abjectly. The dog in the very act of trying to sneak in
at the door, sat down hurriedly to hunt for fleas.'

'"Did you speak to me?" asked Jim very low, and bending forward, not so much towards me but at me, if you
know what I mean. I said "No" at once. Something in the
sound of that quiet tone of his warned me to be on my
defence. I watched him. It was very much like a meeting in
a wood, only more uncertain in its issue, since he could
possibly want neither my money nor my life – nothing that
I could simply give up or defend with a clear conscience.
"You say you didn't," he said, very sombre. "But I heard."
"Some mistake," I protested, utterly at a loss, and never
taking my eyes off him. To watch his face was like watching
a darkening sky before a clap of thunder, shade upon shade
imperceptibly coming on, the gloom growing mysteriously
intense in the calm of maturing violence.

' "As far as I know, I haven't opened my lips in your hearing," I affirmed with perfect truth. I was getting a little angry, too, at the absurdity of this encounter. It strikes me now I have never in my life been so near a beating – I mean it literally; a beating with fists. I suppose I had some hazy prescience of that eventuality being in the air. Not that he was actively threatening me. On the contrary, he was strangely passive – don't you know? but he was lowering, and, though not exceptionally big, he looked generally fit to demolish a wall. The most reassuring symptom I noticed was a kind of slow and ponderous hesitation, which I took as a tribute to the evident sincerity of my manner and of my tone. We faced each other. In the court the assault case was proceeding. I caught the words: "Well – buffalo – stick – in the greatness of my fear. . . ."

' "What did you mean by staring at me all the morning?" said Jim at last. He looked up and looked down again. "Did you expect us all to sit with downcast eyes out of regard for your susceptibilities?" I retorted sharply. I was not going to submit meekly to any of his nonsense. He raised his eyes again, and this time continued to look me straight in the face. "No. That's all right," he pronounced with an air of deliberating with himself upon the truth of this statement – "that's all right. I am going through with that. Only" – and there he spoke a little faster – "I won't let any man call me names outside this court. There was a fellow with you. You spoke to him – oh, yes – I know; 'tis all very fine. You spoke to him, but you meant me to hear. . . ."

'I assured him he was under some extraordinary delusion. I had no conception how it came about. "You thought I would be afraid to resent this," he said, with just a faint tinge of bitterness. I was interested enough to discern the slightest shades of expression, but I was not in the least enlightened; yet I don't know what in these words, or perhaps just the intonation of that phrase, induced me suddenly to make all possible allowances for him. I ceased to be annoyed at my unexpected predicament. It was some

mistake on his part; he was blundering and I had an intu-
ition that the blunder was of an odious, of an unfortunate
nature. I was anxious to end this scene on grounds of
decency, just as one is anxious to cut short some unprovoked
and abominable confidence. The funniest part was, that in
the midst of all these considerations of the higher order I
was conscious of a certain trepidation as to the possibility –
nay, likelihood – of this encounter ending in some disreputable brawl which could not possibly be explained, and
would make me ridiculous. I did not hanker after a three
days' celebrity as the man who got a black eye or something
of the sort from the mate of the *Patna*. He, in all probability, did not care what he did, or at any rate would be
fully justified in his own eyes. It took no magician to see he
was amazingly angry about something, for all his quiet and
even torpid demeanour. I don't deny I was extremely desir-
ous to pacify him at all costs, had I only known what to do.
But I didn't know, as you may well imagine. It was blackness without a single gleam. We confronted each other in
silence. He hung fire for about fifteen seconds, then made a
step nearer, and I made ready to ward off a blow, though
I don't think I moved a muscle. "If you were as big as two
men and as strong as six," he said very softly, "I would tell
you what I think of you. You . . ." "Stop!" I exclaimed. This
checked him for a second. "Before you tell me what you
think of me," I went on, quickly, "will you kindly tell me
what it is I've said or done?" During the pause that ensued
he surveyed me with indignation, while I made supernatural efforts of memory, in which I was hindered by the
oriental voice within the court-room expostulating with
impassioned volubility against a charge of falsehood. Then
we spoke almost together. "I will soon show you I am not,"
he said, in a tone suggestive of a crisis. "I declare I don't
know," I protested earnestly at the same time. He tried to
crush me by the scorn of his glance. "Now that you see I am
not afraid you try to crawl out of it," he said. "Who's a cur
now – hey?" Then, at last, I understood.

'He had been scanning my features as though looking for a place where he would plant his fist. "I will allow no man," . . . he mumbled, threateningly. It was, indeed, a hideous mistake; he had given himself away utterly. I can't give you an idea how shocked I was. I suppose he saw some reflection of my feelings in my face, because his expression changed just a little. "Good God!" I stammered, "you don't think I . . ." "But I am sure I've heard," he persisted, raising his voice for the first time since the beginning of this deplorable scene. Then with a shade of disdain he added, "It wasn't you, then? Very well; I'll find the other." "Don't be a fool," I cried in exasperation; "it wasn't that at all." "I've heard," he said again with an unshaken and sombre perseverance.

'There may be those who could have laughed at his pertinacity. I didn't. Oh, I didn't! There had never been a man so mercilessly shown up by his own natural impulse. A single word had stripped him of his discretion – of that discretion which is more necessary to the decencies of our inner being than clothing is to the decorum of our body. "Don't be a fool," I repeated. "But the other man said it, you don't deny that?" he pronounced, distinctly, and looking in my face without flinching. "No, I don't deny," said I, returning his gaze. At last his eyes followed downwards the direction of my pointing finger. He appeared at first uncomprehending, then confounded, and at last amazed and scared as though a dog had been a monster and he had never seen a dog before. "Nobody dreamt of insulting you," I said.

'He contemplated the wretched animal, that moved no more than an effigy: it sat with ears pricked and its sharp muzzle pointed into the doorway, and suddenly snapped at a fly like a piece of mechanism.

'I looked at him. The red of his fair sunburnt complexion deepened suddenly under the down of his cheeks, invaded his forehead, spread to the roots of his curly hair. His ears became intensely crimson, and even the clear blue of his eyes was darkened many shades by the rush of blood to his head. His lips pouted a little, trembling as though he had been on the point of bursting into tears. I perceived he was incapable of pronouncing a word from the excess of his humiliation. From disappointment too – who knows? Perhaps he looked forward to that hammering he was going to give me for rehabilitation, for appeasement? Who can tell what relief he expected from this chance of a row? He was naïve enough to expect anything; but he had given himself away for nothing in this case. He had been frank with himself – let alone with me – in the wild hope of arriving in that way at some effective refutation, and the stars had been ironically unpropitious. He made an inarticulate noise in his throat like a man imperfectly stunned by a blow on the head. It was pitiful.

'I didn't catch up again with him till well outside the gate. I had even to trot a bit at the last, but when, out of breath at his elbow, I taxed him with running away, he said, "Never!" and at once turned at bay. I explained I never meant to say he was running away from *me*. "From no man – from not a single man on earth," he affirmed with a stubborn mien. I forebore to point out the one obvious exception which would hold good for the bravest of us; I thought he would find out by himself very soon. He looked at me patiently while I was thinking of something to say, but I could find nothing on the spur of the moment, and he began to walk on. I kept up, and anxious not to lose him, I said hurriedly that I couldn't think of leaving him under a false impression of my – of my – I stammered. The stupidity of the phrase appalled me while I was trying to finish it, but the power of sentences has nothing to do with their sense or the logic of their construction. My idiotic mumble seemed to please him. He cut it short by saying, with courteous placidity that argued an immense power of self-control or else a wonderful elasticity of spirits – "Altogether my mistake." I marvelled greatly at this expression: he might have been alluding to some trifling

occurrence. Hadn't he understood its deplorable meaning?
"You may well forgive me," he continued, and went on a
little moodily, "All these staring people in court seemed
such fools that – that it might have been as I supposed."

'This opened suddenly a new view of him to my wonder.
I looked at him curiously and met his unabashed and
impenetrable eyes. "I can't put up with this kind of
thing," he said, very simply, "and I don't mean to. In court
it's different; I've got to stand that – and I can do it too."

'I don't pretend I understood him. The views he let me
have of himself were like those glimpses through the shifting rents in a thick fog – bits of vivid and vanishing detail,
giving no connected idea of the general aspect of a country.
They fed one's curiosity without satisfying it; they were no
good for purposes of orientation. Upon the whole he was
misleading. That's how I summed him up to myself after he
left me late in the evening. I had been staying at the
Malabar House for a few days, and on my pressing invita-
tion he dined with me there.'

# CHAPTER SEVEN

'An outward-bound mail-boat had come in that afternoon, and the big dining-room of the hotel was more than half full of people with a hundred pounds round-the-world tickets in their pockets. There were married couples looking domesticated and bored with each other in the midst of their travels; there were small parties and large parties, and lone individuals dining solemnly or feasting boisterously, but all thinking, conversing, joking, or scowling as was their wont at home; and just as intelligently receptive of new impressions as their trunks upstairs. Henceforth they would be labelled as having passed through this and that place, and so would be their luggage. They would cherish this distinction of their persons, and preserve the gummed tickets on their portmanteaus as documentary evidence, as the only permanent trace of their improving enterprise. The dark-faced servants tripped without noise over the vast and polished floor; now and then a girl's laugh would be heard, as innocent and empty as her mind, or, in a sudden hush of crockery, a few words in an affected drawl from some wit embroidering for the benefit of a grinning tableful the last funny story of shipboard scandal. Two nomadic old maids, dressed up to kill, worked acrimoniously through the bill of fare, whispering to each other with faded lips, wooden-faced and bizarre, like two sumptuous scarecrows. A little wine opened Jim's heart and loosened his tongue. His appetite was good, too, I noticed. He seemed to have buried somewhere the opening episode of our acquaintance. It was like a thing of which there would be no more question in this world. And all the time I had before

71

me these blue, boyish eyes looking straight into mine, this
young face, these capable shoulders, the open bronzed
forehead with a white line under the roots of clustering
fair hair, this appearance appealing at sight to all my sympathies: this frank aspect, the artless smile, the youthful
seriousness. He was of the right sort; he was one of us. He
talked soberly, with a sort of composed unreserve, and with
a quiet bearing that might have been the outcome of manly
self-control, of impudence, of callousness, of a colossal
unconsciousness, of a gigantic deception. Who can tell!
From our tone we might have been discussing a third
person, a football match, last year's weather. My mind
floated in a sea of conjectures till the turn of the conversation enabled me, without being offensive, to remark that,
upon the whole, this inquiry must have been pretty trying
to him. He darted his arm across the tablecloth, and clutching my hand by the side of my plate, glared fixedly. I *was*
startled. "It must be awfully hard," I stammered, confused
by this display of speechless feeling. "It is – hell," he burst
out in a muffled voice.

'This movement and these words caused two well-
groomed male globe-trotters at a neighbouring table to
look up in alarm from their iced pudding. I rose, and we
passed into the front gallery for coffee and cigars.

'On little octagon tables candles burned in glass globes;
clumps of stiff-leaved plants separated sets of cosy wicker
chairs; and between the pairs of columns, whose reddish
shafts caught in a long row the sheen from the tall windows,
the night, glittering and sombre, seemed to hang like a
splendid drapery. The riding lights of ships winked afar like
setting stars, and the hills across the roadstead resembled
rounded black masses of arrested thunder-clouds.

' "I couldn't clear out," Jim began. "The skipper did – that's
all very well for him. I couldn't, and I wouldn't. They all got
out of it in one way or another, but it wouldn't do for me."

'I listened with concentrated attention, not daring to stir
in my chair; I wanted to know – and to this day I don't

know, I can only guess. He would be confident and depressed all in the same breath, as if some conviction of innate blamelessness had checked the truth writhing within him at every turn. He began by saying, in the tone in which a man would admit his inability to jump a twenty-foot wall, that he could never go home now; and this declaration recalled to my mind what Brierly had said, "that the old parson in Essex seemed to fancy his sailor son not a little."

'I can't tell you whether Jim knew he was especially "fancied," but the tone of his references to "my Dad" was calculated to give me a notion that the good old rural dean was about the finest man that ever had been worried by the cares of a large family since the beginning of the world. This, though never stated, was implied with an anxiety that there should be no mistake about it, which was really very true and charming, but added a poignant sense of lives far off to the other elements of the story. "He has seen it all in the home papers by this time," said Jim. "I can never face the poor old chap." I did not dare to lift my eyes at this till I heard him add, "I could never explain. He wouldn't understand." Then I looked up. He was smoking reflectively, and after a moment, rousing himself, began to talk again. He discovered at once a desire that I should not confound him with his partners in – in crime, let us call it. He was not one of them; he was altogether of another sort. I gave no sign of dissent. I had no intention, for the sake of barren truth, to rob him of the smallest particle of any saving grace that would come in his way. I didn't know how much of it he believed himself. I didn't know what he was playing up to – if he was playing up to anything at all – and I suspect he did not know either; for it is my belief no man ever understands quite his own artful dodges to escape from the grim shadow of self-knowledge. I made no sound all the time he was wondering what he had better do after "that stupid inquiry was over."

'Apparently he shared Brierly's contemptuous opinion of these proceedings ordained by law. He would not know where to turn, he confessed, clearly thinking aloud rather than talking to me. Certificate gone, career broken, no money to get away, no work that he could obtain as far as he could see. At home he could perhaps get something; but it meant going to his people for help, and that he would not do. He saw nothing for it but ship before the mast – could get perhaps a quartermaster's billet in some steamer. Would do for a quartermaster.... "Do you think you would?" I asked, pitilessly. He jumped up, and going to the stone balustrade looked out into the night. In a moment he was back, towering above my chair with his youthful face clouded yet by the pain of a conquered emotion. He had understood very well I did not doubt his ability to steer a ship. In a voice that quavered a bit he asked me, "Why did I say that? I had been 'no end kind' to him. I had not even laughed at him when" – here he began to mumble – "that mistake, you know – made a confounded ass of myself." I broke in by saying rather warmly that for me such a mistake was not a matter to laugh at. He sat down and drank deliberately some coffee, emptying the small cup to the last drop. "That does not mean I admit for a moment the cap fitted," he declared, distinctly. "No?" I said. "No," he affirmed with quiet decision. "Do you know what *you* would have done? Do you? And you don't think yourself" ... he gulped something ... "you don't think yourself a – a – cur?"

'And with this – upon my honour! – he looked up at me inquisitively. It was a question it appears – a *bonâ-fide* question! However, he didn't wait for an answer. Before I could recover he went on, with his eyes straight before him, as if reading off something written on the body of the night. "It is all in being ready. I wasn't; not – not then. I don't want to excuse myself; but I would like to explain – I would like somebody to understand – somebody – one person at least! You! Why not you?"

'It was solemn, and a little ridiculous, too, as they always are, those struggles of an individual trying to save from the

fire his idea of what his moral identity should be, this
precious notion of a convention, only one of the rules of
the game, nothing more, but all the same so terribly effective by its assumption of unlimited power over natural
instincts, by the awful penalties of its failure. He began
his story quietly enough. On board that Dale Line steamer
that had picked up these four floating in a boat upon the
discreet sunset glow of the sea, they had been after the first
day looked askance upon. The fat skipper told some story,
the others had been silent, and at first it had been accepted.
You don't cross-examine poor castaways you had the good
luck to save, if not from cruel death, then at least from cruel
suffering. Afterwards, with time to think it over, it might
have struck the officers of the *Avondale* that there was
"something fishy" in the affair; but of course they would
keep their doubts to themselves. They had picked up the
captain, the mate, and two engineers of the steamer *Patna*
sunk at sea, and that, very properly, was enough for them. I
did not ask Jim about the nature of his feelings during the
ten days he spent on board. From the way he narrated that
part I was at liberty to infer he was partly stunned by the
discovery he had made – the discovery about himself – and
no doubt was at work trying to explain it away to the only
man who was capable of appreciating all its tremendous
magnitude. You must understand he did not try to min-
imise its importance. Of that I am sure; and therein lies his
distinction. As to what sensations he experienced when he
got ashore and heard the unforeseen conclusion of the tale
in which he had taken such a pitiful part, he told me
nothing of them, and it is difficult to imagine. I wonder
whether he felt the ground cut from under his feet? I
wonder? But no doubt he managed to get a fresh foothold
very soon. He was ashore a whole fortnight waiting in the
Sailors' Home, and as there were six or seven men staying
there at the time, I had heard of him a little. Their languid
opinion seemed to be that in addition to his other short-
comings, he was a sulky brute. He had passed these days on

the verandah, buried in a long chair, and coming out of his
place of sepulture only at meal-times or late at night, when
he wandered on the quays all by himself, detached from his
surroundings, irresolute and silent, like a ghost without a
home to haunt. "I don't think I've spoken three words to a
living soul in all that time," he said, making me very sorry
for him; and directly he added, "One of these fellows would
have been sure to blurt out something I had made up my
mind not to put up with, and I didn't want a row. No! Not
then. I was too – too... I had no heart for it." "So that
bulkhead held out after all," I remarked, cheerfully. "Yes,"
he murmured, "it held. And yet I swear to you I felt it bulge
under my hand." "It's extraordinary what strains old iron
will stand sometimes," I said. Thrown back in his seat, his
legs stiffly out and arms hanging down, he nodded slightly
several times. You could not conceive a sadder spectacle.
Suddenly he lifted his head; he sat up; he slapped his thigh,
"Ah! what a chance missed! My God! what a chance
missed!" he blazed out, but the ring of the last "missed"
resembled a cry wrung out by pain.

'He was silent again with a still, far-away look of fierce
yearning after that missed distinction, with his nostrils for
an instant dilated, sniffing the intoxicating breath of that
wasted opportunity. If you think I was either surprised or
shocked you do me an injustice in more ways than one! Ah,
he was an imaginative beggar! He would give himself away;
he would give himself up. I could see in his glance darted
into the night all his inner being carried on, projected
headlong into the fanciful realm of recklessly heroic aspirations. He had no leisure to regret what he had lost, he was
so wholly and naturally concerned for what he had failed to
obtain. He was very far away from me who watched him
across three feet of space. With every instant he was penetrating deeper into the impossible world of romantic
achievements. He got to the heart of it at last! A strange
look of beatitude overspread his features, his eyes sparkled
in the light of the candle burning between us; he positively

smiled! He had penetrated to the very heart – to the very heart. It was an ecstatic smile that your faces – or mine either – will never wear, my dear boys. I whisked him back by saying, "If you had stuck to the ship, you mean!"

'He turned upon me, his eyes suddenly amazed and full of pain, with a bewildered, startled, suffering face, as though he had tumbled down from a star. Neither you nor I will ever look like this on any man. He shuddered profoundly, as if a cold finger-tip had touched his heart. Last of all he sighed.

'I was not in a merciful mood. He provoked one by his contradictory indiscretions. "It is unfortunate you didn't know beforehand!" I said with every unkind intention; but the perfidious shaft fell harmless – dropped at his feet like a spent arrow, as it were, and he did not think of picking it up. Perhaps he had not even seen it. Presently, lolling at ease, he said, "Dash it all! I tell you it bulged. I was holding up my lamp along the angle-iron in the lower deck when a flake of rust as big as the palm of my hand fell off the plate, all of itself." He passed his hand over his forehead. "The thing stirred and jumped off like something alive while I was looking at it." "That made you feel pretty bad," I observed, casually. "Do you suppose," he said, "that I was thinking of myself, with a hundred and sixty people at my back, all fast asleep in that fore-'tween-deck alone – and more of them aft; more on the deck – sleeping – knowing nothing about it – three times as many as there were boats for, even if there had been time? I expected to see the iron open out as I stood there and the rush of water going over them as they lay.... What could I do – what?"

'I can easily picture him to myself in the peopled gloom of the cavernous place, with the light of the bulk-lamp falling on a small portion of the bulkhead that had the weight of the ocean on the other side, and the breathing of unconscious sleepers in his ears. I can see him glaring at the iron, startled by the falling rust, overburdened by the knowledge of an imminent death. This, I gathered, was the second time he had been sent forward by that skipper of his, who, I rather think, wanted to keep him away from the bridge. He told me that his first impulse was to shout and straight away make all those people leap out of sleep into terror; but such an overwhelming sense of his helplessness came over him that he was not able to produce a sound. This is, I suppose, what people mean by the tongue cleaving to the roof of the mouth. "Too dry," was the concise expression he used in reference to this state. Without a sound, then, he scrambled out on deck through the number one hatch. A wind-sail rigged down there swung against him accidentally, and he remembered that the light touch of the canvas on his face nearly knocked him off the hatchway ladder.

'He confessed that his knees wobbled a good deal as he stood on the foredeck looking at another sleeping crowd. The engines having been stopped by that time, the steam was blowing off. Its deep rumble made the whole night vibrate like a bass string. The ship trembled to it.

'He saw here and there a head lifted off a mat, a vague form uprise in sitting posture, listen sleepily for a moment, sink down again into the billowy confusion of boxes, steam-winches, ventilators. He was aware all these people did not know enough to take intelligent notice of that strange noise. The ship of iron, the men with white faces, all the sights, all the sounds, everything on board to that ignorant and pious multitude was strange alike, and as trustworthy as it would for ever remain incomprehensible. It occurred to him that the fact was fortunate. The idea of it was simply terrible.

'You must remember he believed, as any other man would have done in his place, that the ship would go down at any moment; the bulging, rust-eaten plates that kept back the ocean, fatally must give way, all at once like an undermined dam, and let in a sudden and overwhelming flood. He stood still looking at these recumbent bodies, a doomed man aware of his fate, surveying the silent company of the dead. They *were* dead! Nothing could save them! There were boats enough for half of them perhaps, but there was no time. No time! No time! It did not seem worth while to open his lips, to stir hand or foot. Before he could shout three words, or make three steps, he would be floundering in a sea whitened awfully by the desperate struggles of human beings, clamorous with the distress of cries for help. There was no help. He imagined what would happen perfectly; he went through it all motionless by the hatchway with the lamp in his hand – he went through it to the very last harrowing detail. I think he went through it again while he was telling me these things he could not tell the court.

' "I saw as clearly as I see you now that there was nothing I could do. It seemed to take all life out of my limbs. I thought I might just as well stand where I was and wait. I did not think I had many seconds..." Suddenly the steam ceased blowing off. The noise, he remarked, had been distracting, but the silence at once became intolerably oppressive.

' "I thought I would choke before I got drowned," he said.

'He protested he did not think of saving himself. The only distinct thought formed, vanishing, and reforming in his brain, was: eight hundred people and seven boats; eight hundred people and seven boats.

' "Somebody was speaking aloud inside my head," he said a little wildly. "Eight hundred people and seven boats – and no time! Just think of it." He leaned towards me across the little table, and I tried to avoid his stare. "Do you think I was afraid of death?" he asked in a voice very fierce and low. He brought down his open hand with a bang that made the coffee-cups dance. "I am ready to swear I was not – I was not.... By God – no!" He hitched himself upright and crossed his arms; his chin fell on his breast.

'The soft clashes of crockery reached us faintly through the high windows. There was a burst of voices, and several men came out in high good-humour into the gallery. They were exchanging jocular reminiscences of the donkeys in Cairo. A pale anxious youth stepping softly on long legs was being chaffed by a strutting and rubicund globe-trotter about his purchases in the bazaar. "No, really – do you think I've been done to that extent?" he inquired very earnest and deliberate. The band moved away, dropping into chairs as they went; matches flared, illuminating for a second faces without the ghost of an expression and the flat glaze of white shirt-fronts; the hum of many conversations animated with the ardour of feasting sounded to me absurd and infinitely remote.

'"Some of the crew were sleeping on the number one hatch within reach of my arm," began Jim again.

'You must know they kept Kalashee watch in that ship, all hands sleeping through the night, and only the reliefs of quartermasters and look-out men being called. He was tempted to grip and shake the shoulder of the nearest lascar, but he didn't. Something held his arms down along his sides. He was not afraid – oh no! only he just couldn't – that's all. He was not afraid of death perhaps, but I'll tell you what, he was afraid of the emergency. His confounded imagination had evoked for him all the horrors of panic, the trampling rush, the pitiful screams, boats swamped – all the appalling incidents of a disaster at sea he had ever heard of. He might have been resigned to die but I suspect he wanted to die without added terrors, quietly, in a sort of peaceful trance. A certain readiness to perish is not so very rare, but it is seldom that you meet men whose souls, steeled in the impenetrable armour of resolution, are ready to fight a losing battle to the last, the desire of peace waxes stronger as hope declines, till at last it conquers the very desire of life. Which of us here has not observed this, or maybe experienced something of that feeling in his own person – this extreme weariness of emotions, the vanity of effort, the yearning for rest? Those striving with unreasonable forces know it well, – the shipwrecked castaways in boats, wanderers lost in a desert, men battling against the unthinking might of nature, or the stupid brutality of crowds.'

# CHAPTER EIGHT

'How long he stood stock-still by the hatch expecting every moment to feel the ship dip under his feet and the rush of water to take him at the back and toss him like a chip. I cannot say. Not very long – two minutes perhaps. A couple of men he could not make out began to converse drowsily, and also, he could not tell where, he detected a curious noise of shuffling feet. Above these faint sounds there was that awful stillness preceding a catastrophe, that trying silence of the moment before the crash; then it came into his head that perhaps he would have time to rush along and cut all the lanyards of the gripes, so that the boats would float off as the ship went down.

'The *Patna* had a long bridge, and all the boats were up there, four on one side and three on the other – the smallest of them on the port-side and nearly abreast of the steering gear. He assured me, with evident anxiety to be believed, that he had been most careful to keep them ready for instant service. He knew his duty. I dare say he was a good enough mate as far as that went. "I always believed in being prepared for the worst," he commented, staring anxiously in my face. I nodded my approval of the sound principle, averting my eyes before the subtle unsoundness of the man.

'He started unsteadily to run. He had to step over legs, avoid stumbling against the heads. Suddenly some one caught hold of his coat from below, and a distressed voice spoke under his elbow. The light of the lamp he carried in his right hand fell upon an upturned dark face whose eyes entreated him together with the voice. He had picked up enough of the language to understand the word water, repeated several times in a tone of insistence, of prayer, almost of despair. He gave a jerk to get away, and felt an arm embrace his leg.

'"The beggar clung to me like a drowning man," he said, impressively. "Water, water! What water did he mean? What did he know? As calmly as I could I ordered him to let go. He was stopping me, time was pressing, other men began to stir; I wanted time – time to cut the boats adrift. He got hold of my hand now, and I felt that he would begin to shout. It flashed upon me it was enough to start a panic, and I hauled off with my free arm and slung the lamp in his face. The glass jingled, the light went out, but the blow made him let go, and I ran off – I wanted to get at the boats; I wanted to get at the boats. He leaped after me from behind. I turned on him. He would not keep quiet; he tried to shout; I had half throttled him before I made out what he wanted. He wanted some water – water to drink; they were on strict allowance, you know, and he had with him a young boy I had noticed several times. His child was sick – and thirsty. He had caught sight of me as I passed by, and was begging for a little water. That's all. We were under the bridge, in the dark. He kept on snatching at my wrists; there was no getting rid of him. I dashed into my berth, grabbed my water-bottle, and thrust it into his hands. He vanished. I didn't find out till then how much I was in want of a drink myself." He leaned on one elbow with a hand over his eyes.

'I felt a creepy sensation all down my backbone; there was something peculiar in all this. The fingers of the hand that shaded his brow trembled slightly. He broke the short silence.

'"These things happen only once to a man and ... Ah! well! When I got on the bridge at last the beggars were getting one of the boats off the chocks. A boat! I was running up the ladder when a heavy blow fell on my shoulder, just missing my head. It didn't stop me, and the chief engineer – they had got him out of his bunk by then –

raised the boat-stretcher again. Somehow I had no mind to be surprised at anything. All this seemed natural – and awful – and awful. I dodged that miserable maniac, lifted him off the deck as though he had been a little child, and he started whispering in my arms: "Don't! don't! I thought you were one of them niggers." I flung him away, he skidded along the bridge and knocked the legs from under the little chap – the second. The skipper, busy about the boat, looked round and came at me head down, growling like a wild beast. I flinched no more than a stone. I was as solid standing there as this," he tapped lightly with his knuckles the wall beside his chair. "It was as though I had heard it all, seen it all, gone through it all twenty times already. I wasn't afraid of them. I drew back my fist and he stopped short, muttering –

'"'Ah! it's you. Lend a hand quick.'

'"That's what he said. Quick! As if anybody could be quick enough. Aren't you going to do something?" I asked. "'Yes. Clear out,' he snarled over his shoulder.

'"I don't think I understood then what he meant. The other two had picked themselves up by that time, and they rushed together to the boat. They tramped, they wheezed, they shoved, they cursed the boat, the ship, each other – cursed me. All in mutters. I didn't move, I didn't speak. I watched the slant of the ship. She was as still as if landed on the blocks in a dry dock – only she was like this." He held up his hand, palm under, the tips of the fingers inclined downwards. "Like this," he repeated. "I could see the line of the horizon before me, as clear as a bell, above her stem-head; I could see the water far off there black and sparkling, and still – still as a pond, deadly still, more still than ever sea was before – more still than I could bear to look at. Have you watched a ship floating head down, checked in sinking by a sheet of old iron too rotten to stand being shored up. Have you? Oh yes, shored up? I thought of that – I thought of every mortal thing; but can you shore up a bulkhead in five minutes – or in fifty for that matter? Where was

I going to get men that would go down below? And the
timber – the timber! Would you have had the courage to
swing the maul for the first blow if you had seen that
bulkhead? Don't say you would: you had not seen it;
nobody would. Hang it – to do a thing like that you must
believe there is a chance, one in a thousand, at least, some
ghost of a chance; and you would not have believed.
Nobody would have believed. You think me a cur for
standing there, but what would you have done? What!
You can't tell – nobody can tell. One must have time to
turn round. What would you have me do? Where was the
kindness in making crazy with fright all those people
I could not save single-handed – that nothing could save?
Look here! As true as I sit on this chair before you..."

'He drew quick breaths at every few words and shot
quick glances at my face, as though in his anguish he
were watchful of the effect. He was not speaking to me,
he was only speaking before me, in a dispute with an
invisible personality, an antagonistic and inseparable partner of his existence – another possessor of his soul. These
were issues beyond the competency of a court of inquiry: it
was a subtle and momentous quarrel as to the true essence
of life, and did not want a judge. He wanted an ally, a
helper, an accomplice. I felt the risk I ran of being circum-
vented, blinded, decoyed, bullied, perhaps, into taking a
definite part in a dispute impossible of decision if one had
to be fair to all the phantoms in possession – to the reput-
able that had its claims and to the disreputable that had its
exigencies. I can't explain to you who haven't seen him and
who hear his words only at second hand the mixed nature
of my feelings. It seemed to me I was being made to
comprehend the Inconceivable – and I know of nothing
to compare with the discomfort of such a sensation. I was
made to look at the convention that lurks in all truth and on
the essential sincerity of falsehood. He appealed to all sides
at once – to the side turned perpetually to the light of day,
and to that side of us which, like the other hemisphere of

the moon, exists stealthily in perpetual darkness, with only a fearful ashy light falling at times on the edge. He swayed me. I own to it, I own up. The occasion was obscure, insignificant – what you will: a lost youngster, one in a million – but then he was one of us; an incident as completely devoid of importance as the flooding of an ant-heap, and yet the mystery of his attitude got hold of me as though he had been an individual in the forefront of his kind, as if the obscure truth involved were momentous enough to affect mankind's conception of itself . . . .'

Marlow paused to put new life into his expiring cheroot, seemed to forget all about the story, and abruptly began again.

'My fault of course. One has no business really to get interested. It's a weakness of mine. His was of another kind. My weakness consists in not having a discriminating eye for the incidental – for the externals – no eye for the hod of the rag-picker or the fine linen of the next man. Next man – that's it. I have met so many men,' he pursued, with momentary sadness – 'met them, too, with a certain – certain – impact, let us say; like this fellow, for instance – and in each case all I could see was merely the human being. A confounded democratic quality of vision which may be better than total blindness, but has been of no advantage to me, I can assure you. Men expect one to take into account their fine linen. But I never could get up any enthusiasm about these things. Oh! it's a failing; it's a failing; and then comes a soft evening; a lot of men too indolent for whist – and a story . . . .'

He paused again to wait for an encouraging remark perhaps, but nobody spoke; only the host, as if reluctantly performing a duty, murmured –

'You are so subtle, Marlow.'

'Who? I?' said Marlow in a low voice. 'Oh, no! But *he* was; and try as I may for the success of this yarn I am missing innumerable shades – they were so fine, so difficult to render in colourless words. Because he complicated

matters by being so simple, too – the simplest poor
devil!...By Jove! he was amazing. There he sat telling
me that just as I saw him before my eyes he wouldn't be
afraid to face anything – and believing in it, too. I tell you it
was fabulously innocent and it was enormous, enormous! I
watched him covertly, just as though I had suspected him of
an intention to take a jolly good rise out of me. He was
confident that, on the square, "on the square, mind!" there
was nothing he couldn't meet. Ever since he had been "so
high" – "quite a little chap," he had been preparing himself
for all the difficulties that can beset one on land and water.
He confessed proudly to this kind of foresight. He had
been elaborating dangers and defences, expecting the
worst, rehearsing his best. He must have led a most exalted
existence. Can you fancy it? A succession of adventures, so
much glory, such a victorious progress! and the deep sense
of his sagacity crowning every day of his inner life. He
forgot himself; his eyes shone; and with every word my
heart, searched by the light of his absurdity, was growing
heavier in my breast. I had no mind to laugh, and lest I
should smile I made for myself a stolid face. He gave signs
of irritation.

'"It is always the unexpected that happens," I said in
a propitiatory tone. My obtuseness provoked him into a
contemptuous "Pshaw!" I suppose he meant that the unexpected couldn't touch him; nothing less than the
unconceivable itself could get over his perfect state of pre-
paration. He had been taken unawares – and he whispered
to himself a malediction upon the waters and the firma-
ment, upon the ship, upon the men. Everything had
betrayed him! He had been tricked into that sort of high-
minded resignation which prevented him lifting as much as
his little finger, while these others who had a very clear
perception of the actual necessity were tumbling against
each other and sweating desperately over that boat business. Something had gone wrong there at the last moment.
It appears that in their flurry they had contrived in some

mysterious way to get the sliding bolt of the foremost boat-
chock jammed tight, and forthwith had gone out of the
remnants of their minds over the deadly nature of that
accident. It must have been a pretty sight, the fierce industry of these beggars toiling on a motionless ship that
floated quietly in the silence of a world asleep, fighting
against time for the freeing of that boat, grovelling on all-
fours, standing up in despair, tugging, pushing, snarling at
each other venomously, ready to kill, ready to weep, and
only kept from flying at each other's throats by the fear of
death that stood silent behind them like an inflexible and
cold-eyed taskmaster. Oh, yes! It must have been a pretty
sight. He saw it all, he could talk about it with scorn and
bitterness; he had a minute knowledge of it by means of
some sixth sense, I conclude, because he swore to me he
had remained apart without a glance at them and at the
boat – without one single glance. And I believe him.
I should think he was too busy watching the threatening
slant of the ship, the suspended menace discovered in the
midst of the most perfect security – fascinated by the sword
hanging by a hair over his imaginative head.

'Nothing in the world moved before his eyes, and he
could depict to himself without hindrance the sudden
swing upwards of the dark sky-line, the sudden tilt up of
the vast plain of the sea, the swift still rise, the brutal fling,
the grasp of the abyss, the struggle without hope, the starlight closing over his head for ever like the vault of a tomb –
the revolt of his young life – the black end. He could! By
Jove! who couldn't? And you must remember he was a
finished artist in that peculiar way, he was a gifted poor
devil with the faculty of swift and forestalling vision. The
sights it showed him had turned him into cold stone from
the soles of his feet to the nape of his neck; but there was a
hot dance of thoughts in his head, a dance of lame, blind,
mute thoughts – a whirl of awful cripples. Didn't I tell you
he confessed himself before me as though I had the power
to bind and to loose? He burrowed deep, deep, in the hope

of my absolution, which would have been of no good to him. This was one of those cases which no solemn deception can palliate, which no man can help; where his very Maker seems to abandon a sinner to his own devices.

'He stood on the starboard side of the bridge, as far as he could get from the struggle for the boat, which went on with the agitation of madness and the stealthiness of a conspiracy. The two Malays had meantime remained holding to the wheel. Just picture to yourselves the actors in that, thank God! unique, episode of the sea, four beside themselves with fierce and secret exertions, and three looking on in complete immobility, above the awnings covering the profound ignorance of hundreds of human beings, with their weariness, with their dreams, with their hopes, arrested, held by an invisible hand on the brink of annihilation. For that they were so, makes no doubt to me: given the state of the ship, this was the deadliest possible description of accident that could happen. These beggars by the boat had every reason to go distracted with funk. Frankly, had I been there I would not have given as much as a counterfeit farthing for the ship's chance to keep above water to the end of each successive second. And still she floated! These sleeping pilgrims were destined to accomplish their whole pilgrimage to the bitterness of some other end. It was as if the Omnipotence whose mercy they confessed had needed their humble testimony on earth for a while longer, and had looked down to make a sign, "Thou shalt not!" to the ocean. Their escape would trouble me as a prodigiously inexplicable event, did I not know how tough old iron can be — as tough sometimes as the spirit of some men we meet now and then, worn to a shadow and breasting the weight of life. Not the least wonder of these twenty minutes, to my mind, is the behaviour of the two helmsmen. They were amongst the native batch of all sorts brought over from Aden to give evidence at the inquiry. One of them, labouring under intense bashfulness, was very young, and with his smooth, yellow, cheery countenance looked even younger than he was. I remember perfectly Brierly asking him, through the interpreter, what he thought of it at the time, and the interpreter, after a short colloquy, turning to the court with an important air –

'"He says he thought nothing."

'The other with patient blinking eyes, a blue cotton handkerchief, faded with much washing, bound with a smart twist over a lot of grey wisps, his face shrunk into grim hollows, his brown skin made darker by a mesh of wrinkles, explained that he had a knowledge of some evil thing befalling the ship, but there had been no order; he could not remember an order; why should he leave the helm? To some further questions he jerked back his spare shoulders, and declared it never came into his mind then that the white men were about to leave the ship through fear of death. He did not believe it now. There might have been secret reasons. He wagged his old chin knowingly. Aha! secret reasons. He was a man of great experience, and he wanted *that* white Tuan to know – he turned towards Brierly, who didn't raise his head – that he had acquired a knowledge of many things by serving white men on the sea for a great number of years – and, suddenly, with shaky excitement he poured upon our spell-bound attention a lot of queer-sounding names, names of dead-and-gone skippers, names of forgotten country ships, names of familiar and distorted sound, as if the hand of dumb time had been at work on them for ages. They stopped him at last. A silence fell upon the court, – a silence that remained unbroken for at least a minute, and passed gently into a deep murmur. This episode was *the* sensation of the second day's proceedings – affecting all the audience, affecting everybody except Jim, who was sitting moodily at the end of the first bench, and never looked up at this extraordinary and damning witness that seemed possessed of some mysterious theory of defence.

'So these two lascars stuck to the helm of that ship without steerage-way, where death would have found them if such had been their destiny. The whites did not give them half a glance, had probably forgotten their existence. Assuredly Jim did not remember it. He remembered he could do nothing; he could do nothing, now he was alone. There was nothing to do but to sink with the ship. No use making a disturbance about it. Was there? He waited upstanding, without a sound, stiffened in the idea of some sort of heroic discretion. The first engineer ran cautiously across the bridge to tug at his sleeve.

'"Come and help!. For God's sake, come and help!"

'He ran back to the boat on the points of his toes, and returned directly to worry at his sleeve, begging and cursing at the same time.

'"I believe he would have kissed my hands," said Jim, savagely, "and, next moment, he starts foaming and whispering in my face, 'If I had the time I would like to crack your skull for you.' I pushed him away. Suddenly he caught hold of me round the neck. Damn him! I hit him. I hit out without looking. 'Won't you save your own life – you infernal coward?' he sobs. Coward! He called me an infernal coward! Ha! ha! ha! ha! He called me – ha! ha! ha! . . ."

'He had thrown himself back and was shaking with laughter. I had never in my life heard anything so bitter as that noise. It felt like a blight on all the merriment about donkeys, pyramids, bazaars, or what not. Along the whole dim length of the gallery the voices dropped, the pale blotches of faces turned our way with one accord, and the silence became so profound that the clear tinkle of a teaspoon falling on the tesselated floor of the verandah rang out like a tiny and silvery scream.

'"You mustn't laugh like this, with all these people about," I remonstrated. "It isn't nice for them, you know."

'He gave no sign of having heard at first, but after a while, with a stare that, missing me altogether, seemed to probe the heart of some awful vision, he muttered carelessly – "Oh! they'll think I am drunk."

'And after that you would have thought from his appearance he would never make a sound again. But – no fear! He could no more stop telling now than he could have stopped living by the mere exertion of his will.'

# CHAPTER NINE

'"I was saying to myself, 'Sink – curse you! Sink!'" These were the words with which he began again. He wanted it over. He was severely left alone, and he formulated in his head this address to the ship in a tone of imprecation, while at the same time he enjoyed the privilege of witnessing scenes – as far as I can judge – of low comedy. They were still at that bolt. The skipper was ordering. "Get under and try to lift;" and the others naturally shirked. You understand that to be squeezed flat under the keel of a boat wasn't a desirable position to be caught in if the ship went down suddenly. "Why don't you – you the strongest?" whined the little engineer. "Gott- for-dam! I am too thick," spluttered the skipper in despair. It was funny enough to make angels weep. They stood idle for a moment, and suddenly the chief engineer rushed again at Jim.

'"Come and help, man! Are you mad to throw your only chance away? Come and help, man! Man! Look there – look!"

'And at last Jim looked astern where the other pointed with maniacal insistence. He saw a silent black squall which had eaten up already one-third of the sky. You know how these squalls come up there about that time of the year. First you see a darkening of the horizon – no more; then a cloud rises opaque like a wall. A straight edge of vapour lined with sickly whitish gleams flies up from the southwest, swallowing the stars in whole constellations; its shadow flies over the waters, and confounds sea and sky into one abyss of obscurity. And all is still. No thunder, no wind, no sound; not a flicker of lightning. Then in the tenebrous immensity a livid arch appears; a swell or two like undulations of the very darkness run past, and suddenly, wind and rain strike together with a peculiar impetuosity as if they had burst through something solid. Such a cloud had come up while they weren't looking. They had just noticed it, and were perfectly justified in surmising that if in absolute stillness there was some chance for the ship to keep afloat a few minutes longer, the least disturbance of the sea would make an end of her instantly. Her first nod to the swell that precedes the burst of such a squall would be also her last, would become a plunge, would, so to speak, be prolonged into a long dive, down, down to the bottom. Hence these new capers of their fright, these new antics in which they displayed their extreme aversion to die.

'"It was black, black," pursued Jim with moody steadiness. "It had sneaked upon us from behind. The infernal thing! I suppose there had been at the back of my head some hope yet. I don't know. But that was all over anyhow. It maddened me to see myself caught like this. I was angry, as though I had been trapped. I *was* trapped! The night was hot, too, I remember. Not a breath of air."

'He remembered so well that, gasping in the chair, he seemed to sweat and choke before my eyes. No doubt it maddened him; it knocked him over afresh – in a manner of speaking – but it made him also remember that important purpose which had sent him rushing on that bridge only to slip clean out of his mind. He had intended to cut the lifeboats clear of the ship. He whipped out his knife and went to work slashing as though he had seen nothing, had heard nothing, had known of no one on board. They thought him hopelessly wrong-headed and crazy, but dared not protest noisily against this useless loss of time. When he had done he returned to the very same spot from which he had started. The chief was there, ready with a clutch at him to whisper close to his head, scathingly, as though he wanted to bite his ear –

'"You silly fool! do you think you'll get the ghost of a show when all that lot of brutes is in the water? Why, they will batter your head for you from these boats."

'He wrung his hands, ignored, at Jim's elbow. The skipper kept up a nervous shuffle in one place and mumbled, "Hammer! hammer! Mein Gott! Get a hammer."

'The little engineer whimpered like a child, but broken arm and all, he turned out the least craven of the lot as it seems, and, actually, mustered enough pluck to run an errand to the engine-room. No trifle it must be owned in fairness to him. Jim told me he darted desperate looks like a cornered man, gave one low wail, and dashed off. He was back instantly clambering, hammer in hand, and without a pause flung himself at the bolt. The others gave up Jim at once and ran off to assist. He heard the tap, tap of the hammer, the sound of the released chock falling over. The boat was clear. Only then he turned to look – only then. But he kept his distance – he kept his distance. He wanted me to know he had kept his distance; that there was nothing in common between him and these men – who had the hammer. Nothing whatever. It is more than probable he thought himself cut off from them by a space that could not be traversed, by an obstacle that could not be overcome, by a chasm without bottom. He was as far as he could get from them – the whole breadth of the ship.

'His feet were glued to that remote spot and his eyes to their indistinct group bowed together and swaying strangely in the common torment of fear. A hand-lamp lashed to a stanchion above a little table rigged up on the bridge – the *Patna* had no chart-room amidships – threw a light on their labouring shoulders, on their arched and bobbing backs. They pushed at the bow of the boat; they pushed out into the night; they pushed, and would no more look back at him. They had given him up as if indeed he had been too far, too hopelessly separated from themselves, to be worth an appealing word, a glance, or a sign. They had no leisure to look back upon his passive heroism, to feel the sting of his abstention. The boat was heavy; they pushed at the bow with no breath to spare for an encouraging word: but the turmoil of terror that had scattered their self-control like chaff before the wind, converted their desperate exertions into a bit of fooling, upon my word fit for knockabout clowns in a farce. They pushed with their hands, with their heads, they pushed for dear life with all the weight of their bodies, they pushed with all the might of their souls – only no sooner had they succeeded in canting the stem clear of the davit than they would leave off like one man and start a wild scramble into her. As a natural consequence the boat would swing in abruptly, driving them back, helpless and jostling against each other. They would stand nonplussed for a while, exchanging in fierce whispers all the infamous names they could call to mind, and go at it again. Three times this occurred. He described it to me with morose thoughtfulness. He hadn't lost a single movement of that comic business. "I loathed them. I hated them. I had to look at all that," he said without emphasis, turning upon me a sombrely watchful glance. "Was ever there any one so shamefully tried!"

'He took his head in his hands for a moment, like a man driven to distraction by some unspeakable outrage. These were things he could not explain to the court – and not even to me; but I would have been little fitted for the reception of his confidences had I not been able at times to understand the pauses between the words. In this assault upon his fortitude there was the jeering intention of a spiteful and vile vengeance; there was an element of burlesque in his ordeal – a degradation of funny grimaces in the approach of death or dishonour.

'He related facts which I have not forgotten, but at this distance of time I couldn't recall his very words: I only remember that he managed wonderfully to convey the brooding rancour of his mind into the bare recital of events. Twice, he told me, he shut his eyes in the certitude that the end was upon him already, and twice he had to open them again. Each time he noted the darkening of the great stillness. The shadow of the silent cloud had fallen upon the ship from the zenith, and seemed to have extinguished every sound of her teeming life. He could no longer hear the voices under the awnings. He told me that each time he closed his eyes a flash of thought showed him that crowd of bodies, laid out for death, as plain as daylight. When he opened them, it was to see the dim struggle of four men fighting like mad with a stubborn boat. "They would fall back before it time after time, stand swearing at each other, and suddenly make another rush in a bunch. . . . Enough to make you die laughing," he commented with downcast eyes; then raising them for a moment to my face with a dismal smile, "I ought to have a merry life of it, by God! for I shall see that funny sight a good many times yet before I die." His eyes fell again. "See and hear. . . . See and hear," he repeated twice, at long intervals, filled by vacant staring.

'He roused himself.

'"I made up my mind to keep my eyes shut," he said, "and I couldn't. I couldn't, and I don't care who knows it. Let them go through that kind of thing before they talk. Just let them – and do better – that's all. The second time my eyelids flew open and my mouth too. I had felt the ship move. She just dipped her bows – and lifted them gently – and slow! everlastingly slow; and ever so little. She hadn't done that much for days. The cloud had raced ahead, and this first swell seemed to travel upon a sea of lead. There was no life in that stir. It managed, though, to knock over something in my head. What would you have done? You are sure of yourself – aren't you? What would you do if you felt now – this minute – the house here move, just move a little under your chair. Leap! By heavens! you would take one spring from where you sit and land in that clump of bushes yonder."

'He flung his arm out at the night beyond the stone balustrade. I held my peace. He looked at me very steadily, very severe. There could be no mistake: I was being bullied

now, and it behoved me to make no sign lest by a gesture or
a word I should be drawn into a fatal admission about
myself which would have had some bearing on the case.
I was not disposed to take any risk of that sort. Don't forget
I had him before me, and really he was too much like one of
us not to be dangerous. But if you want to know I don't
mind telling you that I did, with a rapid glance, estimate
the distance to the mass of denser blackness in the middle
of the grassplot before the verandah. He exaggerated.
I would have landed short by several feet – and that's the
only thing of which I am fairly certain.

'The last moment had come, as he thought, and he did
not move. His feet remained glued to the planks if his
thoughts were knocking about loose in his head. It was at
this moment, too, that he saw one of the men around the
boat step backwards suddenly, clutch at the air with raised
arms, totter and collapse. He didn't exactly fall, he only slid
gently into a sitting posture, all hunched up and with his
shoulders propped against the side of the engine-room
skylight. "That was the donkey-man. A haggard, white-
faced chap with a ragged moustache. Acted third engineer," he explained.

'"Dead," I said. We had heard something of that in
court.

'"So they say," he pronounced with sombre indifference.
"Of course I never knew. Weak heart. The man had been
complaining of being out of sorts for some time before.
Excitement. Over-exertion. Devil only knows. Ha! ha! ha!
It was easy to see he did not want to die either. Droll, isn't
it? May I be shot if he hadn't been fooled into killing
himself! Fooled – neither more nor less. Fooled into it,
by heavens! just as I ... Ah! If he had only kept still; if he
had only told them to go to the devil when they came to
rush him out of his bunk because the ship was sinking! If he
had only stood by with his hands in his pockets and called
them names!"

'He got up, shook his fist, glared at me, and sat down.

'"A chance missed, eh?" I murmured.

'"Why don't you laugh?" he said. "A joke hatched in hell. Weak heart! . . . I wish sometimes mine had been."

'This irritated me. "Do you?" I exclaimed with deep-rooted irony. "Yes! Can't *you* understand?" he cried. "I don't know what more you could wish for," I said, angrily. He gave me an utterly uncomprehending glance. This shaft had also gone wide of the mark, and he was not the man to bother about stray arrows. Upon my word, he was too unsuspecting; he was not fair game. I was glad that my missile had been thrown away, – that he had not even heard the twang of the bow.

'Of course he could not know at the time the man was dead. The next minute – his last on board – was crowded with a tumult of events and sensations which beat about him like the sea upon a rock. I use the simile advisedly, because from his relation I am forced to believe he had preserved through it all a strange illusion of passiveness, as though he had not acted but had suffered himself to be handled by the infernal powers who had selected him for the victim of their practical joke. The first thing that came to him was the grinding surge of the heavy davits swinging out at last – a jar which seemed to enter his body from the deck through the soles of his feet, and travel up his spine to the crown of his head. Then, the squall being very near now, another and a heavier swell lifted the passive hull in a threatening heave that checked his breath, while his brain and his heart together were pierced as with daggers by panic-stricken screams. "Let go! For God's sake, let go! Let go! She's going." Following upon that the boat falls ripped through the blocks, and a lot of men began to talk in startled tones under the awnings. "When these beggars did break out, their yelps were enough to wake the dead," he said. Next after the splashing shock of the boat literally dropped in the water, came the hollow noises of stamping and tumbling in her, mingled with confused shouts: "Unhook! Unhook! Shove! Unhook! Shove for your life!

Here's the squall down on us. . . ." He heard, high above his head, the faint muttering of the wind; he heard below his feet a cry of pain. A lost voice alongside started cursing a swivel hook. The ship began to buzz fore and aft like a disturbed hive, and, as quietly as he was telling me all of this – because just then he was very quiet in attitude, in face, in voice – he went on to say without the slightest warning as it were, "I stumbled over his legs."

'This was the first I heard of his having moved at all. I could not restrain a grunt of surprise. Something had started him off at last, but of the exact moment, of the cause that tore him out of his immobility, he knew no more than the uprooted tree knows of the wind that laid it low. All this had come to him: the sounds, the sights, the legs of the dead man – by Jove! The infernal joke was being crammed devilishly down his throat, but – look you – he was not going to admit of any sort of swallowing motion in his gullet. It's extraordinary how he could cast upon you the spirit of his illusion. I listened as if to a tale of black magic at work upon a corpse.

'"He went over sideways, very gently, and this is the last thing I remember seeing on board," he continued. "I did not care what he did. It looked as though he were picking himself up: I thought he was picking himself up, of course: I expected him to bolt past me over the rail and drop into the boat after the others. I could hear them knocking about, down there, and a voice as if crying up a shaft called out 'George.' Then three voices together raised a yell. They came to me separately: one bleated, another screamed, one howled. Ough!"

'He shivered a little, and I beheld him rise slowly as if a steady hand from above had been pulling him out of the chair by his hair. Up, slowly – to his full height, and when his knees had locked stiff the hand let him go, and he swayed a little on his feet. There was a suggestion of awful stillness in his face, in his movements, in his very voice when he said "They shouted" – and involuntarily I pricked up my ears for the ghost of that shout that would be heard directly through the false effect of silence. "There were eight hundred people in that ship," he said, impaling me to the back of my seat with an awful blank stare. "Eight hundred living people, and they were yelling after the one dead man to come down and be saved. 'Jump, George! Jump! Oh, jump!' I stood by with my hand on the davit. I was very quiet. It had come over pitch dark. You could see neither sky nor sea. I heard the boat alongside go bump, bump, and not another sound down there for a while, but the ship under me was full of talking noises. Suddenly the skipper howled, 'Mein Gott! The squall! The squall! Shove off!' With the first hiss of rain, and the first gust of wind, they screamed, 'Jump, George! We'll catch you! Jump!' The ship began a slow plunge; the rain swept over her like a broken sea; my cap flew off my head; my breath was driven back into my throat. I heard as if I had been on the top of a tower another wild screech, 'Geo-o-o-orge! Oh, jump!' She was going down, down, head first under me...."

'He raised his hand deliberately to his face, and made picking motions with his fingers as though he had been bothered with cobwebs, and afterwards he looked into the open palm for quite half a second before he blurted out –

'"I had jumped..." He checked himself, averted his gaze.... "It seems," he added.

'His clear blue eyes turned to me with a piteous stare, and looking at him standing before me, dumfounded and hurt, I was oppressed by a sad sense of resigned wisdom, mingled with the amused and profound pity of an old man helpless before a childish disaster.

'"Looks like it," I muttered.

'"I knew nothing about it till I looked up," he explained, hastily. And that's possible, too. You had to listen to him as you would to a small boy in trouble. He didn't know. It had happened somehow. It would never happen again. He had landed partly on somebody and fallen across a thwart. He felt as though all his ribs on his left side must be broken;

then he rolled over, and saw vaguely the ship he had deserted uprising above him, with the red side-light glowing large in the rain like a fire on the brow of a hill seen through a mist. "She seemed higher than a wall; she looked like a cliff over the boat. . . . I wished I could die," he cried. "There was no going back. It was as if I had jumped into a well — into an everlasting deep hole. . . ." '

# CHAPTER TEN

'HE LOCKED his fingers together and tore them apart.
Nothing could be more true: he had indeed jumped into an
everlasting deep hole. He had tumbled from a height he
could never scale again. By that time the boat had gone
driving forward past the bows. It was too dark just then for
them to see each other, and, moreover, they were blinded
and half drowned with rain. He told me it was like being
swept by a flood through a cavern. They turned their backs
to the squall; the skipper, it seems, got an oar over the stern
to keep the boat before it, and for two or three minutes the
end of the world had come through a deluge in a pitchy
blackness. The sea hissed "like twenty thousand kettles."
That's his simile, not mine. I fancy there was not much
wind after the first gust; and he himself had admitted at the
inquiry that the sea never got up that night to any extent.
He crouched down in the bows and stole a furtive glance
back. He saw just one yellow gleam of the masthead light
high up and blurred like a last star ready to dissolve. "It
terrified me to see it still there," he said. That's what he
said. What terrified him was the thought that the drowning was not over yet. No doubt he wanted to be done with
that abomination as quickly as possible. Nobody in the boat
made a sound. In the dark she seemed to fly, but of course
she could not have had much way. Then the shower
swept ahead, and the great, distracting, hissing noise
followed the rain into distance and died out. There was
nothing to be heard then but the slight wash about the
boat's sides. Somebody's teeth were chattering violently. A
hand touched his back. A faint voice said, "You there?"
Another cried out, shakily, "She's gone!" and they all stood

up together to look astern. They saw no lights. All was black. A thin cold drizzle was driving into their faces. The boat lurched slightly. The teeth chattered faster, stopped, and began again twice before the man could master his shiver sufficiently to say, "Ju-ju-st in ti-ti-me. . . . Brrrr." He recognised the voice of the chief engineer saying surlily, "I saw her go down. I happened to turn my head." The wind had dropped almost completely.

'They watched in the dark with their heads half turned to windward as if expecting to hear cries. At first he was thankful the night had covered up the scene before his eyes, and then to know of it and yet to have seen and heard nothing appeared somehow the culminating-point of an awful misfortune. "Strange, isn't it?" he murmured, interrupting himself in his disjointed narrative.

'It did not seem so strange to me. He must have had an unconscious conviction that the reality could not be half as bad, not half as anguishing, appalling, and vengeful as the created terror of his imagination. I believe that, in this first moment, his heart was wrung with all the suffering, that his soul knew the accumulated savour of all the fear, all the horror, all the despair of eight hundred human beings pounced upon in the night by a sudden and violent death, else why should he have said, "It seemed to me that I must jump out of that accursed boat and swim back to see – half a mile – more – any distance – to the very spot . . ."? Why this impulse? Do you see the significance? Why back to the very spot? Why not drown alongside – if he meant drowning? why back to the very spot, to see – as if his imagination had to be soothed by the assurance that all was over before death could bring relief? I defy any one of you to offer another explanation. It was one of those bizarre and exciting glimpses through the fog. It was an extraordinary disclosure. He let it out as the most natural thing one could say. He fought down that impulse and then he became conscious of the silence. He mentioned this to me. A silence of the sea, of the sky, merged into one indefinite immensity still as death around these saved, palpitating lives. "You might have heard a pin drop in the boat," he said with a queer contraction of his lips, like a man trying to master his sensibilities while relating some extremely moving fact. A silence! God alone, who had willed him as he was, knows what he made of it in his heart. "I didn't think any spot on earth could be so still," he said. "You couldn't distinguish the sea from the sky; there was nothing to see and nothing to hear. Not a glimmer, not a shape, not a sound. You could have believed that every bit of dry land had gone to the bottom; that every man on earth but I and these beggars in the boat had got drowned." He leaned over the table with his knuckles propped amongst coffee-cups, liqueur-glasses, cigar-ends. "I seemed to believe it. Everything was gone and – all was over..." he fetched a deep sigh... "with me." '

Marlow sat up abruptly and flung away his cheroot with force. It made a darting red trail like a toy rocket fired through the drapery of creepers. Nobody stirred.

'Hey, what do you think of it?' he cried with sudden animation. 'Wasn't he true to himself, wasn't he? His saved life was over for want of ground under his feet, for want of sights for his eyes, for want of voices in his ears. Annihilation – hey! And all the time it was only a clouded sky, a sea that did not break, the air that did not stir. Only a night; only a silence.

'It lasted for a while, and then they were suddenly and unanimously moved to make a noise over their escape. "I knew from the first she would go." "Not a minute too soon." "A narrow squeak, b'gosh!" He said nothing, but the breeze that had dropped came back, a gentle draught freshened steadily, and the sea joined its murmuring voice to this talkative reaction succeeding the dumb moments of awe. She was gone! She was gone! Not a doubt of it. Nobody could have helped. They repeated the same words over and over again as though they couldn't stop themselves. Never doubted she would go. The lights were gone. No mistake. The lights were gone. Couldn't expect anything else. She had to go.....He noticed that they talked as though they had left behind them nothing but an empty ship. They concluded she would not have been long when she once started. It seemed to cause them some sort of satisfaction. They assured each other that she couldn't have been long about it – "Just shot down like a flat-iron." The chief engineer declared that the masthead light at the moment of sinking seemed to drop "like a lighted match you throw down." At this the second laughed hysterically. "I am g-g-glad, I am gla-a-a-d." His teeth went on "like an electric rattle," said Jim, "and all at once he began to cry. He wept and blubbered like a child, catching his breath and sobbing 'Oh, dear! oh, dear! oh, dear!' He would be quiet for a while and start suddenly, 'Oh, my poor arm! oh, my poor a-a-a-arm!' I felt I could knock him down. Some of them sat in the stern-sheets. I could just make out their shapes. Voices came to me, mumble, mumble, grunt, grunt. All this seemed very hard to bear. I was cold, too. And I could do nothing. I thought that if I moved I would have to go over the side and..."

'His hand groped stealthily, came in contact with a liqueur-glass, and was withdrawn suddenly as if it had touched a red-hot coal. I pushed the bottle slightly. "Won't you have some more?" I asked. He looked at me angrily. "Don't you think I can tell you what there is to tell without screwing myself up?" he asked. The squad of globe-trotters had gone to bed. We were alone but for a vague white form erect in the shadow, that, being looked at, cringed forward, hesitated, backed away silently. It was getting late, but I did not hurry my guest.

'In the midst of his forlorn state he heard his companions begin to abuse some one. "What kept you from jumping, you lunatic?" said a scolding voice. The chief engineer left the stern-sheets, and could be heard clambering forward as if with hostile intentions against "the greatest idiot that ever was." The skipper shouted with rasping effort offensive epithets from where he sat at the oars. He lifted his head at that uproar, and heard the name "George," while a hand in the dark struck him on the breast. "What have you got to say for yourself, you fool?" queried somebody, with a sort of virtuous fury. "They were after me," he said. "They were abusing me – abusing me … by the name of George."

'He paused to stare, tried to smile, turned his eyes away and went on. "That little second puts his head right under my nose, 'Why, it's that blasted mate!' 'What!' howls the skipper from the other end of the boat. 'No!' shrieks the chief. And he, too, stopped to look at my face."

'The wind had left the boat suddenly. The rain began to fall again, and the soft, uninterrupted, a little mysterious sound with which the sea receives a shower arose on all sides in the night. "They were too taken aback to say anything more at first," he narrated steadily, "and what could I have to say to them?" He faltered for a moment, and made an effort to go on. "They called me horrible names." His voice, sinking to a whisper, now and then would leap up suddenly, hardened by the passion of scorn, as though he had been talking of secret abominations. "Never mind what they called me," he said, grimly. "I could hear hate in their voices. A good thing, too. They could not forgive me for being in that boat. They hated it. It made them mad. …" He laughed short. … "But it kept me from – Look! I was sitting with my arms crossed, on the gunwale! …" He perched himself smartly on the edge of the table and crossed his arms. … "Like this – see? One little tilt backwards and I would have been gone – after the others. One little tilt – the least bit – the least bit." He frowned, and tapping his forehead with the tip of his middle finger, "It was there all the time," he said, impressively. "All the time – that notion. And the rain – cold, thick, cold as melted snow – colder – on my thin cotton clothes – I'll never be so cold again in my life, I know. And the sky was black, too – all

black. Not a star, not a light anywhere. Nothing outside
that confounded boat and those two yapping before me like
a couple of mean mongrels at a tree'd thief. Yap! yap! What
you doing here? You're a fine sort! Too much of a bloomin'
gentleman to put his hand to it. Come out of your trance,
did you? To sneak in? Did you? Yap! yap! You ain't fit to
live! Yap! yap! Two of them together trying to out-bark
each other. The other would bay from the stern through
the rain – couldn't see him – couldn't make out – some of
his filthy jargon. Yap! yap! Bow-ow-ow-ow-ow! Yap! yap!
It was sweet to hear them; it kept me alive, I tell you. It has
saved my life. At it they went, as if trying to drive me
overboard with the noise!... I wonder you had pluck
enough to jump. You ain't wanted here. If I had known
who it was, I would have tipped you over – you skunk.
What have you done with the other? Where did you get
the pluck to jump – you coward? What's to prevent us
three from firing you overboard?... They were out of
breath; the shower passed away upon the sea. Then nothing. There was nothing round the boat, not even a sound.
Wanted to see me overboard, did they? Upon my soul! I
think they would have had their wish if they had only kept
quiet. Fire me overboard! Would they? 'Try,' I said. 'I would
for twopence.' 'Too good for you,' they screeched together.
It was so dark that it was only when one or the other
of them moved that I was quite sure of seeing him. By
heavens! I only wish they had tried."

'I couldn't help exclaiming, "What an extraordinary
affair!"

'"Not bad – eh?" he said, as if in some sort astounded.
"They pretended to think I had done away with that
donkey-man for some reason or other. Why should
I? And how the devil was I to know? Didn't I get somehow into that boat? into that boat – I..." The muscles
round his lips contracted into an unconscious grimace
that tore through the mask of his usual expression – something violent, short-lived and illuminating like a twist of

lightning that admits the eye for an instant into the secret convolutions of a cloud. "I did. I was plainly there with them – wasn't I? Isn't it awful a man should be driven to do a thing like that – and be responsible? What did I know about their George they were howling after? I remembered I had seen him curled up on the deck. 'Murdering coward!' the chief kept on calling me. He didn't seem able to remember any other two words. I didn't care, only his noise began to worry me. 'Shut up,' I said. At that he collected himself for a confounded screech. 'You killed him. You killed him.' 'No,' I shouted, 'but I will kill you directly.' I jumped up, and he fell backwards over a thwart with an awful loud thump. I don't know why. Too dark. Tried to step back, I suppose. I stood still facing aft, and the wretched little second began to whine, 'You ain't going to hit a chap with a broken arm – and you call yourself a gentleman, too.' I heard a heavy tramp – one – two – and wheezy grunting. The other beast was coming at me, clattering his oar over the stern. I saw him moving, big, big – as you see a man in a mist, in a dream. 'Come on,' I cried. I would have tumbled him over like a bale of shakings. He stopped, muttered to himself, and went back. Perhaps he had heard the wind. I didn't. It was the last heavy gust we had. He went back to his oar. I was sorry. I would have tried to – to..."

'He opened and closed his curved fingers, and his hands had an eager and cruel flutter. "Steady, steady," I murmured.

'"Eh? What? I am not excited," he remonstrated, awfully hurt, and with a convulsive jerk of his elbow knocked over the cognac-bottle. I started forward, scraping my chair. He bounced off the table as if a mine had been exploded behind his back, and half turned before he alighted, crouching on his feet to show me a startled pair of eyes and a face white about the nostrils. A look of intense annoyance succeeded. "Awfully sorry. How clumsy of me!" he mumbled very vexed, while the pungent odour of spilt alcohol enveloped us suddenly with an atmosphere of a low drinking-bout in the cool, pure darkness of the night. The lights had been put out in the dining-hall; our candle glimmered solitary in the long gallery, and the columns had turned black from pediment to capital. On the vivid stars the high corner of the Harbour Office stood out distinct across the Esplanade, as though the sombre pile had glided nearer to see and hear.

'He assumed an air of indifference.

'"I dare say I am less calm now than I was then. I was ready for anything. These were trifles. . . ."

'"You had a lively time of it in that boat," I remarked.

'"I was ready," he repeated. "After the ship's lights had gone, anything might have happened in that boat – anything in the world – and the world no wiser. I felt this, and I was pleased. It was just dark enough, too. We were like men walled up quick in a roomy grave. No concern with anything on earth. Nobody to pass an opinion. Nothing mattered." For the third time during this conversation he laughed harshly, but there was no one about to suspect him of being only drunk. "No fear, no law, no sounds, no eyes – not even our own, till – till sunrise at least."

'I was struck by the suggestive truth of his words. There is something peculiar in a small boat upon the wide sea. Over the lives borne from under the shadow of death there seems to fall the shadow of madness. When your ship fails you, your whole world seems to fail you; the world that made you, restrained you, taken care of you. It is as if the souls of men floating on an abyss and in touch with immensity had been set free for any excess of heroism, absurdity, or abomination. Of course, as with belief, thought, love, hate, conviction, or even the visual aspect of material things, there are as many shipwrecks as there are men, and in this one there was something abject which made the isolation more complete – there was a villainy of circumstances that cut these men off more completely from the rest of mankind, whose ideal of conduct had never undergone the trial of a fiendish and appalling joke. They were exasperated with him for being a half-hearted shirker: he focussed on them his hatred of the whole thing; he would have liked to take a signal revenge for the abhorrent opportunity they had put in his way. Trust a boat on the high seas to bring out the Irrational that lurks at the bottom of every thought, sentiment, sensation, emotion. It was part of the burlesque meanness pervading that particular disaster at sea that they did not come to blows. It was all threats, all a terribly effective feint, a sham from beginning to end, planned by the tremendous disdain of the Dark Powers whose real terrors, always on the verge of triumph, are perpetually foiled by the steadfastness of men. I asked, after waiting for a while, "Well, what happened?" A futile question. I knew too much already to hope for the grace of a single uplifting touch, for the favour of hinted madness, of shadowed horror. "Nothing," he said. "I meant business, but they meant noise only. Nothing happened."

'And the rising sun found him just as he had jumped up first in the bows of the boat. What a persistence of readiness! He had been holding the tiller in his hand, too, all the night. They had dropped the rudder overboard while attempting to ship it, and I suppose the tiller got kicked forward somehow while they were rushing up and down that boat trying to do all sorts of things at once so as to get clear of the side. It was a long heavy piece of hard wood, and apparently he had been clutching it for six hours or so. If you don't call that being ready! Can you imagine him, silent and on his feet half the night, his face to the gusts of rain, staring at sombre forms, watchful of vague movements, straining his ears to catch rare low murmurs in the stern-sheets! Firmness of courage or effort of fear? What do you think? And the endurance is undeniable, too. Six hours more or less on the defensive; six hours of alert immobility while the boat drove slowly or floated arrested according to the caprice of the wind; while the sea, calmed, slept at last; while the clouds passed above his head; while the sky from an immensity lustreless and black, diminished to a sombre and lustrous vault, scintillated with a greater brilliance, faded to the east, paled at the zenith; while the dark shapes blotting the low stars astern got outlines, relief; became shoulders, heads, faces, features, – confronted him with dreary stares, had dishevelled hair, torn clothes, blinked red eyelids at the white dawn. "They looked as though they had been knocking about drunk in gutters for a week," he described graphically; and then he muttered something about the sunrise being of a kind that foretells a calm day. You know that sailor habit of referring to the weather in every connection. And on my side his few mumbled words were enough to make me see the lower limb of the sun clearing the line of the horizon, the tremble of a vast ripple running over all the visible expanse of the sea, as if the waters had shuddered, giving birth to the globe of light, while the last puff of the breeze would stir the air in a sigh of relief.

'"They sat in the stern shoulder to shoulder, with the skipper in the middle, like three dirty owls, and stared at me," I heard him say with an intention of hate that distilled a corrosive virtue into the commonplace words like a drop of powerful poison falling into a glass of water; but my thoughts dwelt upon that sunrise. I could imagine under the pellucid emptiness of the sky these four men imprisoned in the solitude of the sea, the lonely sun, regardless of the speck of life, ascending the clear curve of the heaven as if to gaze ardently from a greater height at his own splendour reflected in the still ocean. "They called out to me from aft," said Jim, "as though we had been chums together. I heard them. They were begging me to be sensible and drop that 'blooming piece of wood.' Why *would* I carry on so? They hadn't done me any harm – had they? There had been no harm. . . . No harm!"

'His face crimsoned as though he could not get rid of the air in his lungs.

'"No harm!" he burst out. "I leave it to you. You can understand. Can't you? You see it – don't you? No harm! Good God! What more could they have done? Oh, yes, I know very well – I jumped. Certainly. I jumped! I told you I jumped; but I tell you they were too much for any man. It was their doing as plainly as if they had reached up with a boat-hook and pulled me over. Can't you see it? You must see it. Come. Speak – straight out."

'His uneasy eyes fastened upon mine, questioned, begged, challenged, entreated. For the life of me I couldn't help murmuring, "You've been tried." "More than is fair," he caught up, swiftly. "I wasn't given half a chance – with a gang like that. And now they were friendly – oh, so damnably friendly! Chums, shipmates. All in the same boat. Make the best of it. They hadn't meant anything. They didn't care a hang for George. George had gone back to his berth for something at the last moment and got caught. The man was a manifest fool. Very sad, of course. . . . Their eyes looked at me; their lips moved; they wagged their heads at the other end of the boat – three of them; they beckoned – to me. Why not? Hadn't I jumped? I said nothing. There are no words for the sort of things I wanted to say. If I had opened my lips just then I would have simply howled like an animal. I was asking myself when I would wake up. They urged me aloud to come aft and hear quietly what the skipper had to say. We were sure to be picked up before the evening – right in the track of all the Canal traffic; there was smoke to the northwest now."

'"It gave me an awful shock to see this faint, faint blur, this low trail of brown mist through which you could see the boundary of sea and sky. I called out to them that I could hear very well where I was. The skipper started swearing, as hoarse as a crow. He wasn't going to talk at the top of his voice for *my* accommodation. 'Are you afraid they will hear you on shore?' I asked. He glared as if he would have liked to claw me to pieces. The chief engineer advised him to humour me. He said I wasn't right in my head yet.

The other rose astern, like a thick pillar of flesh – and talked – talked...."

'Jim remained thoughtful. "Well?" I said. "What did I care what story they agreed to make up?" he cried, recklessly. "They could tell what they jolly well liked. It was their business. I knew the story. Nothing they could make people believe could alter it for me. I let him talk, argue – talk, argue. He went on and on and on. Suddenly I felt my legs give way under me. I was sick, tired – tired to death. I let fall the tiller, turned my back on them, and sat down on the foremost thwart. I had enough. They called to me to know if I understood – wasn't it true, every word of it? It was true, by God! after their fashion. I did not turn my head. I heard them palavering together. 'The silly ass won't say anything.' 'Oh, he understands well enough.' 'Let him be; he will be all right.' 'What can he do?' What could I do? Weren't we all in the same boat? I tried to be deaf. The smoke had disappeared to the northward. It was a dead calm. They had a drink from the water-breaker, and I drank, too. Afterwards they made a great business of spreading the boat-sail over the gunwales. Would I keep a look-out? They crept under, out of my sight, thank God! I felt weary, weary, done up, as if I hadn't had one hour's sleep since the day I was born. I couldn't see the water for the glitter of the sunshine. From time to time one of them would creep out, stand up to take a look all round, and get under again. I could hear spells of snoring below the sail. Some of them could sleep. One of them at least. I couldn't! All was light, light, and the boat seemed to be falling through it. Now and then I would feel quite surprised to find myself sitting on a thwart...."

'He began to walk with measured steps to and fro before my chair, one hand in his trousers-pocket, his head bent thoughtfully, and his right arm at long intervals raised for a gesture that seemed to put out of his way an invisible intruder.

' "I suppose you think I was going mad," he began in a changed tone. "And well you may, if you remember I had lost my cap. The sun crept all the way from east to west over my bare head, but that day I could not come to any harm, I suppose. The sun could not make me mad...." His right arm put aside the idea of madness...."Neither could it kill me...." Again his arm repulsed a shadow.... "*That* rested with me."

' "Did it?" I said, inexpressibly amazed at this new turn, and I looked at him with the same sort of feeling I might be fairly conceived to experience had he, after spinning round on his heel, presented an altogether new face.

' "I didn't get brain fever, I did not drop dead either," he went on. "I didn't bother myself at all about the sun over my head. I was thinking as coolly as any man that ever sat thinking in the shade. That greasy beast of a skipper poked his big cropped head from under the canvas and screwed his fishy eyes up at me. 'Donnerwetter! you will die,' he growled, and drew in like a turtle. I had seen him. I had heard him. He didn't interrupt me. I was thinking just then that I wouldn't."

'He tried to sound my thought with an attentive glance dropped on me in passing. "Do you mean to say you had been deliberating with yourself whether you would die?" I asked in as impenetrable a tone as I could command. He nodded without stopping. "Yes, it had come to that as I sat there alone," he said. He passed on a few steps to the imaginary end of his beat, and when he flung round to come back both his hands were thrust deep into his pockets. He stopped short in front of my chair and looked down. "Don't you believe it?" he inquired with tense curiosity. I was moved to make a solemn declaration of my readiness to believe implicitly anything he thought fit to tell me.'

# CHAPTER ELEVEN

'HE HEARD me out with his head on one side, and I had another glimpse through a rent in the mist in which he moved and had his being. The dim candle spluttered within the ball of glass, and that was all I had to see him by; at his back was the dark night with the clear stars, whose distant glitter disposed in retreating planes lured the eye into the depths of a greater darkness; and yet a mysterious light seemed to show me his boyish head, as if in that moment the youth within him had, for a moment, gleamed and expired. "You are an awful good sort to listen like this," he said. "It does me good. You don't know what it is to me. You don't" . . . words seemed to fail him. It was a distinct glimpse. He was a youngster of the sort you like to see about you; of the sort you like to imagine yourself to have been; of the sort whose appearance claims the fellowship of these illusions you had thought gone out, extinct, cold, and which, as if rekindled at the approach of another flame, give a flutter deep, deep down somewhere, give a flutter of light . . . of heat! . . . Yes; I had a glimpse of him then . . . and it was not the last of that kind. . . . "You don't know what it is for a fellow in my position to be believed – make a clean breast of it to an elder man. It is so difficult – so awfully unfair – so hard to understand."

'The mists were closing again. I don't know how old I appeared to him – and how much wise. Not half as old as I felt just then; not half as uselessly wise as I knew myself to be. Surely in no other craft as in that of the sea do the hearts of those already launched to sink or swim go out so much to the youth on the brink, looking with shining eyes upon that glitter of the vast surface which is only a reflection of his

116

own glances full of fire. There is such magnificent vagueness in the expectations that had driven each of us to sea, such a glorious indefiniteness, such a beautiful greed of adventures that are their own and only reward! What we get – well, we won't talk of that; but can one of us restrain a smile? In no other kind of life is the illusion more wide of reality – in no other is the beginning *all* illusion – the disenchantment more swift – the subjugation more complete. Hadn't we all commenced with the same desire, ended with the same knowledge, carried the memory of the same cherished glamour through the sordid days of imprecation? What wonder that when some heavy prod gets home the bond is found to be close; that besides the fellowship of the craft there is felt the strength of a wider feeling – the feeling that binds a man to a child. He was there before me, believing that age and wisdom can find a remedy against the pain of truth, giving me a glimpse of himself as a young fellow in a scrape that is the very devil of a scrape, the sort of scrape greybeards wag at solemnly while they hide a smile. And he had been deliberating upon death – confound him! He had found *that* to meditate about because he thought he had saved his life, while all its glamour had gone with the ship in the night. What more natural! It was tragic enough and funny enough in all conscience to call aloud for compassion, and in what was I better than the rest of us to refuse him my pity? And even as I looked at him the mists rolled into the rent, and his voice spoke –

'"I was so lost, you know. It was the sort of thing one does not expect to happen to one. It was not like a fight, for instance."

'"It was not," I admitted. He appeared changed as if he had suddenly matured.

'"One couldn't be sure," he muttered.

'"Ah! You were not sure," I said, and was placated by the sound of a faint sigh that passed between us like the flight of a bird in the night.

'"Well, I wasn't," he said, courageously. "It was something like that wretched story they made up. It was not a lie – but it wasn't truth all the same. It was something.... One knows a downright lie. There was not the thickness of a sheet of paper between the right and wrong of this affair."

'"How much more did you want?" I asked; but I think I spoke so low that he did not catch what I said. He had advanced his argument as though life had been a network of paths separated by chasms. His voice sounded reasonable.

'"Suppose I had not – I mean to say, suppose I had stuck to the ship? Well. How much longer? Say a minute – half a minute. Come. In thirty seconds, as it seemed certain then, I would have been overboard; and do you think I would not have laid hold of the first thing that came in my way – oar, life-buoy, grating – anything? Wouldn't you?"

'"And be saved," I interjected.

'"I would have meant to be," he retorted. "And that's more than I meant when I"... he shivered as if about to swallow some nauseous drug... "jumped," he pronounced with a convulsive effort, whose stress, as if propagated by the waves of the air, made my body stir a little in the chair. He fixed me with lowering eyes. "Don't you believe me?" he cried. "I swear!... Confound it! You got me here to talk, and... You must!... You said you would believe." "Of course I do," I protested in a matter-of-fact tone which produced a calming effect. "Forgive me," he said. "Of course I wouldn't have talked to you about all this if you had not been a gentleman. I ought to have known... I am – I am – a gentleman, too..." "Yes, yes," I said, hastily. He was looking me squarely in the face and withdrew his gaze slowly. "Now you understand why I didn't after all... didn't go out in that way. I wasn't going to be frightened at what I had done. And, anyhow, if I had stuck to the ship I would have done my best to be saved. Men have been known to float for hours – in the open sea – and be picked up not much the worse for it. I might have lasted it out better than

many others. There's nothing the matter with *my* heart."
He withdrew his right fist from his pocket, and the blow he
struck on his chest resounded like a muffled detonation in
the night.

'"No," I said. He meditated, with his legs slightly apart
and his chin sunk. "A hair's-breadth," he muttered. "Not
the breadth of a hair between this and that. And at the
time..."

'"It is difficult to see a hair at midnight," I put in, a little
viciously I fear. Don't you see what I mean by the solidarity
of the craft? I was aggrieved against him, as though he had
cheated me – me! – of a splendid opportunity to keep up the
illusion of my beginnings, as though he had robbed our
common life of the last spark of its glamour. "And so you
cleared out – at once."

'"Jumped," he corrected me incisively. "Jumped – mind!"
he repeated, and I wondered at the evident but obscure
intention. "Well, yes! Perhaps I could not see then. But
I had plenty of time and any amount of light in that boat.
And I could think, too. Nobody would know, of course, but
this did not make it any easier for me. You've got to believe
that, too. I did not want all this talk.... No... Yes...
I won't lie... I wanted it: it is the very thing I wanted –
there. Do you think you or anybody could have made me if
I... I am – I am not afraid to tell. And I wasn't afraid to
think either. I looked it in the face. I wasn't going to run
away. At first – at night, if it hadn't been for these fellows
I might have... No! by heavens! I was not going to
give them that satisfaction. They had done enough.
They made up a story, and believed it for all I know. But
I knew the truth, and I would live it down – alone, with
myself. I wasn't going to give in to such a beastly unfair
thing. What did it prove after all? I was confoundedly cut
up. Sick of life – to tell you the truth; but what would have
been the good to shirk it – in – in – that way? That was not
the way. I believe – I believe it would have – it would have
ended – nothing."

'He had been walking up and down, but with the last word he turned short at me.

'"What do *you* believe?" he asked with violence. A pause ensued, and suddenly I felt myself overcome by a profound and hopeless fatigue, as though his voice had startled me out of a dream of wandering through empty spaces whose immensity had harassed my soul and exhausted my body.

'"... Would have ended nothing," he muttered over me obstinately, after a little while. "No! the proper thing was to face it out — alone for myself — wait for another chance — find out..."'

# CHAPTER TWELVE

'ALL around everything was still as far as the ear could reach. The mist of his feelings shifted between us, as if disturbed by his struggles, and in the rifts of the immaterial veil he would appear to my staring eyes distinct of form and pregnant with vague appeal like a symbolic figure in a picture. The chill air of the night seemed to lie on my limbs as heavy as a slab of marble.

'"I see," I murmured, more to prove to myself that I could break my state of numbness than for any other reason.

'"The *Avondale* picked us up just before sunset," he remarked, moodily. "Steamed right straight for us. We had only to sit and wait."

'After a long interval, he said, "They told their story." And again there was that oppressive silence. "Then only I knew what it was I had made up my mind to," he added.

'"You said nothing," I whispered.

'"What could I say?" he asked, in the same low tone.... "Shock slight. Stopped the ship. Ascertained the damage. Took measures to get the boats out without creating a panic. As the first boat was lowered ship went down in a squall. Sank like lead.... What could be more clear"... he hung his head... "and more awful?" His lips quivered while he looked straight into my eyes. "I had jumped – hadn't I?" he asked, dismayed. "That's what I had to live down. The story didn't matter."... He clasped his hands for an instant, glanced right and left into the gloom: "It was like cheating the dead," he stammered.

'"And there were no dead," I said.

121

'He went away from me at this. That is the only way
I can describe it. In a moment I saw his back close to the
balustrade. He stood there for some time, as if admiring the
purity and the peace of the night. Some flowering-shrub in
the garden below spread its powerful scent through the
damp air. He returned to me with hasty steps.

'"And that did not matter," he said, as stubbornly as you
please.

'"Perhaps not," I admitted. I began to have a notion he
was too much for me. After all, what did I know?

'"Dead or not dead, I could not get clear," he said. "I had
to live; hadn't I?"

'"Well, yes – if you take it in that way," I mumbled.

'"I was glad, of course," he threw out carelessly with his
mind fixed on something else. "The exposure," he pronounced, slowly, and lifted his head. "Do you know what
was my first thought when I heard? I was relieved. I was
relieved to learn that those shouts – did I tell you I
had heard shouts? No? Well, I did. Shouts for help... –
blown along with the drizzle. Imagination I suppose. And
yet I can hardly... How stupid.... The others did not.
I asked them afterwards. They all said No. No? And I
was hearing them even then! I might have known – but
I didn't think – I only listened. Very faint screams – day
after day. Then that little half-caste chap here came up and
spoke to me. 'The *Patna*... French gunboat... towed suc-
cessfully to Aden... Investigation... Marine Office...
Sailors' Home... arrangements made for your board and
lodging!' I walked along with him, and I enjoyed the
silence. So there had been no shouting. Imagination. I had
to believe him. I could hear nothing any more. I wonder
how long I could have stood it. It was getting worse,
too... I mean – louder.

'He fell into thought.

'"And I had heard nothing! Well – so be it. But the
lights! The lights did go! We did not see them. They were
not there. If they had been, I would have swam back –

I would have gone back and shouted alongside – I would have begged them to take me on board. . . . I would have had my chance. . . . You doubt me? . . . How do you know how I felt? . . . What right have you to doubt? . . . I very nearly did it as it was – do you understand?" His voice fell. "There was not a glimmer – not a glimmer," he protested, mournfully. "Don't you understand that if there had been, you would not have seen me here? You see me – and you doubt."

'I shook my head negatively. This question of the lights being lost sight of when the boat could not have been more than a quarter of a mile from the ship was a matter for much discussion. Jim stuck to it that there was nothing to be seen after the first shower had cleared away; and the others had affirmed the same thing to the officers of the *Avondale*. Of course people shook their heads and smiled. One old skipper who sat near me in court tickled my ear with his white beard to murmur, "Of course they would lie." As a matter of fact nobody lied; not even the chief engineer with his story of the masthead light dropping like a match you throw down. Not consciously, at least. A man with his liver in such a state might very well have seen a floating spark in the corner of his eye when stealing a hurried glance over his shoulder. They had seen no light of any sort though they were well within range, and they could only explain this in one way: the ship had gone down. It was obvious and comforting. The foreseen fact coming so swiftly had justified their haste. No wonder they did not cast about for any other explanation. Yet the true one was very simple, and as soon as Brierly suggested it the court ceased to bother about the question. If you remember, the ship had been stopped and was lying with her head on the course steered through the night, with her stern canted high and her bows brought low down in the water through the filling of the fore-compartment. Being thus out of trim, when the squall struck her a little on the quarter, she swung head to wind as sharply as though she had been at anchor.

By this change in her position all her lights were in a very
few moments shut off from the boat to leeward. It may very
well be that, had they been seen, they would have had the
effect of a mute appeal – that their glimmer lost in the
darkness of the cloud would have had the mysterious power
of the human glance that can awaken the feelings of
remorse and pity. It would have said, "I am here – still
here" ... and what more can the eye of the most forsaken of
human beings say? But she turned her back on them as if in
disdain of their fate: she had swung round, burdened, to
glare stubbornly at the new danger of the open sea which
she so strangely survived to end her days in a breaking-up
yard, as if it had been her recorded fate to die obscurely
under the blows of many hammers. What were the various
ends their destiny provided for the pilgrims I am unable to
say; but the immediate future brought, at about nine
o'clock next morning, a French gunboat homeward
bound from Réunion. The report of her commander was
public property. He had swept a little out of his course to
ascertain what was the matter with that steamer floating
dangerously by the head upon a still and hazy sea. There
was an ensign, union down, flying at her main gaff (the
serang had the sense to make a signal of distress at daylight); but the cooks were preparing the food in the cook-
ing-boxes forward as usual. The decks were packed as close
as a sheep-pen: there were people perched all along the
rails, jammed on the bridge in a solid mass; hundreds of
eyes stared, and not a sound was heard when the gunboat
ranged abreast, as if all that multitude of lips had been
sealed by a spell.

'The Frenchman hailed, could get no intelligible reply,
and after ascertaining through his binoculars that the
crowd on deck did not look plague-stricken, decided to
send a boat. Two officers came on board, listened to the
serang, tried to talk with the Arab, couldn't make head or
tail of it: but of course the nature of the emergency was
obvious enough. They were also very much struck by

discovering a white man, dead and curled up peacefully on the bridge. "*Fort intrigués par ce cadavre*," as I was informed a long time after by an elderly French lieutenant whom I came across one afternoon in Sydney, by the merest chance, in a sort of café, and who remembered the affair perfectly. Indeed this affair, I may notice in passing, had an extra-ordinary power of defying the shortness of memories and the length of time: it seemed to live, with a sort of uncanny vitality, in the minds of men, on the tips of their tongues. I've had the questionable pleasure of meeting it often, years afterwards, thousands of miles away, emerging from the remotest possible talk, coming to the surface of the most distant allusions. Has it not turned up to-night between us? And I am the only seaman here. I am the only one to whom it is a memory. And yet it has made its way out! But if two men who, unknown to each other, knew of this affair met accidentally on any spot of this earth, the thing would pop up between them as sure as fate, before they parted. I had never seen that Frenchman before, and at the end of an hour we had done with each other for life: he did not seem particularly talkative either; he was a quiet, massive chap in a creased uniform sitting drowsily over a tumbler half full of some dark liquid. His shoulder-straps were a bit tarn-ished, his clean-shaved cheeks were large and sallow; he looked like a man who would be given to taking snuff – don't you know? I won't say he did; but the habit would have fitted that kind of man. It all began by his handing me a number of *Home News*, which I didn't want, across the marble table. I said, "Merci." We exchanged a few apparently innocent remarks, and suddenly, before I knew how it had come about, we were in the midst of it, and he was telling me how much they had been "intrigued by that corpse." It turned out he had been one of the boarding officers.

'In the establishment where we sat one could get a variety of foreign drinks which were kept for the visiting naval officers, and he took a sip of the dark medical-looking stuff, which probably was nothing more nasty than *cassis à l'eau*, and glancing with one eye into the tumbler, shook his head slightly. "*Impossible de comprendre – vous concevez*," he said, with a curious mixture of unconcern and thoughtfulness. I could very easily conceive how impossible it had been for them to understand. Nobody in the gunboat knew enough English to get hold of the story as told by the serang. There was a good deal of noise, too, round the two officers. "They crowded upon us. There was a circle round that dead man (*autour de ce mort*)," he described. "One had to attend to the most pressing. These people were beginning to agitate themselves – *Parbleu!* A mob like that – don't you see?" he interjected with philosophic indulgence. As to the bulkhead, he had advised his commander that the safest thing was to leave it alone, it was so villainous to look at. They got two hawsers on board promptly (*en toute hâte*) and took the *Patna* in tow – stern foremost at that – which, under the circumstances, was not so foolish, since the rudder was too much out of the water to be of any great use for steering, and this manœuvre eased the strain on the bulkhead, whose state, he expounded with stolid glibness, demanded the greatest care (*éxigeait les plus grands ménagements*). I could not help thinking that my new acquaintance must have had a voice in most of these arrangements: he looked a reliable officer, no longer very active, and he was seamanlike, too, in a way, though as he sat there, with his thick fingers clasped lightly on his stomach, he reminded you of one of those snuffy, quiet village priests, into whose ears are poured the sins, the sufferings, the remorse of peasant generations, on whose faces the placid and simple expression is like a veil thrown over the mystery of pain and distress. He ought to have had a threadbare black *soutane* buttoned smoothly up to his ample chin, instead of a frock-coat with shoulder-straps and brass buttons. His broad bosom heaved regularly while he went on telling me that it had been the very devil of a job, as doubtless (*sans doute*) I could figure to myself in my

quality of a seaman (*en votre qualité de marin*). At the end of
the period he inclined his body slightly towards me, and,
pursing his shaved lips, allowed the air to escape with a
gentle hiss. "Luckily," he continued, "the sea was level like
this table, and there was no more wind than there is
here.".... The place struck me as indeed intolerably stuffy,
and very hot; my face burned as though I had been young
enough to be embarrassed and blushing. They had directed
their course, he pursued, to the nearest English port
"*naturellement*," where their responsibility ceased "*Dieu
merci*." ... He blew out his flat cheeks a little ... "Because,
mind you (*notez bien*), all the time of towing we had two
quartermasters stationed with axes by the hawsers, to cut us
clear of our tow in case she ..." He fluttered downwards his
heavy eyelids, making his meaning as plain as
possible.... "What would you! One does what one can
(*on fait ce qu'on peut*)," and for a moment he managed to
invest his ponderous immobility with an air of resignation.
"Two quartermasters – thirty hours – always there. Two!"
he repeated, lifting up his right hand a little, and exhibiting
two fingers. This was absolutely the first gesture I saw him
make. It gave me the opportunity to "note" a starred scar on
the back of his hand – effect of a gunshot clearly; and, as if
my sight had been made more acute by this discovery, I
perceived also the seam of an old wound, beginning a little
below the temple and going out of sight under the short
grey hair at the side of his head – the graze of a spear or the
cut of a sabre. He clasped his hands on his stomach again. "I
remained on board that – that – my memory is going (*s'en
va*). *Ah! Patt-nà. C'est bien ça. Patt-nà. Merci*. It is droll how
one forgets. I stayed on that ship thirty hours...."

   '"You did!" I exclaimed. Still gazing at his hands, he
pursed his lips a little, but this time made no hissing sound.
"It was judged proper," he said, lifting his eyebrows dispassionately, "that one of the officers should remain to keep
an eye open (*pour ouvrir l'œil*)" ... he sighed idly... "and
for communicating by signals with the towing ship – do

you see? – and so on. For the rest, it was my opinion, too. We made our boats ready to drop over – and I also on that ship took measures.... *Enfin!* One has done one's possible. It was a delicate position. Thirty hours. They prepared me some food. As for the wine – go and whistle for it – not a drop." In some extraordinary way, without any marked change in his inert attitude and in the placid expression of his face, he managed to convey the idea of profound disgust. "I – you know – when it comes to eating without my glass of wine – I am nowhere."

'I was afraid he would enlarge upon the grievance, for though he didn't stir a limb or twitch a feature, he made one aware how much he was irritated by the recollection. But he seemed to forget all about it. They delivered their charge to the "port authorities," as he expressed it. He was struck by the calmness with which it had been received. "One might have thought they had such a droll find (*drôle de trouvaille*) brought them every day. You are extraordinary – you others," he commented, with his back propped against the wall, and looking himself as incapable of an emotional display as a sack of meal. There happened to be a man-of-war and an Indian Marine steamer in the harbour at the time, and he did not conceal his admiration of the efficient manner in which the boats of these two ships cleared the *Patna* of her passengers. Indeed his torpid demeanour concealed nothing: it had that mysterious, almost miraculous, power of producing striking effects by means impossible of detection which is the last word of the highest art. "Twenty-five minutes – watch in hand – twenty-five, no more.".... He unclasped and clasped again his fingers without removing his hands from his stomach, and made it infinitely more effective than if he had thrown up his arms to heaven in amazement.... "All that lot (*tout ce monde*) on shore – with their little affairs – nobody left but a guard of seamen (*marins de l'État*) and that interesting corpse (*cet intéressant cadavre*). Twenty-five minutes."... With downcast eyes and his head tilted slightly on one side he seemed to roll knowingly on his tongue the savour of a smart bit of work. He persuaded one without any further demonstration that his approval was eminently worth having, and resuming his hardly interrupted immobility, he went on to inform me that, being under orders to make the best of their way to Toulon, they left in two hours' time, "so that (*de sorte que*) there are many things in this incident of my life (*dans cet épisode de ma vie*) which have remained obscure." '

# CHAPTER THIRTEEN

'AFTER these words, and without a change of attitude, he, so to speak, submitted himself passively to a state of silence. I kept him company; and suddenly, but not abruptly, as if the appointed time had arrived for his moderate and husky voice to come out of his immobility, he pronounced, "*Mon Dieu!* how the time passes!" Nothing could have been more commonplace than this remark; but its utterance coincided for me with a moment of vision. It's extraordinary how we go through life with eyes half shut, with dull ears, with dormant thoughts. Perhaps it's just as well; and it may be that it is this very dulness that makes life to the incalculable majority so supportable and so welcome. Nevertheless, there can be but few of us who had never known one of these rare moments of awakening when we see, hear, understand ever so much – everything – in a flash – before we fall back again into our agreeable somnolence. I raised my eyes when he spoke, and I saw him as though I had never seen him before. I saw his chin sunk on his breast, the clumsy folds of his coat, his clasped hands, his motionless pose, so curiously suggestive of his having been simply left there. Time had passed indeed: it had overtaken him and gone ahead. It had left him hopelessly behind with a few poor gifts: the iron-grey hair, the heavy fatigue of the tanned face, two scars, a pair of tarnished shoulder-straps; one of those steady, reliable men who are the raw material of great reputations, one of those uncounted lives that are buried without drums and trumpets under the foundations of monumental successes. "I am now third lieutenant of the *Victorieuse*" (she was the flagship of the French Pacific squadron at the time), he said, detaching his shoulders from the wall a couple of inches to introduce himself. I bowed slightly on my side of the table, and told him I commanded a merchant vessel at present anchored in Rushcutters' Bay. He had "remarked" her, – a pretty little craft. He was very civil about it in his impassive way. I even fancy he went the length of tilting his head in compliment as he repeated, breathing visibly the while, "Ah, yes. A little craft painted black – very pretty – very pretty (*très coquet*)." After a time he twisted his body slowly to face the glass door on our right. "A dull town (*triste ville*)," he observed, staring into the street. It was a brilliant day; a southerly buster was raging, and we could see the passers-by, men and women, buffeted by the wind on the sidewalks, the sunlit fronts of the houses across the road blurred by the tall whirls of dust. "I descended on shore," he said, "to stretch my legs a little but . . ." He didn't finish, and sank into the depths of his repose. "Pray – tell me," he began, coming up ponderously, "what was there at the bottom of this affair – precisely (*au juste*)? It is curious. That dead man, for instance – and so on."

'"There were living men, too," I said; "much more curious."

'"No doubt, no doubt," he agreed half audibly, then, as if after mature consideration, murmured, "Evidently." I made no difficulty in communicating to him what had interested me most in this affair. It seemed as though he had a right to know: hadn't he spent thirty hours on board the *Patna* – had he not taken the succession, so to speak, had he not done "his possible"? He listened to me, looking more priest-like than ever, and with what – probably on account of his downcast eyes – had the appearance of devout concentration. Once or twice he elevated his eyebrows (but without raising his eyelids), as one would say "The devil!" Once he calmly exclaimed, "Ah, bah!" under his breath, and when I had finished he pursed his lips in a deliberate way and emitted a sort of sorrowful whistle.

'In any one else it might have been an evidence of boredom, a sign of indifference; but he, in his occult way, managed to make his immobility appear profoundly responsive, and as full of valuable thoughts as an egg is of meat. What he said at last was nothing more than a "very interesting," pronounced politely, and not much above a whisper. Before I got over my disappointment he added, but as if speaking to himself, "That's it. That *is* it." His chin seemed to sink lower on his breast, his body to weigh heavier on his seat. I was about to ask him what he meant when a sort of preparatory tremor passed over his whole person, as a faint ripple may be seen upon stagnant water even before the wind is felt. "And so that poor young man ran away along with the others," he said, with grave tranquillity.

'I don't know what made me smile: it is the only genuine smile of mine I can remember in connection with Jim's affair. But somehow this simple statement of the matter sounded funny in French. . . . "*S'est enfui avec les autres,*" had said the lieutenant. And suddenly I began to admire the discrimination of the man. He had made out the point at once: he did get hold of the only thing I cared about. I felt as though I were taking professional opinion on the case. His imperturbable and mature calmness was that of an expert in possession of the facts, and to whom one's perplexities are mere child's-play. "Ah! The young, the young," he said, indulgently. "And after all, one does not die of it." "Die of what?" I asked, swiftly. "Of being afraid." He elucidated his meaning and sipped his drink.

'I perceived that the three last fingers of his wounded hand were stiff and could not move independently of each other, so that he took up his tumbler with an ungainly clutch. "One is always afraid. One may talk, but . . ." He put down the glass awkwardly. . . . "The fear, the fear – look you – it is always there." . . . He touched his breast near a brass button on the very spot where Jim had given a thump to his own when protesting that there was nothing the

matter with his heart. I suppose I made some sign of
dissent, because he insisted, "Yes! yes! One talks, one
talks; this is all very fine; but at the end of the reckoning
one is no cleverer than the next man – and no more brave.
Brave! This is always to be seen. I have rolled my hump
(*roulé ma bosse*)," he said, using the slang expression with
imperturbable seriousness, "in all parts of the world; I have
known brave men – famous ones! *Allez!*"...He drank
carelessly.... "Brave – you conceive – in the Service – one
has got to be – the trade demands it (*le métier veux ça*). Is it
not so?" he appealed to me reasonably. "*Eh bien!* Each of
them – I say each of them, if he were an honest man – *bien
entendu* – would confess that there is a point – there is a
point – for the best of us – there is somewhere a point when
you let go everything (*vous lachez tout*). And you have got to
live with that truth – do you see? Given a certain combination of circumstances, fear is sure to come. Abominable
funk (*un trac épouvantable*). And even for those who do not
believe this truth there is fear all the same – the fear of
themselves. Absolutely so. Trust me. Yes. Yes.... At my
age one knows what one is talking about – *que
diable!*"...He had delivered himself of all this as immovably as though he had been the mouthpiece of abstract
wisdom, but at this point he heightened the effect of
detachment by beginning to twirl his thumbs slowly. "It's
evident – *parbleu!*" he continued; "for, make up your mind
as much as you like, even a simple headache or a fit of
indigestion (*un dérangement d'estomac*) is enough
to...Take me, for instance – I have made my proofs. *Eh
bien!* I, who am speaking to you, once..."

'He drained his glass and returned to his twirling. "No,
no; one does not die of it," he pronounced, finally, and when
I found he did not mean to proceed with the personal
anecdote, I was extremely disappointed; the more so as it
was not the sort of story, you know, one could very well press
him for. I sat silent, and he too, as if nothing could please
him better. Even his thumbs were still now. Suddenly his

lips began to move. "That is so," he resumed, placidly. "Man is born a coward (*L'homme est né poltron*). It is a difficulty – *parbleu!* It would be too easy otherwise. But habit – habit – necessity – do you see? – the eye of others – *voilà*. One puts up with it. And then the example of others who are no better than yourself, and yet make good countenance...."

'His voice ceased.

'"That young man – you will observe – had none of these inducements – at least at the moment," I remarked.

'He raised his eyebrows forgivingly: "I don't say; I don't say. The young man in question might have had the best dispositions – the best dispositions," he repeated, wheezing a little.

'"I am glad to see you taking a lenient view," I said. "His own feeling in the matter was – ah! – hopeful, and ..."

'The shuffle of his feet under the table interrupted me. He drew up his heavy eyelids. Drew up, I say – no other expression can describe the steady deliberation of the act – and at last was disclosed completely to me. I was confronted by two narrow grey circlets, like two tiny steel rings around the profound blackness of the pupils. The sharp glance, coming from that massive body, gave a notion of extreme efficiency, like a razor-edge on a battle-axe. "Pardon," he said, punctiliously. His right hand went up, and he swayed forward. "Allow me ... I contended that one may get on knowing very well that one's courage does not come of itself (*ne vient pas tout seul*). There's nothing much in that to get upset about. One truth the more ought not to make life impossible.... But the honour – the honour, monsieur!... The honour... that is real – that is! And what life may be worth when" ... he got on his feet with a ponderous impetuosity, as a startled ox might scramble up from the grass ... "when the honour is gone – *ah ça! par exemple* – I can offer no opinion. I can offer no opinion – because – monsieur – I know nothing of it."

'I had risen, too, and, trying to throw infinite politeness into our attitudes, we faced each other mutely, like two china dogs on a mantelpiece. Hang the fellow! he had pricked the bubble. The blight of futility that lies in wait for men's speeches had fallen upon our conversation, and made it a thing of empty sounds. "Very well," I said, with a disconcerted smile, "but couldn't it reduce itself to not being found out?" He made as if to retort readily, but when he spoke he had changed his mind. "This, monsieur, is too fine for me – much above me – I don't think about it." He bowed heavily over his cap, which he held before him by the peak, between the thumb and the forefinger of his wounded hand. I bowed, too. We bowed together: we scraped our feet at each other with much ceremony, while a dirty specimen of a waiter looked on critically, as though he had paid for the performance. "Serviteur," said the Frenchman. Another scrape. "Monsieur"..."Monsieur."... The glass door swung behind his burly back. I saw the southerly buster get hold of him and drive him down wind with his hand to his head, his shoulders braced, and the tails of his coat blown hard against his legs.

'I sat down again alone and discouraged – discouraged about Jim's case. If you wonder that after more than three years it had preserved its actuality, you must know that I had seen him only very lately. I had come straight from Samarang, where I had loaded a cargo for Sydney: an utterly uninteresting bit of business, – what Charley here would call one of my rational transactions – and in Samarang I had seen something of Jim. He was then working for De Jongh, on my recommendation. Water-clerk. "My representative afloat," as De Jongh called him. You can't imagine a mode of life more barren of consolation, less capable of being invested with a spark of glamour – unless it be the business of an insurance canvasser. Little Bob Stanton – Charley here knew him well – had gone through that experience. The same who got drowned afterwards trying to save a lady's-maid in the *Sephora* disaster. A case of collision on a hazy morning off the Spanish coast you may remember. All the passengers had been packed tidily into the boats and shoved clear of the ship when Bob sheered alongside again and scrambled back on deck to fetch that girl. How she had been left behind I can't make out; anyhow, she had gone completely crazy – wouldn't leave the ship – held to the rail like grim death. The wrestling-match could be seen plainly from the boats; but poor Bob was the shortest chief mate in the merchant service, and the woman stood five feet ten in her shoes and was as strong as a horse, I've been told. So it went on, pull devil, pull baker, the wretched girl screaming all the time, and Bob letting out a yell now and then to warn his boat to keep well clear of the ship. One of the hands told me, hiding a smile at the recollection, "It was for all the world, sir, like a naughty youngster fighting with his mother." The same old chap said that "At the last we could see that Mr Stanton had given up hauling at the gal, and just stood by looking at her, watchful like. We thought afterwards he must 've been reckoning that, maybe, the rush of water would tear her away from the rail by and by and give him a show to save her. We daren't come alongside for our life; and after a bit the old ship went down all on a sudden with a lurch to starboard – plop. The suck in was something awful. We never saw anything alive or dead come up." Poor Bob's spell of shore-life had been one of the complications of a love affair, I believe. He fondly hoped he had done with the sea for ever, and made sure he had got hold of all the bliss on earth, but it came to canvassing in the end. Some cousin of his in Liverpool put him up to it. He used to tell us his experiences in that line. He made us laugh till we cried, and, not altogether displeased at the effect, undersized and bearded to the waist like a gnome, he would tiptoe amongst us and say, "It's all very well for you beggars to laugh, but my immortal soul was shrivelled down to the size of a parched pea after a week of that work." I don't know how Jim's soul accommodated itself to the new conditions of his life – I

was kept too busy in getting him something to do that
would keep body and soul together – but I am pretty certain
his adventurous fancy was suffering all the pangs of starvation. It had certainly nothing to feed upon in this new
calling. It was distressing to see him at it, though he tackled
it with a stubborn serenity for which I must give him full
credit. I kept my eye on his shabby plodding with a sort of
notion that it was a punishment for the heroics of his fancy
– an expiation for his craving after more glamour than he
could carry. He had loved too well to imagine himself a
glorious racehorse, and now he was condemned to toil
without honour like a costermonger's donkey. He did it
very well. He shut himself in, put his head down, said never
a word. Very well; very well indeed – except for certain
fantastic and violent outbreaks, on the deplorable occasions
when the irrepressible *Patna* case cropped up.
Unfortunately that scandal of the Eastern seas would not
die out. And this is the reason why I could never feel I had
done with Jim for good.

'I sat thinking of him after the French lieutenant had
left, not, however, in connection with De Jongh's cool and
gloomy backshop, where we had hurriedly shaken hands
not very long ago, but as I had seen him years before in the
last flickers of the candle, alone with me in the long gallery
of the Malabar House, with the chill and the darkness of
the night at his back. The respectable sword of his country's
law was suspended over his head. To-morrow – or was it
to-day? (midnight had slipped by long before we parted) –
the marble-faced police magistrate, after distributing fines
and terms of imprisonment in the assault-and-battery case,
would take up the awful weapon and smite his bowed neck.
Our communion in the night was uncommonly like a last
vigil with a condemned man. He was guilty, too. He was
guilty – as I had told myself repeatedly, guilty and done for;
nevertheless, I wished to spare him the mere detail of a
formal execution. I don't pretend to explain the reasons of
my desire – I don't think I could; but if you haven't got a

sort of notion by this time, then I must have been very
obscure in my narrative, or you too sleepy to seize upon the
sense of my words. I don't defend my morality. There was
no morality in the impulse which induced me to lay before
him Brierly's plan of evasion – I may call it – in all its
primitive simplicity. There were the rupees – absolutely
ready in my pocket and very much at his service. Oh! a loan;
a loan of course – and if an introduction to a man (in
Rangoon) who could put some work in his way... Why!
with the greatest pleasure. I had pen, ink, and paper in my
room on the first floor. And even while I was speaking I was
impatient to begin the letter: day, month, year, 2:30
a.m.... for the sake of our old friendship I ask you to put
some work in the way of Mr James So-and-so, in whom,
&c., &c.... I was even ready to write in that strain about
him. If he had not enlisted my sympathies he had done
better for himself – he had gone to the very fount and
origin of that sentiment, he had reached the secret sensibility of my egoism. I am concealing nothing from you,
because were I to do so my action would appear more
unintelligible than any man's action has the right to be,
and – in the second place – to-morrow you shall forget my
sincerity along with the other lessons of the past. In this
transaction, to speak grossly and precisely, I was the irre-
proachable man; but the subtle intentions of my immoral-
ity were defeated by the moral simplicity of the criminal.
No doubt he was selfish, too, but his selfishness had a
higher origin, a more lofty aim. I discovered that, say
what I would, he was eager to go through the ceremony
of execution; and I didn't say much, for I felt that in
argument his youth would tell against me heavily: he
believed where I had already ceased to doubt. There was
something fine in the wildness of his unexpressed, hardly
formulated hope. "Clear out! Couldn't think of it," he said,
with a shake of the head. "I make you an offer for which
I neither demand nor expect any sort of gratitude," I said;
"you shall repay the money when convenient, and..."

"Awfully good of you," he muttered without looking up. I watched him narrowly: the future must have appeared horribly uncertain to him; but he did not falter, as though indeed there had been nothing wrong with his heart. I felt angry – not for the first time that night. "The whole wretched business," I said, "is bitter enough, I should think, for a man of your kind ..." "It is, it is," he whispered twice, with his eyes fixed on the floor. It was heartrending. He towered above the light, and I could see the down on his cheek, the colour mantling warm under the smooth skin of his face. Believe me or not, I say it was outrageously heart-rending. It provoked me to brutality. "Yes," I said; "and allow me to confess that I am totally unable to imagine what advantage you can expect from this licking of the dregs." "Advantage!" he murmured out of his stillness. "I am dashed if I do," I said, enraged. "I've been trying to tell you all there is in it," he went on, slowly, as if meditating something unanswerable. "But after all, it is *my* trouble." I opened my mouth to retort, and discovered suddenly that I'd lost all confidence in myself; and it was as if he, too, had given me up, for he mumbled like a man thinking half aloud. "Went away ... went into hospitals. ... Not one of them would face it. ... They! ..." He moved his hand slightly to imply disdain. "But I've got to get over this thing, and I mustn't shirk any of it or ... I won't shirk any of it." He was silent. He gazed as though he had been haunted. His unconscious face reflected the passing expressions of scorn, of despair, of resolution, – reflected them in turn, as a magic mirror would reflect the gliding passage of unearthly shapes. He lived surrounded by deceitful ghosts, by austere shades. "Oh! nonsense, my dear fellow," I began. He had a movement of impatience. "You don't seem to understand," he said, incisively; then looking at me without a wink, "I may have jumped, but I don't run away." "I meant no offence," I said; and added stupidly, "Better men than you have found it expedient to run, at times." He coloured all over, while in my confusion I half-choked myself with my own tongue. "Perhaps so," he said at last; "I am not good enough; I can't afford it. I am bound to fight this thing down – I am fighting it *now*." I got out of my chair and felt stiff all over. The silence was embarrassing, and to put an end to it I imagined nothing better but to remark, "I had no idea it was so late," in an airy tone.... "I daresay you have had enough of this," he said, brusquely: "and to tell you the truth" – he began to look round for his hat – "so have I."

'Well! he had refused this unique offer. He had struck aside my helping hand; he was ready to go now, and beyond the balustrade the night seemed to wait for him very still, as though he had been marked down for its prey. I heard his voice. "Ah! here it is." He had found his hat. For a few seconds we hung in the wind. "What will you do after – after..." I asked very low. "Go to the dogs as likely as not," he answered in a gruff mutter. I had recovered my wits in a measure, and judged best to take it lightly. "Pray remember," I said, "that I should like very much to see you again before you go." "I don't know what's to prevent you. The damned thing won't make me invisible," he said with intense bitterness, – "no such luck." And then at the moment of taking leave he treated me to a ghastly muddle of dubious stammers and movements, to an awful display of hesitations. God forgive him – me! He had taken it into his fanciful head that I was likely to make some difficulty as to shaking hands. It was too awful for words. I believe I shouted suddenly at him as you would bellow to a man you saw about to walk over a cliff; I remember our voices being raised, the appearance of a miserable grin on his face, a crushing clutch on my hand, a nervous laugh. The candle spluttered out, and the thing was over at last, with a groan that floated up to me in the dark. He got himself away somehow. The night swallowed his form. He was a horrible bungler. Horrible. I heard the quick crunch-crunch of the gravel under his boots. He was running. Absolutely running, with nowhere to go to. And he was not yet four-and-twenty.'

# CHAPTER FOURTEEN

'I SLEPT little, hurried over my breakfast, and after a slight hesitation gave up my early morning visit to my ship. It was really very wrong of me, because, though my chief mate was an excellent man all round, he was the victim of such black imaginings that if he did not get a letter from his wife at the expected time he would go quite distracted with rage and jealousy, lose all grip on the work, quarrel with all hands, and either weep in his cabin or develop such a ferocity of temper as all but drove the crew to the verge of mutiny. The thing had always seemed inexplicable to me: they had been married thirteen years; I had a glimpse of her once, and, honestly, I couldn't conceive a man abandoned enough to plunge into sin for the sake of such an unattractive person. I don't know whether I have not done wrong by refraining from putting that view before poor Selvin: the man made a little hell on earth for himself, and I also suffered indirectly, but some sort of, no doubt, false delicacy prevented me. The marital relations of seamen would make an interesting subject, and I could tell you instances. . . . However, this is not the place, nor the time, and we are concerned with Jim – who was unmarried. If his imaginative conscience or his pride; if all the extravagant ghosts and austere shades that were the disastrous familiars of his youth would not let him run away from the block, I, who of course can't be suspected of such familiars, was irresistibly impelled to go and see his head roll off. I wended my way towards the court. I didn't hope to be very much impressed or edified, or interested or even frightened – though, as long as there is any life before one, a jolly good fright now and then is a salutary discipline. But neither did I expect to be so awfully depressed.

The bitterness of his punishment was in its chill and mean atmosphere. The real significance of crime is in its being a breach of faith with the community of mankind, and from that point of view he was no mean traitor, but his execution was a hole-and-corner affair. There was no high scaffolding, no scarlet cloth (did they have scarlet cloth on Tower Hill? They should have had), no awe-stricken multitude to be horrified at his guilt and be moved to tears at his fate – no air of sombre retribution. There was, as I walked along, the clear sunshine, a brilliance too passionate to be consoling, the streets full of jumbled bits of colour like a damaged kaleidoscope: yellow, green, blue, dazzling white, the brown nudity of an undraped shoulder, a bullock-cart with a red canopy, a company of native infantry in a drab body with dark heads marching in dusty laced boots, a native policeman in a sombre uniform of scanty cut and belted in patent leather, who looked up at me with orientally pitiful eyes as though his migrating spirit were suffering exceedingly from that unforeseen – what d'ye call 'em? – avatar – incarnation. Under the shade of a lonely tree in the courtyard, the villagers connected with the assault case sat in a picturesque group, looking like a chromo-lithograph of a camp in a book of Eastern travel. One missed the obligatory thread of smoke in the foreground and the pack-animals grazing. A blank yellow wall rose behind overtopping the tree, reflecting the glare. The court-room was sombre, seemed more vast. High up in the dim space the punkahs were swaying short to and fro, to and fro. Here and there a draped figure, dwarfed by the bare walls, remained without stirring amongst the rows of empty benches, as if absorbed in pious meditation. The plaintiff, who had been beaten, an obese chocolate-coloured man with shaved head, one fat breast bare and a bright yellow caste-mark above the bridge of his nose, sat in pompous immobility: only his eyes glittered, rolling in the gloom, and the nostrils dilated and collapsed violently as he breathed. Brierly dropped into his seat looking done up, as though he had spent the night in sprinting on a cinder-track. The pious sailing-ship skipper appeared excited and made uneasy movements, as if restraining with difficulty an impulse to stand up and exhort us earnestly to prayer and repentance. The head of the magistrate, delicately pale under the neatly arranged hair, resembled the head of a hopeless invalid after he had been washed and brushed and propped up in bed. He moved aside the vase of flowers – a bunch of purple with a few pink blossoms on long stalks – and seizing in both hands a long sheet of bluish paper, ran his eye over it, propped his forearms on the edge of the desk, and began to read aloud in an even, distinct, and careless voice.

'By Jove! For all my foolishness about scaffolds and heads rolling off – I assure you it was infinitely worse than a beheading. A heavy sense of finality brooded over all this, unrelieved by the hope of rest and safety following the fall of the axe. These proceedings had all the cold vengefulness of a death-sentence, had all the cruelty of a sentence of exile. This is how I looked at it that morning – and even now I seem to see an undeniable vestige of truth in that exaggerated view of a common occurrence. You may imagine how strongly I felt this at the time. Perhaps it is for that reason that I could not bring myself to admit the finality. The thing was always with me, I was always eager to take opinion on it, as though it had not been practically settled: individual opinion – international opinion – by Jove! That Frenchman's, for instance. His own country's pronouncement was uttered in the passionless and definite phraseology a machine would use, if machines could speak. The head of the magistrate was half hidden by the paper, his brow was like alabaster.

'There were several questions before the Court. The first as to whether the ship was in every respect fit and sea-worthy for the voyage. The court found she was not. The next point, I remember, was, whether up to the time of the accident the ship had been navigated with proper and seamanlike care. They said Yes to that, goodness knows why, and then they declared that there was no evidence to show the exact cause of the accident. A floating derelict probably. I myself remember that a Norwegian barque bound out with a cargo of pitch-pine had been given up as missing about that time, and it was just the sort of craft that would capsize in a squall and float bottom up for months – a kind of maritime ghoul on the prowl to kill ships in the dark. Such wandering corpses are common enough in the North Atlantic, which is haunted by all the terrors of the sea, – fogs, icebergs, dead ships bent upon mischief, and long sinister gales that fasten upon one like a vampire till all the strength and the spirit and even hope are gone, and one feels like the empty shell of a man. But there – in those seas – the incident was rare enough to resemble a special arrangement of a malevolent providence, which, unless it had for its object the killing of a donkeyman and the bringing of worse than death upon Jim, appeared an utterly aimless piece of devilry. This view occurring to me took off my attention. For a time I was aware of the magistrate's voice as a sound merely; but in a moment it shaped itself into distinct words..."in utter disregard of their plain duty," it said. The next sentence escaped me somehow, and then..."abandoning in the moment of danger the lives and property confided to their charge"... went on the voice evenly, and stopped. A pair of eyes under the white forehead shot darkly a glance above the edge of the paper. I looked for Jim hurriedly, as though I had expected him to disappear. He was very still – but he was there. He sat pink and fair and extremely attentive. "Therefore, ..." began the voice emphatically. He stared with parted lips, hanging upon the words of the man behind the desk. These came out into the stillness wafted on the wind made by the punkahs, and I, watching for their effect upon him, caught only the fragments of official language.... "The Court ... Gustav So-and-so master ...

native of Germany... James So-and-so ... mate ... certifi-
cates cancelled." A silence fell. The magistrate had dropped
the paper, and leaning sideways on the arm of his chair,
began to talk with Brierly easily. People started to move
out; others were pushing in, and I also made for the door.
Outside I stood still, and when Jim passed me on his way to
the gate, I caught at his arm and detained him. The look he
gave discomposed me, as though I had been responsible for
his state: he looked at me as if I had been the embodied evil
of life. "It's all over," I stammered. "Yes," he said, thickly.
"And now let no man..." He jerked his arm out of my
grasp. I watched his back as he went away. It was a long
street, and he remained in sight for some time. He walked
rather slow, and straddling his legs a little, as if he had
found it difficult to keep a straight line. Just before I lost
him I fancied he staggered a bit.

'"Man overboard," said a deep voice behind me. Turning
round, I saw a fellow I knew slightly, a West Australian;
Chester was his name. He, too, had been looking after Jim.
He was a man with an immense girth of chest, a rugged,
clean-shaved face of mahogany colour, and two blunt tufts
of iron-grey, thick wiry hairs on his upper lip. He had been
pearler, wrecker, trader, whaler, too, I believe; in his own
words – anything and everything a man may be at sea, but a
pirate. The Pacific, north and south, was his proper hunt-
ing-ground; but he had wandered so far afield looking for a
cheap steamer to buy. Lately he had discovered – so he said
– a guano island somewhere, but its approaches were dangerous, and the anchorage, such as it was, could not be
considered safe, to say the least of it. "As good as a gold-
mine," he would exclaim. "Right bang in the middle of the
Walpole Reefs, and if it's true enough that you can get no
holding-ground anywhere in less than forty fathom, then
what of that? There are the hurricanes, too. But it's a first-
rate thing. As good as a gold-mine – better! Yet there's not a
fool of them that will see it. I can't get a skipper or a
shipowner to go near the place. So I made up my mind to

cart the blessed stuff myself." . . . This was what he required a steamer for, and I knew he was just then negotiating enthusiastically with a Parsee firm for an old, brig-rigged, sea-anachronism of ninety horse-power. We had met and spoken together several times. He looked knowingly after Jim. "Takes it to heart?" he asked, scornfully. "Very much," I said. "Then he's no good," he opined. "What's all the to-do about? A bit of ass's skin. That never yet made a man. You must see things exactly as they are – if you don't, you may just as well give in at once. You will never do anything in this world. Look at me. I made it a practice never to take anything to heart." "Yes," I said, "you see things as they are." "I wish I could see my partner coming along, that's what I wish to see," he said. "Know my partner? Old Robinson. Yes; *the* Robinson. Don't *you* know? The notorious Robinson. The man who smuggled more opium and bagged more seals in his time than any loose Johnny now alive. They say he used to board the sealing-schooners up Alaska way when the fog was so thick that the Lord God, He alone, could tell one man from another. Holy-Terror Robinson. That's the man. He is with me in that guano thing. The best chance he ever came across in his life." He put his lips to my ear. "Cannibal? – well, they used to give him the name years and years ago. You remember the story? A shipwreck on the west side of Stewart Island; that's right; seven of them got ashore, and it seems they did not get on very well together. Some men are too cantankerous for anything – don't know how to make the best of a bad job – don't see things as they arc – as they *are*, my boy! And then what's the consequence? Obvious! Trouble, trouble; as likely as not a knock on the head; and serve 'em right, too. That sort is the most useful when it's dead. The story goes that a boat of Her Majesty's ship *Wolverine* found him kneeling on the kelp, naked as the day he was born, and chanting some psalm-tune or other; light snow was falling at the time. He waited till the boat was an oar's length from the shore, and then up and away. They chased him for an hour up and down the boulders, till a marine flung a stone that took him behind the ear providentially and knocked him senseless. Alone? Of course. But that's like that tale of sealing-schooners; the Lord God knows the right and the wrong of that story. The cutter did not investigate much. They wrapped him in a boat-cloak and took him off as quick as they could, with a dark night coming on, the weather threatening, and the ship firing recall guns every five minutes. Three weeks afterwards he was as well as ever. He didn't allow any fuss that was made on shore to upset him; he just shut his lips tight, and let people screech. It was bad enough to have lost his ship, and all he was worth besides, without paying attention to the hard names they called him. That's the man for me." He lifted his arm for a signal to some one down the street. "He's got a little money, so I had to let him into my thing. Had to! It would have been sinful to throw away such a find, and I was cleaned out myself. It cut me to the quick, but I could see the matter just as it was, and if I *must* share – thinks I – with any man, then give me Robinson. I left him at breakfast in the hotel to come to court, because I've an idea.... Ah! Good morning, Captain Robinson.... Friend of mine, Captain Robinson."

'An emaciated patriarch in a suit of white drill, a solah topi with a green-lined rim on a head trembling with age, joined us after crossing the street in a trotting shuffle, and stood propped with both hands on the handle of an umbrella. A white beard with amber streaks hung lumpily down to his waist. He blinked his creased eyelids at me in a bewildered way. "How do you do? how do you do?" he piped, amiably, and tottered. "A little deaf," said Chester aside. "Did you drag him over six thousand miles to get a cheap steamer?" I asked. "I would have taken him twice round the world as soon as look at him," said Chester with immense energy. "The steamer will be the making of us, my lad. Is it my fault that every skipper and shipowner in the whole of blessed Australasia turns out a blamed fool? Once

I talked for three hours to a man in Auckland. 'Send a ship,' I said, 'send a ship. I'll give you half of the first cargo for yourself, free gratis for nothing – just to make a good start.' Says he, 'I wouldn't do it if there was no other place on earth to send a ship to.' Perfect ass, of course. Rocks, currents, no anchorage, sheer cliff to lay to, no insurance company would take the risk, didn't see how he could get loaded under three years. Ass! I nearly went on my knees to him. 'But look at the thing as it is,' says I. 'Damn rocks and hurricanes. Look at it as it is. There's guano there, Queensland sugar-planters would fight for – fight for on the quay, I tell you.'... What can you do with a fool?... 'That's one of your little jokes, Chester,' he says.... Joke! I could have wept. Ask Captain Robinson here.... And there was another shipowning fellow – a fat chap in a white waistcoat in Wellington, who seemed to think I was up to some swindle or other. 'I don't know what sort of fool you're looking for,' he says, 'but I am busy just now. Good morning.' I longed to take him in my two hands and smash him through the window of his own office. But I didn't. I was as mild as a curate. 'Think of it,' says I. '*Do* think it over. I'll call to-morrow.' He grunted something about being 'out all day.' On the stairs I felt ready to beat my head against the wall from vexation. Captain Robinson here can tell you. It was awful to think of all that lovely stuff lying waste under the sun – stuff that would send the sugar-cane shooting sky-high. The making of Queensland! The making of Queensland! And in Brisbane, where I went to have a last try, they gave me the name of a lunatic. Idiots! The only sensible man I came across was the cabman who drove me about. A broken-down swell he was, I fancy. Hey! Captain Robinson? You remember I told you about my cabby in Brisbane – don't you? The chap had a wonderful eye for things. He saw it all in a jiffy. It was a real pleasure to talk with him. One evening after a devil of a day amongst shipowners I felt so bad that, says I, 'I must get drunk. Come along; I must get drunk, or I'll go mad.' 'I am your man,' he says; 'go ahead.' I don't know what I would have done without him. Hey! Captain Robinson."

'He poked the ribs of his partner. "He! he! he!" laughed the Ancient, looked aimlessly down the street, then peered at me doubtfully with sad, dim pupils. . . . "He! he! he!" . . . He leaned heavier on the umbrella, and dropped his gaze on the ground. I needn't tell you I had tried to get away several times, but Chester had foiled every attempt by simply catching hold of my coat. "One minute. I've a notion." "What's your infernal notion?" I exploded at last. "If you think I am going in with you . . ." "No, no, my boy. Too late, if you wanted ever so much. We've got a steamer." "You've got the ghost of a steamer," I said. "Good enough for a start – there's no superior nonsense about us. Is there, Captain Robinson?" "No! no! no!" croaked the old man without lifting his eyes, and the senile tremble of his head became almost fierce with determination. "I understand you know that young chap," said Chester, with a nod at the street from which Jim had disappeared long ago. "He's been having grub with you in the Malabar last night – so I was told."

'I said that was true, and after remarking that he, too, liked to live well and in style, only that, for the present, he had to be saving of every penny – "none too many for the business! Isn't that so, Captain Robinson?" – he squared his shoulders and stroked his dumpy moustache, while the notorious Robinson, coughing at his side, clung more than ever to the handle of the umbrella, and seemed ready to subside passively into a heap of old bones. "You see, the old chap has all the money," whispered Chester, confidentially. "I've been cleaned out trying to engineer the dratted thing. But wait a bit, wait a bit. The good time is coming.". . . He seemed suddenly astonished at the signs of impatience I gave. "Oh, crakee!" he cried; "I am telling you of the biggest thing that ever was, and you . . ." "I have an appointment," I pleaded mildly. "What of that?" he asked with genuine surprise; "let it wait." "That's exactly what I am doing now," I remarked; "hadn't you better tell me what it is you want?" "Buy twenty hotels like that," he growled to himself; "and every joker boarding in them, too – twenty times over." He lifted his head smartly. "I want that young chap." "I don't understand," I said. "He's no good, is he?" said Chester, crisply. "I know nothing about it," I protested. "Why, you told me yourself he was taking it to heart," argued Chester. "Well, in my opinion a chap who . . . Anyhow, he can't be much good; but then you see I am on the look-out for somebody, and I've just got a thing that will suit him. I'll give him a job on my island." He nodded significantly. "I'm going to dump forty coolies there – if I've got to steal 'em. Somebody must work the stuff. Oh! I mean to act square: wooden shed, corrugated-iron roof – I know a man in Hobart who will take my bill at six months for the materials. I do. Honour bright. Then there's the water-supply. I'll have to fly round and get somebody to trust me for half-a-dozen second-hand iron tanks. Catch rain-water, hey? Let him take charge. Make him supreme boss over the coolies. Good idea, isn't it? What do you say?" "There are whole years when not a drop of rain falls on Walpole," I said, too amazed to laugh. He bit his lip and seemed bothered. "Oh, well, I will fix up something for them – or land a supply. Hang it all! That's not the question.

'I said nothing. I had a rapid vision of Jim perched on a shadowless rock, up to his knees in guano, with the screams of sea-birds in his ears, the incandescent ball of the sun above his head; the empty sky and the empty ocean all a-quiver, simmering together in the heat as far as the eye could reach. "I wouldn't advise my worst enemy . . ." I began. "What's the matter with you?" cried Chester; "I mean to give him a good screw – that is, as soon as the thing is set going, of course. It's as easy as falling off a log. Simply nothing to do; two six-shooters in his belt. . . . Surely he wouldn't be afraid of anything forty coolies could do – with two six-shooters and he the only armed man, too! It's much

better than it looks. I want you to help me to talk him over."
"No!" I shouted. Old Robinson lifted his bleared eyes
dismally for a moment, Chester looked at me with infinite
contempt. "So you wouldn't advise him?" he uttered,
slowly. "Certainly not," I answered, as indignant as though
he had requested me to help murder somebody; "moreover,
I am sure he wouldn't. He is badly cut up, but he isn't mad
as far as I know." "He is no earthly good for anything,"
Chester mused aloud. "He would just have done for me. If
you only could see a thing as it is, you would see it's the very
thing for him. And besides . . . Why! it's the most splendid,
sure chance . . ." He got angry suddenly. "I must have a
man. There! . . ." He stamped his foot and smiled unpleasantly. "Anyhow, I could guarantee the island wouldn't sink
under him – and I believe he is a bit particular on that
point." "Good morning," I said, curtly. He looked at me as
though I had been an incomprehensible fool. . . . "Must be
moving, Captain Robinson," he yelled suddenly into the
old man's ear. "These Parsee Johnnies are waiting for us to
clinch the bargain." He took his partner under the arm
with a firm grip, swung him round, and, unexpectedly,
leered at me over his shoulder. "I was trying to do him a
kindness," he asserted, with an air and tone that made my
blood boil. "Thank you for nothing – in his name," I
rejoined. "Oh! you are devilish smart," he sneered; "but
you are like the rest of them. Too much in the clouds. See
what *you* will do with him." "I don't know that I want to do
anything with him." "Don't you?" he spluttered; his grey
moustache bristled with anger, and by his side the notorious Robinson, propped on the umbrella, stood with his
back to me, as patient and still as a worn-out cab-horse. "I
haven't found a guano island," I said. "It's my belief you
wouldn't know one if you were led right up to it by the
hand," he riposted quickly; "and in this world you've got to
see a thing first, before you can make use of it. Got to see it
through and through at that, neither more nor less." "And
get others to see it, too," I insinuated, with a glance at the

bowed back by his side. Chester snorted at me. "His eyes are right enough – don't you worry. He ain't a puppy." "Oh, dear, no!" I said. "Come along, Captain Robinson," he shouted, with a sort of bullying deference under the rim of the old man's hat; the Holy Terror gave a submissive little jump. The ghost of a steamer was waiting for them, Fortune on that fair isle! They made a curious pair of Argonauts. Chester strode on leisurely, well set up, portly, and of conquering mien; the other, long, wasted, drooping, and hooked to his arm, shuffled his withered shanks with desperate haste.'

# CHAPTER FIFTEEN

'I DID not start in search of Jim at once, only because I had really an appointment which I could not neglect. Then, as ill-luck would have it, in my agent's office I was fastened upon by a fellow fresh from Madagascar with a little scheme for a wonderful piece of business. It had something to do with cattle and cartridges and a Prince Ravonalo something; but the pivot of the whole affair was the stupidity of some admiral – Admiral Pierre, I think. Everything turned on that, and the chap couldn't find words strong enough to express his confidence. He had globular eyes starting out of his head with a fishy glitter, bumps on his forehead, and wore his long hair brushed back without a parting. He had a favourite phrase which he kept on repeating triumphantly, "The minimum of risk with the maximum of profit is my motto. What?" He made my head ache, spoiled my tiffin, but got his own out of me all right; and as soon as I had shaken him off, I made straight for the water-side. I caught sight of Jim leaning over the parapet of the quay. Three native boatmen quarrelling over five annas were making an awful row at his elbow. He didn't hear me come up, but spun round as if the slight contact of my finger had released a catch. "I was looking," he stammered. I don't remember what I said, not much anyhow, but he made no difficulty in following me to the hotel.

'He followed me as manageable as a little child, with an obedient air, with no sort of manifestation, rather as though he had been waiting for me there to come along and carry him off. I need not have been so surprised as I was at his tractability. On all the round earth, which to some

seems so big and that others affect to consider as rather
smaller than a mustard-seed, he had no place where he
could – what shall I say? – where he could withdraw. That's
it! Withdraw – be alone with his loneliness. He walked by
my side very calm, glancing here and there, and once
turned his head to look after a Sidiboy fireman in a cutaway
coat and yellowish trousers, whose black face had silky
gleams like a lump of anthracite coal. I doubt, however,
whether he saw anything, or even remained all the time
aware of my companionship, because if I had not edged
him to the left here, or pulled him to the right there,
I believe he would have gone straight before him in any
direction till stopped by a wall or some other obstacle.
I steered him into my bedroom, and sat down at once to
write letters. This was the only place in the world (unless,
perhaps, the Walpole Reef – but that was not so handy)
where he could have it out with himself without being
bothered by the rest of the universe. The damned thing –
as he had expressed it – had not made him invisible, but
I behaved exactly as though he were. No sooner in my
chair I bent over my writing-desk like a medieval scribe,
and, but for the movement of the hand holding the pen,
remained anxiously quiet. I can't say I was frightened; but I
certainly kept as still as if there had been something dangerous in the room, that at the first hint of a movement on my
part would be provoked to pounce upon me. There was not
much in the room – you know how these bed-rooms are – a
sort of four-poster bedstead under a mosquito-net, two or
three chairs, the table I was writing at, a bare floor. A glass
door opened on an upstairs verandah, and he stood with his
face to it, having a hard time with all possible privacy. Dusk
fell; I lit a candle with the greatest economy of movement
and as much prudence as though it were an illegal proceeding. There is no doubt that he had a very hard time of it, and
so had I, even to the point, I must own, of wishing him to the
devil, or on Walpole Reef at least. It occurred to me once or
twice that, after all, Chester was, perhaps, the man to deal

effectively with such a disaster. That strange idealist had
found a practical use for it at once – unerringly, as it were. It
was enough to make one suspect that, maybe, he really
could see the true aspect of things that appeared mysterious
or utterly hopeless to less imaginative persons. I wrote and
wrote; I liquidated all the arrears of my correspondence,
and then went on writing to people who had no reason
whatever to expect from me a gossipy letter about nothing
at all. At times I stole a sidelong glance. He was rooted to
the spot, but convulsive shudders ran down his back; his
shoulders would heave suddenly. He was fighting, he was
fighting – mostly for his breath, as it seemed. The massive
shadows, cast all one way from the straight flame of the
candle, seemed possessed of gloomy consciousness; the
immobility of the furniture had to my furtive eye an air of
attention. I was becoming fanciful in the midst of my
industrious scribbling; and though, when the scratching
of my pen stopped for a moment, there was complete
silence and stillness in the room, I suffered from that
profound disturbance and confusion of thought which is
caused by a violent and menacing uproar – of a heavy gale at
sea, for instance. Some of you may know what I mean, –
that mingled anxiety, distress, and irritation with a sort of
craven feeling creeping in – not pleasant to acknowledge,
but which gives a quiet special merit to one's endurance. I
don't claim any merit for standing the stress of Jim's emotions; I could take refuge in the letters; I could have written
to strangers if necessary. Suddenly, as I was taking up a
fresh sheet of notepaper, I heard a low sound, the first
sound that, since we had been shut up together, had come
to my ears in the dim stillness of the room. I remained with
my head down, with my hand arrested. Those who have
kept vigil by a sick-bed have heard such faint sounds in the
stillness of the night watches, sounds wrung from a racked
body, from a weary soul. He pushed the glass door with
such force that all the panes rang: he stepped out, and I held
my breath, straining my ears without knowing what else

I expected to hear. He was really taking too much to heart an empty formality which to Chester's rigorous criticism seemed unworthy the notice of a man who could see things as they were. An empty formality; a piece of parchment. Well, well. As to the inaccessible guano deposit, that was another story altogether. One could intelligibly break one's heart over that. A feeble burst of many voices mingled with the tinkle of silver and glass floated up from the dining-room below; through the open door the outer edge of the light from my candle fell on his back faintly; beyond all was black; he stood on the brink of a vast obscurity, like a lonely figure by the shore of a sombre and hopeless ocean. There was the Walpole Reef in it – to be sure – a speck in the dark void, a straw for the drowning man. My compassion for him took the shape of the thought that I wouldn't have liked his people to see him at that moment. I found it trying myself. His back was no longer shaken by his gasps; he stood straight as an arrow, faintly visible and still; and the meaning of this stillness sank to the bottom of my soul like lead into the water, and made it so heavy that for a second I wished heartily that the only course left open for me were to pay for his funeral. Even the law had done with him. To bury him would have been such an easy kindness! It would have been so much in accordance with the wisdom of life, which consists in putting out of sight all the reminders of our folly, of our weakness, of our mortality; all that makes against our efficiency – the memory of our failures, the hints of our undying fears, the bodies of our dead friends. Perhaps he did take it too much to heart. And if so then – Chester's offer. . . . At this point I took up a fresh sheet and began to write resolutely. There was nothing but myself between him and the dark ocean. I had a sense of responsibility. If I spoke, would that motionless and suffering youth leap into the obscurity – clutch at the straw? I found out how difficult it may be sometimes to make a sound. There is a weird power in a spoken word. And why the devil not? I was asking myself persistently while I drove on with my writing. All at once, on the blank page, under the very point of the pen, the two figures of Chester and his antique partner, very distinct and complete, would dodge into view with stride and gestures, as if reproduced in the field of some optical toy. I would watch them for a while. No! They were too phantasmal and extravagant to enter into any one's fate. And a word carries far – very far – deals destruction through time as the bullets go flying through space. I said nothing; and he, out there with his back to the light, as if bound and gagged by all the invisible foes of man, made no stir and made no sound.'

# CHAPTER SIXTEEN

'The time was coming when I should see him loved, trusted, admired, with a legend of strength and prowess forming round his name as though he had been the stuff of a hero. It's true – I assure you; as true as I'm sitting here talking about him in vain. He, on his side, had that faculty of beholding at a hint the face of his desire and the shape of his dream, without which the earth would know no lover and no adventurer. He captured much honour and an Arcadian happiness (I won't say anything about innocence) in the bush, and it was as good to him as the honour and the Arcadian happiness of the streets to another man. Felicity, felicity – how shall I say it? – is quaffed out of a golden cup in every latitude: the flavour is with you – with you alone, and you can make it as intoxicating as you please. He was of the sort that would drink deep, as you may guess from what went before. I found him, if not exactly intoxicated, then at least flushed with the elixir at his lips. He had not obtained it at once. There had been, as you know, a period of probation amongst infernal ship-chandlers, during which he had suffered and I had worried about – about – my trust – you may call it. I don't know that I am completely reassured now, after beholding him in all his brilliance. That was my last view of him – in a strong light, dominating, and yet in complete accord with his surroundings – with the life of the forests and with the life of men. I own that I was impressed, but I must admit to myself that after all this is not the lasting impression. He was protected by his isolation, alone of his own superior kind, in close touch with Nature, that keeps faith on such easy terms with her lovers. But I cannot fix before my eye the image of his safety. I shall always remember him as seen through the open door of my room, taking, perhaps, too much to heart the mere consequences of his failure. I am pleased, of course, that some good — and even some splendour — came out of my endeavours; but at times it seems to me it would have been better for my peace of mind if I had not stood between him and Chester's confoundedly generous offer. I wonder what his exuberant imagination would have made of Walpole islet — that most hopelessly forsaken crumb of dry land on the face of the waters. It is not likely I would ever have heard, for I must tell you that Chester, after calling at some Australian port to patch up his brig-rigged sea-anachronism, steamed out into the Pacific with a crew of twenty-two hands all told, and the only news having a possible bearing upon the mystery of his fate was the news of a hurricane which is supposed to have swept in its course over the Walpole shoals, a month or so afterwards. Not a vestige of the Argonauts ever turned up; not a sound came out of the waste. Finis! The Pacific is the most discreet of live, hot-tempered oceans: the chilly Antarctic can keep a secret, too, but more in the manner of a grave.

'And there is a sense of blessed finality in such discretion, which is what we all more or less sincerely are ready to admit — for what else is it that makes the idea of death supportable? End! Finis! the potent word that exorcises from the house of life the haunting shadow of fate. This is what — notwithstanding the testimony of my eyes and his own earnest assurances — I miss when I look back upon Jim's success. While there's life there is hope, truly; but there is fear, too. I don't mean to say that I regret my action, nor will I pretend that I can't sleep o'nights in consequence; still the idea obtrudes itself that he made so much of his disgrace while it is the guilt alone that matters. He was not — if I may say so — clear to me. He was not clear. And there is a suspicion he was not clear to himself either. There were his fine sensibilities, his fine feelings, his fine longings — a sort of sublimated, idealised selfishness. He was — if you allow me to say so – very fine; very fine – and very unfortunate. A little coarser nature would not have borne the strain; it would have had to come to terms with itself – with a sigh, with a grunt, or even with a guffaw; a still coarser one would have remained invulnerably ignorant and completely uninteresting.

'But he was too interesting or too unfortunate to be thrown to the dogs, or even to Chester. I felt this while I sat with my face over the paper and he fought and gasped, struggling for his breath in that terribly stealthy way, in my room; I felt it when he rushed out on the verandah as if to fling himself over – and didn't; I felt it more and more all the time he remained outside, faintly lighted on the background of night, as if standing on the shore of a sombre and hopeless sea.

'An abrupt heavy rumble made me lift my head. The noise seemed to roll away, and suddenly a searching and violent glare fell on the blind face of the night. The sustained and dazzling flickers seemed to last for an unconscionable time. The growl of the thunder increased steadily while I looked at him, distinct and black, planted solidly upon the shores of a sea of light. At the moment of greatest brilliance the darkness leaped back with a culminating crash, and he vanished before my dazzled eyes as utterly as though he had been blown to atoms. A blustering sigh passed; furious hands seemed to tear at the shrubs, shake the tops of the trees below, slam doors, break windowpanes, all along the front of the building. He stepped in, closing the door behind him, and found me bending over the table: my sudden anxiety as to what he would say was very great, and akin to a fright. "May I have a cigarette?" he asked. I gave a push to the box without raising my head. "I want – want – tobacco," he muttered. I became extremely buoyant. "Just a moment," I grunted, pleasantly. He took a few steps here and there. "That's over," I heard him say. A single distant clap of thunder came from the sea like a gun of distress. "The monsoon breaks up early this year," he remarked, conversationally, somewhere behind me. This encouraged me to turn round, which I did as soon as I had finished addressing the last envelope. He was smoking greedily in the middle of the room, and though he heard the stir I made, he remained with his back to me for a time.

"Come – I carried it off pretty well," he said, wheeling suddenly. "Something's paid off – not much. I wonder what's to come." His face did not show any emotion, only it appeared a little darkened and swollen, as though he had been holding his breath. He smiled reluctantly as it were, and went on while I gazed up at him mutely.... "Thank you, though – your room – jolly convenient – for a chap – badly hipped."... The rain pattered and swished in the garden; a water-pipe (it must have had a hole in it) performed just outside the window a parody of blubbering woe with funny sobs and gurgling lamentations, interrupted by jerky spasms of silence.... "A bit of shelter," he mumbled and ceased.

'A flash of faded lightning darted in through the black framework of the windows and ebbed out without any noise. I was thinking how I had best approach him (I did not want to be flung off again) when he gave a little laugh. "No better than a vagabond now"... the end of the cigarette smouldered between his fingers... "without a single – single," he pronounced slowly; "and yet..." He paused; the rain fell with redoubled violence. "Some day one's bound to come upon some sort of chance to get it all back again. Must!" he whispered, distinctly, glaring at my boots.

'I did not even know what it was he wished so much to regain, what it was he had so terribly missed. It might have been so much that it was impossible to say. A piece of ass's skin, according to Chester.... He looked up at me inquisitively. "Perhaps. If life's long enough," I muttered through my teeth with unreasonable animosity. "Don't reckon too much on it.

'"Jove! I feel as if nothing could ever touch me," he said in a tone of sombre conviction. "If this business couldn't knock me over, then there's no fear of there being not enough time to – climb out, and . . ." He looked upwards.

'It struck me that it is from such as he that the great army of waifs and strays is recruited, the army that marches down, down into all the gutters of the earth. As soon as he left my room, that "bit of shelter," he would take his place in the ranks, and begin the journey towards the bottomless pit. I at least had no illusions; but it was I, too, who a moment ago had been so sure of the power of words, and now was afraid to speak, in the same way one dares not move for fear of losing a slippery hold. It is when we try to grapple with another man's intimate need that we perceive how incomprehensible, wavering, and misty are the beings that share with us the sight of the stars and the warmth of the sun. It is as if loneliness were a hard and absolute condition of existence; the envelope of flesh and blood on which our eyes are fixed melts before the out-stretched hand, and there remains only the capricious, unconsolable, and elusive spirit that no eye can follow, no hand can grasp. It was the fear of losing him that kept me silent, for it was borne upon me suddenly and with un-accountable force that should I let him slip away into the darkness I would never forgive myself.

'"Well. Thanks – once more. You've been – er – uncommonly – really there's no word to . . . Uncommonly! I don't know why, I am sure. I am afraid I don't feel as grateful as I would if the whole thing hadn't been so brutally sprung on me. Because at bottom . . . you, yourself . . ." He stuttered.

'"Possibly," I struck in. He frowned.

'"All the same, one is responsible." He watched me like a hawk.

'"And that's true, too," I said.

'"Well. I've gone with it to the end, and I don't intend to let any man cast it in my teeth without – without – resenting it." He clenched his fist.

'"There's yourself," I said with a smile – mirthless enough, God knows – but he looked at me menacingly.

"That's my business," he said. An air of indomitable resolution came and went upon his face like a vain and passing
shadow. Next moment he looked a dear good boy in trouble, as before. He flung away the cigarette. "Good-bye," he
said, with the sudden haste of a man who had lingered too
long in view of a pressing bit of work waiting for him; and
then for a second or so he made not the slightest movement. The downpour fell with the heavy uninterrupted
rush of a sweeping flood, with a sound of unchecked overwhelming fury that called to one's mind the images of
collapsing bridges, of uprooted trees, of undermined
mountains. No man could breast the colossal and headlong
stream that seemed to break and swirl against the dim
stillness in which we were precariously sheltered as if on
an island. The perforated pipe gurgled, choked, spat, and
splashed in odious ridicule of a swimmer fighting for his
life. "It is raining," I remonstrated, "and I..." "Rain or
shine," he began, brusquely, checked himself, and walked
to the window. "Perfect deluge," he muttered after a while:
he leaned his forehead on the glass. "It's dark, too."

'"Yes, it is very dark," I said.

'He pivoted on his heels, crossed the room, and had
actually opened the door leading into the corridor before
I leaped up from my chair. "Wait," I cried, "I want you
to..." "I can't dine with you again to-night," he flung at
me, with one leg out of the room already. "I haven't the
slightest intention to ask you," I shouted. At this he drew
back his foot, but remained mistrustfully in the very doorway. I lost no time in entreating him earnestly not to be
absurd; to come in and shut the door.'

# CHAPTER SEVENTEEN

'HE came in at last; but I believe it was mostly the rain that did it; it was falling just then with a devastating violence which quieted down gradually while we talked. His manner was very sober and set; his bearing was that of a naturally taciturn man possessed by an idea. My talk was of the material aspect of his position; it had the sole aim of saving him from the degradation, ruin, and despair that out there close so swiftly upon a friendless, homeless man; I pleaded with him to accept my help; I argued reasonably: and every time I looked up at that absorbed smooth face, so grave and youthful, I had a disturbing sense of being no help but rather an obstacle to some mysterious, inexplicable, impalpable striving of his wounded spirit.

'"I suppose you intend to eat and drink and to sleep under shelter in the usual way," I remember saying with irritation. "You say you won't touch the money that is due to you."...He came as near as his sort can to making a gesture of horror. (There were three weeks and five days' pay owing him as mate of the *Patna*.) "Well, that's too little to matter anyhow; but what will you do to-morrow? Where will you turn? You must live..." "That isn't the thing," was the comment that escaped him under his breath. I ignored it, and went on combating what I assumed to be the scruples of an exaggerated delicacy. "On every conceivable ground," I concluded, "you must let me help you." "You can't," he said very simply and gently, and holding fast to some deep idea which I could detect shimmering like a pool of water in the dark, but which I despaired of ever approaching near enough to fathom. I surveyed his well-proportioned bulk. "At any rate," I said, "I am able to help what I can see of you. I don't pretend to do more." He shook his head sceptically without looking at me. I got very warm. "But I can," I insisted. "I can do even more. I *am* doing more. I am trusting you..." "The money..." he began. "Upon my word you deserve being told to go to the devil," I cried, forcing the note of indignation. He was startled, smiled, and I pressed my attack home. "It isn't a question of money at all. You are too superficial," I said (and at the same time I was thinking to myself: Well, here goes! And perhaps he is after all). "Look at the letter I want you to take. I am writing to a man of whom I've never asked a favour, and I am writing about you in terms that one only ventures to use when speaking of an intimate friend. I make myself unreservedly responsible for you. That's what I am doing. And really if you will only reflect a little what that means..."

'He lifted his head. The rain had passed away; only the water-pipe went on shedding tears with an absurd drip, drip outside the window. It was very quiet in the room, whose shadows huddled together in corners, away from the still flame of the candle flaring upright in the shape of a dagger; his face after a while seemed suffused by a reflection of a soft light as if the dawn had broken already.

'"Jove!" he gasped out. "It is noble of you!"

'Had he suddenly put out his tongue at me in derision, I could not have felt more humiliated. I thought to myself – Serve me right for a sneaking humbug.... His eyes shone straight into my face, but I perceived it was not a mocking brightness. All at once he sprang into jerky agitation, like one of those flat wooden figures that are worked by a string. His arms went up, then came down with a slap. He became another man altogether. "And I had never seen," he shouted; then suddenly bit his lip and frowned. "What a bally ass I've been," he said very slow in an awed tone.... "You are a brick," he cried next in a muffled voice. He snatched my hand as though he had just then seen it for the first time, and dropped it at once. "Why! this is what I –

you – I . . ." he stammered, and then with a return of his old stolid, I may say mulish, manner he began heavily, "I would be a brute now if I . . ." and then his voice seemed to break. "That's all right," I said. I was almost alarmed by this display of feeling, through which pierced a strange elation. I had pulled the string accidentally, as it were; I did not fully understand the working of the toy. "I must go now," he said. "Jove! You *have* helped me. Can't sit still. The very thing . . ." He looked at me with puzzled admiration. "The very thing . . ."

'Of course it was the thing. It was ten to one that I had saved him from starvation – of that peculiar sort that is almost invariably associated with drink. This was all. I had not a single illusion on that score, but looking at him, I allowed myself to wonder at the nature of the one he had, within the last three minutes, so evidently taken into his bosom. I had forced into his hand the means to carry on decently the serious business of life, to get food, drink, and shelter of the customary kind while his wounded spirit, like a bird with a broken wing, might hop and flutter into some hole to die quietly of inanition there. This is what I had thrust upon him: a definitely small thing; and – behold! – by the manner of its reception it loomed in the dim light of the candle like a big, indistinct, perhaps a dangerous shadow. "You don't mind me not saying anything appropriate," he burst out. "There isn't anything one could say. Last night already you had done me no end of good. Listening to me – you know. I give you my word I've thought more than once the top of my head would fly off . . ." He darted – positively darted – here and there, rammed his hands into his pockets, jerked them out again, flung his cap on his head. I had no idea it was in him to be so airily brisk. I thought of a dry leaf imprisoned in an eddy of wind, while a mysterious apprehension, a load of indefinite doubt, weighed me down in my chair. He stood stock-still, as if struck motionless by a discovery. "You have given me confidence," he declared, soberly. "Oh! for God's sake, my dear fellow – don't!"

I entreated, as though he had hurt me. "All right. I'll shut up now and henceforth. Can't prevent me thinking though.... Never mind!... I'll show yet..." He went to the door in a hurry, paused with his head down, and came back, stepping deliberately. "I always thought that if a fellow could begin with a clean slate... And now you... in a measure... yes... clean slate." I waved my hand, and he marched out without looking back; the sound of his footfalls died out gradually behind the closed door – the unhesitating tread of a man walking in broad daylight.

'But as to me, left alone with the solitary candle, I remained strangely unenlightened. I was no longer young enough to behold at every turn the magnificence that besets our insignificant footsteps in good and in evil. I smiled to think that, after all, it was yet he, of us two, who had the light. And I felt sad. A clean slate, did he say? As if the initial word of each our destiny were not graven in imperishable characters upon the face of a rock.'

# CHAPTER EIGHTEEN

'SIX months afterwards my friend (he was a cynical, more than middle-aged bachelor, with a reputation for eccentricity, and owned a rice-mill) wrote to me, and judging, from the warmth of my recommendation, that I would like to hear, enlarged a little upon Jim's perfections. These were apparently of a quiet and effective sort. "Not having been able so far to find more in my heart than a resigned toleration for any individual of my kind, I have lived till now alone in a house that even in this steaming climate could be considered as too big for one man. I have had him to live with me for some time past. It seems I haven't made a mistake." It seemed to me on reading this letter that my friend had found in his heart more than tolerance for Jim, – that there were the beginnings of active liking. Of course he stated his grounds in a characteristic way. For one thing, Jim kept his freshness in the climate. Had he been a girl – my friend wrote – one could have said he was blooming – blooming modestly – like a violet, not like some of these blatant tropical flowers. He had been in the house for six weeks, and had not as yet attempted to slap him on the back, or address him as "old boy," or try to make him feel a superannuated fossil. He had nothing of the exasperating young man's chatter. He was good-tempered, had not much to say for himself, was not clever by any means, thank goodness – wrote my friend. It appeared, however, that Jim was clever enough to be quietly appreciative of his wit, while, on the other hand, he amused him by his naïveness. "The dew is yet on him, and since I had the bright idea of giving him a room in the house and having him at meals I feel less withered myself. The other day he

168

took it into his head to cross the room with no other
purpose but to open a door for me; and I felt more in
touch with mankind than I had been for years.
Ridiculous, isn't it? Of course I guess there is something –
some awful little scrape – which you know all about – but if
I am sure that it is terribly heinous, I fancy one could
manage to forgive it. For my part, I declare I am unable
to imagine him guilty of anything much worse than rob-
bing an orchard. Is *it* much worse? Perhaps you ought to
have told me; but it is such a long time since we both turned
saints that you may have forgotten we, too, had sinned in
our time? It may be that some day I shall have to ask you,
and then I shall expect to be told. I don't care to question
him myself till I have some idea what it is. Moreover, it's
too soon as yet. Let him open the door a few times more for
me...." Thus my friend. I was trebly pleased – at Jim's
shaping so well, at the tone of the letter, at my own cleverness. Evidently I had known what I was doing. I had read
characters aright, and so on. And what if something unexpected and wonderful were to come of it? That evening,
reposing in a deck-chair under the shade of my own poop
awning (it was in Hong-Kong harbour), I laid on Jim's
behalf the first stone of a castle in Spain.

'I made a trip to the northward, and when I returned I
found another letter from my friend waiting for me. It was
the first envelope I tore open. "There are no spoons missing, as far as I know," ran the first line; "I haven't been
interested enough to inquire. He is gone, leaving on the
breakfast-table a formal little note of apology, which is
either silly or heartless. Probably both – and it's all one to
me. Allow me to say, lest you should have some more
mysterious young men in reserve, that I have shut up
shop, definitely and for ever. This is the last eccentricity I
shall be guilty of. Do not imagine for a moment that I care a
hang; but he is very much regretted at tennis-parties, and
for my own sake I've told a plausible lie at the club...." I
flung the letter aside and started looking through the batch

on my table, till I came upon Jim's handwriting. Would you believe it? One chance in a hundred! But it is always that hundredth chance! That little second engineer of the *Patna* had turned up in a more or less destitute state, and got a temporary job of looking after the machinery of the mill. "I couldn't stand the familiarity of the little beast," Jim wrote from a seaport seven hundred miles south of the place where he should have been in clover. "I am now for the time with Egström & Blake, ship-chandlers, as their – well – runner, to call the thing by its right name. For reference I gave them your name, which they know of course, and if you could write a word in my favour it would be a permanent employment." I was utterly crushed under the ruins of my castle, but of course I wrote as desired. Before the end of the year my new charter took me that way, and I had an opportunity of seeing him.

'He was still with Egström & Blake, and we met in what they called "our parlour" opening out of the store. He had that moment come in from boarding a ship, and confronted me head down, ready for a tussle. "What have you got to say for yourself?" I began as soon as we had shaken hands. "What I wrote you – nothing more," he said stubbornly. "Did the fellow blab – or what?" I asked. He looked up at me with a troubled smile. "Oh, no! He didn't. He made it a kind of confidential business between us. He was most damnably mysterious whenever I came over to the mill; he would wink at me in a respectful manner – as much as to say, 'We know what we know.' Infernally fawning and familiar – and that sort of thing." He threw himself into a chair and stared down his legs. "One day we happened to be alone and the fellow had the cheek to say, 'Well, Mr James' – I was called Mr James there as if I had been the son – 'here we are together once more. This is better than the old ship – ain't it?' . . . Wasn't it appalling, eh? I looked at him, and he put on a knowing air. 'Don't you be uneasy, sir,' he says. 'I know a gentleman when I see one, and I know how a gentleman feels. I hope, though, you will be keeping me on

this job. I had a hard time of it, too, along of that rotten
old *Patna* racket.' Jove! It was awful. I don't know what
I should have said or done if I had not just then heard Mr
Denver calling me in the passage. It was tiffin-time, and we
walked together across the yard and through the garden to
the bungalow. He began to chaff me in his kindly way... I
believe he liked me..."

'Jim was silent for a while.

'"I know he liked me. That's what made it so hard. Such
a splendid man! That morning he slipped his hand under
my arm.... He, too, was familiar with me." He burst into a
short laugh, and dropped his chin on his breast. "Pah!
When I remembered how that mean little beast had been
talking to me," he began suddenly in a vibrating voice, "I
couldn't bear to think of myself... I suppose you know..."
I nodded.... "More like a father," he cried; his voice sank.
"I would have had to tell him. I couldn't let it go on – could
I?" "Well?" I murmured, after waiting a while. "I preferred
to go," he said, slowly; "this thing must be buried."

'We could hear in the shop Blake upbraiding Egström in
an abusive, strained voice. They had been associated for
many years, and every day from the moment the doors were
opened to the last minute before closing, Blake, a little man
with sleek, jetty hair and unhappy, beady eyes, could be
heard rowing his partner incessantly with a sort of scathing
and plaintive fury. The sound of that everlasting scolding
was part of the place like the other fixtures; even strangers
would very soon come to disregard it completely unless it
be perhaps to mutter "Nuisance," or to get up suddenly and
shut the door of the "parlour." Egström himself, a raw-
boned, heavy Scandinavian, with a busy manner and
immense blonde whiskers, went on directing his people,
checking parcels, making out bills or writing letters at a
stand-up desk in the shop, and comported himself in that
clatter exactly as though he had been stone-deaf. Now and
again he would emit a bothered perfunctory "Sssh," which
neither produced nor was expected to produce the slightest

effect. "They are very decent to me here," said Jim. "Blake's a little cad, but Egström's all right." He stood up quickly, and walking with measured steps to a tripod telescope standing in the window and pointed at the roadstead, he applied his eye to it. "There's that ship which had been becalmed outside all the morning has got a breeze now and is coming in," he remarked, patiently; "I must go and board." We shook hands in silence, and he turned to go. "Jim!" I cried. He looked round with his hand on the lock. "You – you have thrown away something like a fortune." He came back to me all the way from the door. "Such a splendid old chap," he said. "How could I? How could I?" His lips twitched. "*Here* it does not matter." "Oh! you – you —" I began, and had to cast about for a suitable word, but before I became aware that there was no name that would just do, he was gone. I heard outside Egström's deep gentle voice saying cheerily, "That's the *Sarah W. Granger*, Jimmy. You must manage to be first abroad"; and directly Blake struck in, screaming after the manner of an outraged cockatoo, "Tell the captain we've got some of his mail here. That'll fetch him. D'ye hear, Mister What's-your-name?" And there was Jim answering Egström with something boyish in his tone. "All right. I'll make a race of it." He seemed to take refuge in the boat-sailing part of that sorry business.

'I did not see him again that trip, but on my next (I had a six months' charter) I went up to the store. Ten yards away from the door Blake's scolding met my ears, and when I came in he gave me a glance of utter wretchedness; Egström, all smiles, advanced, extending a large bony hand. "Glad to see you, captain.... Sssh.... Been thinking you were about due back here. What did you say, sir? ... Sssh.... Oh! him! He has left us. Come into the parlour." ... After the slam of the door Blake's strained voice became faint, as the voice of one scolding desperately in a wilderness.... "Put us to a great inconvenience, too. Used us badly – I must say..." "Where's he gone to? Do

you know?" I asked. "No. It's no use asking either," said
Egström, standing bewhiskered and obliging before me
with his arms hanging down his sides clumsily and a thin
silver watch-chain looped very low on a rucked-up blue
serge waistcoat. "A man like that don't go anywhere in
particular." I was too concerned at the news to ask for the
explanation of that pronouncement, and he went on. "He
left – let's see – the very day a steamer with returning
pilgrims from the Red Sea put in here with two blades of
her propeller gone. Three weeks ago now." "Wasn't there
something said about the *Patna* case?" I asked, fearing the
worst. He gave a start, and looked at me as if I had been a
sorcerer. "Why, yes! How do you know? Some of them
were talking about it here. There was a captain or two, the
manager of Vanlo's engineering shop at the harbour, two or
three others, and myself. Jim was in here, too, having a
sandwich and a glass of beer; when we are busy – you see,
captain – there's no time for a proper tiffin. He was standing by this table eating sandwiches, and the rest of us were
round the telescope watching that steamer come in; and by
and by Vanlo's manager began to talk about the chief of the
*Patna*; he had done some repairs for him once, and from
that he went on to tell us what an old ruin she was, and the
money that had been made out of her. He came to mention
her last voyage, and then we all struck in. Some said one
thing and some another – not much – what you or any
other man might say; and there was some laughing.
Captain O'Brien of the *Sarah W. Granger*, a large, noisy
old man with a stick – he was sitting listening to us in this
arm-chair here – he let drive suddenly with his stick at the
floor, and roars out, 'Skunks!'...Made us all jump. Vanlo's
manager winks at us and asks, 'What's the matter, Captain
O'Brien?' 'Matter! matter!' the old man began to shout;
'what are you Injuns laughing at? It's no laughing matter.
It's a disgrace to human natur' – that's what it is. I would
despise being seen in the same room with one of those men.
Yes, sir!' He seemed to catch my eye like, and I had to speak

out of civility. 'Skunks!' says I, 'of course, Captain O'Brien, and I wouldn't care to have them here myself, so you're quite safe in this room, Captain O'Brien. Have a little something cool to drink.' 'Dam' your drink, Egström,' says he, with a twinkle in his eye; 'when I want a drink I will shout for it. I am going to quit. It stinks here now.' At this all the others burst out laughing, and out they go after the old man. And then, sir, that blasted Jim he puts down the sandwich he had in his hand and walks round the table to me; there was his glass of beer poured out quite full. 'I am off,' he says – just like this. 'It isn't half-past one yet,' says I; 'you might snatch a smoke first.' I thought he meant it was time for him to go down to his work. When I understood what he was up to, my arms fell – so! Can't get a man like that every day, you know, sir; a regular devil for sailing a boat; ready to go out miles to sea to meet ships in any sort of weather. More than once a captain would come in here full of it, and the first thing he would say would be, 'That's a reckless sort of a lunatic you've got for water-clerk, Egström. I was feeling my way in at daylight under short canvas when there comes flying out of the mist right under my forefoot a boat half under water, sprays going over the masthead, two frightened niggers on the bottom boards, a yelling fiend at the tiller. Hey! hey! Ship ahoy! ahoy! Captain! Hey! hey! Egström & Blake's man first to speak to you! Hey! hey! Egström & Blake! Hallo! hey! whoop! Kick the niggers – out reefs – a squall on at the time – shoots ahead whooping and yelling to me to make sail and he would give me a lead in – more like a demon than a man. Never saw a boat handled like that in all my life. Couldn't have been drunk – was he? Such a quiet, soft-spoken chap, too – blush like a girl when he came on board. . . .' I tell you, Captain Marlow, nobody had a chance against us with a strange ship when Jim was out. The other ship-chandlers just kept their old customers, and . . ."

'Egström appeared overcome with emotion.

' "Why, sir – it seemed as though he wouldn't mind going a hundred miles out to sea in an old shoe to nab a ship for the firm. If the business had been his own and all to make yet, he couldn't have done more in that way. And now . . . all at once . . . like this! Thinks I to myself: 'Oho! a rise in the screw – that's the trouble – is it? All right,' says I, 'no need of all that fuss with me, Jimmy. Just mention your figure. Anything in reason.' He looks at me as if he wanted to swallow something that stuck in his throat. 'I can't stop with you.' 'What's that blooming joke?' I asks. He shakes his head, and I could see in his eye he was as good as gone already, sir. So I turned to him and slanged him till all was blue. 'What is it you're running away from?' I asks. 'Who has been getting at you? What scared you? You haven't as much sense as a rat; they don't clear out from a good ship. Where do you expect to get a better berth? – you this and you that.' I made him look sick, I can tell you. 'This business ain't going to sink,' says I. He gave a big jump. 'Good-bye,' he says, nodding at me like a lord; 'you ain't half a bad chap, Egström. I give you my word that if you knew my reasons you wouldn't care to keep me.' 'That's the biggest lie you ever told in your life,' says I; 'I know my own mind.' He made me so mad that I had to laugh. 'Can't you really stop long enough to drink this glass of beer here, you funny beggar, you?' I don't know what came over him; he didn't seem able to find the door; something comical, I can tell you, captain. I drank the beer myself. 'Well, if you're in such a hurry, here's luck to you in your own drink,' says I; 'only, you mark my words, if you keep up this game you'll very soon find that the earth ain't big enough to hold you – that's all.' He gave me one black look, and out he rushed with a face fit to scare little children." '

'Egström snorted bitterly, and combed one auburn whisker with knotty fingers. 'Haven't been able to get a man that was any good since. It's nothing but worry, worry, worry in business. And where might you have come across him, captain, if it's fair to ask?'

'"He was the mate of the *Patna* that voyage," I said, feeling that I owed some explanation. For a time Egström remained very still, with his fingers plunged in the hair at the side of his face, and then exploded. "And who the devil cares about that?" "I daresay no one," I began . . . "And what the devil is he – anyhow – for to go on like this?" He stuffed suddenly his left whisker into his mouth and stood amazed. "Jee!" he exclaimed, "I told him the earth wouldn't be big enough to hold his caper." '

# CHAPTER NINETEEN

'I HAVE told you these two episodes at length to show his manner of dealing with himself under the new conditions of his life. There were many others of the sort, more than I could count on the fingers of my two hands.

'They were all equally tinged by a high-minded absurdity of intention which made their futility profound and touching. To fling away your daily bread so as to get your hands free for a grapple with a ghost may be an act of prosaic heroism. Men had done it before (though we who have lived know full well that it is not the haunted soul but the hungry body that makes an outcast), and men who had eaten and meant to eat every day had applauded the creditable folly. He was indeed unfortunate, for all his recklessness could not carry him out from under the shadow. There was always a doubt of his courage. The truth seems to be that it is impossible to lay the ghost of a fact. You can face it or shirk it – and I have come across a man or two who could wink at their familiar shades. Obviously Jim was not of the winking sort; but what I could never make up my mind about was whether his line of conduct amounted to shirking his ghost or to facing him out.

'I strained my mental eyesight only to discover that, as with the complexion of all our actions, the shade of difference was so delicate that it was impossible to say. It might have been flight and it might have been a mode of combat. To the common mind he became known as a rolling stone, because this was the funniest part; he did after a time become perfectly known, and even notorious, within the circle of his wanderings (which had a diameter of, say, three thousand miles), in the same way as an eccentric character

177

is known to a whole countryside. For instance, in Bankok, where he found employment with Yucker Brothers, charterers and teak merchants, it was almost pathetic to see him go about in sunshine hugging his secret, which was known to the very up-country logs on the river. Schomberg, the keeper of the hotel where he boarded, a hirsute Alsatian of manly bearing and an irrepressible retailer of all the scandalous gossip of the place, would, with both elbows on the table, impart an adorned version of the story to any guest who cared to imbibe knowledge along with the more costly liquors. "And, mind you, the nicest fellow you could meet," would be his generous conclusion; "quite superior." It says a lot for the casual crowd that frequented Schomberg's establishment that Jim managed to hang out in Bankok for a whole six months. I remarked that people, perfect strangers, took to him as one takes to a nice child. His manner was reserved, but it was as though his personal appearance, his hair, his eyes, his smile, made friends for him wherever he went. And, of course, he was no fool. I heard Siegmund Yucker (native of Switzerland), a gentle creature ravaged by a cruel dyspepsia, and so frightfully lame that his head swung through a quarter of a circle at every step he took, declare appreciatively that for one so young he was "of great gabasidy," as though it had been a mere question of cubic contents. "Why not send him up country?" I suggested anxiously. (Yucker Brothers had concessions and teak forests in the interior.) "If he has capacity, as you say, he will soon get hold of the work. And physically he is very fit. His health is always excellent." "Ach! It's a great ting in dis goundry to be vree vrom tispep-shia," sighed poor Yucker enviously, casting a stealthy glance at the pit of his ruined stomach. I left him drumming pensively on his desk and muttering, "Es ist ein idee. Es ist ein idee." Unfortunately, that very evening an unpleasant affair took place in the hotel.

'I don't know that I blame Jim very much, but it was a truly regrettable incident. It belonged to the lamentable

species of bar-room scuffles, and the other party to it was a
cross-eyed Dane of sorts whose visiting card recited under
his misbegotten name: first lieutenant in the Royal Siamese
Navy. The fellow, of course, was utterly hopeless at bil-
liards, but did not like to be beaten, I suppose. He had had
enough to drink to turn nasty after the sixth game, and
make some scornful remark at Jim's expense. Most of the
people there didn't hear what was said, and those who had
heard seemed to have had all precise recollection scared out
of them by the appalling nature of the consequences that
immediately ensued. It was very lucky for the Dane that he
could swim, because the room opened on a verandah and
the Menam flowed below very wide and black. A boat-load
of Chinamen, bound, as likely as not, on some thieving
expedition, fished out the officer of the King of Siam, and
Jim turned up at about midnight on board my ship without
a hat. "Everybody in the room seemed to know," he said,
gasping yet from the contest, as it were. He was rather
sorry, on general principles, for what had happened,
though in this case there had been, he said, "no option."
But what dismayed him was to find the nature of his
burden as well known to everybody as though he had
gone about all that time carrying it on his shoulders.
Naturally after this he couldn't remain in the place. He
was universally condemned for the brutal violence, so
unbecoming a man in his delicate position; some maintained he had been disgracefully drunk at the time; others
criticised his want of tact. Even Schomberg was very much
annoyed. "He is a very nice young man," he said, argumen-
tatively, to me, "but the lieutenant is a first-rate fellow, too.
He dines every night at my *table d'hôte*, you know. And
there's a billiard-cue broken. I can't allow that. First thing
this morning I went over with my apologies to the lieutenant, and I think I've made it all right for myself; but only
think, captain, if everybody started such games! Why, the
man might have been drowned! And here I can't run out
into the next street and buy a new cue. I've got to write to

Europe for them. No, no! A temper like that won't do!"... He was extremely sore on the subject.

'This was the worst incident of all in his – his retreat. Nobody could deplore it more than myself; for if, as somebody said hearing him mentioned, "Oh, yes! I know. He has knocked about a good deal out here," yet he had somehow avoided being battered and chipped in the process. This last affair, however, made me seriously uneasy, because if his exquisite sensibilities were to go the length of involving him in pot-house shindies, he would lose his name of an inoffensive, if aggravating, fool, and acquire that of a common loafer. For all my confidence in him I could not help reflecting that in such cases from the name to the thing itself is but a step. I suppose you will understand that by that time I could not think of washing my hands of him. I took him away from Bankok in my ship, and we had a longish passage. It was pitiful to see how he shrank within himself. A seaman, even if a mere passenger, takes an interest in a ship, and looks at the sea-life around him with the critical enjoyment of a painter, for instance, looking at another man's work. In every sense of the expression he is "on deck"; but my Jim, for the most part, skulked down below as though he had been a stowaway. He infected me so that I avoided speaking on professional matters, such as would suggest themselves naturally to two sailors during a passage. For whole days we did not exchange a word; I felt extremely unwilling to give orders to my officers in his presence. Often, when alone with him on deck or in the cabin, we didn't know what to do with our eyes.

'I placed him with De Jongh, as you know, glad enough to dispose of him in any way, yet persuaded that his position was now growing intolerable. He had lost some of that elasticity which had enabled him to rebound back into his uncompromising position after every overthrow. One day, coming ashore, I saw him standing on the quay; the water of the roadstead and the sea in the offing made one smooth ascending plane, and the outermost ships at anchor seemed to ride motionless in the sky. He was waiting for his boat, which was being loaded at our feet with packages of small stores for some vessel ready to leave. After exchanging greetings, we remained silent – side by side. "Jove!" he said, suddenly, "this is killing work."

'He smiled at me; I must say he generally could manage a smile. I made no reply. I knew very well he was not alluding to his duties; he had an easy time of it with De Jongh. Nevertheless, as soon as he had spoken I became completely convinced that the work was killing. I did not even look at him. "Would you like," said I, "to leave this part of the world altogether; try California or the West Coast? I'll see what I can do..." He interrupted me a little scornfully. "What difference would it make?"...I felt at once convinced that he was right. It would make no difference; it was not relief he wanted; I seemed to perceive dimly that what he wanted, what he was, as it were, waiting for, was something not easy to define – something in the nature of an opportunity. I had given him many opportunities, but they had been merely opportunities to earn his bread. Yet what more could any man do? The position struck me as hopeless, and poor Brierly's saying recurred to me, "Let him creep twenty feet underground and stay there." Better that, I thought, than this waiting above ground for the impossible. Yet one could not be sure even of that. There and then, before his boat was three oars' lengths away from the quay, I had made up my mind to go and consult Stein in the evening.

'This Stein was a wealthy and respected merchant. His "house" (because it was a house, Stein & Co., and there was some sort of partner who, as Stein said, "looked after the Moluccas") had a large inter-island business, with a lot of trading posts established in the most out-of-the-way places for collecting the produce. His wealth and his respectability were not exactly the reasons why I was anxious to seek his advice. I desired to confide my difficulty to him because he was one of the most trustworthy men I had ever known. The gentle light of a simple unwearied, as it were, and intelligent good-nature illumined his long hairless face. It had deep downward folds, and was pale as of a man who had always led a sedentary life – which was indeed very far from being the case. His hair was thin, and brushed back from a massive and lofty forehead. One fancied that at twenty he must have looked very much like what he was now at threescore. It was a student's face; only the eyebrows nearly all white, thick and bushy, together with the resolute searching glance that came from under them, were not in accord with his, I may say, learned appearance. He was tall and loose-jointed; his slight stoop, together with an inno-cent smile, made him appear benevolently ready to lend you his ear; his long arms with pale big hands had rare deliberate gestures of a pointing out, demonstrating kind. I speak of him at length, because under this exterior, and in conjunction with an upright and indulgent nature, this man possessed an intrepidity of spirit and a physical cour-age that could have been called reckless had it not been like a natural function of the body – say good digestion, for instance – completely unconscious of itself. It is sometimes said of a man that he carries his life in his hand. Such a saying would have been inadequate if applied to him; during the early part of his existence in the East he had been playing ball with it. All this was in the past, but I knew the story of his life and the origin of his fortune. He was also a naturalist of some distinction, or perhaps I should say a learned collector. Entomology was his special study. His collection of *Buprestidae* and *Longicorns* – beetles all – horrible miniature monsters, looking malevolent in death and immobility, and his cabinet of butterflies, beautiful and hovering under the glass of cases on lifeless wings, had spread his fame far over the earth. The name of this merchant, adventurer, sometime adviser of a Malay sultan (to whom he never alluded otherwise than as "my poor Mohammed Bonso"), had, on account of a few bushels of dead insects, become known to learned persons in Europe, who could have had no conception, and certainly would not have cared to know anything, of his life or character. I, who knew, considered him an eminently suitable person to receive my confidences about Jim's difficulties as well as my own.'

# CHAPTER TWENTY

'Late in the evening I entered his study, after traversing an imposing but empty dining-room very dimly lit. The house was silent. I was preceded by an elderly grim Javanese servant in a sort of livery of white jacket and yellow sarong, who, after throwing the door open, exclaimed low, "O master!" and stepping aside, vanished in a mysterious way as though he had been a ghost only momentarily embodied for that particular service. Stein turned round with the chair, and in the same movement his spectacles seemed to get pushed up on his forehead. He welcomed me in his quiet and humorous voice. Only one corner of the vast room, the corner in which stood his writing-desk, was strongly lighted by a shaded reading-lamp, and the rest of the spacious apartment melted into shapeless gloom like a cavern. Narrow shelves filled with dark boxes of uniform shape and colour ran round the walls, not from floor to ceiling, but in a sombre belt about four feet broad. Catacombs of beetles. Wooden tablets were hung above at irregular intervals. The light reached one of them, and the word *Coleoptera* written in gold letters glittered mysteriously upon a vast dimness. The glass cases containing the collection of butterflies were ranged in three long rows upon slender-legged little tables. One of these cases had been removed from its place and stood on the desk, which was bestrewn with oblong slips of paper blackened with minute handwriting.

'"So you see me – so," he said. His hand hovered over the case where a butterfly in solitary grandeur spread out dark bronze wings, seven inches or more across, with exquisite white veinings and a gorgeous border of yellow spots.

184

"Only one specimen like this they have in *your* London, and then – no more. To my small native town this my collection I shall bequeath. Something of me. The best."

'He bent forward in the chair and gazed intently, his chin over the front of the case. I stood at his back. "Marvellous," he whispered, and seemed to forget my presence. His history was curious. He had been born in Bavaria, and when a youth of twenty-two had taken an active part in the revolutionary movement of 1848. Heavily compromised, he managed to make his escape, and at first found a refuge with a poor republican watch-maker in Trieste. From there he made his way to Tripoli with a stock of cheap watches to hawk about, – not a very great opening truly, but it turned out lucky enough, because it was there he came upon a Dutch traveller – a rather famous man, I believe, but I don't remember his name. It was that naturalist who, engaging him as a sort of assistant, took him to the East. They travelled in the Archipelago together and separately, collecting insects and birds, for four years or more. Then the naturalist went home, and Stein, having no home to go to, remained with an old trader he had come across in his journeys in the interior of Celebes – if Celebes may be said to have an interior. This old Scotsman, the only white man allowed to reside in the country at the time, was a privileged friend of the chief ruler of Wajo States, who was a woman. I often heard Stein relate how that chap, who was slightly paralysed on one side, had introduced him to the native court a short time before another stroke carried him off. He was a heavy man with a patriarchal white beard, and of imposing stature. He came into the council-hall where all the rajahs, pangerans, and headmen were assembled, with the queen, a fat wrinkled woman (very free in her speech, Stein said), reclining on a high couch under a canopy. He dragged his leg, thumping with his stick, and grasped Stein's arm, leading him right up to the couch. "Look, queen, and you rajahs, this is my son," he proclaimed in a stentorian voice. "I have traded with your fathers, and when I die he shall trade with you and your sons."

'By means of this simple formality Stein inherited the Scotsman's privileged position and all his stock-in-trade, together with a fortified house on the banks of the only navigable river in the country. Shortly afterwards the old queen, who was so free in her speech, died, and the country became disturbed by various pretenders to the throne. Stein joined the party of a younger son, the one of whom thirty years later he never spoke otherwise but as "my poor Mohammed Bonso." They both became the heroes of innumerable exploits; they had wonderful adventures, and once stood a siege in the Scotsman's house for a month, with only a score of followers against a whole army. I believe the natives talk of that war to this day. Meantime, it seems, Stein never failed to annex on his own account every butterfly or beetle he could lay hands on. After some eight years of war, negotiations, false truces, sudden outbreaks, reconciliation, treachery, and so on, and just as peace seemed at last permanently established, his "poor Mohammed Bonso" was assassinated at the gate of his own royal residence while dismounting in the highest spirits on his return from a successful deer-hunt. This event rendered Stein's position extremely insecure, but he would have stayed perhaps had it not been that a short time afterwards he lost Mohammed's sister ("my dear wife the princess," he used to say solemnly), by whom he had had a daughter – mother and child both dying within three days of each other from some infectious fever. He left the country, which this cruel loss had made unbearable to him. Thus ended the first and adventurous part of his existence. What followed was so different that, but for the reality of sorrow which remained with him, this strange part must have resembled a dream. He had a little money; he started life afresh, and in the course of years acquired a considerable fortune. At first he had travelled a good deal amongst the islands, but age had stolen upon him, and of late he seldom left his spacious house three miles out of town, with an extensive garden, and surrounded by stables, offices, and bamboo cottages for his servants and dependants, of whom he had many. He drove in his buggy every morning to town, where he had an office with white and Chinese clerks. He owned a small fleet of schooners and native craft, and dealt in island produce on a large scale. For the rest he lived solitary, but not misanthropic, with his books and his collection, classing and arranging specimens, corresponding with entomologists in Europe, writing up a descriptive catalogue of his treasures. Such was the history of the man whom I had come to consult upon Jim's case without any definite hope. Simply to hear what he would have to say would have been a relief. I was very anxious, but I respected the intense, almost passionate, absorption with which he looked at a butterfly, as though on the bronze sheen of these frail wings, in the white tracings, in the gorgeous markings, he could see other things, an image of something as perishable and defying destruction as these delicate and lifeless tissues displaying a splendour unmarred by death.

'"Marvellous!" he repeated, looking up at me, "Look! The beauty – but that is nothing – look at the accuracy, the harmony. And so fragile! And so strong! And so exact! This is Nature – the balance of colossal forces. Every star is so – and every blade of grass stands *so* – and the mighty Kosmos in perfect equilibrium produces – this. This wonder; this masterpiece of Nature – the great artist."

'"Never heard an entomologist go on like this," I observed, cheerfully. "Masterpiece! And what of man?"

'"Man is amazing, but he is not a masterpiece," he said, keeping his eyes fixed on the glass case. "Perhaps the artist was a little mad. Eh? What do you think? Sometimes it seems to me that man is come where he is not wanted, where there is no place for him; for if not, why should he want all the place? Why should he run about here and there making a great noise about himself, talking about the stars, disturbing the blades of grass? . . ."

'"Catching butterflies," I chimed in.

'He smiled, threw himself back in his chair, and stretched his legs. "Sit down," he said. "I captured this rare specimen myself one very fine morning. And I had a very big emotion. You don't know what it is for a collector to capture such a rare specimen. You can't know."

'I smiled at my ease in a rocking-chair. His eyes seemed to look far beyond the wall at which they stared; and he narrated how, one night, a messenger arrived from his "poor Mohammed," requiring his presence at the "residenz" – as he called it – which was distant some nine or ten miles by a bridle-path over a cultivated plain, with patches of forest here and there. Early in the morning he started from his fortified house, after embracing his little Emma, and leaving the "princess," his wife, in command. He described how she came with him as far as the gate, walking with one hand on the neck of his horse; she had on a white jacket, gold pins in her hair, and a brown leather belt over her left shoulder with a revolver in it. "She talked as women will talk," he said, "telling me to be careful, and to try to get back before dark, and what a great wickedness it was for me to go alone. We were at war, and the country was not safe; my men were putting up bullet-proof shutters to the house and loading their rifles, and she begged me to have no fear for her. She could defend the house against anybody till I returned. And I laughed with pleasure a little. I liked to see her so brave and young and strong. I, too, was young then. At the gate she caught hold of my hand and gave it one squeeze and fell back. I made my horse stand still outside till I heard the bars of the gate put up behind me. There was a great enemy of mine, a great noble – and a great rascal, too – roaming with a band in the neighbour-hood. I cantered for four or five miles; there had been rain in the night, but the mists had gone up, up – and the face of the earth was clean; it lay smiling to me, so fresh and innocent – like a little child. Suddenly somebody fires a volley – twenty shots at least it seemed to me. I hear bullets sing in my ear, and my hat jumps to the back of my head. It was a little intrigue, you understand. They got my poor Mohammed to send for me and then laid that ambush. I see it all in a minute, and I think — This wants a little management. My pony snort, jump, and stand, and I fall slowly forward with my head on his mane. He begins to walk, and with one eye I could see over his neck a faint cloud of smoke hanging in front of a clump of bamboos to my left. I think — Aha! my friends, why you not wait long enough before you shoot? This is not yet *gelungen*. Oh, no! I get hold of my revolver with my right hand – quiet – quiet. After all, there were only seven of these rascals. They get up from the grass and start running with their sarongs tucked up, waving spears above their heads, and yelling to each other to look out and catch the horse, because I was dead. I let them come as close as the door here, and then bang, bang, bang – take aim each time, too. One more shot I fire at a man's back, but I miss. Too far already. And then I sit alone on my horse with the clean earth smiling at me, and there are the bodies of three men lying on the ground. One was curled up like a dog, another on his back had an arm over his eyes as if to keep off the sun, and the third man he draws up his leg very slowly and makes it with one kick straight again. I watch him very carefully from my horse, but there is no more – *bleibt ganz ruhig* – keep still, so. And as I looked at his face for some sign of life I observed something like a faint shadow pass over his forehead. It was the shadow of this butterfly. Look at the form of the wing. This species fly high with a strong flight. I raised my eyes and I saw him fluttering away. I think — Can it be possible? And then I lost him. I dismounted and went on very slow, leading my horse and holding my revolver with one hand and my eyes darting up and down and right and left, everywhere! At last I saw him sitting on a small heap of dirt ten feet away. At once my heart began to beat quick. I let go my horse, keep my revolver in one hand, and with the other snatch my soft felt hat off my head. One step. Steady. Another step. Flop! I got him! When I got up I shook like a leaf with excitement, and when I opened these beautiful wings and made sure what a rare and so extraordinary perfect specimen I had, my head went round and my legs became so weak with emotion that I had to sit on the ground. I had greatly desired to possess myself of a speci-men of that species when collecting for the professor. I took long journeys and underwent great privations; I had dreamed of him in my sleep, and here suddenly I had him in my fingers – for myself! In the words of the poet" (he pronounced it "boet") –

> "'So halt' ich's endlich denn in meinen Händen,
> Und nenn' es in gewissem Sinne mein.'"

He gave to the last word the emphasis of a suddenly lowered voice, and withdrew his eyes slowly from my face. He began to charge a long-stemmed pipe busily and in silence, then, pausing with his thumb on the orifice of the bowl, looked again at me significantly.

'"Yes, my good friend. On that day I had nothing to desire; I had greatly annoyed my principal enemy; I was young, strong; I had friendship; I had the love" (he said "lof") "of woman, a child I had, to make my heart very full – and even what I had once dreamed in my sleep had come into my hand, too!"

'He struck a match, which flared violently. His thought-ful placid face twitched once.

'"Friend, wife, child," he said, slowly, gazing at the small flame – "phoo!" The match was blown out. He sighed and turned again to the glass case. The frail and beautiful wings quivered faintly, as if his breath had for an instant called back to life that gorgeous object of his dreams.

'"The work," he began, suddenly, pointing to the scat-tered slips, and in his usual gentle and cheery tone, "is making great progress. I have been this rare specimen describing. . . . Na! And what is your good news?"

'"To tell you the truth, Stein," I said with an effort that surprised me, "I came here to describe a specimen. . . ."

'"Butterfly?" he asked, with an unbelieving and humorous eagerness.

'"Nothing so perfect," I answered, feeling suddenly dispirited with all sorts of doubts. "A man!"

'"Ach so!" he murmured, and his smiling countenance, turned to me, became grave. Then after looking at me for a while he said slowly, "Well – I am a man, too."

'Here you have him as he was; he knew how to be so generously encouraging as to make a scrupulous man hesitate on the brink of confidence; but if I did hesitate it was not for long.

'He heard me out, sitting with crossed legs. Sometimes his head would disappear completely in a great eruption of smoke, and a sympathetic growl would come out from the cloud. When I finished he uncrossed his legs, laid down his pipe, leaned forward towards me earnestly with his elbows on the arms of his chair, the tips of his fingers together.

'"I understand very well. He is romantic."

'He had diagnosed the case for me, and at first I was quite startled to find how simple it was; and indeed our conference resembled so much a medical consultation – Stein, of learned aspect, sitting in an arm-chair before his desk; I, anxious, in another, facing him, but a little to one side – that it seemed natural to ask –

'"What's good for it?"

'He lifted up a long forefinger.

'"There is only one remedy! One thing alone can us from being ourselves cure!" The finger came down on the desk with a smart rap. The case which he had made to look so simple before became if possible still simpler – and altogether hopeless. There was a pause. "Yes," said I, "strictly speaking, the question is not how to get cured, but how to live."

'He approved with his head, a little sadly as it seemed. "*Ja! ja!* In general, adapting the words of your great poet: That is the question...." He went on nodding sympathetically.... "How to be! *Ach!* How to be."

'He stood up with the tips of his fingers resting on the desk.

'"We want in so many different ways to be," he began again. "This magnificent butterfly finds a little heap of dirt and sits still on it; but man he will never on his heap of mud keep still. He want to be so, and again he want to be so...." He moved his hand up, then down...."He wants to be a saint, and he wants to be a devil – and every time he shuts his eyes he sees himself as a very fine fellow – so fine as he can never be.... In a dream...."

'He lowered the glass lid, the automatic lock clicked sharply, and taking up the case in both hands he bore it religiously away to its place, passing out of the bright circle of the lamp into the ring of fainter light – into shapeless dusk at last. It had an odd effect – as if these few steps had carried him out of this concrete and perplexed world. His tall form, as though robbed of its substance, hovered noiselessly over invisible things with stooping and indefinite movements; his voice, heard in that remoteness where he could be glimpsed mysteriously busy with immaterial cares, was no longer incisive, seemed to roll voluminous and grave – mellowed by distance.

'"And because you not always can keep your eyes shut there comes the real trouble – the heart pain – the world pain. I tell you, my friend, it is not good for you to find you cannot make your dream come true, for the reason that you not strong enough are, or not clever enough. *Ja!* ... And all the time you are such a fine fellow, too! *Wie? Was? Gott in Himmel!* How can that be? Ha! ha! ha!"

'The shadow prowling amongst the graves of butterflies laughed boisterously.

'"Yes! Very funny this terrible thing is. A man that is born falls into a dream like a man who falls into the sea. If

he tries to climb out into the air as inexperienced people
endeavour to do, he drowns – *nicht wahr?* ... No! I tell you!
The way is to the destructive element submit yourself, and
with the exertions of your hands and feet in the water make
the deep, deep sea keep you up. So if you ask me – how to
be?"

'His voice leaped up extraordinarily strong, as though
away there in the dusk he had been inspired by some
whisper of knowledge. "I will tell you! For that, too, there
is only one way."

'With a hasty swish swish of his slippers he loomed up in
the ring of faint light, and suddenly appeared in the bright
circle of the lamp. His extended hand aimed at my breast
like a pistol; his deep-set eyes seemed to pierce through me,
but his twitching lips uttered no word, and the austere
exaltation of a certitude seen in the dusk vanished from
his face. The hand that had been pointing at my breast fell,
and by-and-by, coming a step nearer, he laid it gently on my
shoulder. There were things, he said mournfully, that perhaps could never be told, only he had lived so much alone
that sometimes he forgot – he forgot. The light had
destroyed the assurance which had inspired him in the
distant shadows. He sat down and, with both elbows on
the desk, rubbed his forehead. "And yet it is true – it is true.
In the destructive element immerse."... He spoke in a
subdued tone, without looking at me, one hand on each
side of his face. "That was the way. To follow the dream,
and again to follow the dream – and so – *ewig – usque ad
finem*...." The whisper of his conviction seemed to open
before me a vast and uncertain expanse, as of a crepuscular
horizon on a plain at dawn – or was it, perchance, at the
coming of the night? One had not the courage to decide;
but it was a charming and deceptive light, throwing the
impalpable poesy of its dimness over pitfalls – over graves.
His life had begun in sacrifice, in enthusiasm for generous
ideas; he had travelled very far, on various ways, on strange
paths, and whatever he followed it had been without

faltering, and therefore without shame and without regret. In so far he was right. That was the way, no doubt. Yet for all that the great plain on which men wander amongst graves and pitfalls remained very desolate under the impalpable poesy of its crepuscular light, overshadowed in the centre, circled with a bright edge as if surrounded by an abyss full of flames. When at last I broke the silence it was to express the opinion that no one could be more romantic than himself.

'He shook his head slowly, and afterwards looked at me with a patient and inquiring glance. It was a shame, he said. There we were sitting and talking like two boys, instead of putting our heads together to find something practical – a practical remedy – for the evil – for the great evil – he repeated, with a humorous and indulgent smile. For all that, our talk did not grow more practical. We avoided pronouncing Jim's name as though we had tried to keep flesh and blood out of our discussion, or he were nothing but an erring spirit, a suffering and nameless shade. "Na!" said Stein, rising. "To-night you sleep here, and in the morning we shall do something practical – practical. . . ." He lit a two-branched candlestick and led the way. We passed through empty dark rooms, escorted by gleams from the lights Stein carried. They glided along the waxed floors, sweeping here and there over the polished surface of the table, leaped upon a fragmentary curve of a piece of furniture, or flashed perpendicularly in and out of distant mirrors, while the forms of two men and the flicker of two flames could be seen for a moment stealing silently across the depths of a crystalline void. He walked slowly a pace in advance with stooping courtesy; there was a profound, as it were a listening, quietude on his face; the long flaxen locks mixed with white threads were scattered thinly upon his slightly bowed neck.

' "He is romantic – romantic," he repeated. "And that is very bad – very bad. . . . Very good, too," he added. "But *is* he?" I queried.

'"*Gewiss*," he said, and stood still holding up the candelabrum, but without looking at me. "Evident! What is it that by inward pain makes him know himself? What is it that for you and me makes him – exist?"

'At that moment it was difficult to believe in Jim's existence – starting from a country parsonage, blurred by crowds of men as by clouds of dust, silenced by the clashing claims of life and death in a material world – but his imperishable reality came to me with a convincing, with an irresistible force! I saw it vividly, as though in our progress through the lofty silent rooms amongst fleeting gleams of light and the sudden revelations of human figures stealing with flickering flames within unfathomable and pellucid depths, we had approached nearer to absolute Truth, which, like Beauty itself, floats elusive, obscure, half submerged, in the silent still waters of mystery. "Perhaps he is," I admitted with a slight laugh, whose unexpectedly loud reverberation made me lower my voice directly; "but I am sure you are." With his head dropping on his breast and the light held high he began to walk again. "Well – I exist, too," he said.

'He preceded me. My eyes followed his movements, but what I did see was not the head of the firm, the welcome guest at afternoon receptions, the correspondent of learned societies, the entertainer of stray naturalists; I saw only the reality of his destiny, which he had known how to follow with unfaltering footsteps, that life begun in humble surroundings, rich in generous enthusiasms, in friendship, love, war – in all the exalted elements of romance. At the door of my room he faced me. "Yes," I said, as though carrying on a discussion, "and amongst other things you dreamed foolishly of a certain butterfly; but when one fine morning your dream came in your way you did not let the splendid opportunity escape. Did you? Whereas he..." Stein lifted his hand. "And do you know how many opportunities I let escape; how many dreams I had lost that had come in my way?" He shook his head regretfully. "It seems to me that some would have been very fine – if I had made them come true. Do you know how many? Perhaps I myself don't know." "Whether his were fine or not," I said, "he knows of one which he certainly did not catch." "Everybody knows of one or two like that," said Stein; "and that is the trouble – the great trouble...."

'He shook hands on the threshold, peered into my room under his raised arm. "Sleep well. And tomorrow we must do something practical – practical...."

'Though his own room was beyond mine I saw him return the way he came. He was going back to his butterflies.'

# CHAPTER TWENTY-ONE

'I DON'T suppose any of you had ever heard of Patusan?'
Marlow resumed, after a silence occupied in the careful
lighting of a cigar. 'It does not matter; there's many a
heavenly body in the lot crowding upon us of a night that
mankind had never heard of, it being outside the sphere of
its activities and of no earthly importance to anybody but to
the astronomers who are paid to talk learnedly about its
composition, weight, path – the irregularities of its conduct, the aberrations of its light – a sort of scientific
scandal-mongering. Thus with Patusan. It was referred to
knowingly in the inner government circles in Batavia,
especially as to its irregularities and aberrations, and it
was known by name to some few, very few, in the mercantile world. Nobody, however, had been there, and I suspect
no one desired to go there in person, just as an astronomer,
I should fancy, would strongly object to being transported
into a distant heavenly body, where, parted from his earthly
emoluments, he would be bewildered by the view of an
unfamiliar heavens. However, neither heavenly bodies nor
astronomers have anything to do with Patusan. It was Jim
who went there. I only meant you to understand that had
Stein arranged to send him into a star of the fifth
magnitude the change could not have been greater. He
left his earthly failings behind him and that sort of reputation he had, and there was a totally new set of conditions
for his imaginative faculty to work upon. Entirely new,
entirely remarkable. And he got hold of them in a remarkable way.

'Stein was the man who knew more about Patusan than
anybody else. More than was known in the government

circles I suspect. I have no doubt he had been there, either in his butterfly-hunting days or later on, when he tried in his incorrigible way to season with a pinch of romance the fattening dishes of his commercial kitchen. There were very few places in the Archipelago he had not seen in the original dusk of their being, before light (and even electric light) had been carried into them for the sake of better morality and – and – well – the greater profit, too. It was at breakfast of the morning following our talk about Jim that he mentioned the place, after I had quoted poor Brierly's remark: "Let him creep twenty feet underground and stay there." He looked up at me with interested attention, as though I had been a rare insect. "This could be done, too," he remarked, sipping his coffee. "Bury him in some sort," I explained. "One doesn't like to do it of course, but it would be the best thing, seeing what he is." "Yes; he is young," Stein mused. "The youngest human being now in existence," I affirmed. "*Schön*. There's Patusan," he went on in the same tone. . . ."And the woman is dead now," he added incomprehensibly.

'Of course I don't know that story; I can only guess that once before Patusan had been used as a grave for some sin, transgression, or misfortune. It is impossible to suspect Stein. The only woman that had ever existed for him was the Malay girl he called "My wife the princess," or, more rarely in moments of expansion, "the mother of my Emma." Who was the woman he had mentioned in connection with Patusan I can't say; but from his allusions I understand she had been an educated and very good-looking Dutch-Malay girl, with a tragic or perhaps only a pitiful history, whose most painful part no doubt was her marriage with a Malacca Portuguese who had been clerk in some commercial house in the Dutch colonies. I gathered from Stein that this man was an unsatisfactory person in more ways than one, all being more or less indefinite and offensive. It was solely for his wife's sake that Stein had appointed him manager of Stein & Co.'s trading post in

Patusan; but commercially the arrangement was not a success, at any rate for the firm, and now the woman had died, Stein was disposed to try another agent there. The Portuguese, whose name was Cornelius, considered himself a very deserving but ill-used person, entitled by his abilities to a better position. This man Jim would have to relieve. "But I don't think he will go away from the place," remarked Stein. "That has nothing to do with me. It was only for the sake of the woman that I... But as I think there is a daughter left, I shall let him, if he likes to stay, keep the old house."

'Patusan is a remote district of a native-ruled State, and the chief settlement bears the same name. At a point on the river about forty miles from the sea, where the first houses come into view, there can be seen rising above the level of the forests the summits of two steep hills very close together, and separated by what looks like a deep fissure, the cleavage of some mighty stroke. As a matter of fact, the valley between is nothing but a narrow ravine; the appearance from the settlement is of one irregularly conical hill split in two, and with the two halves leaning slightly apart. On the third day after the full, the moon, as seen from the open space in front of Jim's house (he had a very fine house in the native style when I visited him), rose exactly behind these hills, its diffused light at first throwing the two masses into intensely black relief, and then the nearly perfect disc, glowing ruddily, appeared, gliding upwards between the sides of the chasm, till it floated away above the summits, as if escaping from a yawning grave in gentle triumph. "Wonderful effect," said Jim by my side. "Worth seeing. Is it not?"

'And this question was put with a note of personal pride that made me smile, as though he had had a hand in regulating that unique spectacle. He had regulated so many things in Patusan! Things that would have appeared as much beyond his control as the motions of the moon and the stars.

'It was inconceivable. That was the distinctive quality of the part into which Stein and I had tumbled him unwittingly, with no other notion than to get him out of the way; out of his own way, be it understood. That was our main purpose, though, I own, I might have had another motive which had influenced me a little. I was about to go home for a time; and it may be I desired, more than I was aware of myself, to dispose of him – to dispose of him, you understand – before I left. I was going home, and he had come to me from there, with his miserable trouble and his shadowy claim, like a man panting under a burden in a mist. I cannot say I had ever seen him distinctly – not even to this day, after I had my last view of him; but it seemed to me that the less I understood the more I was bound to him in the name of that doubt which is the inseparable part of our knowledge. I did not know so much more about myself. And then, I repeat, I was going home – to that home distant enough for all its hearthstones to be like one hearthstone, by which the humblest of us has the right to sit. We wander in our thousands over the face of the earth, the illustrious and the obscure, earning beyond the seas our fame, our money, or only a crust of bread; but it seems to me that for each of us going home must be like going to render an account. We return to face our superiors, our kindred, our friends – those whom we obey, and those whom we love; but even they who have neither, the most free, lonely, irresponsible and bereft of ties, – even those for whom home holds no dear face, no familiar voice, – even they have to meet the spirit that dwells within the land, under its sky, in its air, in its valleys, and on its rises, in its fields, in its waters and its trees – a mute friend, judge, and inspirer. Say what you like, to get its joy, to breathe its peace, to face its truth, one must return with a clear consciousness. All this may seem to you sheer sentimentalism; and indeed very few of us have the will or the capacity to look consciously under the surface of familiar emotions. There are the girls we love, the men we look up to, the tenderness, the friendships, the opportunities, the pleasures! But the fact remains that you must touch your reward with clean hands, lest it turn to dead leaves, to thorns, in your grasp. I think it is the lonely, without a fireside or an affection they may call their own, those who return not to a dwelling but to the land itself, to meet its disembodied, eternal, and unchangeable spirit – it is those who understand best its severity, its saving power, the grace of its secular right to our fidelity, to our obedience. Yes! few of us understand, but we all feel it though, and I say *all* without exception, because those who do not feel do not count. Each blade of grass has its spot on earth whence it draws its life, its strength; and so is man rooted to the land from which he draws his faith together with his life. I don't know how much Jim understood; but I know he felt, he felt confusedly but powerfully, the demand of some such truth or some such illusion – I don't care how you call it, there is so little difference, and the difference means so little. The thing is that in virtue of his feeling he mattered. He would never go home now. Not he. Never. Had he been capable of picturesque manifestations he would have shuddered at the thought and made you shudder, too. But he was not of that sort, though he was expressive enough in his way. Before the idea of going home he would grow desperately stiff and immovable, with lowered chin and pouted lips, and with those candid blue eyes of his glowering darkly under a frown, as if before something unbearable, as if before something revolting. There was imagination in that hard skull of his, over which the thick clustering hair fitted like a cap. As to me, I have no imagination (I would be more certain about him to-day, if I had), and I do not mean to imply that I figured to myself the spirit of the land uprising above the white cliffs of Dover, to ask me what I – returning with no bones broken, so to speak – had done with my very young brother. I could not make such a mistake. I knew very well he was of those about whom there is no inquiry; I had seen better men go out, disappear, vanish utterly, without provoking a

sound of curiosity or sorrow. The spirit of the land, as
becomes the ruler of great enterprises, is careless of innumerable lives. Woe to the stragglers! We exist only in so
far as we hang together. He had straggled in a way; he had
not hung on; but he was aware of it with an intensity that
made him touching, just as a man's more intense life makes
his death more touching than the death of a tree. I happened to be handy, and I happened to be touched. That's all
there is to it. I was concerned as to the way he would go out.
It would have hurt me if, for instance, he had taken to
drink. The earth is so small that I was afraid of, some day,
being waylaid by a blear-eyed, swollen-faced, besmirched
loafer, with no soles to his canvas shoes, and with a flutter
of rags about the elbows, who, on the strength of old
acquaintance, would ask for a loan of five dollars. You
know the awful jaunty bearing of these scarecrows coming
to you from a decent past, the rasping careless voice, the
half-averted impudent glances – those meetings more trying to a man who believes in the solidarity of our lives than
the sight of an impenitent deathbed to a priest. That, to tell
you the truth, was the only danger I could see for him and
for me; but I also mistrusted my want of imagination. It
might even come to something worse, in some way it was
beyond my powers of fancy to foresee. He wouldn't let me
forget how imaginative he was, and your imaginative people swing farther in any direction, as if given a longer scope
of cable in the uneasy anchorage of life. They do. They take
to drink, too. It may be I was belittling him by such a fear.
How could I tell? Even Stein could say no more than that
he was romantic. I only knew he was one of us. And what
business had he to be romantic? I am telling you so much
about my own instinctive feelings and bemused reflections
because there remains so little to be told of him. He existed
for me, and after all it is only through me that he exists for
you. I've led him out by the hand; I have paraded him
before you. Were my commonplace fears unjust? I won't
say – not even now. You may be able to tell better, since the

proverb has it that the onlookers see most of the game. At any rate, they were superfluous. He did not go out, not at all; on the contrary, he came on wonderfully, came on straight as a die and in excellent form, which showed that he could stay as well as spurt. I ought to be delighted, for it is a victory in which I had taken my part; but I am not so pleased as I would have expected to be. I ask myself whether his rush had really carried him out of that mist in which he loomed interesting if not very big, with floating outlines – a straggler yearning inconsolably for his humble place in the ranks. And besides, the last word is not said, – probably shall never be said. Are not our lives too short for that full utterance which through all our stammerings is of course our only and abiding intention? I have given up expecting those last words, whose ring, if they could only be pronounced, would shake both heaven and earth. There is never time to say our last word – the last word of our love, of our desire, faith, remorse, submission, revolt. The heaven and the earth must not be shaken. I suppose – at least, not by us who know so many truths about either. My last words about Jim shall be few. I affirm he had achieved greatness; but the thing would be dwarfed in the telling, or rather in the hearing. Frankly, it is not my words that I mistrust but your minds. I could be eloquent were I not afraid you fellows had starved your imaginations to feed your bodies. I do not mean to be offensive; it is respectable to have no illusions – and safe – and profitable – and dull. Yet you, too, in your time must have known the intensity of life, that light of glamour created in the shock of trifles, as amazing as the glow of sparks struck from a cold stone – and as short-lived, alas!'

# CHAPTER TWENTY-TWO

'THE conquest of love, honour, men's confidence – the pride of it, the power of it, are fit materials for a heroic tale; only our minds are struck by the externals of such a success, and to Jim's successes there were no externals. Thirty miles of forest shut it off from the sight of an indifferent world, and the noise of the white surf along the coast overpowered the voice of fame. The stream of civilisation, as if divided on a headland a hundred miles north of Patusan, branches east and south-east, leaving its plains and valleys, its old trees and its old mankind, neglected and isolated, such as an insignificant and crumbling islet between the two branches of a mighty, devouring stream. You find the name of the country pretty often in collections of old voyages. The seventeenth-century traders went there for pepper, because the passion for pepper seemed to burn like a flame of love in the breast of Dutch and English adventurers about the time of James the First. Where wouldn't they go for pepper! For a bag of pepper they would cut each other's throats without hesitation, and would forswear their souls, of which they were so careful otherwise: the bizarre obstinacy of that desire made them defy death in a thousand shapes; the unknown seas, the loathsome and strange diseases; wounds, captivity, hunger, pestilence, and despair. It made them great! By heavens! it made them heroic; and it made them pathetic, too, in their craving for trade with the inflexible death levying its toll on young and old. It seems impossible to believe that mere greed could hold men to such a steadfastness of purpose, to such a blind persistence in endeavour and sacrifice. And indeed those who adventured their persons and lives risked all they had for a slender reward. They left their bones to lie bleaching on distant shores, so that wealth might flow to the living at home. To us, their less tried successors, they appear magnified, not as agents of trade but as instruments of a recorded destiny, pushing out into the unknown in obedience to an inward voice, to an impulse beating in the blood, to a dream of the future. They were wonderful; and it must be owned they were ready for the wonderful. They recorded it complacently in their sufferings, in the aspect of the seas, in the customs of strange nations, in the glory of splendid rulers.

'In Patusan they had found lots of pepper, and had been impressed by the magnificence and the wisdom of the Sultan; but somehow, after a century of checkered intercourse, the country seems to drop gradually out of the trade. Perhaps the pepper had given out. Be it as it may, nobody cares for it now; the glory has departed, the Sultan is an imbecile youth with two thumbs on his left hand and an uncertain and beggarly revenue extorted from a miserable population and stolen from him by his many uncles.

'This of course I have from Stein. He gave me their names and a short sketch of the life and character of each. He was as full of information about native States as an official report, but infinitely more amusing. He *had* to know. He traded in so many, and in some districts – as in Patusan, for instance – his firm was the only one to have an agency by special permit from the Dutch authorities. The Government trusted his discretion, and it was understood that he took all the risks. The men he employed understood that, too, but he made it worth their while apparently. He was perfectly frank with me over the breakfast-table in the morning. As far as he was aware (the last news was thirteen months old, he stated precisely), utter insecurity for life and property was the normal condition. There were in Patusan antagonistic forces, and one of them was Rajah Allang, the worst of the Sultan's uncles, the governor of the river, who did the extorting and the stealing, and ground down to the point of extinction the country-born Malays, who, utterly defenceless, had not even the resource of emigrating, – "for indeed," as Stein remarked, "where could they go, and how could they get away?" No doubt they did not even desire to get away. The world (which is circumscribed by lofty impassable mountains) has been given into the hand of the high-born, and *this* Rajah they knew: he was of their own royal house. I had the pleasure of meeting the gentleman later on. He was a dirty, little, used-up old man with evil eyes and a weak mouth, who swallowed an opium pill every two hours, and in defiance of common decency wore his hair uncovered and falling in wild stringy locks about his wizened grimy face. When giving audience he would clamber upon a sort of narrow stage erected in a hall like a ruinous barn with a rotten bamboo floor, through the cracks of which you could see twelve or fifteen feet below the heaps of refuse and garbage of all kinds lying under the house. That is where and how he received us when, accompanied by Jim, I paid him a visit of ceremony. There were about forty people in the room, and perhaps three times as many in the great courtyard below. There was constant movement, coming and going, pushing and murmuring, at our backs. A few youths in gay silks glared from the distance; the majority, slaves and humble dependants, were half naked, in ragged sarongs, dirty with ashes and mudstains. I had never seen Jim look so grave, so self-possessed, in an impenetrable, impressive way. In the midst of these dark-faced men, his stalwart figure in white apparel, the gleaming clusters of his fair hair, seemed to catch all the sunshine that trickled through the cracks in the closed shutters of that dim hall, with its walls of mats and a roof of thatch. He appeared like a creature not only of another kind but of another essence. Had they not seen him come up in a canoe they might have thought he had descended upon them from the clouds. He did, however, come in a crazy dug-out, sitting (very still and with his knees together, for fear of overturning the thing) – sitting on a tin box – which I had lent him – nursing on his lap a revolver of the Navy pattern – presented by me on parting – which, through an interposition of Providence, or through some wrong-headed notion, that was just like him, or else from sheer instinctive sagacity, he had decided to carry unloaded. That's how he ascended the Patusan river. Nothing could have been more prosaic and more unsafe, more extravagantly casual, more lonely. Strange, this fatality that would cast the complexion of a flight upon all his acts, of impulsive unreflecting desertion – of a jump into the unknown.

'It is precisely the casualness of it that strikes me most. Neither Stein nor I had a clear conception of what might be on the other side when we, metaphorically speaking, took him up and hove him over the wall with scant ceremony. At the moment I merely wished to achieve his disappearance. Stein characteristically enough had a sentimental motive. He had a notion of paying off (in kind, I suppose) the old debt he had never forgotten. Indeed he had been all his life especially friendly to anybody from the British Isles. His late benefactor, it is true, was a Scot – even to the length of being called Alexander M'Neil – and Jim came from a long way south of the Tweed; but at the distance of six or seven thousand miles Great Britain, though never diminished, looks foreshortened enough even to its own children to rob such details of their importance. Stein was excusable, and his hinted intentions were so generous that I begged him most earnestly to keep them secret for a time. I felt that no consideration of personal advantage should be allowed to influence Jim; that not even the risk of such influence should be run. We had to deal with another sort of reality. He wanted a refuge, and a refuge at the cost of danger should be offered him – nothing more.

'Upon every other point I was perfectly frank with him, and I even (as I believed at the time) exaggerated the danger of the undertaking. As a matter of fact I did not do it justice; his first day in Patusan was nearly his last –

would have been his last if he had not been so reckless or so hard on himself and had condescended to load that revolver. I remember, as I unfolded our precious scheme for his retreat, how his stubborn but weary resignation was gradually replaced by surprise, interest, wonder, and by boyish eagerness. This was a chance he had been dreaming of. He couldn't think how he merited that I . . . He would be shot if he could see to what he owed. . . . And it was Stein, Stein the merchant, who . . . but of course it was me he had to . . . I cut him short. He was not articulate, and his gratitude caused me inexplicable pain. I told him that if he owed this chance to any one especially, it was to an old Scot of whom he had never heard, who had died many years ago, of whom little was remembered besides a roaring voice and a rough sort of honesty. There was really no one to receive his thanks. Stein was passing on to a young man the help he had received in his own young days, and I had done no more than to mention his name. Upon this he coloured, and, twisting a bit of paper in his fingers, he remarked bashfully that I had always trusted him.

'I admitted that such was the case, and added after a pause that I wished he had been able to follow my example. "You think I don't?" he asked uneasily, and remarked in a mutter that one had to get some sort of show first; then brightening up, and in a loud voice he protested he would give me no occasion to regret my confidence, which – which . . .

'"Do not misapprehend," I interrupted. "It is not in your power to make me regret anything." There would be no regrets; but if there were, it would be altogether my own affair: on the other hand, I wished him to understand clearly that this arrangement, this – this – experiment, was his own doing; he was responsible for it and no one elsc. "Why? Why," he stammered, "this is the very thing that I . . ." I begged him not to be dense, and he looked more puzzled than ever. He was in a fair way to make life intolerable to himself. . . . "Do you think so?" he asked, disturbed; but in a moment added confidently, "I was going on though. Was I not?" It was impossible to be angry with him: I could not help a smile, and told him that in the old days people who went on like this were on the way of becoming hermits in a wilderness. "Hermits be hanged!" he commented with engaging impulsiveness. Of course he didn't mind a wilderness. . . . "I was glad of it," I said. That was where he would be going to. He would find it lively enough, I ventured to promise. "Yes, yes," he said, keenly. He had shown a desire, I continued inflexibly, to go out and shut the door after him. . . . "Did I?" he interrupted in a strange access of gloom that seemed to envelop him from head to foot like the shadow of a passing cloud. He was wonderfully expressive after all. Wonderfully! "Did I?" he repeated, bitterly. "You can't say I made much noise about it. And I can keep it up, too – only, confound it! you show me a door." . . . "Very well. Pass on," I struck in. I could make him a solemn promise that it would be shut behind him with a vengeance. His fate, whatever it was, would be ignored, because the country, for all its rotten state, was not judged ripe for interference. Once he got in, it would be for the outside world as though he had never existed. He would have nothing but the soles of his two feet to stand upon, and he would have first to find his ground at that. "Never existed – that's it, by Jove!" he murmured to himself. His eyes, fastened upon my lips, sparkled. If he had thoroughly understood the conditions, I concluded, he had better jump into the first gharry he could see and drive on to Stein's house for his final instructions. He flung out of the room before I had fairly finished speaking.

# CHAPTER TWENTY-THREE

'He did not return till next morning. He had been kept to dinner and for the night. There never had been such a wonderful man as Mr Stein. He had in his pocket a letter for Cornelius ("the Johnnie who's going to get the sack," he explained with a momentary drop in his elation), and he exhibited with glee a silver ring, such as natives use, worn down very thin and showing faint traces of chasing.

'This was his introduction to an old chap called Doramin – one of the principal men out there – a big pot – who had been Mr Stein's friend in that country where he had all these adventures. Mr Stein called him "war-comrade." War-comrade was good. Wasn't it? And didn't Mr Stein speak English wonderfully well? Said he had learned it in Celebes – of all places! That was awfully funny. Was it not? He did speak with an accent – a twang – did I notice? That chap Doramin had given him the ring. They had exchanged presents when they parted for the last time. Sort of promising eternal friendship. He called it fine – did I not? They had to make a dash for dear life out of the country when that Mohammed – Mohammed – What's-his-name had been killed. I knew the story, of course. Seemed a beastly shame, didn't it?...

'He ran on like this, forgetting his plate, with a knife and fork in hand (he had found me at tiffin), slightly flushed, and with his eyes darkened many shades, which was with him a sign of excitement. The ring was a sort of credential – ("It's like something you read of in books," he threw in appreciatively) and Doramin would do his best for him. Mr Stein had been the means of saving that chap's life on some occasion; purely by accident, Mr Stein had said, but he – Jim – had his own opinion about that. Mr Stein was just the man to look out for such accidents. No matter. Accident or purpose, this would serve his turn immensely. Hoped to goodness the jolly old beggar had not gone off the hooks meantime. Mr Stein could not tell. There had been no news for more than a year; they were kicking up no end of an all-fired row amongst themselves, and the river was closed. Jolly awkward, this; but, no fear; he would manage to find a crack to get in.

'He impressed, almost frightened, me with his elated rattle. He was voluble like a youngster on the eve of a long holiday with a prospect of delightful scrapes, and such an attitude of mind in a grown man and in this connection had in it something phenomenal, a little mad, dangerous, unsafe. I was on the point of entreating him to take things seriously when he dropped his knife and fork (he had begun eating, or rather swallowing food, as it were, unconsciously), and began a search all round his plate. The ring! The ring! Where the devil...Ah! Here it was.... He closed his big hand on it, and tried all his pockets one after another. Jove! wouldn't do to lose the thing. He meditated gravely over his fist. Had it? Would hang the bally affair round his neck! And he proceeded to do this immediately, producing a string (which looked like a bit of a cotton shoe-lace) for the purpose. There! That would do the trick! It would be the deuce if... He seemed to catch sight of my face for the first time, and it steadied him a little. I probably didn't realise, he said with a naïve gravity, how much importance he attached to that token. It meant a friend; and it is a good thing to have a friend. He knew something about that. He nodded at me expressively, but before my disclaiming gesture he leaned his head on his hand and for a while sat silent, playing thoughtfully with the bread-crumbs on the cloth.... "Slam the door – that was jolly well put," he cried, and jumping up, began to pace the room, reminding me by the set of the shoulders, the turn of his head, the head-long and uneven stride, of that night when he had paced thus, confessing, explaining – what you will – but, in the last instance, living – living before me, under his own little cloud, with all his unconscious subtlety which could draw consolation from the very source of sorrow. It was the same mood, the same and different, like a fickle companion that to-day guiding you on the true path, with the same eyes, the same step, the same impulse, to-morrow will lead you hopelessly astray. His tread was assured, his straying, darkened eyes seemed to search the room for something. One of his footfalls somehow sounded louder than the other – the fault of his boots probably – and gave a curious impression of an invisible halt in his gait. One of his hands was rammed deep into his trousers-pocket, the other waved suddenly above his head. "Slam the door!" he shouted. "I've been waiting for that. I'll show yet...I'll...I'm ready for any confounded thing....I've been dreaming of it... Jove! Get out of this. Jove! This is luck at last....You wait. I'll..."

'He tossed his head fearlessly, and I confess that for the first and last time in our acquaintance I perceived myself unexpectedly to be thoroughly sick of him. Why these vapourings? He was stumping about the room flourishing his arm absurdly, and now and then feeling on his breast for the ring under his clothes. Where was the sense of such exaltation in a man appointed to be a trading-clerk, and in a place where there was no trade – at that? Why hurl defiance at the universe? This was not a proper frame of mind to approach any undertaking; an improper frame of mind not only for him, I said, but for any man. He stood still over me. Did I think so? he asked, by no means subdued, and with a smile in which I seemed to detect suddenly something insolent. But then I am twenty years his senior. Youth *is* insolent; it is its right – its necessity; it has got to assert itself, and all assertion in this world of doubts is a defiance, is an insolence. He went off into a far corner, and coming back, he, figuratively speaking, turned to rend me. I spoke like that because I – even I, who had been no end kind to him – even I remembered – remembered – against him – what – what had happened. And what about others – the – the – world? Where's the wonder he wanted to get out, meant to get out, meant to stay out – by heavens! And I talked about proper frames of mind!"

'"It is not I or the world who remember," I shouted. "It is you – you, who remember."

'He did not flinch, and went on with heat, "Forget everything, everybody, everybody." . . . His voice fell. . . . "But you," he added.

'"Yes – me, too – if it would help," I said, also in a low tone. After this we remained silent and languid for a time as if exhausted. Then he began again, composedly, and told me that Mr Stein had instructed him to wait for a month or so, to see whether it was possible for him to remain, before he began building a new house for himself, so as to avoid "vain expense." He did make use of funny expressions – Stein did. "Vain expense" was good. . . . Remain? Why! of course. He would hang on. Let him only get in – that's all; he would answer for it he would remain. Never get out. It was easy enough to remain.

'"Don't be foolhardy," I said, rendered uneasy by his threatening tone. "If you only live long enough you will want to come back."

'"Come back to what?" he asked, absently, with his eyes fixed upon the face of a clock on the wall.

'I was silent for a while. "Is it to be never, then?" I said. "Never," he repeated, dreamily, without looking at me, and then flew into sudden activity. "Jove! Two o'clock, and I sail at four!"

'It was true. A brigantine of Stein's was leaving for the westward that afternoon, and he had been instructed to take his passage in her, only no orders to delay the sailing had been given. I suppose Stein forgot. He made a rush to get his things while I went aboard my ship, where he promised to call on his way to the outer roadster. He turned up accordingly in a great hurry and with a small leather valise in his hand. This wouldn't do, and I offered him an old tin trunk of mine supposed to be water-tight, or at least damp-tight. He effected the transfer by the simple process of shooting out the contents of his valise as you would empty a sack of wheat. I saw three books in the tumble; two small, in dark covers, and a thick green-and-gold volume – a half-crown complete Shakespeare. "You read this?" I asked. "Yes. Best thing to cheer up a fellow," he said, hastily. I was struck by this appreciation, but there was no time for Shakespearian talk. A heavy revolver and two small boxes of cartridges were laying on the cuddy-table. "Pray take this," I said. "It may help you to remain." No sooner were these words out of my mouth than I perceived what grim meaning they could bear. "May help you to get in," I corrected myself, remorsefully. He, however, was not troubled by obscure meanings; he thanked me effusively and bolted out, calling Good-bye over his shoulder. I heard his voice through the ship's side urging his boatmen to give way, and looking out of the stern-port I saw the boat rounding under the counter. He sat in her leaning forward, exciting his men with voice and gestures; and as he had kept the revolver in his hand and seemed to be presenting it at their heads, I shall never forget the scared faces of the four Javanese, and the frantic swing of their stroke which snatched that vision from under my eyes. Then turning away, the first thing I saw were the two boxes of cartridges on the cuddy-table. He had forgotten to take them.

'I ordered my gig manned at once; but Jim's rowers, under the impression that their lives hung on a thread while they had that madman in the boat, made such excellent time that before I had traversed half the distance between the two vessels I caught sight of him clambering over the rail, and of his box being passed up. All the brigantine's canvas was loose, her mainsail was set, and the windlass was just beginning to clink as I stepped upon her deck: her master, a dapper little half-caste of forty or so, in a blue flannel suit, with lively eyes, his round face the colour of lemon-peel, and with a thin little black moustache drooping on each side of his thick, dark lips, came forward smirking. He turned out, notwithstanding his self-satisfied and cheery exterior, to be of a careworn temperament. In answer to a remark of mine (while Jim had gone below for a moment) he said, "Oh, yes. Patusan." He was going to carry the gentleman to the mouth of the river, but would "never ascend." His flowing English seemed to be derived from a dictionary compiled by a lunatic. Had Mr Stein desired him to "ascend," he would have "reverentially" – (I think he wanted to say respectfully – but devil only knows) – "reverentially made objects for the safety of properties." If disregarded, he would have presented "resignation to quit." Twelve months ago he had made his last voyage there, and though Mr Cornelius "propitiated many offertories" to Mr Rajah Allang and the "principal populations," on conditions which made the trade "a snare and ashes in the mouth," yet his ship had been fired upon from the woods by "irresponsive parties" all the way down the river; which causing his crew "from exposure to limb to remain silent in hidings," the brigantine was nearly stranded on a sandbank at the bar, where she "would have been perishable beyond the act of man." The angry disgust at the recollection, the pride of his fluency, to which he turned an attentive ear, struggled for the possession of his broad simple face. He scowled and beamed at me, and watched with satisfaction the undeniable effect of his phraseology. Dark frowns ran swiftly over the placid sea, and the brigantine, with her fore-topsail to the mast and her main-boom amidships, seemed bewildered amongst the cat's-paws. He told me further, gnashing his teeth, that the Rajah was a "laughable hyæna" (can't imagine how he got hold of hyænas); while somebody else was many times falser than the "weapons of a crocodile." Keeping one eye on the movements of his crew forward, he let loose his volubility – comparing the place to a "cage of beasts made ravenous by long impenitence." I fancy he meant impunity. He had no intention, he cried, to "exhibit himself to be made attached purposefully to robbery." The long-drawn wails, giving the time for the pull of the men catting the anchor, came to an end, and he lowered his voice. "Plenty too much enough of Patusan," he concluded, with energy.

'I heard afterwards he had been so indiscreet as to get himself tied up by the neck with a rattan halter to a post planted in the middle of a mud-hole before the Rajah's house. He spent the best part of a day and a whole night in that unwholesome situation, but there is every reason to believe the thing had been meant as a sort of joke. He brooded for a while over that horrid memory, I suppose, and then addressed in a quarrelsome tone the man coming aft to the helm. When he turned to me again it was to speak judicially, without passion. He would take the gentleman to the mouth of the river at Batu Kring (Patusan town "being situated internally," he remarked, "thirty miles"). But in his eyes, he continued – a tone of bored, weary conviction replacing his previous voluble delivery – the gentleman was already "in the similitude of a corpse." "What? What do you say?" I asked. He assumed a startlingly ferocious demeanour, and imitated to perfection the act of stabbing from behind. "Already like the body of one deported," he explained, with the insufferably conceited air of his kind after what they imagine a display of cleverness. Behind him I perceived Jim smiling silently at me, and with a raised hand checking the exclamation on my lips.

'Then, while the half-caste, bursting with importance, shouted his orders, while the yards swung creaking and the heavy boom came surging over, Jim and I, alone as it were, to leeward of the mainsail, clasped each other's hands and exchanged the last hurried words. My heart was freed from that dull resentment which had existed side by side with interest in his fate. The absurd chatter of the half-caste had given more reality to the miserable dangers of his path than

Stein's careful statements. On that occasion the sort of formality that had been always present in our intercourse vanished from our speech; I believe I called him "dear boy," and he tacked on the words "old man" to some half-uttered expression of gratitude, as though his risk set off against my years had made us more equal in age and in feeling. There was a moment of real and profound intimacy, unexpected and short-lived like a glimpse of some everlasting, of some saving truth. He exerted himself to soothe me as though he had been the more mature of the two. "All right, all right," he said, rapidly, and with feeling. "I promise to take care of myself. Yes; I won't take any risks. Not a single blessed risk. Of course not. I mean to hang out. Don't you worry. Jove! I feel as if nothing could touch me. Why! this is luck from the word Go. I wouldn't spoil such a magnificent chance!" ... A magnificent chance! Well, it *was* magnificent, but chances are what men make them, and how was I to know? As he had said, even I – even I remembered – his – his misfortunes against him. It was true. And the best thing for him was to go.

'My gig had dropped in the wake of the brigantine, and I saw him aft detached upon the light of the westering sun, raising his cap high above his head. I heard an indistinct shout, "You – shall – hear – of – me." Of me, or from me, I don't know which. I think it must have been *of* me. My eyes were too dazzled by the glitter of the sea below his feet to see him clearly; but I can assure you no man could have appeared less "in the similitude of a corpse," as that half-caste croaker had put it. I could see the little wretch's face, the shape and colour of a ripe pumpkin, poked out somewhere under Jim's elbow. He, too, raised his arm as if for a downward thrust. *Absit omen!*'

# CHAPTER TWENTY-FOUR

'THE coast of Patusan (I saw it nearly two years afterwards) is straight and sombre, and faces a misty ocean. Red trails are seen like cataracts of rust streaming under the dark-green foliage of bushes and creepers clothing the low cliffs. Swampy plains open out at the mouth of rivers, with a view of jagged blue peaks beyond the vast forests. In the offing a chain of islands, dark, crumbling shapes, stand out in the everlasting sunlit haze like the remnants of a wall breached by the sea.

'There is a village of fisher-folk at the mouth of the Batu Kring branch of the estuary. The river, which had been closed so long, was open then, and Stein's little schooner, in which I had my passage, worked her way up in three tides without being exposed to a fusillade from "irresponsive parties." Such a state of affairs belonged already to ancient history, if I could believe the elderly headman of the fishing village, who came on board to act as a sort of pilot. He talked to me (the second white man he had ever seen) with confidence, and most of his talk was about the first white man he had ever seen. He called him Tuan Jim, and the tone of his references was made remarkable by a strange mixture of familiarity and awe. They, in the village, were under that lord's special protection, which showed that Jim bore no grudge. If he had warned me that I would hear of him it was perfectly true. I was hearing of him. There was already a story that the tide had turned two hours before its time to help him on his journey up the river. The talkative old man himself had steered the canoe and had marvelled at the phenomenon. Moreover, all the glory was in his family. His son and his son-in-law had paddled; but they were only youths without experience, who did not notice the speed of the canoe till he pointed out to them the amazing fact.

'Jim's coming to that fishing village was a blessing; but to them, as to many of us, the blessing came heralded by terrors. So many generations had been released since the last white man had visited the river that the very tradition had been lost. The appearance of the being that descended upon them and demanded inflexibly to be taken up to Patusan was discomposing; his insistence was alarming; his generosity more than suspicious. It was an unheard-of request. There was no precedent. What would the Rajah say to this? What would he do to them? The best part of the night was spent in consultation; but the immediate risk from the anger of that strange man seemed so great that at last a cranky dug-out was got ready. The women shrieked with grief as it put off. A fearless old hag cursed the stranger.

'He sat in it, as I've told you, on his tin box, nursing the unloaded revolver on his lap. He sat with precaution – than which there is nothing more fatiguing – and thus entered the land he was destined to fill with the fame of his virtues, from the blue peaks inland to the white ribbon of surf on the coast. At the first bend he lost sight of the sea with its labouring waves for ever rising, sinking, and vanishing to rise again – the very image of struggling mankind – and faced the immovable forests rooted deep in the soil, soaring towards the sunshine, everlasting in the shadowy might of their tradition, like life itself. And his opportunity sat veiled by his side like an Eastern bride waiting to be uncovered by the hand of the master. He, too, was the heir of a shadowy and mighty tradition! He told me, however, that he had never in his life felt so depressed and tired as in that canoe. All the movement he dared to allow himself was to reach, as it were by stealth, after the shell of half a cocoa-nut floating between his shoes, and bale some of the water out with a carefully restrained action. He discovered how hard the lid of a block-tin case was to sit upon. He had heroic health; but several times during that journey he experienced fits of giddiness, and between whiles he speculated hazily as to the size of the blister the sun was raising on his back. For amusement he tried by looking ahead to decide whether the muddy object he saw lying on the water's edge was a log of wood or an alligator. Only very soon he had to give that up. No fun in it. Always alligator. One of them flopped into the river and all but capsized the canoe. But this excitement was over directly. Then in a long empty reach he was very grateful to a troop of monkeys who came right down on the bank and made an insulting hullabaloo on his passage. Such was the way in which he was approaching greatness as genuine as any man ever achieved. Principally, he longed for sunset; and meantime his three paddlers were preparing to put into execution their plan of delivering him up to the Rajah.

'"I suppose I must have been stupid with fatigue, or perhaps I did doze off for a time," he said. The first thing he knew was his canoe coming to the bank. He became instantaneously aware of the forest having been left behind, of the first houses being visible higher up, of a stockade on his left, and of his boatmen leaping out together upon a low point of land and taking to their heels. Instinctively he leaped out after them. At first he thought himself deserted for some inconceivable reason, but he heard excited shouts, a gate swung open, and a lot of people poured out, making towards him. At the same time a boat full of armed men appeared on the river and came alongside his empty canoe, thus shutting off his retreat.

'"I was too startled to be quite cool – don't you know? and if that revolver had been loaded I would have shot somebody – perhaps two, three bodies, and that would have been the end of me. But it wasn't. . ." "Why not?" I asked. "Well, I couldn't fight the whole population, and I wasn't coming to them as if I were afraid of my life," he said, with just a faint hint of his stubborn sulkiness in the glance he gave me. I refrained from pointing out to him that they could not have known the chambers were actually empty. He had to satisfy himself in his own way.... "Anyhow it wasn't," he repeated, good-humouredly, "and so I just stood still and asked them what was the matter. That seemed to strike them dumb. I saw some of these thieves going off with my box. That long-legged old scoundrel Kassim (I'll show him to you to-morrow) ran out fussing to me about the Rajah wanting to see me. I said, 'All right'; I, too, wanted to see the Rajah, and I simply walked in through the gate and – and – here I am." He laughed, and then with unexpected emphasis, "And do you know what's the best in it?" he asked. "I'll tell you. It's the knowledge that had I been wiped out it is this place that would have been the loser."

'He spoke thus to me before his house on that evening I've mentioned – after we had watched the moon float away above the chasm between the hills like an ascending spirit out of a grave; its sheen descended, cold and pale, like the ghost of dead sunlight. There is something haunting in the light of the moon; it has all the dispassionateness of a disembodied soul, and something of its inconceivable mystery. It is to our sunshine, which – say what you like – is all we have to live by, what the echo is to the sound: misleading and confusing whether the note be mocking or sad. It robs all forms of matter – which, after all, is our domain – of their substance, and gives a sinister reality to shadows alone. And the shadows were very real around us, but Jim by my side looked very stalwart, as though nothing – not even the occult power of moonlight – could rob him of his reality in my eyes. Perhaps, indeed, nothing could touch him since he had survived the assault of the dark powers. All was silent, all was still; even on the river the moonbeams slept as on a pool. It was the moment of high water, a moment of immobility that accentuated the utter isolation of this lost corner of the earth. The houses crowding along the wide shining sweep without ripple or glitter, stepping into the water in a line of jostling, vague, grey, silvery forms mingled with black masses of shadow, were like a spectral herd of shapeless creatures pressing forward to drink in a spectral and lifeless stream. Here and there a red gleam twinkled within the bamboo walls, warm, like a living spark, significant of human affections, of shelter, of repose.

'He confessed to me that he often watched these tiny warm gleams go out one by one, that he loved to see people go to sleep under his eyes, confident in the security of to-morrow. "Peaceful here, eh?" he asked. He was not eloquent, but there was a deep meaning in the words that followed. "Look at these houses; there's not one where I am not trusted. Jove! I told you I would hang on. Ask any man, woman, or child..." He paused. "Well, I am all right anyhow."

'I observed quickly that he had found that out in the end. I had been sure of it, I added. He shook his head. "Were you?" He pressed my arm lightly above the elbow. "Well, then – you were right."

'There was elation and pride, there was awe almost, in that low exclamation. "Jove!" he cried, "only think what it is to me." Again he pressed my arm. "And you asked me whether I thought of leaving. Good God! I! want to leave! Especially now after what you told me of Mr Stein's...Leave! Why! That's what I was afraid of. It would have been – it would have been harder than dying. No – on my word. Don't laugh. I must feel – every day, every time I open my eyes – that I am trusted – that nobody has a right – don't you know? Leave! For where? What for? To get what?"

'I had told him (indeed it was the main object of my visit) that it was Stein's intention to present him at once with the house and the stock of trading goods, on certain easy conditions which would make the transaction perfectly regular and valid. He began to snort and plunge at first. "Confound your delicacy!" I shouted. "It isn't Stein at all. It's giving you what you had made for yourself. And in any case keep your remarks for M'Neil – when you meet him in the other world. I hope it won't happen soon...." He had to give in to my arguments, because all his conquests, the trust, the fame, the friendships, the love – all these things that made him master had made him a captive, too. He looked with an owner's eye at the peace of the evening, at the river, at the houses, at the everlasting life of the forests, at the life of the old mankind, at the secrets of the land, at the pride of his own heart: but it was they that possessed him and made him their own to the innermost thought, to the slightest stir of blood, to his last breath.

'It was something to be proud of. I, too, was proud – for him, if not so certain of the fabulous value of the bargain. It was wonderful. It was not so much of his fearlessness that I thought. It is strange how little account I took of it: as if it had been something too conventional to be at the root of the matter. No. I was more struck by the other gifts he had displayed. He had proved his grasp of the unfamiliar situation, his intellectual alertness in that field of thought. There was his readiness, too! Amazing. And all this had come to him in a manner like keen scent to a well-bred hound. He was not eloquent, but there was a dignity in this constitutional reticence, there was a high seriousness in his stammerings. He had still his old trick of stubborn blushing. Now and then, though, a word, a sentence, would escape him that showed how deeply, how solemnly, he felt about that work which had given him the certitude of rehabilitation. That is why he seemed to love the land and the people with a sort of fierce egoism, with a contemptuous tenderness.

# CHAPTER TWENTY-FIVE

'"THIS is where I was prisoner for three days," he murmured to me (it was on the occasion of our visit to the Rajah), while we were making our way slowly through a kind of awestruck riot of dependants across Tunku Allang's courtyard. "Filthy place, isn't it? And I couldn't get anything to eat either, unless I made a row about it, and then it was only a small plate of rice and a fried fish not much bigger than a stickleback – confound them! Jove! *I've* been hungry prowling inside this stinking enclosure with some of these vagabonds shoving their mugs right under my nose. I had given up that famous revolver of yours at the first demand. Glad to get rid of the bally thing. Look like a fool walking about with an empty shooting-iron in my hand." At that moment we came into the presence, and he became unflinchingly grave and complimentary with his late captor. Oh! magnificent! I want to laugh when I think of it. But I was impressed, too. The old disreputable Tunku Allang could not help showing his fear (he was no hero, for all the tales of his hot youth he was fond of telling); and at the same time there was a wistful confidence in his manner towards his late prisoner. Note! Even where he would be most hated he was still trusted. Jim – as far as I could follow the conversation – was improving the occasion by the delivery of a lecture. Some poor villagers had been waylaid and robbed while on their way to Doramin's house with a few pieces of gum or beeswax which they wished to exchange for rice. "It was Doramin who was a thief," burst out the Rajah. A shaking fury seemed to enter that old frail body. He writhed weirdly on his mat, gesticulating with his hands and feet, tossing the tangled strings of his

224

mop – an important incarnation of rage. There were staring
eyes and dropping jaws all around us. Jim began to speak.
Resolutely, coolly, and for some time he enlarged upon the
text that no man should be prevented from getting his food
and his children's food honestly. The other sat like a tailor
at his board, one palm on each knee, his head low, and
fixing Jim through the grey hair that fell over his very eyes.
When Jim had done there was a great stillness. Nobody
seemed to breathe even; no one made a sound till the old
Rajah sighed faintly, and looking up, with a toss of his
head, said quickly, "You hear, my people! No more of
these little games." This decree was received in profound
silence. A rather heavy man, evidently in a position of
confidence, with intelligent eyes, a bony, broad, very dark
face, and a cheerily officious manner (I learned later on he
was the executioner), presented to us two cups of coffee on
a brass tray, which he took from the hands of an inferior
attendant. "You needn't drink," muttered Jim very rapidly. I
didn't perceive the meaning at first, and only looked at him.
He took a good sip and sat composedly, holding the saucer
in his left hand. In a moment I felt excessively annoyed.
"Why the devil," I whispered, smiling at him amiably, "do
you expose me to such a stupid risk?" I drank, of course,
there was nothing for it, while he gave no sign, and almost
immediately afterwards we took our leave. While we were
going down the courtyard to our boat, escorted by the
intelligent and cheery executioner, Jim said he was very
sorry. It was the barest chance, of course. Personally he
thought nothing of poison. The remotest chance. He was –
he assured me – considered to be infinitely more useful
than dangerous, and so . . . "But the Rajah is afraid of you
abominably. Anybody can see that," I argued, with, I own, a
certain peevishness, and all the time watching anxiously for
the first twist of some sort of ghastly colic. I was awfully
disgusted. "If I am to do any good here and preserve my
position," he said, taking his seat by my side in the boat,
"I must stand the risk: I take it once every month, at least.

Many people trust me to do that – for them. Afraid of me! That's just it. Most likely he is afraid of me because I am not afraid of his coffee." Then showing me a place on the north front of the stockade where the pointed tops of several stakes were broken, "This is where I leaped over on my third day in Patusan. They haven't put new stakes there yet. Good leap, eh?" A moment later we passed the mouth of a muddy creek. "This is my second leap. I had a bit of a run and took this one flying, but fell short. Thought I would leave my skin there. Lost my shoes struggling. And all the time I was thinking to myself how beastly it would be to get a jab with a bally long spear while sticking in the mud like this. I remember how sick I felt wriggling in that slime. I mean really sick – as if I had bitten something rotten."

'That's how it was – and the opportunity ran by his side, leaped over the gap, floundered in the mud . . . still veiled. The unexpectedness of his coming was the only thing, you understand, that saved him from being at once despatched with krises and flung into the river. They had him, but it was like getting hold of an apparition, a wraith, a portent. What did it mean? What to do with it? Was it too late to conciliate him? Hadn't he better be killed without more delay? But what would happen then? Wretched old Allang went nearly mad with apprehension and through the difficulty of making up his mind. Several times the council was broken up, and the advisers made a break helter-skelter for the door and out on to the verandah. One – it is said – even jumped down to the ground – fifteen feet, I should judge – and broke his leg. The royal governor of Patusan had bizarre mannerisms, and one of them was to introduce boastful rhapsodies into every arduous discussion, when, getting gradually excited, he would end by flying off his perch with a kris in his hand. But, barring such interruptions, the deliberations upon Jim's fate went on night and day.

'Meanwhile he wandered about the courtyard, shunned by some, glared at by others, but watched by all, and practically at the mercy of the first casual ragamuffin with a chopper, in there. He took possession of a small tumble-down shed to sleep in; the effluvia of filth and rotten matter incommoded him greatly: it seems he had not lost his appetite though, because – he told me – he had been hungry all the blessed time. Now and again "some fussy ass" deputed from the council-room would come out running to him, and in honeyed tones would administer amazing interrogatories: "Were the Dutch coming to take the country? Would the white man like to go back down the river? What was the object of coming to such a miserable country? The Rajah wanted to know whether the white man could repair a watch?" They did actually bring out to him a nickel clock of New England make, and out of sheer unbearable boredom he busied himself in trying to get the alarum to work. It was apparently when thus occupied in his shed that the true perception of his extreme peril dawned upon him. He dropped the thing – he says – "like a hot potato," and walked out hastily, without the slightest idea of what he would, or indeed could, do. He only knew that the position was intolerable. He strolled aimlessly beyond a sort of ramshackle little granary on posts, and his eyes fell on the broken stakes of the palisade; and then – he says – at once, without any mental process as it were, without any stir of emotion, he set about his escape as if executing a plan matured for a month. He walked off carelessly to give himself a good run, and when he faced about there was some dignitary, with two spearmen in attendance, close at his elbow ready with a question. He started off "from under his very nose," went over "like a bird," and landed on the other side with a fall that jarred all his bones and seemed to split his head. He picked himself up instantly. He never thought of anything at the time; all he could remember – he said – was a great yell; the first houses of Patusan were before him four hundred yards away; he saw the creek, and as it were mechanically put on more pace. The earth seemed fairly to fly backwards under his feet. He took off from the last dry spot, felt himself flying through the air, felt himself, without any shock, planted upright in an extremely soft and sticky mudbank. It was only when he tried to move his legs and found he couldn't that, in his own words, "he came to himself." He began to think of the "bally long spears." As a matter of fact, considering that the people inside the stockade had to run to the gate, then get down to the landing-place, get into boats, and pull round a point of land, he had more advance than he imagined. Besides, it being low water, the creek was without water – you couldn't call it dry – and practically he was safe for a time from everything but a very long shot perhaps. The higher firm ground was about six feet in front of him. "I thought I would have to die there all the same," he said. He reached and grabbed desperately with his hands, and only succeeded in gathering a horrible cold shiny heap of slime against his breast – up to his very chin. It seemed to him he was burying himself alive, and then he struck out madly, scattering the mud with his fists. It fell on his head, on his face, over his eyes, into his mouth. He told me that he remembered suddenly the courtyard, as you remember a place where you had been very happy years ago. He longed – so he said – to be back there again, mending the clock. Mending the clock – that was the idea. He made efforts, tremendous sobbing, gasping efforts, efforts that seemed to burst his eyeballs in their sockets and make him blind, and culminating into one mighty supreme effort in the darkness to crack the earth asunder, to throw it off his limbs – and he felt himself creeping feebly up the bank. He lay full length on the firm ground and saw the light, the sky. Then as a sort of happy thought the notion came to him that he would go to sleep. He will have it that he *did* actually go to sleep; that he slept – perhaps for a minute, perhaps for twenty seconds, or only for one second, but he recollects distinctly the violent convulsive start of awakening. He remained lying still for a while, and then he arose muddy

from head to foot and stood there, thinking he was alone of
his kind for hundreds of miles, alone, with no help, no
sympathy, no pity to expect from any one, like a hunted
animal. The first houses were not more than twenty yards
from him; and it was the desperate screaming of a frightened woman trying to carry off a child that started him
again. He pelted straight on in his socks, beplastered with
filth out of all semblance to a human being. He traversed
more than half the length of the settlement. The nimbler
women fled right and left, the slower men just dropped
whatever they had in their hands, and remained petrified
with dropping jaws. He was a flying terror. He says he
noticed the little children trying to run for life, falling on
their little stomachs and kicking. He swerved between two
houses up a slope, clambered in desperation over a barri-
cade of felled trees (there wasn't a week without some fight
in Patusan at that time), burst through a fence into a maize-
patch, where a scared boy flung a stick at him, blundered
upon a path, and ran all at once into the arms of several
startled men. He just had breath enough to gasp out,
"Doramin! Doramin!" He remembers being half-carried,
half-rushed to the top of the slope, and in a vast enclosure
with palms and fruit-trees being run up to a large man
sitting massively in a chair in the midst of the greatest
possible commotion and excitement. He fumbled in mud
and clothes to produce the ring, and, finding himself suddenly on his back, wondered who had knocked him down.
They had simply let him go – don't you know? – but he
couldn't stand. At the foot of the slope random shots were
fired, and above the roofs of the settlement there rose a dull
roar of amazement. But he was safe. Doramin's people were
barricading the gate and pouring water down his throat;
Doramin's old wife, full of business and commiseration,
was issuing shrill orders to her girls. "The old woman," he
said, softly, "made a to-do over me as if I had been her own
son. They put me into an immense bed – her state bed –
and she ran in and out wiping her eyes to give me pats on

the back. I must have been a pitiful object. I just lay there like a log for I don't know how long."

'He seemed to have a great liking for Doramin's old wife. She on her side had taken a motherly fancy to him. She had a round, nut-brown, soft face, all fine wrinkles, large, bright red lips (she chewed betel assiduously), and screwed-up, winking, benevolent eyes. She was constantly in movement, scolding busily and ordering unceasingly a troop of young women with clear brown faces and big grave eyes, her daughters, her servants, her slave-girls. You know how it is in these households: it's generally impossible to tell the difference. She was very spare, and even her ample outer garment, fastened in front with jewelled clasps, had somehow a skimpy effect. Her dark bare feet were thrust into yellow straw slippers of Chinese make. I have seen her myself flitting about with her extremely thick, long, grey hair falling about her shoulders. She uttered homely shrewd sayings, was of noble birth, and was eccentric and arbitrary. In the afternoon she would sit in a very roomy arm-chair, opposite her husband, gazing steadily through a wide opening in the wall which gave an extensive view of the settlement and the river.

'She invariably tucked up her feet under her, but old Doramin sat squarely, sat imposingly as a mountain sits on a plain. He was only of the *nakhoda* or merchant class, but the respect shown to him and the dignity of his bearing were very striking. He was the chief of the second power in Patusan. The immigrants from Celebes (about sixty families that, with dependants and so on, could muster some two hundred men "wearing the kris") had elected him years ago for their head. The men of that race are intelligent, enterprising, revengeful, but with a more frank courage than the other Malays, and restless under oppression. They formed the party opposed to the Rajah. Of course the quarrels were for trade. This was the primary cause of faction fights, of the sudden outbreaks that would fill this or that part of the settlement with smoke, flame, the noise of shots and shrieks. Villages were burnt, men were dragged into the Rajah's stockade to be killed or tortured for the crime of trading with anybody else but himself. Only a day or two before Jim's arrival several heads of households in the very fishing village that was afterwards taken under his especial protection had been driven over the cliffs by a party of the Rajah's spearmen, on suspicion of having been collecting edible birds' nests for a Celebes trader. Rajah Allang pretended to be the only trader in his country, and the penalty for the breach of the monopoly was death; but his idea of trading was indistinguishable from the commonest forms of robbery. His cruelty and rapacity had no other bounds than his cowardice, and he was afraid of the organised power of the Celebes men, only – till Jim came – he was not afraid enough to keep quiet. He struck at them through his subjects, and thought himself pathetically in the right. The situation was complicated by a wandering stranger, an Arab half-breed, who, I believe, on purely religious grounds, had incited the tribes in the interior (the bushfolk, as Jim himself called them) to rise, and had established himself in a fortified camp on the summit of one of the twin hills. He hung over the town of Patusan like a hawk over a poultry-yard, but he devastated the open country. Whole villages, deserted, rotted on their blackened posts over the banks of clear streams, dropping piecemeal into the water the grass of their walls, the leaves of their roofs, with a curious effect of natural decay as if they had been a form of vegetation stricken by a blight at its very root. The two parties in Patusan were not sure which one this partisan most desired to plunder. The Rajah intrigued with him feebly. Some of the Bugis settlers, weary with endless insecurity, were half inclined to call him in. The younger spirits amongst them, chaffing, advised to "get Sherif Ali with his wild men and drive the Rajah Allang out of the country." Doramin restrained them with difficulty. He was growing old, and, though his influence had not diminished, the situation was getting beyond him. This was the state of affairs when Jim, bolting from the Rajah's stockade, appeared before the chief of the Bugis, produced the ring, and was received, in a manner of speaking, into the heart of the community.

# CHAPTER TWENTY-SIX

'DORAMIN was one of the most remarkable men of his race I had ever seen. His bulk for a Malay was immense, but he did not look merely fat; he looked imposing, monumental. This motionless body, clad in rich stuffs, coloured silks, gold embroideries; this huge head, enfolded in a red-and-gold head-kerchief; the flat, big, round face, wrinkled, furrowed, with two semicircular heavy folds starting on each side of wide, fierce nostrils, and enclosing a thick-lipped mouth; the throat like a bull; the vast corrugated brow overhanging the starting proud eyes – made a whole that, once seen, can never be forgotten. His impassive repose (he seldom stirred a limb when once he sat down) was like a display of dignity. He was never known to raise his voice. It was a hoarse and powerful murmur, slightly veiled as if heard from a distance. When he walked, two short, sturdy young fellows, naked to the waist, in white sarongs and with black skull-caps on the backs of their heads, sustained his elbows; they would ease him down and stand behind his chair till he wanted to rise, when he would turn his head slowly, as if with difficulty, to the right and to the left, and then they would catch him under his armpits and help him up. For all that, there was nothing of a cripple about him: on the contrary, all his ponderous movements were like manifestations of a mighty deliberate force. It was generally believed he consulted his wife as to public affairs; but nobody, as far as I know, had ever heard them exchange a single word. When they sat in state by the wide opening it was in silence. They could see below them in the declining light the vast expanse of the forest country, a dark sleeping sea of sombre green undulating as far as the

violet and purple range of mountains; the shining sinuosity
of the river like an immense letter S of beaten silver; the
brown ribbon of houses following the sweep of both banks,
overtopped by the twin hills uprising above the nearer tree-
tops. They were wonderfully contrasted: she, light, delicate, spare, quick, a little witch-like, with a touch of
motherly fussiness in her repose; he, facing her, immense
and heavy, like a figure of a man roughly fashioned of stone,
with something magnanimous and ruthless in his immobility. The son of these old people was a most distinguished youth.

'They had him late in life. Perhaps he was not really so
young as he looked. Four- or five-and-twenty is not so
young when a man is already father of a family at eighteen.
When he entered the large room, lined and carpeted with
fine mats, and with a high ceiling of white sheeting, where
the couple sat in state surrounded by a most deferential
retinue, he would make his way straight to Doramin, to
kiss his hand – which the other abandoned to him majes-
tically – and then would step across to stand by his mother's
chair. I suppose I may say they idolised him, but I never
caught them giving him an overt glance. Those, it is true,
were public functions. The room was generally thronged.
The solemn formality of greetings and leave-takings, the
profound respect expressed in gestures, on the faces, in the
low whispers, is simply indescribable. "It's well worth seeing," Jim had assured me while we were crossing the river,
on our way back. "They are like people in a book, aren't
they?" he said triumphantly. "And Dain Waris – their son –
is the best friend (barring you) I ever had. What Mr Stein
would call a good 'war-comrade.' I was in luck. Jove! I was
in luck when I tumbled amongst them at my last gasp." He
meditated with bowed head, then rousing himself he
added:

'"Of course I didn't go to sleep over it, but..." He
paused again. "It seemed to come to me," he murmured.
"All at once I saw what I had to do..."

'There was no doubt that it had come to him; and it had come through the war, too, as is natural, since this power that came to him was the power to make peace. It is in this sense alone that might so often *is* right. You must not think he had seen his way at once. When he arrived the Bugis community was in a most critical position. "They were all afraid," he said to me – "each man afraid for himself; while I could see as plain as possible that they must do something at once, if they did not want to go under one after another, what between the Rajah and that vagabond Sherif." But to see that was nothing. When he got his idea he had to drive it into reluctant minds, through the bulwarks of fear, of selfishness. He drove it in at last. And that was nothing. He had to devise the means. He devised them – an audacious plan; and his task was only half done. He had to inspire with his own confidence a lot of people who had hidden and absurd reasons to hang back; he had to conciliate imbecile jealousies, and argue away all sorts of senseless mistrusts. Without the weight of Doramin's authority, and his son's fiery enthusiasm, he would have failed. Dain Waris, the distinguished youth, was the first to believe in him; theirs was one of those strange, profound, rare friendships between brown and white, in which the very difference of race seems to draw two human beings closer by some mystic element of sympathy. Of Dain Waris, his own people said with pride that he knew how to fight like a white man. This was true; he had that sort of courage – the courage in the open, I may say – but he had also a European mind. You meet them sometimes like that, and are surprised to discover unexpectedly a familiar turn of thought, an unobscured vision, a tenacity of purpose, a touch of altruism. Of small stature, but admirably well proportioned, Dain Waris had a proud carriage, a polished, easy bearing, a temperament like a clear flame. His dusky face, with big black eyes, was in action expressive, and in repose thoughtful. He was of a silent disposition; a firm glance, an ironic smile, a courteous deliberation of manner seemed to hint at great reserves of intelligence and power. Such beings open to the Western eye, so often concerned with mere surfaces, the hidden possibilities of races and lands over which hangs the mystery of unrecorded ages. He not only trusted Jim, he understood him, I firmly believe. I speak of him because he had captivated me. His – if I may say so – his caustic placidity, and, at the same time, his intelligent sympathy with Jim's aspirations, appealed to me. I seemed to behold the very origin of friendship. If Jim took the lead, the other had captivated his leader. In fact, Jim the leader was a captive in every sense. The land, the people, the friendship, the love, were like the jealous guardians of his body. Every day added a link to the fetters of that strange freedom. I felt convinced of it, as from day to day I learned more of the story.

'The story! Haven't I heard the story? I've heard it on the march, in camp (he made me scour the country after invisible game); I've listened to a good part of it on one of the twin summits, after climbing the last hundred feet or so on my hands and knees. Our escort (we had volunteer followers from village to village) had camped meantime on a bit of level ground half-way up the slope, and in the still breathless evening the smell of wood-smoke reached our nostrils from below with the penetrating delicacy of some choice scent. Voices also ascended, wonderful in their distinct and immaterial clearness. Jim sat on the trunk of a felled tree, and pulling out his pipe began to smoke. A new growth of grass and bushes was springing up; there were traces of an earthwork under a mass of thorny twigs. "It all started from here," he said, after a long and meditative silence. On the other hill, two hundred yards across a sombre precipice, I saw a line of high blackened stakes, showing here and there ruinously – the remnants of Sherif Ali's impregnable camp.

'But it had been taken though. That had been his idea. He had mounted Doramin's old ordnance on the top of that hill; two rusty iron 7-pounders, a lot of small brass cannon – currency cannon. But if the brass guns represent wealth, they can also, when crammed recklessly to the muzzle, send a solid shot to some little distance. The thing was to get them up there. He showed me where he had fastened the cables, explained how he had improvised a rude capstan out of a hollowed long turning upon a pointed stake, indicated with the bowl of his pipe the outline of the earthwork. The last hundred feet of the ascent had been the most difficult. He had made himself responsible for success on his own head. He had induced the war party to work hard all night. Big fires lighted at intervals blazed all down the slope, "but up here," he explained, "the hoisting gang had to fly around in the dark." From the top he saw men moving on the hill-side like ants at work. He himself on that night had kept on rushing down and climbing up like a squirrel, directing, encouraging, watching all along the line. Old Doramin had himself carried up the hill in his arm-chair. They put him down on the level place upon the slope, and he sat there in the light of one of the big fires – "amazing old chap – real old chieftain," said Jim, "with his little fierce eyes – a pair of immense flintlock pistols on his knees. Magnificent things, ebony, silver-mounted, with beautiful locks and a calibre like an old blunderbuss. A present from Stein, it seems – in exchange for that ring, you know. Used to belong to good old M'Neil. God only knows how *he* came by them. There he sat, moving neither hand nor foot, a flame of dry brushwood behind him, and lots of people rushing about, shouting and pulling round him – the most solemn, imposing old chap you can imagine. *He* wouldn't have had much chance if Sherif Ali had let his infernal crew loose at us and stampeded my lot. Eh? Anyhow, he had come up there to die if anything went wrong. No mistake! Jove! It thrilled me to see him there – like a rock. But the Sherif must have thought us mad, and never troubled to come and see how we got on. Nobody believed it could be done. Why! I think the very chaps who pulled and shoved and sweated over it did not believe it could be done! Upon my word I don't think they did...."

'He stood erect, the smouldering brier-wood in his clutch, with a smile on his lips and a sparkle in his boyish eyes. I sat on the stump of a tree at his feet, and below us stretched the land, the great expanse of the forests, sombre under the sunshine, rolling like a sea, with glints of winding rivers, the grey spots of villages, and here and there a clearing, like an islet of light amongst the dark waves of continuous tree-tops. A brooding gloom lay over this vast and monotonous landscape; the light fell on it as if into an abyss. The land devoured the sunshine; only far off, along the coast, the empty ocean, smooth and polished within the faint haze, seemed to rise up to the sky in a wall of steel.

'And there I was with him, high in the sunshine on the top of that historic hill of his. He dominated the forest, the secular gloom, the old mankind. He was like a figure set up on a pedestal, to represent in his persistent youth the power, and perhaps the virtues, of races that never grow old, that have emerged from the gloom. I don't know why he should always have appeared to me symbolic. Perhaps this is the real cause of my interest in his fate. I don't know whether it was exactly fair to him to remember the incident which had given a new direction to his life, but at that very moment I remembered very distinctly. It was like a shadow in the light.'

# CHAPTER TWENTY-SEVEN

'ALREADY the legend had gifted him with supernatural powers. Yes, it was said, there had been many ropes cunningly disposed, and a strange contrivance that turned by the efforts of many men, and each gun went up tearing slowly through the bushes, like a wild pig rooting its way in the undergrowth, but . . . and the wisest shook their heads. There was something occult in all this, no doubt; for what is the strength of ropes and of men's arms? There is a rebellious soul in things which must be overcome by powerful charms and incantations. Thus old Sura – a very respectable householder of Patusan – with whom I had a quiet chat one evening. However, Sura was a professional sorcerer also, who attended all the rice sowings and reapings for miles around for the purpose of subduing the stubborn soul of things. This occupation he seemed to think a most arduous one, and perhaps the souls of things are more stubborn than the souls of men. As to the simple folk of outlying villages, they believed and said (as the most natural thing in the world) that Jim had carried the guns up the hill on his back – two at a time.

'This would make Jim stamp his foot in vexation and exclaim with an exasperated little laugh. "What can you do with such silly beggars? They will sit up half the night talking bally rot, and the greater the lie the more they seem to like it." You could trace the subtle influence of his surroundings in this irritation. It was part of his captivity. The earnestness of his denials was amusing, and at last I said, "My dear fellow, you don't suppose *I* believe this." He looked at me quite startled. "Well, no! I suppose not," he said, and burst into a Homeric peal of laughter. "Well, anyhow the guns were there, and went off together at sunrise. Jove! You should have seen the splinters fly," he cried. By his side Dain Waris, listening with a quiet smile, dropped his eyelids and shuffled his feet a little. It appears that the success in mounting the guns had given Jim's people such a feeling of confidence that he ventured to leave the battery under charge of two elderly Bugis who had seen some fighting in their day, and went to join Dain Waris and the storming party who were concealed in the ravine. In the small hours they began creeping up, and when two-thirds of the way up, lay in the wet grass waiting for the appearance of the sun, which was the agreed signal. He told me with what impatient anguishing emotion he watched the swift coming of the dawn; how, heated with the work and the climbing, he felt the cold dew chilling his very bones; how afraid he was he would begin to shiver and shake like a leaf before the time came for the advance. "It was the slowest half-hour in my life," he declared. Gradually the silent stockade came out on the sky above him. Men scattered all down the slope were crouching amongst the dark stones and dripping bushes. Dain Waris was lying flattened by his side. "We looked at each other," Jim said, resting a gentle hand on his friend's shoulder. "He smiled at me as cheery as you please, and I dared not stir my lips for fear I would break out into a shivering fit. 'Pon my word, it's true! I had been streaming with perspiration when we took cover – so you may imagine..." He declared, and I believe him, that he had no fears as to the result. He was only anxious as to his ability to repress these shivers. He didn't bother about the result. He was bound to get to the top of that hill and stay there, whatever might happen. There could be no going back for him. Those people had trusted him implicitly. Him alone! His bare word....

'I remember how, at this point, he paused with his eyes fixed upon me. "As far as he knew, they never had an occasion to regret it yet," he said. "Never. He hoped to

God they never would. Meantime – worse luck! – they had
got into the habit of taking his word for anything and
everything. I could have no idea! Why? Only the other
day an old fool he had never seen in his life came from some
village miles away to find out if he should divorce his wife.
Fact. Solemn word. That's the sort of thing.... He
wouldn't have believed it. Would I? Squatted on the
verandah chewing betel-nut, sighing and spitting all over
the place for more than an hour, and as glum as an under-
taker before he came out with that dashed conundrum.
That's the kind of thing that isn't so funny as it looks. What
was a fellow to say? – Good wife? – Yes. Good wife – old
though; started a confounded long story about some brass
pots. Been living together for fifteen years – twenty years –
could not tell. A long, long time. Good wife. Beat her a
little – not much – just a little, when she was young. Had to
– for the sake of his honour. Suddenly in her old age she
goes and lends three brass pots to her sister's son's wife, and
begins to abuse him every day in a loud voice. His enemies
jeered at him; his face was utterly blackened. Pots totally
lost. Awfully cut up about it. Impossible to fathom a story
like that; told him to go home, and promised to come along
myself and settle it all. It's all very well to grin, but it was
the dashedest nuisance! A day's journey through the forest,
another day lost in coaxing a lot of silly villagers to get at
the rights of the affair. There was the making of a sanguin-
ary shindy in the thing. Every bally idiot took sides with
one family or the other, and one half of the village was
ready to go for the other half with anything that came
handy. Honour bright! No joke!... Instead of attending
to their bally crops. Got him the infernal pots back of
course – and pacified all hands. No trouble to settle it. Of
course not. Could settle the deadliest quarrel in the country
by crooking his little finger. The trouble was to get at the
truth of anything. Was not sure to this day whether he had
been fair to all parties. It worried him. And the talk! Jove!
There didn't seem to be any head or tail to it. Rather storm

a twenty-foot-high old stockade any day. Much! Child's
play to that other job. Wouldn't take so long either. Well,
yes; a funny set out, upon the whole – the fool looked old
enough to be his grandfather. But from another point of
view it was no joke. His word decided everything – ever
since the smashing of Sherif Ali. An awful responsibility,"
he repeated. "No, really – joking apart, had it been three
lives instead of three rotten brass pots it would have been
the same...."

'Thus he illustrated the moral effect of his victory in war.
It was in truth immense. It had led him from strife to peace,
and through death into the innermost life of the people;
but the gloom of the land spread out under the sunshine
preserved its appearance of inscrutable, of secular repose.
The sound of his fresh young voice – it's extraordinary how
very few signs of wear he showed – floated lightly, and
passed away over the unchanged face of the forests like the
sound of the big guns on that cold dewy morning when he
had no other concern on earth but the proper control of the
chills in his body. With the first slant of sun-rays along
these immovable tree-tops the summit of one hill wreathed
itself, with heavy reports, in white clouds of smoke, and the
other burst into an amazing noise of yells, war-cries, shouts
of anger, of surprise, of dismay. Jim and Dain Waris were
the first to lay their hands on the stakes. The popular story
has it that Jim with a touch of one finger had thrown down
the gate. He was, of course, anxious to disclaim this
achievement. The whole stockade – he would insist on
explaining to you – was a poor affair (Sherif Ali trusted
mainly to the inaccessible position); and, anyway, the
thing had been already knocked to pieces and only hung
together by a miracle. He put his shoulder to it like a little
fool and went in head over heels. Jove! If it hadn't been for
Dain Waris, a pock-marked tattooed vagabond would
have pinned him with his spear to a baulk of timber like
one of Stein's beetles. The third man in, it seems, had been
Tamb' Itam, Jim's own servant. This was a Malay from the

north, a stranger who had wandered into Patusan, and had been forcibly detained by Rajah Allang as paddler of one of the state boats. He had made a bolt of it at the first opportunity, and finding a precarious refuge (but very little to eat) amongst the Bugis settlers, had attached himself to Jim's person. His complexion was very dark, his face flat, his eyes prominent and injected with bile. There was something excessive, almost fanatical, in his devotion to his "white lord." He was inseparable from Jim like a morose shadow. On state occasions he would tread on his master's heels, one hand on the haft of his kris, keeping the common people at a distance by his truculent brooding glances. Jim had made him the head-man of his establishment, and all Patusan respected and courted him as a person of much influence. At the taking of the stockade he had distinguished himself greatly by the methodical ferocity of his fighting. The storming-party had come on so quick – Jim said – that notwithstanding the panic of the garrison, there was a "hot five minutes hand-to-hand inside that stockade, till some bally ass set fire to the shelters of boughs and dry grass, and we all had to clear out for dear life."

'The rout, it seems, had been complete. Doramin waiting immovably in his chair on the hillside, with the smoke of the guns spreading slowly above his big head, received the news with a deep grunt. When informed that his son was safe and leading the pursuit, he, without another sound, made a mighty effort to rise; his attendants hurried to his help, and, held up reverently, he shuffled with great dignity into a bit of shade where he laid himself down to sleep covered entirely with a piece of white sheeting. In Patusan the excitement was intense. Jim told me that from the hill, turning his back on the stockade with its embers, black ashes, and half-consumed corpses, he could see time after time the open spaces between the houses on both sides of the stream fill suddenly with a seething rush of people and get empty in a moment. His ears caught feebly from below the tremendous din of gongs and drums; the wild shouts of the crowd reached him in bursts of faint roaring. A lot of streamers made a flutter as of little white, red, yellow birds amongst the brown ridges of roofs. "You must have enjoyed it," I murmured, feeling the stir of sympathetic emotion.

'"It was... it was immense! Immense!" he cried aloud, flinging his arms open. The sudden movement startled me as though I had seen him bare the secrets of his breast to the sunshine, to the brooding forests, to the steely sea. Below us the town reposed in easy curves upon the banks of a stream whose current seemed to sleep. "Immense!" he repeated for a third time, speaking in a whisper, for himself alone.

'Immense! No doubt it was immense; the seal of success upon his words, the conquered ground for the soles of his feet, the blind trust of men, the belief in himself snatched from the fire, the solitude of his achievement. All this, as I've warned you, gets dwarfed in the telling. I can't with mere words convey to you the impression of his total and utter isolation. I know, of course, he was in every sense alone of his kind there, but the unsuspected qualities of his nature had brought him in such close touch with his surroundings that this isolation seemed only the effect of his power. His loneliness added to his stature. There was nothing within sight to compare him with, as though he had been one of those exceptional men who can be only measured by the greatness of their fame; and his fame, remember, was the greatest thing around for many a day's journey. You would have to paddle, pole, or track a long weary way through the jungle before you passed beyond the reach of its voice. Its voice was not the trumpeting of the disreputable goddess we all know – not blatant – not brazen. It took its tone from the stillness and gloom of the land without a past, where his word was the one truth of every passing day. It shared something of the nature of that silence through which it accompanied you into

unexplored depths, heard continuously by your side, penetrating, far-reaching – tinged with wonder and mystery on
the lips of whispering men.

# CHAPTER TWENTY-EIGHT

'THE defeated Sherif Ali fled the country without making another stand, and when the miserable hunted villagers began to crawl out of the jungle back to their rotting houses, it was Jim who, in consultation with Dain Waris, appointed the headmen. Thus he became the virtual ruler of the land. As to old Tunku Allang, his fears at first had known no bounds. It is said that at the intelligence of the successful storming of the hill he flung himself, face down, on the bamboo floor of his audience-hall, and lay motionless for a whole night and a whole day, uttering stifled sounds of such an appalling nature that no man dared approach his prostrate form nearer than a spear's length. Already he could see himself driven ignominiously out of Patusan, wandering abandoned, stripped, without opium, without his women, without followers, a fair game for the first comer to kill. After Sherif Ali his turn would come, and who could resist an attack led by such a devil? And indeed he owed his life and such authority as he still possessed at the time of my visit to Jim's idea of what was fair alone. The Bugis had been extremely anxious to pay off old scores, and the impassive old Doramin cherished the hope of yet seeing his son ruler of Patusan. During one of our interviews he deliberately allowed me to get a glimpse of this secret ambition. Nothing could be finer in its way than the dignified wariness of his approaches. He himself – he began by declaring – had used his strength in his young days, but now he had grown old and tired. . . . With his imposing bulk and haughty little eyes darting sagacious, inquisitive glances, he reminded one irresistibly of a cunning old elephant; the slow rise and fall of his vast breast

went on powerful and regular, like the heave of a calm sea.
He, too, as he protested, had an unbounded confidence in
Tuan Jim's wisdom. If he could only obtain a promise! One
word would be enough!... His breathing silences, the low
rumblings of his voice, recalled the last efforts of a spent
thunderstorm.

'I tried to put the subject aside. It was difficult, for there
could be no question that Jim had the power; in his new
sphere there did not seem to be anything that was not his to
hold or to give. But that, I repeat, was nothing in com-
parison with the notion, which occurred to me, while
I listened with a show of attention, that he seemed to have
come very near at last to mastering his fate. Doramin was
anxious about the future of the country, and I was struck by
the turn he gave to the argument. The land remains where
God had put it; but white men – he said – they come to us
and in a little while they go. They go away. Those they leave
behind do not know when to look for their return. They go
to their own land, to their people, and so this white man,
too, would.... I don't know what induced me to commit
myself at this point by a vigorous "No, no." The whole
extent of this indiscretion became apparent when
Doramin, turning full upon me his face, whose expression,
fixed in rugged deep folds, remained unalterable, like a
huge brown mask, said that this was good news indeed,
reflectively; and then wanted to know why.

'His little, motherly witch of a wife sat on my other
hand, with her head covered and her feet tucked up, gazing
through the great shutter-hole. I could only see a straying
lock of grey hair, a high cheek-bone, the slight masticating
motion of the sharp chin. Without removing her eyes from
the vast prospect of forests stretching as far as the hills, she
asked me in a pitying voice why was it that he so young had
wandered from his home, coming so far, through so many
dangers? Had he no household there, no kinsmen in his
own country? Had he no old mother, who would always
remember his face?...

'I was completely unprepared for this. I could only mutter and shake my head vaguely. Afterwards I am perfectly aware I cut a very poor figure trying to extricate myself out of this difficulty. From that moment, however, the old *nakhoda* became taciturn. He was not very pleased, I fear, and evidently I had given him food for thought. Strangely enough, on the evening of that very day (which was my last in Patusan) I was once more confronted with the same question, with the unanswerable why of Jim's fate. And this brings me to the story of his love.

'I suppose you think it is a story that you can imagine for yourselves. We have heard so many such stories, and the majority of us don't believe them to be stories of love at all. For the most part we look upon them as stories of opportunities: episodes of passion at best, or perhaps only of youth and temptation, doomed to forgetfulness in the end, even if they pass through the reality of tenderness and regret. This view mostly is right, and perhaps in this case, too.... Yet I don't know. To tell this story is by no means so easy as it should be – were the ordinary standpoint adequate. Apparently it is a story very much like the others: for me, however, there is visible in its background the melancholy figure of a woman, the shadow of a cruel wisdom buried in a lonely grave, looking on wistfully, helplessly, with sealed lips. The grave itself, as I came upon it during an early morning stroll, was a rather shapeless brown mound, with an inlaid neat border of white lumps of coral at the base, and enclosed within a circular fence made of split saplings, with the bark left on. A garland of leaves and flowers was woven about the heads of the slender posts – and the flowers were fresh.

'Thus, whether the shadow is of my imagination or not, I can at all events point out the significant fact of an unforgotten grave. When I tell you besides that Jim with his own hands had worked at the rustic fence, you will perceive directly the difference, the individual side of the story. There is in his espousal of memory and affection

belonging to another human being something characteristic of his seriousness. He had a conscience, and it was a
romantic conscience. Through her whole life the wife of
the unspeakable Cornelius had no other companion, confidant, and friend but her daughter. How the poor woman
had come to marry the awful Malacca Portuguese – after
the separation from the father of her girl – and how that
separation had been brought about, whether by death,
which can be sometimes merciful, or by the merciless
pressure of conventions, is a mystery to me. From the little
which Stein (who knew so many stories) had let drop in my
hearing, I am convinced that she was no ordinary woman.
Her own father had been a white; a high official; one of the
brilliantly endowed men who are not dull enough to nurse a
success, and whose careers so often end under a cloud.
I suppose she, too, must have lacked the saving dullness –
and her career ended in Patusan. Our common fate . . . for
where is the man – I mean a real sentient man – who does
not remember vaguely having been deserted in the fullness
of possession by some one or something more precious
than life? . . . our common fate fastens upon the women
with a peculiar cruelty. It does not punish like a master,
but inflicts lingering torment, as if to gratify a secret,
unappeasable spite. One would think that, appointed to
rule on earth, it seeks to revenge itself upon the beings that
come nearest to rising above the trammels of earthly caution; for it is only women who manage to put at times into
their love an element just palpable enough to give one a
fright – an extra-terrestrial touch. I ask myself with wonder
– how the world can look to them – whether it has the
shape and substance *we* know, the air *we* breathe!
Sometimes I fancy it must be a region of unreasonable
sublimities seething with the excitement of their adventurous souls, lighted by the glory of all possible risks and
renunciations. However, I suspect there are very few
women in the world, though of course I am aware of the
multitudes of mankind and of the equality of sexes in point

of numbers – that is. But I am sure that the mother was as much of a woman as the daughter seemed to be. I cannot help picturing to myself these two, at first the young woman and the child, then the old woman and the young girl, the awful sameness and the swift passage of time, the barrier of forest, the solitude and the turmoil round these two lonely lives, and every word spoken between them penetrated with sad meaning. There must have been confidences, not so much of fact, I suppose, as of innermost feelings – regrets – fears – warnings, no doubt: warnings that the younger did not fully understand till the elder was dead – and Jim came along. Then I am sure she understood much – not everything – the fear mostly it seems. Jim called her by a word that means precious, in the sense of a precious gem – jewel. Pretty, isn't it? But he was capable of anything. He was equal to his fortune, as he – after all – must have been equal to his misfortune. Jewel he called her; and he would say this as he might have said "Jane," don't you know – with a marital, homelike, peaceful effect. I heard the name for the first time ten minutes after I had landed in his courtyard, when, after nearly shaking my arm off, he darted up the steps and began to make a joyous, boyish disturbance at the door under the heavy eaves. "Jewel! O Jewel! Quick! Here's a friend come,"... and suddenly peering at me in the dim verandah, he mumbled earnestly, "You know – this – no confounded nonsense about it – can't tell you how much I owe to her – and so – you understand – I – exactly as if..." His hurried, anxious whispers were cut short by the flitting of a white form within the house, a faint exclamation, and a childlike but energetic little face with delicate features and a profound, attentive glance peeped out of the inner gloom, like a bird out of the recess of a nest. I was struck by the name, of course; but it was not till later on that I connected it with an astonishing rumour that had met me on my journey, at a little place on the coast about 230 miles south of Patusan river. Stein's schooner, in which I had my passage, put in there, to collect some produce, and going ashore, I found to my great surprise that the wretched locality could boast of a third-class deputy-assistant resident, a big, fat, greasy, blinking fellow of mixed descent, with turned-out, shiny lips. I found him lying extended on his back in a cane chair, odiously unbuttoned, with a large green leaf of some sort on the top of his steaming head, and another in his hand which he used lazily as a fan.... Going to Patusan? Oh, yes. Stein's Trading Company. He knew. Had a permission. No business of his. It was not so bad there now, he remarked negligently, and, he went on drawling, "There's some sort of white vagabond had got in there, I hear.... Eh? What you say? Friends of yours? So!... Then it was true there was one of these *vordamte* – What was he up to? Found his way in, the rascal. Eh? I had not been sure. Patusan – they cut throats there – no business of ours." He interrupted himself to groan. "Phoo! Almighty! The heat! The heat! Well, then, there might be something in the story, too, after all, and..." He shut one of his beastly glassy eyes (the eyelid went on quivering), while he leered at me atrociously with the other. "Look here," says he, mysteriously, "if – do you understand? – if he has really got hold of something fairly good – none of your bits of green glass – understand? – I am a government official – you tell the rascal ... Eh? What? Friend of yours?" ... He continued wallowing calmly in the chair.... "You said so; that's just it; and I am pleased to give you the hint. I suppose you, too, would like to get something out of it? Don't interrupt. You just tell him I've heard the tale, but to my government I have made no report. Not yet. See? Why make a report? Eh? Tell him to come to me if they let him get alive out of the country. He had better look out for himself. Eh? I promise to ask no questions. On the quiet – you understand? You, too – you shall get something from me. Small commission for the trouble. Don't interrupt. I am a government official, and make no report. That's business. Understand? I know some good people that will buy anything worth having, and can give him more money than the scoundrel ever saw in his life. I know his sort." He fixed me steadfastly with both his eyes open, while I stood over him utterly amazed, and asking myself whether he was mad or drunk. He perspired, puffed, moaning feebly, and scratching himself with such horrible composure that I could not bear the sight long enough to find out. Next day, talking casually with the people of the little native court of the place, I discovered that a story was travelling slowly down the coast about a mysterious white man in Patusan who had got hold of an extraordinary gem – namely, an emerald of an enormous size, and altogether priceless. The emerald seems to appeal more to the Eastern imagination than any other precious stone. The white man had obtained it, I was told, partly by the exercise of his wonderful strength and partly by cunning, from the ruler of a distant country, whence he had fled instantly, arriving in Patusan in utmost distress, but frightening the people by his extreme ferocity, which nothing seemed able to subdue. Most of my informants were of the opinion that the stone was probably unlucky, – like the famous stone of the Sultan of Succadana, which in the old times had brought wars and untold calamities upon that country. Perhaps it was the same stone – one couldn't say. Indeed the story of a fabulously large emerald is as old as the arrival of the first white men in the Archipelago; and the belief in it is so persistent that less than forty years ago there had been an official Dutch inquiry into the truth of it. Such a jewel – it was explained to me by the old fellow from whom I heard most of this amazing Jim-myth – a sort of scribe to the wretched little Rajah of the place; – such a jewel, he said, cocking his poor purblind eyes up at me (he was sitting on the cabin floor out of respect), is best preserved by being concealed about the person of a woman. Yet it is not every woman that would do. She must be young – he sighed deeply – and insensible to the seductions of love. He shook his head sceptically. But such a woman seemed to be actually in existence. He had been told of a tall girl, whom the white man treated with great respect and care, and who never went forth from the house unattended. People said the white man could be seen with her almost any day; they walked side by side, openly, he holding her arm under his – pressed to his side – thus – in a most extraordinary way. This might be a lie, he conceded, for it was indeed a strange thing for any one to do: on the other hand, there could be no doubt she wore the white man's jewel concealed upon her bosom.'

# CHAPTER TWENTY-NINE

'This was the theory of Jim's marital evening walks. I made a third on more than one occasion, unpleasantly aware every time of Cornelius, who nursed the aggrieved sense of his legal paternity, slinking in the neighbourhood with that peculiar twist of his mouth as if he were perpetually on the point of gnashing his teeth. But do you notice how, three hundred miles beyond the end of telegraph cables and mail-boat lines, the haggard utilitarian lies of our civilisation wither and die, to be replaced by pure exercises of imagination, that have the futility, often the charm, and sometimes the deep hidden truthfulness, of works of art? Romance had singled Jim for its own – and that was the true part of the story, which otherwise was all wrong. He did not hide his jewel. In fact, he was extremely proud of it.

'It comes to me now that I had, on the whole, seen very little of her. What I remember best is the even, olive pallor of her complexion, and the intense blue-black gleams of her hair, flowing abundantly from under a small crimson cap she wore far back on her shapely head. Her movements were free, assured, and she blushed a dusky red. While Jim and I were talking, she would come and go with rapid glances at us, leaving on her passage an impression of grace and charm and a distinct suggestion of watchfulness. Her manner presented a curious combination of shyness and audacity. Every pretty smile was succeeded swiftly by a look of silent, repressed anxiety, as if put to flight by the recollection of some abiding danger. At times she would sit down with us and, with her soft cheek dimpled by the knuckles of her little hand, she would listen to our talk; her big clear eyes would remain fastened on our lips, as though each pronounced word had a visible shape. Her mother had taught her to read and write; she had learned a good bit of English from Jim, and she spoke it most amusingly, with his own clipping, boyish intonation. Her tenderness hovered over him like a flutter of wings. She lived so completely in his contemplation that she had acquired something of his outward aspect, something that recalled him in her movements, in the way she stretched her arm, turned her head, directed her glances. Her vigilant affection had an intensity that made it almost perceptible to the senses; it seemed actually to exist in the ambient matter of space, to envelop him like a peculiar fragrance, to dwell in the sunshine like a tremulous, subdued, and impassioned note. I suppose you think that I, too, am romantic, but it is a mistake. I am relating to you the sober impressions of a bit of youth, of a strange uneasy romance that had come in my way. I observed with interest the work of his – well – good fortune. He was jealously loved, but why she should be jealous, and of what, I could not tell. The land, the people, the forests were her accomplices, guarding him with vigilant accord, with an air of seclusion, of mystery, of invincible possession. There was no appeal, as it were; he was imprisoned within the very freedom of his power, and she, though ready to make a footstool of her head for his feet, guarded her conquest inflexibly – as though he were hard to keep. The very Tamb' Itam, marching on our journeys upon the heels of his white lord, with his head thrown back, truculent and beweaponed like a janissary, with kris, chopper, and lance (besides carrying Jim's gun); even Tamb' Itam allowed himself to put on the airs of uncompromising guardianship, like a surly devoted jailer ready to lay down his life for his captive. On the evenings when we sat up late his silent, indistinct form would pass and repass under the verandah, with noiseless footsteps, or lifting my head I would unexpectedly make him out standing rigidly erect in the shadow. As a general rule he would vanish after a time, without a sound; but when we rose he would spring up close to us as if from the ground, ready for any orders Jim might wish to give. The girl, too, I believe, never went to sleep till we had separated for the night. More than once I saw her and Jim through the window of my room come out together quietly and lean on the rough balustrade – two white forms very close, his arm about her waist, her head on his shoulder. Their soft murmurs reached me, penetrating, tender, with a calm sad note in the stillness of the night, like a self-communion of one being carried on in two tones. Later on, tossing on my bed under the mosquito-net, I was sure to hear slight creakings, faint breathing, a throat cleared cautiously – and I would know that Tamb' Itam was still on the prowl. Though he had (by the favour of the white lord) a house in the compound, had "taken wife," and had lately been blessed with a child, I believe that, during my stay at all events, he slept on the verandah every night. It was very difficult to make this faithful and grim retainer talk. Even Jim himself was answered in jerky short sentences, under protest as it were. Talking, he seemed to imply, was no business of his. The longest speech I heard him volunteer was one morning when, suddenly extending his hand towards the courtyard, he pointed at Cornelius and said, "Here comes the Nazarene." I don't think he was addressing me, though I stood at his side; his object seemed rather to awaken the indignant attention of the universe. Some muttered allusions, which followed, to dogs and the smell of roast-meat, struck me as singularly felicitous. The court-yard, a large square space, was one torrid blaze of sunshine, and, bathed in intense light, Cornelius was creeping across in full view with an inexpressible effect of stealthiness, of dark and secret slinking. He reminded one of everything that is unsavoury. His slow laborious walk resembled the creeping of a repulsive beetle, the legs alone moving with horrid industry while the body glided evenly. I suppose he made straight enough for the place where he wanted to get to, but his progress with one shoulder carried forward seemed oblique. He was often seen circling slowly amongst the sheds, as if following a scent; passing before the verandah with upward stealthy glances; disappearing without haste round the corner of some hut. That he seemed free of the place demonstrated Jim's absurd carelessness or else his infinite disdain, for Cornelius had played a very dubious part (to say the least of it) in a certain episode which might have ended fatally for Jim. As a matter of fact, it had redounded to his glory. But everything redounded to his glory; and it was the irony of his good fortune that he, who had been too careful of it once, seemed to bear a charmed life.

'You must know he had left Doramin's place very soon after his arrival – much too soon, in fact, for his safety, and of course a long time before the war. In this he was actuated by a sense of duty; he had to look after Stein's business, he said. Hadn't he? To that end, with an utter disregard of his personal safety, he crossed the river and took up his quarters with Cornelius. How the latter had managed to exist through the troubled times I can't say. As Stein's agent, after all, he must have had Doramin's protection in a measure; and in one way or another he had managed to wriggle through all the deadly complications, while I have no doubt that his conduct, whatever line he was forced to take, was marked by that abjectness which was like the stamp of the man. That was his characteristic; he was fundamentally and outwardly abject, as other men are markedly of a generous, distinguished, or venerable appearance. It was the element of his nature which permeated all his acts and passions and emotions; he raged abjectly, smiled abjectly, was abjectly sad; his civilities and his indignations were alike abject. I am sure his love would have been the most abject of sentiments – but can one imagine a loathsome insect in love? And his loathsomeness, too, was abject, so that a simply disgusting person would have appeared noble by his side. He has his place neither in the background nor in the foreground of the story; he is simply seen skulking on its outskirts, enigmatical and unclean, tainting the fragrance of its youth and of its naïveness.

'His position in any case could not have been other than extremely miserable, yet it may very well be that he found some advantages in it. Jim told me he had been received at first with an abject display of the most amicable sentiments. "The fellow apparently couldn't contain himself for joy," said Jim with disgust. "He flew at me every morning to shake both my hands – confound him! but I could never tell whether there would be any breakfast. If I got three meals in two days I considered myself jolly lucky, and he made me sign a chit for ten dollars every week. Said he was sure Mr Stein did not mean him to keep me for nothing. Well – he kept me on nothing as near as possible. Put it down to the unsettled state of the country, and made as if to tear his hair out, begging my pardon twenty times a day, so that I had at last to entreat him not to worry. It made me sick. Half the roof of his house had fallen in, and the whole place had a mangy look, with wisps of dry grass sticking out and the corners of broken mats flapping on every wall. He did his best to make out that Mr Stein owed him money on the last three years' trading, but his books were all torn, and some were missing. He tried to hint it was his late wife's fault. Disgusting scoundrel! At last I had to forbid him to mention his late wife at all. It made Jewel cry. I couldn't discover what became of all the trade-goods; there was nothing in the store but rats, having a high old time amongst a litter of brown paper and old sacking. I was assured on every hand that he had a lot of money buried somewhere, but of course could get nothing out of him. It was the most miserable existence I led there in that wretched house. I tried to do my duty by Stein, but I had also other matters to think of. When I escaped to Doramin old Tunku Allang got frightened and returned all my things. It was done in a roundabout way, and with no end of mystery, through a Chinaman who keeps a small shop here; but as soon as I left the Bugis quarter and went to live with Cornelius it began to be said openly that the Rajah had made up his mind to have me killed before long. Pleasant, wasn't it? And I couldn't see what there was to prevent him if he really *had* made up his mind. The worst of it was, I couldn't help feeling I wasn't doing any good either for Stein or for myself. Oh! it was beastly – the whole six weeks of it."'

# CHAPTER THIRTY

'HE TOLD me further that he didn't know what made him hang on – but of course we may guess. He sympathised deeply with the defenceless girl, at the mercy of that "mean, cowardly scoundrel." It appears Cornelius led her an awful life, stopping only short of actual ill-usage, for which he had not the pluck, I suppose. He insisted upon her calling him father – "and with respect, too – with respect," he would scream, shaking a little yellow fist in her face. "I am a respectable man, and what are you? Tell me – what are you? You think I am going to bring up somebody else's child and not to be treated with respect? You ought to be glad I let you. Come – say Yes, father.... No?... You wait a bit." Thereupon he would begin to abuse the dead woman, till the girl would run off with her hands to her head. He pursued her, dashing in and out and round the house and amongst the sheds, would drive her into some corner, where she would fall on her knees stopping her ears, and then he would stand at a distance and declaim filthy denunciations at her back for half an hour at a stretch. "Your mother was a devil, a deceitful devil – and you, too, are a devil," he would shriek in a final outburst, pick up a bit of dry earth or a handful of mud (there was plenty of mud around thc house), and fling it into her hair. Sometimes, though, she would hold out full of scorn, confronting him in silence, her face sombre and contracted, and only now and then uttering a word or two that would make the other jump and writhe with the sting. Jim told me these scenes were terrible. It was indeed a strange thing to come upon in a wilderness. The endlessness of such a subtly cruel situation was appalling – if you think of it. The respectable

Cornelius (Inchi 'Nelyus the Malays called him, with a grimace that meant many things) was a much-disappointed man. I don't know what he had expected would be done for him in consideration of his marriage; but evidently the liberty to steal, and embezzle, and appropriate to himself for many years and in any way that suited him best, the goods of Stein's Trading Company (Stein kept the supply up unfalteringly as long as he could get his skippers to take it there) did not seem to him a fair equivalent for the sacrifice of his honourable name. Jim would have enjoyed exceedingly thrashing Cornelius within an inch of his life; on the other hand, the scenes were of so painful a character, so abominable, that his impulse would be to get out of earshot, in order to spare the girl's feelings. They left her agitated, speechless, clutching her bosom now and then with a stony, desperate face, and then Jim would lounge up and say unhappily, "Now – come – really – what's the use – you must try to eat a bit," or give some such mark of sympathy. Cornelius would keep on slinking through the doorways, across the verandah and back again, as mute as a fish, and with malevolent, mistrustful, underhand glances. "I can stop his game," Jim said to her once. "Just say the word." And do you know what she answered? She said – Jim told me impressively – that if she had not been sure he was intensely wretched himself, she would have found the courage to kill him with her own hands. "Just fancy that! The poor devil of a girl, almost a child, being driven to talk like that," he exclaimed in horror. It seemed impossible to save her not only from that mean rascal but even from herself! It wasn't that he pitied her so much, he affirmed; it was more than pity; it was as if he had something on his conscience, while that life went on. To leave the house would have appeared a base desertion. He had understood at last that there was nothing to expect from a longer stay, neither accounts nor money, nor truth of any sort, but he stayed on, exasperating Cornelius to the verge, I won't say of insanity, but almost of courage. Meantime he felt all sorts of dangers gathering obscurely about him. Doramin had sent over twice a trusty servant to tell him seriously that he could do nothing for his safety unless he would recross the river again and live amongst the Bugis as at first. People of every condition used to call, often in the dead of night, in order to disclose to him plots for his assassination. He was to be poisoned. He was to be stabbed in the bath-house. Arrangements were being made to have him shot from a boat on the river. Each of these informants professed himself to be his very good friend. It was enough – he told me – to spoil a fellow's rest for ever. Something of the kind was extremely possible – nay, probable – but the lying warnings gave him only the sense of deadly scheming going on all around him, on all sides, in the dark. Nothing more calculated to shake the best of nerve. Finally, one night, Cornelius himself, with a great apparatus of alarm and secrecy, unfolded in solemn wheedling tones a little plan wherein for one hundred dollars – or even for eighty; let's say eighty – he, Cornelius, would procure a trustworthy man to smuggle Jim out of the river, all safe. There was nothing else for it now – if Jim cared a pin for his life. What's eighty dollars? A trifle. An insignificant sum. While he, Cornelius, who had to remain behind, was absolutely courting death by his proof of devotion to Mr Stein's young friend. The sight of his abject grimacing was – Jim told me – very hard to bear: he clutched at his hair, beat his breast, rocked himself to and fro with his hands pressed to his stomach, and actually pretended to shed tears. "Your blood be on your own head," he squeaked at last, and rushed out. It is a curious question how far Cornelius was sincere in that performance. Jim confessed to me that he did not sleep a wink after the fellow had gone. He lay on his back on a thin mat spread over the bamboo flooring, trying idly to make out the bare rafters, and listening to the rustlings in the torn thatch. A star suddenly twinkled through a hole in the roof. His brain was in a whirl; but, nevertheless, it was on that very night that he matured his plan for overcoming Sherif Ali. It had been the thought of all the moments he could spare from the hopeless investigation into Stein's affairs, but the notion – he says – came to him then all at once. He could see, as it were, the guns mounted on the top of the hill. He got very hot and excited lying there; sleep was out of the question more than ever. He jumped up, and went out barefooted on the verandah. Walking silently, he came upon the girl, motionless against the wall, as if on the watch. In his then state of mind it did not surprise him to see her up, nor yet to hear her ask in an anxious whisper where Cornelius could be. He simply said he did not know. She moaned a little, and peered into the *campong*. Everything was very quiet. He was possessed by his new idea, and so full of it that he could not help telling the girl all about it at once. She listened, clapped her hands lightly, whispered softly her admiration, but was evidently on the alert all the time. It seems he had been used to make a confidant of her all along – and that she on her part could and did give him a lot of useful hints as to Patusan affairs there is no doubt. He assured me more than once that he had never found himself the worse for her advice. At any rate, he was proceeding to explain his plan fully to her there and then, when she pressed his arm once, and vanished from his side. Then Cornelius appeared from somewhere, and, perceiving Jim, ducked sideways, as though he had been shot at, and afterwards stood very still in the dusk. At last he came forward prudently, like a suspicious cat. "There were some fishermen there – with fish," he said in a shaky voice. "To sell fish – you understand." . . . It must have been then two o'clock in the morning – a likely time for anybody to hawk fish about!

'Jim, however, let the statement pass, and did not give it a single thought. Other matters occupied his mind, and besides he had neither seen nor heard anything. He contented himself by saying, "Oh!" absently, got a drink of water out of a pitcher standing there, and leaving Cornelius a prey to some inexplicable emotion – that made him

embrace with both arms the worm-eaten rail of the
verandah as if his legs had failed – went in again and lay
down on his mat to think. By-and-by he heard stealthy
footsteps. They stopped. A voice whispered tremulously
through the wall, "Are you asleep?" "No! What is it?" he
answered, briskly, and there was an abrupt movement outside, and then all was still, as if the whisperer had been
startled. Extremely annoyed at this, Jim came out impetuously, and Cornelius with a faint shriek fled along the
verandah as far as the steps, where he hung on to the
broken banister. Very puzzled, Jim called out to him from
the distance to know what the devil he meant. "Have you
given your consideration to what I spoke to you about?"
asked Cornelius, pronouncing the words with difficulty,
like a man in the cold fit of a fever. "No!" shouted Jim in a
passion. "I did not, and I don't intend to. I am going to live
here, in Patusan." "You shall d-d-die h-h-here," answered
Cornelius, still shaking violently, and in a sort of expiring
voice. The whole performance was so absurd and provoking that Jim didn't know whether he ought to be amused or
angry. "Not till I have seen you tucked away, you bet," he
called out, exasperated yet ready to laugh. Half seriously
(being excited with his own thoughts, you know) he went
on shouting, "Nothing can touch me! You can do your
damnedest." Somehow the shadowy Cornelius far off
there seemed to be the hateful embodiment of all the
annoyances and difficulties he had found in his path. He
let himself go – his nerves had been over-wrought for days
– and called him many pretty names, – swindler, liar, sorry
rascal: in fact, carried on in an extraordinary way. He
admits he passed all bounds, that he was quite beside
himself – defied all Patusan to scare him away – declared
he would make them all dance to his own tune yet, and so
on, in a menacing, boasting strain. Perfectly bombastic and
ridiculous, he said. His ears burned at the bare recollection.
Must have been off his chump in some way.... The girl,
who was sitting with us, nodded her little head at me

quickly, frowned faintly, and said, "I heard him," with childlike solemnity. He laughed and blushed. What stopped him at last, he said, was the silence, the complete deathlike silence, of the indistinct figure far over there, that seemed to hang collapsed, doubled over the rail in a weird immobility. He came to his senses, and ceasing suddenly, wondered greatly at himself. He watched for a while. Not a stir, not a sound. "Exactly as if the chap had died while I had been making all that noise," he said. He was so ashamed of himself that he went indoors in a hurry without another word, and flung himself down again. The row seemed to have done him good though, because he went to sleep for the rest of the night like a baby. Hadn't slept like that for weeks. "But *I* didn't sleep," struck in the girl, one elbow on the table and nursing her cheek. "I watched." Her big eyes flashed, rolling a little, and then she fixed them on my face intently.

# CHAPTER THIRTY-ONE

'You may imagine with what interest I listened. All these details were perceived to have some significance twenty-four hours later. In the morning Cornelius made no allusion to the events of the night. "I suppose you will come back to my poor house," he muttered, surlily, slinking up just as Jim was entering the canoe to go over to Doramin's *campong*. Jim only nodded, without looking at him. "You find it good fun, no doubt," muttered the other in a sour tone. Jim spent the day with the old *nakhoda*, preaching the necessity of vigorous action to the principal men of the Bugis community, who had been summoned for a big talk. He remembered with pleasure how very eloquent and persuasive he had been. "I managed to put some backbone into them that time, and no mistake," he said. Sherif Ali's last raid had swept the outskirts of the settlement, and some women belonging to the town had been carried off to the stockade. Sherif Ali's emissaries had been seen in the market-place the day before, strutting about haughtily in white cloaks, and boasting of the Rajah's friendship for their master. One of them stood forward in the shade of a tree, and, leaning on the long barrel of a rifle, exhorted the people to prayer and repentance, advising them to kill all the strangers in their midst, some of whom, he said, were infidels and others even worse – children of Satan in the guise of Moslems. It was reported that several of the Rajah's people amongst the listeners had loudly expressed their approbation. The terror amongst the common people was intense. Jim, immensely pleased with his day's work, crossed the river again before sunset.

'As he had got the Bugis irretrievably committed to action, and had made himself responsible for success on his own head, he was so elated that in the lightness of his heart he absolutely tried to be civil with Cornelius. But Cornelius became wildly jovial in response, and it was almost more than he could stand, he says, to hear his little squeaks of false laughter, to see him wriggle and blink, and suddenly catch hold of his chin and crouch low over the table with a distracted stare. The girl did not show herself, and Jim retired early. When he rose to say good-night, Cornelius jumped up, knocking his chair over, and ducked out of sight as if to pick up something he had dropped. His good-night came huskily from under the table. Jim was amazed to see him emerge out with a dropping jaw, and staring, stupidly frightened eyes. He clutched the edge of the table. "What's the matter? Are you unwell?" asked Jim. "Yes, yes, yes. A great colic in my stomach," says the other; and it is Jim's opinion that it was perfectly true. If so, it was, in view of his contemplated action, an abject sign of a still imperfect callousness for which he must be given all due credit.

'Be it as it may, Jim's slumbers were disturbed by a dream of heavens like brass resounding with a great voice, which called upon him to Awake! Awake! so loud that, notwithstanding his desperate determination to sleep on, he did wake up in reality. The glare of a red spluttering conflagration going on in mid-air fell on his eyes. Coils of black thick smoke curved round the head of some apparition, some unearthly being, all in white, with a severe, drawn, anxious face. After a second or so he recognised the girl. She was holding a dammar torch at arm's-length aloft, and in a persistent, urgent monotone she was repeating, "Get up! Get up! Get up!"

'Suddenly he leaped to his feet; at once she put into his hand a revolver, his own revolver, which had been hanging on a nail, but loaded this time. He gripped it in silence, bewildered, blinking in the light. He wondered what he could do for her.

'She asked rapidly and very low, "Can you face four men with this?" He laughed while narrating this part at the recollection of his polite alacrity. It seems he made a great display of it. "Certainly – of course – certainly – command me." He was not properly awake, and had a notion of being very civil in these extraordinary circumstances, of showing his unquestioning, devoted readiness. She left the room, and he followed her; in the passage they disturbed an old hag who did the casual cooking of the household, though she was so decrepit as to be hardly able to understand human speech. She got up and hobbled behind them, mumbling toothlessly. On the verandah a hammock of sailcloth, belonging to Cornelius, swayed lightly to the touch of Jim's elbow. It was empty.

'The Patusan establishment, like all the posts of Stein's Trading Company, had originally consisted of four buildings. Two of them were represented by two heaps of sticks, broken bamboos, rotten thatch, over which the four corner-posts of hardwood leaned sadly at different angles: the principal storeroom, however, stood yet, facing the agent's house. It was an oblong hut, built of mud and clay: it had at one end a wide door of stout planking, which so far had not come off the hinges, and in one of the side walls there was a square aperture, a sort of window, with three wooden bars. Before descending the few steps the girl turned her face over her shoulder and said quickly, "You were to be set upon while you slept." Jim tells me he experienced a sense of deception. It was the old story. He was weary of these attempts upon his life. He had had his fill of these alarms. He was sick of them. He assured me he was angry with the girl for deceiving him. He had followed her under the impression that it was she who wanted his help, and now he had half a mind to turn on his heel and go back in disgust. "Do you know," he commented, profoundly, "I rather think I was not quite myself for whole weeks on end about that time." "Oh, yes. You were though," I couldn't help contradicting.

'But she moved on swiftly, and he followed her into the courtyard. All its fences had fallen in a long time ago; the neighbours' buffaloes would pace in the morning across the open space, snorting profoundly, without haste; the very jungle was invading it already. Jim and the girl stopped in the rank grass. The light in which they stood made a dense blackness all round, and only above their heads there was an opulent glitter of stars. He told me it was a beautiful night – quite cool, with a little stir of breeze from the river. It seems he noticed its friendly beauty. Remember this is a love-story I am telling you now. A lovely night that seemed to breathe on them a soft caress. The flame of the torch streamed now and then with a fluttering noise like a flag, and for a time this was the only sound. "They are in the storeroom waiting," whispered the girl; "they are waiting for the signal." "Who's to give it?" he asked. She shook the torch, which blazed up after a shower of sparks. "Only you have been sleeping so restlessly," she continued in a murmur. "I watched your sleep, too." "You!" he exclaimed, craning his neck to look about him. "You think I watched on this night only!" she said, with a sort of despairing indignation.

'He says it was as if he had received a blow on the chest. He gasped. He thought he had been an awful brute somehow, and he felt remorseful, touched, happy, elated. This, let me remind you again, is a love story; you can see it by the imbecility, not a repulsive imbecility, the exalted imbecility of these proceedings, this station in torchlight, as if they had come there on purpose to have it out for the edification of concealed murderers. If Sherif Ali's emissaries had been possessed – as Jim remarked – of a pennyworth of spunk, this was the time to make a rush. His heart was thumping – not with fear – but he seemed to hear the grass rustle, and he stepped smartly out of the light. Something dark, imperfectly seen, flitted rapidly out of sight. He called out in a strong voice, "Cornelius! O Cornelius!" A profound silence succeeded: his voice did not seem to have carried twenty feet. Again the girl was by his side. "Fly!" she said. The old woman was coming up; her broken figure hovered in crippled little jumps on the edge of the light; they heard her mumbling, and a light, moaning sigh. "Fly!" repeated the girl, excitedly. "They are frightened now – this light – the voices. They know you are awake now – they know you are big, strong, fearless..." "If I am all that," he began, but she interrupted him. "Yes – to-night! But what of to-morrow night? Of the next night? Of the night after – of all the many, many nights? Can I be always watching?" A sobbing catch of her breath affected him beyond the power of words.

'He told me that he had never felt so small, so powerless – and as to courage, what was the good of it? he thought. He was so helpless that even flight seemed of no use; and though she kept on whispering, "Go to Doramin, go to Doramin," with feverish insistence, he realised that for him there was no refuge from that loneliness which centupled all his dangers except – in her. "I thought," he said to me, "that if I went away from her it would be the end of every-thing somehow." Only as they couldn't stop there for ever in the middle of that courtyard, he made up his mind to go and look into the storehouse. He let her follow him with-out thinking of any protest, as if they had been indissolubly united. "I am fearless – am I?" he muttered through his teeth. She restrained his arm. "Wait till you hear my voice," she said, and, torch in hand, ran lightly round the corner. He remained alone in the darkness, his face to the door: not a sound, not a breath came from the other side. The old hag let out a dreary groan somewhere behind his back. He heard a high-pitched almost screaming call from the girl. "Now! Push!" He pushed violently; the door swung with a creak and a clatter, disclosing to his intense astonishment the low dungeon-like interior illuminated by a lurid, wavering glare. A turmoil of smoke eddied down upon an empty wooden crate in the middle of the floor, a litter of rags and straw tried to soar, but only stirred feebly in the draught. She had thrust the light through the bars of the window. He saw her bare round arm extended and rigid, holding up the torch with the steadiness of an iron bracket. A conical ragged heap of old mats cumbered a distant corner almost to the ceiling, and that was all.

'He explained to me that he was bitterly disappointed at this. His fortitude had been tried by so many warnings, he had been for weeks surrounded by so many hints of danger, that he wanted the relief of some reality, of something tangible that he could meet. "It would have cleared the air for a couple of hours at least, if you know what I mean," he said to me. "Jove! I had been living for days with a stone on my chest." Now at last he had thought he would get hold of something, and – nothing! Not a trace, not a sign of anybody. He had raised his weapon as the door flew open, but now his arm fell. "Fire! Defend yourself," the girl outside cried in an agonising voice. She, being in the dark and with her arm thrust in to the shoulder through the small hole, couldn't see what was going on, and she dared not withdraw the torch now to run round. "There's nobody here!" yelled Jim, contemptuously, but his impulse to burst into a resentful exasperated laugh died without a sound: he had perceived in the very act of turning away that he was exchanging glances with a pair of eyes in the heap of mats. He saw a shifting gleam of whites. "Come out!" he cried in a fury, a little doubtful, and a dark-faced head, a head without a body, shaped itself in the rubbish, a strangely detached head, that looked at him with a steady scowl. Next moment the whole mound stirred, and with a low grunt a man emerged swiftly, and bounded towards Jim. Behind him the mats as it were jumped and flew, his right arm was raised with a crooked elbow, and the dull blade of a kris protruded from his fist held off, a little above his head. A cloth wound tight round his loins seemed dazzlingly white on his bronze skin; his naked body glistened as if wet.

'Jim noted all this. He told me he was experiencing a feeling of unutterable relief, of vengeful elation. He held his shot, he says, deliberately. He held it for the tenth part of a second, for three strides of the man – an unconscionable time. He held it for the pleasure of saying to himself, That's a dead man! He was absolutely positive and certain. He let him come on because it did not matter. A dead man, anyhow. He noticed the dilated nostrils, the wide eyes, the intent, eager stillness of the face, and then he fired.

'The explosion in that confined space was stunning. He stepped back a pace. He saw the man jerk his head up, fling his arms forward, and drop the kris. He ascertained afterwards that he had shot him through the mouth, a little upwards, the bullet coming out high at the back of the skull. With the impetus of his rush the man drove straight on, his face suddenly gaping disfigured, with his hands open before him gropingly, as though blinded, and landed with terrific violence on his forehead, just short of Jim's bare toes. Jim says he didn't lose the smallest detail of all this. He found himself calm, appeased, without rancour, without uneasiness, as if the death of that man had atoned for everything. The place was getting very full of sooty smoke from the torch, in which the unswaying flame burned blood-red without a flicker. He walked in resolutely, striding over the dead body, and covered with his revolver another naked figure outlined vaguely at the other end. As he was about to pull the trigger, the man threw away with force a short heavy spear, and squatted submissively on his hams, his back to the wall and his clasped hands between his legs. "You want your life?" Jim said. The other made no sound. "How many more of you?" asked Jim again. "Two more, Tuan," said the man very softly, looking with big fascinated eyes into the muzzle of the revolver. Accordingly two more crawled from under the mats, holding out ostentatiously their empty hands.'

# CHAPTER THIRTY-TWO

'JIM took up an advantageous position and shepherded them out in a bunch through the doorway: all that time the torch had remained vertical in the grip of a little hand, without so much as a tremble. The three men obeyed him, perfectly mute, moving automatically. He ranged them in a row. "Link arms!" he ordered. They did so. "The first who withdraws his arm or turns his head is a dead man," he said. "March!" They stepped out together, rigidly; he followed, and at the side the girl, in a trailing white gown, her black hair falling as low as her waist, bore the light. Erect and swaying, she seemed to glide without touching the earth; the only sound was the silky swish and rustle of the long grass. "Stop!" cried Jim.

'The river-bank was steep; a great freshness ascended, the light fell on the edge of smooth dark water frothing without a ripple; right and left the shapes of the houses ran together below the sharp outlines of the roofs. "Take my greetings to Sherif Ali – till I come myself," said Jim. Not one head of the three budged. "Jump!" he thundered. The three splashes made one splash, a shower flew up, black heads bobbed convulsively, and disappeared; but a great blowing and spluttering went on, growing faint, for they were diving industriously, in great fear of a parting shot. Jim turned to the girl, who had been a silent and attentive observer. His heart seemed suddenly to grow too big for his breast and choke him in the hollow of his throat. This probably made him speechless for so long, and after returning his gaze she flung the burning torch with a wide sweep of the arm into the river. The ruddy fiery glare, taking a long flight through the night, sank with a vicious hiss, and the calm soft starlight descended upon them, unchecked.

'He did not tell me what it was he said when at last he recovered his voice. I don't suppose he could be very eloquent. The world was still, the night breathed on them, one of those nights that seem created for the sheltering of tenderness, and there are moments when our souls, as if freed from their dark envelope, glow with an exquisite sensibility that makes certain silences more lucid than speeches. As to the girl, he told me, "She broke down a bit. Excitement – don't you know. Reaction. Deucedly tired she must have been – and all that kind of thing. And – and – hang it all – she was fond of me, don't you see.... I, too... didn't know, of course... never entered my head...."

'There he got up and began to walk about in some agitation. "I – I love her dearly. More than I could tell. Of course one cannot tell. You take a different view of your actions when you come to understand, when you are *made* to understand every day that your existence is necessary – you see, absolutely necessary – to another person. I am made to feel that. Wonderful. But only try to think what her life had been. It is too extravagantly awful! Isn't it? And me finding her here like this – as you may go out for a stroll and come suddenly upon somebody drowning in a lonely dark place. Jove! No time to lose. Well, it is a trust, too... I believe I am equal to it...."

'I must tell you the girl had left us to ourselves some time before. He slapped his chest. "Yes! I feel that, but I believe I am equal to all my luck!" He had the gift of finding a special meaning in everything that happened to him. This was the view he took of his love-affair; it was idyllic, a little solemn, and also true, since his belief had all the unshakable seriousness of youth. Some time after, on another occasion, he said to me, "I've been only two years here, and now, upon my word, I can't conceive being able to live anywhere else. The very thought of the world outside is enough to give me a fright; because, don't you see," he continued, with downcast eyes watching the action of his boot busied in squashing thoroughly a tiny bit of dried mud (we were strolling on the river-bank) – "because I have not forgotten why I came here. Not yet!"

'I refrained from looking at him, but I think I heard a short sigh; we took a turn or two in silence. "Upon my soul and conscience," he began again, "if such a thing can be forgotten, then I think I have a right to dismiss it from my mind. Ask any man here" . . . his voice changed. "Is it not strange," he went on in a gentle, almost yearning tone, "that all these people, all these people who would do anything for me, can never be made to understand? Never! If you disbelieve me I could not call them up. It seems hard, somehow. I am stupid, am I not? What more can I want? If you ask them who is brave – who is true – who is just – who is it they would trust with their lives? – they would say, Tuan Jim. And yet they can never know the real, real truth. . . ."

'That's what he said to me on my last day with him. I did not let a murmur escape me: I felt he was going to say more, and come no nearer to the root of the matter. The sun, whose concentrated glare dwarfs the earth into a restless mote of dust, had sunk behind the forest, and the diffused light from an opal sky seemed to cast upon a world without shadows and without brilliance the illusion of a calm and pensive greatness. I don't know why, listening to him, I should have noted so distinctly the gradual darkening of the river, of the air; the irresistible slow work of the night settling silently on all the visible forms, effacing the outlines, burying the shapes deeper and deeper, like a steady fall of impalpable black dust.

' "Jove!" he began, abruptly, "there are days when a fellow is too absurd for anything; only I know I can tell you what I like. I talk about being done with it – with the bally thing at the back of my head. . . . Forgetting. . . . Hang me if I know! I can think of it quietly. After all, what has it proved? Nothing. I suppose you don't think so. . . ."

'I made a protesting murmur.

'"No matter," he said. "I am satisfied... nearly. I've got to look only at the face of the first man that comes along, to regain my confidence. They can't be made to understand what is going on in me. What of that? Come! I haven't done so badly."

'"Not so badly," I said.

'"But all the same, you wouldn't like to have me aboard your own ship – hey?"

'"Confound you!" I cried. "Stop this."

'"Aha! You see," he cried, crowing, as it were, over me placidly. "Only," he went on, "you just try to tell this to any of them here. They would think you a fool, a liar, or worse. And so I can stand it. I've done a thing or two for them, but this is what they have done for me."

'"My dear chap," I cried, "you shall always remain for them an insoluble mystery." Thereupon we were silent.

'"Mystery," he repeated, before looking up. "Well, then let me always remain here."

'After the sun had set, the darkness seemed to drive upon us, borne in every faint puff of the breeze. In the middle of a hedged path I saw the arrested, gaunt, watchful, and apparently one-legged silhouette of Tamb' Itam; and across the dusky space my eye detected something white moving to and fro behind the supports of the roof. As soon as Jim, with Tamb' Itam at his heels, had started upon his evening rounds, I went up to the house alone, and, unexpectedly, found myself waylaid by the girl, who had been clearly waiting for this opportunity.

'It is hard to tell you what it was precisely she wanted to wrest from me. Obviously it would be something very simple – the simplest impossibility in the world; as, for instance, the exact description of the form of a cloud. She wanted an assurance, a statement, a promise, an explanation – I don't know how to call it: the thing has no name. It was dark under the projecting roof, and all I could see were the flowing lines of her gown, the pale small oval of her face, with the white flash of her teeth, and, turned towards me, the big sombre orbits of her eyes, where there seemed to be a faint stir, such as you may fancy you can detect when you plunge your gaze to the bottom of an immensely deep well. What is it that moves there? you ask yourself. Is it a blind monster or only a lost gleam from the universe? It occurred to me – don't laugh – that all things being dissimilar, she was more inscrutable in her childish ignorance than the Sphinx propounding childish riddles to wayfarers. She had been carried off to Patusan before her eyes were open. She had grown up there; she had seen nothing, she had known nothing, she had no conception of anything. I ask myself whether she were sure that anything else existed. What notions she may have formed of the outside world is to me inconceivable: all that she knew of its inhabitants were a betrayed woman and a sinister pantaloon. Her lover also came to her from there, gifted with irresistible seductions; but what would become of her if he should return to these inconceivable regions that seemed always to claim back their own? Her mother had warned her of this with tears, before she died. . . .

'She had caught hold of my arm firmly, and as soon as I had stopped she had withdrawn her hand in haste. She was audacious and shrinking. She feared nothing, but she was checked by the profound incertitude and the extreme strangeness – a brave person groping in the dark. I belonged to this Unknown that might claim Jim for its own at any moment. I was, as it were, in the secret of its nature and of its intentions; – the confidant of a threatening mystery; – armed with its power perhaps! I believe she supposed I could with a word whisk Jim away out of her very arms; it is my sober conviction she went through agonies of apprehension during my long talks with Jim; through a real and intolerable anguish that might have conceivably driven her into plotting my murder, had the fierceness of her soul been equal to the tremendous situation it had created. This is my impression, and it is all I can give you: the whole thing dawned gradually upon me, and as it got clearer and clearer I was overwhelmed by a slow incredulous amazement. She made me believe her, but there is no word that on my lips could render the effect of the headlong and vehement whisper, of the soft, passionate tones, of the sudden breathless pause and the appealing movement of the white arms extended swiftly. They fell; the ghostly figure swayed like a slender tree in the wind, the pale oval of the face drooped; it was impossible to distinguish her features, the darkness of the eyes was unfathomable; two wide sleeves uprose in the dark like unfolding wings, and she stood silent, holding her head in her hands.'

# CHAPTER THIRTY-THREE

'I was immensely touched: her youth, her ignorance, her pretty beauty, which had the simple charm and the delicate vigour of a wild-flower, her pathetic pleading, her helplessness, appealed to me with almost the strength of her own unreasonable and natural fear. She feared the unknown as we all do, and her ignorance made the unknown infinitely vast. I stood for it, for myself, for you fellows, for all the world that neither cared for Jim nor needed him in the least. I would have been ready enough to answer for the indifference of the teeming earth but for the reflection that he, too, belonged to this mysterious unknown of her fears, and that, however much I stood for, I did not stand for him. This made me hesitate. A murmur of hopeless pain unsealed my lips. I began by protesting that I at least had come with no intention to take Jim away.

'Why did I come, then? After a slight movement she was as still as a marble statue in the night. I tried to explain briefly: friendship, business; if I had any wish in the matter it was rather to see him stay.... "They always leave us," she murmured. The breath of sad wisdom from the grave which her piety wreathed with flowers seemed to pass in a faint sigh.... Nothing, I said, could separate Jim from her.

'It is my firm conviction now; it was my conviction at the time; it was the only possible conclusion from the facts of the case. It was not made more certain by her whispering in a tone in which one speaks to oneself, "He swore this to me." "Did you ask him?" I said.

'She made a step nearer. "No. Never!" She had asked him only to go away. It was that night on the river-bank, after

279

he had killed the man – after she had flung the torch in the water because he was looking at her so. There was too much light, and the danger was over then – for a little time – for a little time. He said then he would not abandon her to Cornelius. She had insisted. She wanted him to leave her. He said that he could not – that it was impossible. He trembled while he said this. She had felt him tremble. . . . One does not require much imagination to see the scene, almost to hear their whispers. She was afraid for him, too. I believe that then she saw in him only a predestined victim of dangers which she understood better than himself. Though by nothing but his mere presence he had mastered her heart, had filled all her thoughts, and had possessed himself of all her affections, she under-estimated his chances of success. It is obvious that at about that time everybody was inclined to under-estimate his chances. Strictly speaking he didn't seem to have any. I know this was Cornelius's view. He confessed that much to me in extenuation of the shady part he had played in Sherif Ali's plot to do away with the infidel. Even Sherif Ali himself, as it seems certain now, had nothing but contempt for the white man. Jim was to be murdered mainly on religious grounds, I believe. A simple act of piety (and so far infinitely meritorious), but otherwise without much importance. In the last part of this opinion Cornelius concurred. "Honourable sir," he argued abjectly on the only occasion he managed to have me to himself – "Honourable sir, how was I to know? Who was he? What could he do to make people believe him? What did Mr Stein mean sending a boy like that to talk big to an old servant? I was ready to save him for eighty dollars. Only eighty dollars. Why didn't the fool go? Was I to get stabbed myself for the sake of a stranger?" He grovelled in spirit before me, with his body doubled up insinuatingly and his hands hovering about my knees, as though he were ready to embrace my legs. "What's eighty dollars? An insignificant sum to give to a defenceless old man ruined for life by a deceased she-devil."

Here he wept. But I anticipate. I didn't that night chance upon Cornelius till I had had it out with the girl.

'She was unselfish when she urged Jim to leave her, and even to leave the country. It was his danger that was foremost in her thoughts – even if she wanted to save herself, too – perhaps unconsciously: but then look at the warning she had, look at the lesson that could be drawn from every moment of the recently ended life in which all her memories were centred. She fell at his feet – she told me so – there by the river, in the discreet light of stars which showed nothing except great masses of silent shadows, indefinite open spaces, and trembling faintly upon the broad stream made it appear as wide as the sea. He had lifted her up. He lifted her up, and then she would struggle no more. Of course not. Strong arms, a tender voice, a stalwart shoulder to rest her poor lonely little head upon. The need – the infinite need – of all this for the aching heart, for the bewildered mind; – the promptings of youth – the necessity of the moment. What would you have? One understands – unless one is incapable of understanding anything under the sun. And so she was content to be lifted up – and held. "You know – Jove! this is serious – no nonsense in it!" as Jim had whispered hurriedly with a troubled concerned face on the threshold of his house. I don't know so much about nonsense, but there was nothing lighthearted in their romance: they came together under the shadow of a life's disaster, like knight and maiden meeting to exchange vows amongst haunted ruins. The starlight was good enough for that story, a light so faint and remote that it cannot resolve shadows into shapes, and show the other shore of a stream. I did look upon the stream that night and from the very place; it rolled silent and as black as Styx: the next day I went away, but I am not likely to forget what it was she wanted to be saved from when she entreated him to leave her while there was time. She told me what it was, calmed – she was now too passionately interested for mere excitement – in a voice as quiet in the obscurity as her white half-lost figure. She told me, "I didn't want to die weeping." I thought I had not heard aright.

'"You did not want to die weeping?" I repeated after her. "Like my mother," she added readily. The outlines of her white shape did not stir in the least. "My mother had wept bitterly before she died," she explained. An inconceivable calmness seemed to have risen from the ground around us, imperceptibly, like the still rise of a flood in the night, obliterating the familiar landmarks of emotions. There came upon me, as though I had felt myself losing my footing in the midst of waters, a sudden dread, the dread of the unknown depths. She went on explaining that, during the last moments, being alone with her mother, she had to leave the side of the couch to go and set her back against the door, in order to keep Cornelius out. He desired to get in, and kept on drumming with both fists, only desisting now and again to shout huskily, "Let me in! Let me in! Let me in!" In a far corner upon a few mats the moribund woman, already speechless and unable to lift her arm, rolled her head over, and with a feeble movement of her hand seemed to command – "No! No!" and the obedient daughter, setting her shoulders with all her strength against the door, was looking on. "The tears fell from her eyes – and then she died," concluded the girl in an imperturbable monotone, which more than anything else, more than the white statuesque immobility of her person, more than mere words could do, troubled my mind profoundly with the passive, irremediable horror of the scene. It had the power to drive me out of my conception of existence, out of that shelter each of us makes for himself to creep under in moments of danger, as a tortoise withdraws within its shell. For a moment I had a view of a world that seemed to wear a vast and dismal aspect of disorder, while, in truth, thanks to our unwearied efforts, it is as sunny an arrangement of small conveniences as the mind of man can conceive. But still – it was only a moment: I went back into my shell directly. One *must* – don't you know? – though

I seemed to have lost all my words in the chaos of dark thoughts I had contemplated for a second or two beyond the pale. These came back, too, very soon, for words also belong to the sheltering conception of light and order which is our refuge. I had them ready at my disposal before she whispered softly, "He swore he would never leave me, when we stood there alone! He swore to me!" . . . "And is it possible that you – you! do not believe him?" I asked, sincerely reproachful, genuinely shocked. Why couldn't she believe? Wherefore this craving for incertitude, this clinging to fear, as if incertitude and fear had been the safeguards of her love. It was monstrous. She should have made for herself a shelter of inexpugnable peace out of that honest affection. She had not the knowledge – not the skill perhaps. The night had come on apace; it had grown pitch-dark where we were, so that without stirring she had faded like the intangible form of a wistful and perverse spirit. And suddenly I heard her quiet whisper again, "Other men had sworn the same thing." It was like a meditative comment on some thoughts full of sadness, of awe. And she added, still lower if possible, "My father did." She paused the time to draw an inaudible breath. "Her father, too." . . . These were the things she knew! At once I said, "Ah! but he is not like that." This, it seemed, she did not intend to dispute; but after a time the strange still whisper wandering dreamily in the air stole into my ears. "Why is he different? Is he better? Is he . . ." "Upon my word of honour," I broke in, "I believe he is." We subdued our tones to a mysterious pitch. Amongst the huts of Jim's workmen (they were mostly liberated slaves from the Sherif's stockade) somebody started a shrill, drawling song. Across the river a big fire (at Doramin's, I think) made a glowing ball, completely isolated in the night. "Is he more true?" she murmured. "Yes," I said. "More true than any other man," she repeated in lingering accents. "Nobody here," I said, "would dream of doubting his word – nobody would dare – except you."

'I think she made a movement at this. "More brave," she
went on in a changed tone. "Fear shall never drive him away
from you," I said a little nervously. The song stopped short
on a shrill note, and was succeeded by several voices talking
in the distance. Jim's voice, too. I was struck by her silence.
"What has he been telling you? He has been telling you
something?" I asked. There was no answer. "What is it he
told you?" I insisted.

' "Do you think I can tell you? How am I to know? How
am I to understand?" she cried at last. There was a stir.
I believe she was wringing her hands. "There is something
he can never forget."

' "So much the better for you," I said, gloomily.

' "What is it? What is it?" She put an extraordinary force
of appeal into her supplicating tone. "He says he had been
afraid. How can I believe this? Am I a mad woman to
believe this? You all remember something! You all go
back to it. What is it? You tell me! What is this thing? Is
it alive? – is it dead? I hate it. It is cruel. Has it got a face and
a voice – this calamity? Will he see it – will he hear it? In his
sleep perhaps when he cannot see me – and then arise and
go. Ah! I shall never forgive him. My mother had forgiven
– but I, never! Will it be a sign – a call?"

'It was a wonderful experience. She mistrusted his very
slumbers – and she seemed to think I could tell her why!
Thus a poor mortal seduced by the charm of an apparition
might have tried to wring from another ghost the tremendous secret of the claim the other world holds over a
disembodied soul astray amongst the passions of this
earth. The very ground on which I stood seemed to melt
under my feet. And it was so simple, too; but if the spirits
evoked by our fears and our unrest have ever to vouch for
each other's constancy before the forlorn magicians that we
are, then I – I alone of us dwellers in the flesh – have
shuddered in the hopeless chill of such a task. A sign, a
call! How telling in its expression was her ignorance. A few
words! How she came to know them, how she came to

pronounce them, I can't imagine. Women find their
inspiration in the stress of moments that for us are merely
awful, absurd, or futile. To discover that she had a voice at
all was enough to strike awe into the heart. Had a spurned
stone cried out in pain it could not have appeared a greater
and more pitiful miracle. These few sounds wandering in
the dark had made their two benighted lives tragic to my
mind. It was impossible to make her understand. I chafed
silently at my impotence. And Jim, too – poor devil! Who
would need him? Who would remember him? He had
what he wanted. His very existence probably had been
forgotten by this time. They had mastered their fates.
They were tragic.

'Her immobility before me was clearly expectant, and
my part was to speak for my brother from the realm of
forgetful shades. I was deeply moved at my responsibility
and at her distress. I would have given anything for the
power to soothe her frail soul, tormenting itself in its
invincible ignorance like a small bird beating about the
cruel wires of a cage. Nothing easier than to say, Have no
fear! Nothing more difficult. How does one kill fear,
I wonder? How do you shoot a spectre through the heart,
slash off its spectral head, take it by its spectral throat? It is
an enterprise you rush into while you dream, and are glad to
make your escape with wet hair and every limb shaking.
The bullet is not run, the blade not forged, the man not
born; even the winged words of truth drop at your feet like
lumps of lead. You require for such a desperate encounter
an enchanted and poisoned shaft dipped in a lie too subtle
to be found on earth. An enterprise for a dream, my
masters!

'I began my exorcism with a heavy heart, with a sort of
sullen anger in it, too. Jim's voice, suddenly raised with a
stern intonation, carried across the courtyard, reproving
the carelessness of some dumb sinner by the river-side.
Nothing – I said, speaking in a distinct murmur – there
could be nothing, in that unknown world she fancied so

eager to rob her of her happiness, there was nothing neither living nor dead, there was no face, no voice, no power, that could tear Jim from her side. I drew breath and she whispered softly, "He told me so." "He told you the truth," I said. "Nothing," she sighed out, and abruptly turned upon me with a barely audible intensity of tone: "Why did you come to us from out there? He speaks of you too often. You make me afraid. Do you – do you want him?" A sort of stealthy fierceness had crept into our hurried mutters. "I shall never come again," I said, bitterly. "And I don't want him. No one wants him." "No one," she repeated in a tone of doubt. "No one," I affirmed, feeling myself swayed by some strange excitement. "You think him strong, wise, courageous, great – why not believe him to be true, too? I shall go to-morrow – and that is the end. You shall never be troubled by a voice from there again. This world you don't know is too big to miss him. You understand? Too big. You've got his heart in your hand. You must feel that. You must know that." "Yes, I know that," she breathed out, hard and still, as a statue might whisper.

'I felt I had done nothing. And what is it that I had wished to do? I am not sure now. At the time I was animated by an inexplicable ardour, as if before some great and necessary task – the influence of the moment upon my mental and emotional state. There are in all our lives such moments, such influences, coming from the outside, as it were, irresistible, incomprehensible – as if brought about by the mysterious conjunctions of the planets. She owned, as I had put it to her, his heart. She had that and everything else – if she could only believe it. What I had to tell her was that in the whole world there was no one who ever would need his heart, his mind, his hand. It was a common fate, and yet it seemed an awful thing to say of any man. She listened without a word, and her stillness now was like the protest of an invincible unbelief. What need she care for the world beyond the forests? I asked. From all the multitudes that peopled the vastness of that unknown there would come, I assured her, as long as he lived, neither a call nor a sign for him. Never. I was carried away. Never! Never! I remember with wonder the sort of dogged fierceness I displayed. I had the illusion of having got the spectre by the throat at last. Indeed the whole real thing has left behind the detailed and amazing impression of a dream. Why should she fear? She knew him to be strong, true, wise, brave. He was all that. Certainly. He was more. He was great – invincible – and the world did not want him, it had forgotten him, it would not even know him.

'I stopped; the silence over Patusan was profound, and the feeble dry sound of a paddle striking the side of a canoe somewhere in the middle of the river seemed to make it infinite. "Why?" she murmured. I felt that sort of rage one feels during a hard tussle. The spectre was trying to slip out of my grasp. "Why?" she repeated louder; "tell me!" And as I remained confounded, she stamped with her foot like a spoilt child. "Why? Speak." "You want to know?" I asked in a fury. "Yes!" she cried. "Because he is not good enough," I said, brutally. During the moment's pause I noticed the fire on the other shore blaze up, dilating the circle of its glow like an amazed stare, and contract suddenly to a red pin-point. I only knew how close to me she had been when I felt the clutch of her fingers on my forearm. Without raising her voice, she threw into it an infinity of scathing contempt, bitterness, and despair.

'"This is the very thing he said.... You lie!"

'The last two words she cried at me in the native dialect. "Hear me out!" I entreated; she caught her breath tremulously, flung my arm away. "Nobody, nobody is good enough," I began with the greatest earnestness. I could hear the sobbing labour of her breath frightfully quickened. I hung my head. What was the use? Footsteps were approaching; I slipped away without another word ...

# CHAPTER THIRTY-FOUR

MARLOW swung his legs out, got up quickly, and staggered a little, as though he had been set down after a rush through space. He leaned his back against the balustrade and faced a disordered array of long cane-chairs. The bodies prone in them seemed started out of their torpor by his movement. One or two sat up as if alarmed; here and there a cigar glowed yet; Marlow looked at them all with the eyes of a man returning from the excessive remoteness of a dream. A throat was cleared; a calm voice encouraged negligently, 'Well.

'Nothing,' said Marlow with a slight start. 'He had told her – that's all. She did not believe him – nothing more. As to myself, I do not know whether it be just, proper, decent for me to rejoice or to be sorry. For my part, I cannot say what I believed – indeed I don't know to this day, and never shall probably. But what did the poor devil believe himself? Truth shall prevail – don't you know *Magna est veritas et*... Yes, when it gets a chance. There is a law, no doubt – and likewise a law regulates your luck in the throwing of dice. It is not Justice the servant of men, but accident, hazard, Fortune – the ally of patient Time – that holds an even and scrupulous balance. Both of us had said the very same thing. Did we both speak the truth – or one of us did – or neither?...

Marlow paused, crossed his arms on his breast, and in a changed tone –

'She said we lied. Poor soul. Well – let's leave it to chance, whose ally is Time, that cannot be hurried, and whose enemy is Death, that will not wait. I had retreated – a little cowed, I must own. I had tried a fall with fear itself

288

and got thrown – of course. I had only succeeded in adding to her anguish the hint of some mysterious collusion, of an inexplicable and incomprehensible conspiracy to keep her for ever in the dark. And it had come easily, naturally, unavoidably, by his act, by her own act! It was as though I had been shown the working of the implacable destiny of which we are the victims – and the tools. It was appalling to think of the girl whom I had left standing there motionless; Jim's footsteps had a fateful sound as he tramped by, without seeing me, in his heavy laced boots. "What? No lights!" he said in a loud, surprised voice. "What are you doing in the dark – you two?" Next moment he caught sight of her, I suppose. "Hallo, girl!" he cried, cheerily. "Hallo, boy!" she answered at once, with amazing pluck.

'This was their usual greeting to each other, and the bit of swagger she would put into her rather high but sweet voice was very droll, pretty, and childlike. It delighted Jim greatly. This was the last occasion on which I heard them exchange this familiar hail, and it struck a chill into my heart. There was the high sweet voice, the pretty effort, the swagger; but it all seemed to die out prematurely, and the playful call sounded like a moan. It was too confoundedly awful. "What have you done with Marlow?" Jim was asking; and then, "Gone down – has he? Funny I didn't meet him. . . . You there, Marlow?"

'I didn't answer. I wasn't going in – not yet at any rate. I really couldn't. While he was calling me I was engaged in making my escape through a little gate leading out upon a stretch of newly cleared ground. No; I couldn't face them yet. I walked hastily with lowered head along a trodden path. The ground rose gently, the few big trees had been felled, the undergrowth had been cut down and the grass fired. He had a mind to try a coffee-plantation there. The big hill, rearing its double summit coal-black in the clear yellow glow of the rising moon, seemed to cast its shadow upon the ground prepared for that experiment. He was going to try ever so many experiments; I had admired his energy, his enterprise, and his shrewdness. Nothing on earth seemed less real now than his plans, his energy, and his enthusiasm; and raising my eyes, I saw part of the moon glittering through the bushes at the bottom of the chasm. For a moment it looked as though the smooth disc, falling from its place in the sky upon the earth, had rolled to the bottom of that precipice: its ascending movement was like a leisurely rebound; it disengaged itself from the tangle of twigs; the bare contorted limb of some tree, growing on the slope, made a black crack right across its face. It threw its level rays afar as if from a cavern, and in this mournful eclipse-like light the stumps of felled trees uprose very dark, the heavy shadows fell at my feet on all sides, my own moving shadow, and across my path the shadow of the solitary grave perpetually garlanded with flowers. In the darkened moonlight the interlaced blossoms took on shapes foreign to one's memory and colours indefinable to the eye, as though they had been special flowers gathered by no man, grown not in this world, and destined for the use of the dead alone. Their powerful scent hung in the warm air, making it thick and heavy like the fumes of incense. The lumps of white coral shone round the dark mound like a chaplet of bleached skulls, and everything around was so quiet that when I stood still all sound and all movements in the world seemed to come to an end.

'It was a great peace, as if the earth had been one grave, and for a time I stood there thinking mostly of the living who, buried in remote places out of the knowledge of mankind, still are fated to share in its tragic or grotesque miseries. In its noble struggles, too – who knows? The human heart is vast enough to contain all the world. It is valiant enough to bear the burden, but where is the courage that would cast it off?

'I suppose I must have fallen into a sentimental mood; I only know that I stood there long enough for the sense of utter solitude to get hold of me so completely that all I had lately seen, all I had heard, and the very human speech itself, seemed to have passed away out of existence, living only for a while longer in my memory, as though I had been the last of mankind. It was a strange and melancholy illusion, evolved half-consciously like all our illusions, which I suspect only to be visions of remote unattainable truth, seen dimly. This was, indeed, one of the lost, forgotten, unknown places of the earth; I had looked under its obscure surface; and I felt that when to-morrow I had left it for ever, it would slip out of existence, to live only in my memory till I myself passed into oblivion. I have that feeling about me now; perhaps it is that feeling which had incited me to tell you the story, to try to hand over to you, as it were, its very existence, its reality – the truth disclosed in a moment of illusion.

'Cornelius broke upon it. He bolted out, vermin-like, from the long grass growing in a depression of the ground. I believe his house was rotting somewhere near by, though I've never seen it, not having been far enough in that direction. He ran towards me upon the path; his feet, shod in dirty white shoes, twinkled on the dark earth; he pulled himself up, and began to whine and cringe under a tall stove-pipe hat. His dried-up little carcass was swallowed up, totally lost, in a suit of black broadcloth. That was his costume for holidays and ceremonies, and it reminded me that this was the fourth Sunday I had spent in Patusan. All the time of my stay I had been vaguely aware of his desire to confide in me, if he only could get me all to himself. He hung about with an eager craving look on his sour yellow little face; but his timidity had kept him back as much as my natural reluctance to have anything to do with such an unsavoury creature. He would have succeeded, nevertheless, had he not been so ready to slink off as soon as you looked at him. He would slink off before Jim's severe gaze, before my own, which I tried to make indifferent, even before Tamb' Itam's surly, superior glance. He was perpetually slinking away; whenever seen he was seen moving off deviously, his face over his shoulder, with either a mistrustful snarl or a woe-begone, piteous, mute aspect; but no assumed expression could conceal this innate irremediable abjectness of his nature, any more than an arrangement of clothing can conceal some monstrous deformity of the body.

'I don't know whether it was the demoralisation of my utter defeat in my encounter with a spectre of fear less than an hour ago, but I let him capture me without even a show of resistance. I was doomed to be the recipient of confidences, and to be confronted with unanswerable questions. It was trying; but the contempt, the unreasoned contempt, the man's appearance provoked, made it easier to bear. He couldn't possibly matter. Nothing mattered, since I had made up my mind that Jim, for whom alone I cared, had at last mastered his fate. He had told me he was satisfied . . . nearly. This is going further than most of us dare. I – who have the right to think myself good enough – dare not. Neither does any of you here, I suppose? . . .

Marlow paused, as if expecting an answer. Nobody spoke.

'Quite right,' he began again. 'Let no soul know, since the truth can be wrung out of us only by some cruel, little, awful catastrophe. But he is one of us, and he could say he was satisfied . . . nearly. Just fancy this! Nearly satisfied. One could almost envy him his catastrophe. Nearly satisfied. After this nothing could matter. It did not matter who suspected him, who trusted him, who loved him, who hated him – especially as it was Cornelius who hated him.

'Yet after all this was a kind of recognition. You shall judge of a man by his foes as well as by his friends, and this enemy of Jim was such as no decent man would be ashamed to own, without, however, making too much of him. This was the view Jim took, and in which I shared; but Jim disregarded him on general grounds. "My dear Marlow," he said, "I feel that if I go straight nothing can touch me. Indeed I do. Now you have been long enough here to have a good look round – and, frankly, don't you think I am pretty

safe? It all depends upon me, and, by Jove! I have lots of
confidence in myself. The worst thing he could do would
be to kill me, I suppose. I don't think for a moment he
would. He couldn't, you know – not if I were myself to
hand him a loaded rifle for the purpose, and then turn my
back on him. That's the sort of thing he is. And suppose he
would – suppose he could? Well – what of that? I didn't
come here flying for my life – did I? I came here to set my
back against the wall, and I am going to stay here..."

'"Till you are *quite* satisfied," I struck in.

'We were sitting at the time under the roof in the stern
of his boat; twenty paddles flashed like one, ten on a side,
striking the water with a single splash, while behind our
backs Tamb' Itam dipped silently right and left, and stared
right down the river, attentive to keep the long canoe in the
greatest strength of the current. Jim bowed his head, and
our last talk seemed to flicker out for good. He was seeing
me off as far as the mouth of the river. The schooner had
left the day before, working down and drifting on the ebb,
while I had prolonged my stay overnight. And now he was
seeing me off.

'Jim had been a little angry with me for mentioning
Cornelius at all. I had not, in truth, said much. The man
was too insignificant to be dangerous, though he was as full
of hate as he could hold. He had called me "honourable sir"
at every second sentence, and had whined at my elbow as he
followed me from the grave of his "late wife" to the gate of
Jim's compound. He declared himself the most unhappy of
men, a victim, crushed like a worm; he entreated me to look
at him. I wouldn't turn my head to do so; but I could see out
of the corner of my eye his obsequious shadow gliding after
mine, while the moon, suspended on our right hand,
seemed to gloat serenely upon the spectacle. He tried to
explain – as I've told you – his share in the events of the
memorable night. It was a matter of expediency. How
could he know who was going to get the upper hand? "I
would have saved him, honourable sir! I would have saved

him for eighty dollars," he protested in dulcet tones, keeping a pace behind me. "He has saved himself," I said, "and he has forgiven you." I heard a sort of tittering, and turned upon him; at once he appeared ready to take to his heels. "What are you laughing at?" I asked, standing still. "Don't be deceived, honourable sir!" he shrieked, seemingly losing all control over his feelings. "*He* save himself! He knows nothing, honourable sir – nothing whatever. Who is he? What does he want here – the big thief? What does he want here? He throws dust into everybody's eyes; he throws dust into your eyes, honourable sir; but he can't throw dust into my eyes. He is a big fool, honourable sir." I laughed contemptuously, and, turning on my heel, began to walk on again. He ran up to my elbow and whispered forcibly, "He's no more than a little child here – like a little child – a little child." Of course I didn't take the slightest notice, and seeing the time pressed, because we were approaching the bamboo fence that glittered over the blackened ground of the clearing, he came to the point. He commenced by being abjectly lachrymose. His great misfortunes had affected his head. He hoped I would kindly forget what nothing but his troubles made him say. He didn't mean anything by it; only the honourable sir did not know what it was to be ruined, broken down, trampled upon. After this introduction he approached the matter near his heart, but in such a rambling, ejaculatory, craven fashion, that for a long time I couldn't make out what he was driving at. He wanted me to intercede with Jim in his favour. It seemed, too, to be some sort of money affair. I heard time and again the words, "Moderate provision – suitable present." He seemed to be claiming value for something, and he even went the length of saying with some warmth that life was not worth having if a man were to be robbed of everything. I did not breathe a word, of course, but neither did I stop my ears. The gist of the affair, which became clear to me gradually, was in this, that he regarded himself as entitled to some money in exchange for the girl. He had brought her up. Somebody else's child. Great trouble and pains – old man now – suitable present. If the honourable sir would say a word. . . . I stood still to look at him with curiosity, and fearful lest I should think him extortionate, I suppose, he hastily brought himself to make a concession. In consideration of a "suitable present" given at once, he would, he declared, be willing to undertake the charge of the girl, "without any other provision – when the time came for the gentleman to go home." His little yellow face, all crumpled as though it had been squeezed together, expressed the most anxious, eager avarice. His voice whined coaxingly, "No more trouble – natural guardian – a sum of money. . . ."

'I stood there and marvelled. That kind of thing, with him, was evidently a vocation. I discovered suddenly in his cringing attitude a sort of assurance, as though he had been all his life dealing in certitudes. He must have thought I was dispassionately considering his proposal, because he became as sweet as honey. "Every gentleman made a provision when the time came to go home," he began, insinuatingly. I slammed the little gate. "In this case, Mr Cornelius," I said, "the time shall never come." He took a few seconds to gather this in. "What!" he fairly squealed. "Why," I continued from my side of the gate, "haven't you heard him say so himself? He will never go home." "Oh! this is too much," he shouted. He would not address me as "honoured sir" any more. He was very still for a time, and then without a trace of humility began very low. "Never go – ah! He – he – he comes here devil knows from where – comes here – devil knows why – to trample on me till I die – ah – trample" (he stamped softly with both feet), "trample like this – nobody knows why – till I die. . . ." His voice became quite extinct; he was bothered by a little cough; he came up close to the fence and told me, dropping into a confidential and piteous tone, that he would *not* be trampled upon. "Patience – patience," he muttered, striking his breast. I had done laughing at him, but unexpectedly he treated me to a wild cracked burst of it. "Ha! ha! ha! We shall see! We shall see! What! Steal from me? Steal from me everything! Everything! Everything!" His head drooped on one shoulder, his hands were hanging before him lightly clasped. One would have thought he had cherished the girl with surpassing love, that his spirit had been crushed and his heart broken by the most cruel of spoliations. Suddenly he lifted his head and shot out an infamous word. "Like her mother – she is like her deceitful mother. Exactly. In her face, too. In her face. The devil!" He leaned his forehead against the fence, and in that position uttered threats and horrible blasphemies in Portuguese in very weak ejaculations, mingled with miserable plaints and groans, coming out with a heave of the shoulders as though he had been overtaken by a deadly fit of sickness. It was an inexpressibly grotesque and vile performance, and I hastened away. He tried to shout something after me. Some disparagement of Jim, I believe – not too loud though, we were too near the house. All I heard distinctly was, "No more than a little child – a little child."

# CHAPTER THIRTY-FIVE

'But next morning, at the first bend of the river shutting off the houses of Patusan, all this dropped out of my sight bodily, with its colour, its design, and its meaning, like a picture created by fancy on a canvas, upon which, after long contemplation, you turn your back for the last time. It remains in the memory motionless, unfaded, with its life arrested, in an unchanging light. There are the ambitions, the fears, the hate, the hopes, and they remain in my mind just as I had seen them – intense and as if for ever suspended in their expression. I had turned away from the picture and was going back to the world where events move, men change, light flickers, life flows in a clear stream, no matter whether over mud or over stones. I wasn't going to dive into it; I would have enough to do to keep my head above the surface. But as to what I was leaving behind, I cannot imagine any alteration. The immense and magnanimous Doramin and his little motherly witch of a wife, gazing together upon the land and nursing secretly their dreams of parental ambition; Tunju Allang, wizened and greatly perplexed; Dain Waris, intelligent and brave, with his faith in Jim, with his firm glance and his ironic friendliness; the girl, absorbed in her frightened, suspicious adoration; Tamb' Itam, surly and faithful; Cornelius, leaning his forehead against the fence under the moonlight – I am certain of them. They exist as if under an enchanter's wand. But the figure round which all these are grouped – that one lives, and I am not certain of him. No magician's wand can immobilise him under my eyes. He is one of us.

'Jim, as I've told you, accompanied me on the first stage of my journey back to the world he had renounced, and the way at times seemed to lead through the very heart of untouched wilderness. The empty reaches sparkled under the high sun; between the high walls of vegetation the heat drowsed upon the water, and the boat, impelled vigorously, cut her way through the air that seemed to have settled dense and warm under the shelter of lofty trees.

'The shadow of the impending separation had already put an immense space between us, and when we spoke it was with an effort, as if to force our low voices across a vast and increasing distance. The boat fairly flew; we sweltered side by side in the stagnant superheated air; the smell of mud, of marsh, the primeval smell of fecund earth, seemed to sting our faces; till suddenly at a bend it was as if a great hand far away had lifted a heavy curtain, had flung open an immense portal. The light itself seemed to stir, the sky above our heads widened, a far-off murmur reached our ears, a freshness enveloped us, filled our lungs, quickened our thoughts, our blood, our regrets – and, straight ahead, the forests sank down against the dark-blue ridge of the sea.

'I breathed deeply, I revelled in the vastness of the opened horizon, in the different atmosphere that seemed to vibrate with a toil of life, with the energy of an impeccable world. This sky and this sea were open to me. The girl was right – there was a sign, a call in them – something to which I responded with every fibre of my being. I let my eyes roam through space, like a man released from bonds who stretches his cramped limbs, runs, leaps, responds to the inspiring elation of freedom. "This is glorious!" I cried, and then I looked at the sinner by my side. He sat with his head sunk on his breast and said "Yes," without raising his eyes, as if afraid to see writ large on the clear sky of the offing the reproach of his romantic conscience.

'I remember the smallest details of that afternoon. We landed on a bit of white beach. It was backed by a low cliff

wooded on the brow, draped in creepers to the very foot.
Below us the plain of the sea, of a serene and intense blue,
stretched with a slight upward tilt to the thread-like horizon drawn at the height of our eyes. Great waves of glitter
blew lightly along the pitted dark surface, as swift as feath-
ers chased by the breeze. A chain of islands sat broken and
massive facing the wide estuary, displayed in a sheet of pale
glassy water reflecting faithfully the contour of the shore.
High in the colourless sunshine a solitary bird, all black,
hovered, dropping and soaring above the same spot with a
slight rocking motion of the wings. A ragged, sooty bunch
of flimsy mat hovels was perched over its own inverted
image upon a crooked multitude of high piles the colour
of ebony. A tiny black canoe put off from amongst them
with two tiny men, all black, who toiled exceedingly, striking down at the pale water: and the canoe seemed to slide
painfully on a mirror. This bunch of miserable hovels was
the fishing village that boasted of the white lord's especial
protection, and the two men crossing over were the old
headman and his son-in-law. They landed and walked up
to us on the white sand, lean, dark-brown as if dried in
smoke, with ashy patches on the skin of their naked
shoulders and breasts. Their heads were bound in dirty
but carefully folded handkerchiefs, and the old man
began at once to state a complaint, voluble, stretching a
lank arm, screwing up at Jim his old bleared eyes confidently. The Rajah's people would not leave them alone;
there had been some trouble about a lot of turtles' eggs his
people had collected on the islets there – and leaning at
arm's-length upon his paddle, he pointed with a brown
skinny hand over the sea. Jim listened for a time without
looking up, and at last told him gently to wait. He would
hear him by-and-by. They withdrew obediently to some
little distance, and sat on their heels, with their paddles
lying before them on the sand; the silvery gleams in their
eyes followed our movements patiently; and the immensity
of the outspread sea, the stillness of the coast, passing north

and south beyond the limits of my vision, made up one colossal Presence watching us four dwarfs isolated on a strip of glistening sand.

'"The trouble is," remarked Jim, moodily, "that for generations these beggars of fishermen in that village there had been considered as the Rajah's personal slaves – and the old rip can't get it into his head that..."'

'He paused. "That you have changed all that," I said.

'"Yes. I've changed all that," he muttered in a gloomy voice.

'"You have had your opportunity," I pursued.

'"Had I?" he said. "Well, yes. I suppose so. Yes. I have got back my confidence in myself – a good name – yet sometimes I wish... No! I shall hold what I've got. Can't expect anything more." He flung his arm out towards the sea. "Not out there anyhow." He stamped his foot upon the sand. "This is my limit, because nothing less will do."

'We continued pacing the beach. "Yes, I've changed all that," he went on, with a sidelong glance at the two patient squatting fishermen; "but only try to think what it would be if I went away. Jove! can't you see it? Hell loose. No! Tomorrow I shall go and take my chance of drinking that silly old Tunku Allang's coffee, and I shall make no end of fuss over these rotten turtles' eggs. No. I can't say – enough. Never. I must go on, go on for ever holding up my end, to feel sure that nothing can touch me. I must stick to their belief in me to feel safe and to – to"... He cast about for a word, seemed to look for it on the sea..."to keep in touch with"... His voice sank suddenly to a murmur..."with those whom, perhaps, I shall never see any more. With – with – you, for instance."

'I was profoundly humbled by his words. "For God's sake," I said, "don't set me up, my dear fellow; just look to yourself." I felt a gratitude, an affection, for that straggler whose eyes had singled me out, keeping my place in the ranks of an insignificant multitude. How little that was to boast of, after all! I turned my burning face away; under the

low sun, glowing, darkened and crimson, like an ember
snatched from the fire, the sea lay outspread, offering all its
immense stillness to the approach of the fiery orb. Twice he
was going to speak, but checked himself: at last, as if he had
found a formula –

'"I shall be faithful," he said, quietly. "I shall be faithful,"
he repeated, without looking at me, but for the first time
letting his eyes wander upon the waters, whose blueness
had changed to a gloomy purple under the fires of sunset.
Ah! he was romantic, romantic. I recalled some words of
Stein's.... "In the destructive element immerse!... To follow the dream, and again to follow the dream – and so –
always – *usque ad finem*..." He was romantic, but none the
less true. Who could tell what forms, what visions, what
faces, what forgiveness he could see in the glow of the
west!... A small boat, leaving the schooner, moved slowly,
with a regular beat of two oars, towards the sandbank to
take me off. "And then there's Jewel," he said, out of the
great silence of earth, sky, and sea, which had mastered my
very thoughts so that his voice made me start. "There's
Jewel." "Yes," I murmured. "I need not tell you what she is
to me," he pursued. "You've seen. In time she will come to
understand..." "I hope so," I interrupted. "She trusts me,
too," he mused, and then changed his tone. "When shall we
meet next, I wonder?" he said.

'"Never – unless you come out," I answered, avoiding his
glance. He didn't seem to be surprised; he kept very quiet
for a while.

'"Good-bye, then," he said, after a pause. "Perhaps it's
just as well."

'We shook hands, and I walked to the boat, which
waited with her nose on the beach. The schooner, her
mainsail set and jib-sheet to windward, curveted on the
purple sea; there was a rosy tinge on her sails. "Will you be
going home again soon?" asked Jim, just as I swung my leg
over the gunwale. "In a year or so if I live," I said. The
forefoot grated on the sand, the boat floated, the wet oars

flashed and dipped once, twice. Jim, at the water's edge, raised his voice. "Tell them..." he began. I signed to the men to cease rowing, and waited in wonder. Tell who? The half-submerged sun faced him; I could see its red gleam in his eyes that looked dumbly at me.... "No – nothing," he said, and with a slight wave of his hand motioned the boat away. I did not look again at the shore till I had clambered on board the schooner.

'By that time the sun had set. The twilight lay over the east, and the coast, turned black, extended infinitely its sombre wall that seemed the very stronghold of the night; the western horizon was one great blaze of gold and crimson in which a big detached cloud floated dark and still, casting a slaty shadow on the water beneath, and I saw Jim on the beach watching the schooner fall off and gather headway.

'The two half-naked fishermen had arisen as soon as I had gone; they were no doubt pouring the plaint of their trifling, miserable, oppressed lives into the ears of the white lord, and no doubt he was listening to it, making it his own, for was it not a part of his luck – the luck "from the word Go" – the luck to which he had assured me he was so completely equal? They, too, I should think, were in luck, and I was sure their pertinacity would be equal to it. Their dark-skinned bodies vanished on the dark background long before I had lost sight of their protector. He was white from head to foot, and remained persistently visible with the stronghold of the night at his back, the sea at his feet, the opportunity by his side – still veiled. What do you say? Was it still veiled? I don't know. For me that white figure in the stillness of coast and sea seemed to stand at the heart of a vast enigma. The twilight was ebbing fast from the sky above his head, the strip of sand had sunk already under his feet, he himself appeared no bigger than a child – then only a speck, a tiny white speck, that seemed to catch all the light left in a darkened world.... And, suddenly, I lost him....'

# CHAPTER THIRTY-SIX

WITH these words Marlow had ended his narrative, and his audience had broken up forthwith, under his abstract, pensive gaze. Men drifted off the verandah in pairs or alone without loss of time, without offering a remark, as if the last image of that incomplete story, its incompleteness itself, and the very tone of the speaker, had made discussion vain and comment impossible. Each of them seemed to carry away his own impression, to carry it away with him like a secret; but there was only one man of all these listeners who was ever to hear the last word of the story. It came to him at home, more than two years later, and it came contained in a thick packet addressed in Marlow's upright and angular handwriting.

The privileged man opened the packet, looked in, then, laying it down, went to the window. His rooms were in the highest flat of a lofty building, and his glance could travel afar beyond the clear panes of glass, as though he were looking out of the lantern of a lighthouse. The slopes of the roofs glistened, the dark broken ridges succeeded each other without end like sombre, uncrested waves, and from the depths of the town under his feet ascended a confused and unceasing mutter. The spires of churches, numerous, scattered haphazard, uprose like beacons on a maze of shoals without a channel; the driving rain mingled with the falling dusk of a winter's evening; and the booming of a big clock on a tower striking the hour, rolled past in voluminous, austere bursts of sound, with a shrill vibrating cry at the core. He drew the heavy curtains.

The light of his shaded reading-lamp slept like a sheltered pool, his footfalls made no sound on the carpet, his

303

wandering days were over. No more horizons as boundless
as hope, no more twilights within the forests as solemn as
temples, in the hot quest of the Ever-undiscovered
Country over the hill, across the stream, beyond the
wave. The hour was striking! No more! No more! – but
the opened packet under the lamp brought back the
sounds, the visions, the very savour of the past – a multitude of fading faces, a tumult of low voices, dying away
upon the shores of distant seas under a passionate and
unconsoling sunshine. He sighed and sat down to read.

At first he saw three distinct enclosures. A good many
pages closely blackened and pinned together; a loose square
sheet of greyish paper with a few words traced in a handwriting he had never seen before, and an explanatory letter
from Marlow. From this last fell another letter, yellowed by
time and frayed on the folds. He picked it up and, laying it
aside, turned to Marlow's message, ran swiftly over the
opening lines, and, checking himself, thereafter read on
deliberately, like one approaching with slow feet and alert
eyes the glimpse of an undiscovered country.

'. . . I don't suppose you've forgotten,' went on the letter.
'You alone have showed an interest in him that survived the
telling of his story, though I remember well you would not
admit he had mastered his fate. You prophesied for him the
disaster of weariness and of disgust with acquired honour,
with the self-appointed task, with the love sprung from
pity and youth. You had said you knew so well "that kind of
thing," its illusory satisfaction, its unavoidable deception.
You said also – I call to mind – that "giving your life up to
them" (*them* meaning all of mankind with skins brown,
yellow, or black in colour) "was like selling your soul to a
brute." You contended that "that kind of thing" was only
endurable and enduring when based on a firm conviction in
the truth of ideas racially our own, in whose name are
established the order, the morality of an ethical progress.
"We want its strength at our backs," you had said. "We
want a belief in its necessity and its justice, to make a

worthy and conscious sacrifice of our lives. Without it the sacrifice is only forgetfulness, the way of offering is no better than the way to perdition." In other words, you maintained that we must fight in the ranks or our lives don't count. Possibly! You ought to know – be it said without malice – you who have rushed into one or two places single-handed and came out cleverly, without singeing your wings. The point, however, is that of all mankind Jim had no dealings but with himself, and the question is whether at the last he had not confessed to a faith mightier than the laws of order and progress.

'I affirm nothing. Perhaps you may pronounce – after you've read. There is much truth – after all – in the common expression "under a cloud." It is impossible to see him clearly – especially as it is through the eyes of others that we take our last look at him. I have no hesitation in imparting to you all I know of the last episode that, as he used to say, had "come to him." One wonders whether this was perhaps that supreme opportunity, that last and satisfying test for which I had always suspected him to be waiting, before he could frame a message to the impeccable world. You remember that when I was leaving him for the last time he had asked whether I would be going home soon, and suddenly cried after me, "Tell them!"...I had waited – curious I'll own, and hopeful, too – only to hear him shout, "No. Nothing." That was all then – and there shall be nothing more; there shall be no message, unless such as each of us can interpret for himself from the language of facts, that are so often more enigmatic than the craftiest arrangement of words. He made, it is true, one more attempt to deliver himself; but that, too, failed, as you may perceive if you look at the sheet of greyish foolscap enclosed here. He had tried to write; do you notice the commonplace hand? It is headed "The Fort, Patusan." I suppose he had carried out his intention of making out of his house a place of defence. It was an excellent plan: a deep ditch, an earth wall topped by a palisade, and at the angles guns mounted on platforms to sweep each side of the square. Doramin had agreed to furnish him the guns; and so each man of his party would know there was a place of safety, upon which every faithful partisan could rally in case of some sudden danger. All this showed his judicious foresight, his faith in the future. What he called "my own people" – the liberated captives of the Sherif – were to make a distinct quarter of Patusan, with their huts and little plots of ground under the walls of the stronghold. Within he would be an invincible host in himself. "The Fort, Patusan." No date, as you observe. What is a number and a name to a day of days? It is also impossible to say whom he had in his mind when he seized the pen: Stein – myself – the world at large – or was this only the aimless startled cry of a solitary man confronted by his fate? "An awful thing has happened," he wrote before he flung the pen down for the first time; look at the ink blot resembling the head of an arrow under these words. After a while he had tried again, scrawling heavily, as if with a hand of lead, another line. "I must now at once..." The pen had sput-tered, and that time he gave it up. There's nothing more; he had seen a broad gulf that neither eye nor voice could span. I can understand this. He was overwhelmed by the inexplicable; he was overwhelmed by his own personality – the gift of that destiny which he had done his best to master.

'I send you also an old letter – a very old letter. It was found carefully preserved in his writing-case. It is from his father, and by the date you can see he must have received it a few days before he joined the *Patna*. Thus it must be the last letter he ever had from home. He had treasured it all these years. The good old parson fancied his sailor-son. I've looked in at a sentence here and there. There is nothing in it except just affection. He tells his "dear James" that the last long letter from him was very "honest and entertain-ing." He would not have him "judge men harshly or has-tily." There are four pages of it, easy morality and family news. Tom had "taken orders." Carrie's husband had "money losses." The old chap goes on equably trusting Providence and the established order of the universe, but alive to its small dangers and its small mercies. One can almost see him, grey-haired and serene in the inviolable shelter of his book-lined, faded, and comfortable study, where for forty years he had conscientiously gone over and over again the round of his little thoughts about faith and virtue, about the conduct of life and the only proper manner of dying; where he had written so many sermons, where he sits talking to his boy, over there, on the other side of the earth. But what of the distance? Virtue is one all over the world, and there is only one faith, one conceivable conduct of life, one manner of dying. He hopes his "dear James" will never forget that "who once gives way to temptation, in the very instant hazards his total depravity and everlasting ruin. Therefore resolve fixedly never, through any possible motives, to do anything which you believe to be wrong." There is also some news of a favourite dog; and a pony, "which all you boys used to ride," had gone blind from old age and had to be shot. The old chap invokes Heaven's blessing; the mother and all the girls then at home send their love. . . . No, there is nothing much in that yellow frayed letter fluttering out of his cherishing grasp after so many years. It was never answered, but who can say what converse he may have held with all these placid, colourless forms of men and women peopling that quiet corner of the world as free of danger or strife as a tomb, and breathing equally the air of undisturbed rectitude. It seems amazing that he should belong to it, he to whom so many things "had come." Nothing ever came to them; they would never be taken unawares, and never be called upon to grapple with fate. Here they all are, evoked by the mild gossip of the father, all these brothers and sisters, bone of his bone and flesh of his flesh, gazing with clear unconscious eyes, while I seem to see him, returned at last, no longer a mere white speck at the heart of an immense mystery, but of full stature, standing disregarded amongst their untroubled shapes, with a stern and romantic aspect, but always mute, dark – under a cloud.

'The story of the last events you shall find in the few pages enclosed here. You must admit that it is romantic beyond the wildest dreams of his boyhood, and yet there is to my mind a sort of profound and terrifying logic in it, as if it were our imagination alone that could set loose upon us the might of an overwhelming destiny. The imprudence of our thoughts recoils upon our heads; who toys with the sword shall perish by the sword. This astounding adventure, of which the most astounding part is that it is true, comes on as an unavoidable consequence. Something of the sort had to happen. You repeat this to yourself while you marvel that such a thing could happen in the year of grace before last. But it has happened – and there is no disputing its logic.

'I put it down here for you as though I had been an eyewitness. My information was fragmentary, but I've fitted the pieces together, and there is enough of them to make an intelligible picture. I wonder how he would have related it himself. He has confided so much in me that at times it seems as though he must come in presently and tell the story in his own words, in his careless yet feeling voice, with his offhand manner, a little puzzled, a little bothered, a little hurt, but now and then by a word or a phrase giving one of these glimpses of his very own self that were never any good for purposes of orientation. It's difficult to believe he will never come. I shall never hear his voice again, nor shall I see his smooth tan-and-pink face with a white line on the forehead, and the youthful eyes darkened by excitement to a profound, unfathomable blue.'

# CHAPTER THIRTY-SEVEN

'It all begins with a remarkable exploit of a man called Brown, who stole with complete success a Spanish schooner out of a small bay near Zamboanga. Till I discovered the fellow my information was incomplete, but most unexpectedly I did come upon him a few hours before he gave up his arrogant ghost. Fortunately he was willing and able to talk between the choking fits of asthma, and his racked body writhed with malicious exultation at the bare thought of Jim. He exulted thus at the idea that he had "paid out the stuck-up beggar after all." He gloated over his action. I had to bear the sunken glare of his fierce crow-footed eyes if I wanted to know; and so I bore it, reflecting how much certain forms of evil are akin to madness, derived from intense egoism, inflamed by resistance, tearing the soul to pieces, and giving factitious vigour to the body. The story also reveals unsuspected depths of cunning in the wretched Cornelius, whose abject and intense hate acts like a subtle inspiration, pointing out an unerring way towards revenge.

'"I could see directly I set my eyes on him what sort of a fool he was," gasped the dying Brown. "He a man! Hell! He was a hollow sham. As if he couldn't have said straight out, 'Hands off my plunder!' blast him! That would have been like a man! Rot his superior soul! He had me there – but he hadn't devil enough in him to make an end of me. Not he! A thing like that letting me off as if I wasn't worth a kick!..." Brown struggled desperately for breath.... "Fraud.... Letting me off.... And so I did make an end of him after all...." He choked again.... "I expect this thing'll kill me, but I shall die easy

now. You...you hear...I don't know your name –
I would give you a five-pound note if – if I had it – for
the news – or my name's not Brown...." He grinned
horribly.... "Gentleman Brown."

'He said all these things in profound gasps, staring at me
with his yellow eyes out of a long, ravaged brown face; he
jerked his left arm; a pepper-and-salt matted beard hung
almost into his lap; a dirty ragged blanket covered his legs.
I had found him out in Bankok through that busybody
Schomberg, the hotelkeeper, who had, confidentially,
directed me where to look. It appears that a sort of loafing,
fuddled vagabond – a white man living amongst the natives
with a Siamese woman – had considered it a great privilege
to give a shelter to the last days of the famous Gentleman
Brown. While he was talking to me in the wretched hovel,
and, as it were, fighting for every minute of his life, the
Siamese woman, with big bare legs and a stupid coarse face,
sat in a dark corner chewing betel stolidly. Now and then
she would get up for the purpose of shooing a chicken away
from the door. The whole hut shook when she walked. An
ugly yellow child, naked and pot-bellied like a little
heathen god, stood at the foot of the couch, finger in
mouth, lost in a profound and calm contemplation of the
dying man.

'He talked feverishly; but in the middle of a word,
perhaps, an invisible hand would take him by the throat,
and he would look at me dumbly with an expression of
doubt and anguish. He seemed to fear that I would get
tired of waiting and go away, leaving him with his tale
untold, with his exultation unexpressed. He died during
the night, I believe, but by that time I had nothing more to
learn.

'So much as to Brown, for the present.

'Eight months before this, coming into Samarang,
I went as usual to see Stein. On the garden side of the
house a Malay on the verandah greeted me shyly, and I
remembered that I had seen him in Patusan, in Jim's house,

amongst other Bugis men who used to come in the evening to talk interminably over their war reminiscences and to discuss State affairs. Jim had pointed him out to me once as a respectable petty trader owning a small seagoing native craft, who had showed himself "one of the best at the taking of the stockade." I was not very surprised to see him, since any Patusan trader venturing as far as Samarang would naturally find his way to Stein's house. I returned his greeting and passed on. At the door of Stein's room I came upon another Malay in whom I recognised Tamb' Itam.

'I asked him at once what he was doing there; it occurred to me that Jim might have come on a visit. I own I was pleased and excited at the thought. Tamb' Itam looked as if he did not know what to say. "Is Tuan Jim inside?" I asked, impatiently. "No," he mumbled, hanging his head for a moment, and then with sudden earnestness, "He would not fight. He would not fight," he repeated twice. As he seemed unable to say anything else, I pushed him aside and went in.

'Stein, tall and stooping, stood alone in the middle of the room between the rows of butterfly cases. "Ach! is it you, my friend?" he said, sadly, peering through his glasses. A drab sack-coat of alpaca hung, unbuttoned, down to his knees. He had a Panama hat on his head, and there were deep furrows on his pale cheeks. "What's the matter now?" I asked, nervously. "There's Tamb' Itam there...." "Come and see the girl. Come and see the girl. She is here," he said, with a half-hearted show of activity. I tried to detain him, but with gentle obstinacy he would take no notice of my eager questions. "She is here, she is here," he repeated, in great perturbation. "They came here two days ago. An old man like me, a stranger – *sehen sie* – cannot do much.... Come this way.... Young hearts are unforgiving...." I could see he was in utmost distress.... "The strength of life in them, the cruel strength of life...." He mumbled, leading me round the house; I followed him, lost in dismal and angry conjectures. At the door of the drawing-room he barred my way. "He loved her very much," he said, interrogatively, and I only nodded, feeling so bitterly disappointed that I would not trust myself to speak. "Very frightful," he murmured. "She can't understand me. I am only a strange old man. Perhaps you ... she knows you. Talk to her. We can't leave it like this. Tell her to forgive him. It was very frightful." "No doubt," I said, exasperated at being in the dark; "but have *you* forgiven him?" He looked at me queerly. "You shall hear," he said, and opening the door, absolutely pushed me in.

'You know Stein's big house and the two immense reception-rooms, uninhabited and uninhabitable, clean, full of solitude and of shining things that look as if never beheld by the eye of man? They are cool on the hottest days, and you enter them as you would a scrubbed cave underground. I passed through one, and in the other I saw the girl sitting at the end of a big mahogany table, on which she rested her head, the face hidden in her arms. The waxed floor reflected her dimly as though it had been a sheet of frozen water. The rattan screens were down, and through the strange greenish gloom made by the foliage of the trees outside, a strong wind blew in gusts, swaying the long draperies of windows and doorways. Her white figure seemed shaped in snow; the pendent crystals of a great chandelier clicked above her head like glittering icicles. She looked up and watched my approach. I was chilled as if these vast apartments had been the cold abode of despair.

'She recognised me at once, and as soon as I had stopped, looking down at her: "He has left me," she said, quietly; "you always leave us – for your own ends." Her face was set. All the heat of life seemed withdrawn within some inaccessible spot in her breast. "It would have been easy to die with him," she went on, and made a slight weary gesture as if giving up the incomprehensible. "He would not! It was like a blindness – and yet it was I who was speaking to him; it was I who stood before his eyes; it was at me that he looked all the time! Ah! you are hard, treacherous, without truth, without compassion. What makes you so wicked? Or is it that you are all mad?"

'I took her hand; it did not respond, and when I dropped it, it hung down to the floor. That indifference, more awful than tears, cries, and reproaches, seemed to defy time and consolation. You felt that nothing you could say would reach the seat of the still and benumbing pain.

'Stein had said, "You shall hear." I did hear. I heard it all, listening with amazement, with awe, to the tones of her inflexible weariness. She could not grasp the real sense of what she was telling me, and her resentment filled me with pity for her – for him, too. I stood rooted to the spot after she had finished. Leaning on her arm, she stared with hard eyes, and the wind passed in gusts, the crystals kept on clicking in the greenish gloom. She went on whispering to herself: "And yet he was looking at me! He could see my face, hear my voice, hear my grief! When I used to sit at his feet, with my cheek against his knee and his hand on my head, the curse of cruelty and madness was already within him, waiting for the day. The day came! . . . and before the sun had set he could not see me any more – he was made blind and deaf and without pity, as you all are. He shall have no tears from me. Never, never. Not one tear. I will not! He went away from me as if I had been worse than death. He fled as if driven by some accursed thing he had heard or seen in his sleep. . . . "

'Her steady eyes seemed to strain after the shape of a man torn out of her arms by the strength of a dream. She made no sign to my silent bow. I was glad to escape.

'I saw her once again, the same afternoon. On leaving her I had gone in search of Stein, whom I could not find indoors; and I wandered out, pursued by distressful thoughts, into the gardens, those famous gardens of Stein, in which you can find every plant and tree of tropical lowlands. I followed the course of the canalised stream, and sat for a long time on a shaded bench near the ornamental pond, where some waterfowl with clipped wings were diving and splashing noisily. The branches of casuarina-trees behind me swayed lightly, incessantly, reminding me of the soughing of fir-trees at home.

'This mournful and restless sound was a fit accompaniment to my meditations. She had said he had been driven away from her by a dream, – and there was no answer one could make her – there seemed to be no forgiveness for such a transgression. And yet is not mankind itself, pushing on its blind way, driven by a dream of its greatness and its power upon the dark paths of excessive cruelty and of excessive devotion? And what is the pursuit of truth, after all?

'When I rose to get back to the house I caught sight of Stein's drab coat through a gap in the foliage, and very soon at a turn of the path I came upon him walking with the girl. Her little hand rested on his forearm, and under the broad, flat rim of his Panama hat he bent over her, greyhaired, paternal, with compassionate and chivalrous deference. I stood aside, but they stopped, facing me. His gaze was bent on the ground at his feet; the girl, erect and slight on his arm, stared sombrely beyond my shoulder with black, clear, motionless eyes. "*Schrecklich*," he murmured. "Terrible! Terrible! What can one do?" He seemed to be appealing to me, but her youth, the length of the days suspended over her head, appealed to me more; and suddenly, even as I realised that nothing could be said, I found myself pleading his cause for her sake. "You must forgive him," I concluded, and my own voice seemed to me muffled, lost in an irresponsive deaf immensity. "We all want to be forgiven," I added after a while.

'"What have I done?" she asked with her lips only.

'"You always mistrusted him," I said.

'"He was like the others," she pronounced slowly.

'"Not like the others," I protested, but she continued evenly, without any feeling –

'"He was false." And suddenly Stein broke in. "No! no! no! My poor child! . . ." He patted her hand lying passively

on his sleeve. "No! no! Not false! True! true! true!" He tried
to look into her stony face. "You don't understand. Ach!
Why you do not understand? ... Terrible," he said to me.
"Some day she *shall* understand."

'"Will *you* explain?" I asked, looking hard at him. They
moved on.

'I watched them. Her gown trailed on the path, her
black hair fell loose. She walked upright and light by the
side of the tall man, whose long shapeless coat hung in
perpendicular folds from the stooping shoulders, whose
feet moved slowly. They disappeared beyond that spinney
(you may remember) where sixteen different kinds of bamboo grow together, all distinguishable to the learned eye.
For my part, I was fascinated by the exquisite grace and
beauty of that fluted grove, crowned with pointed leaves
and feathery heads, the lightness, the vigour, the charm as
distinct as a voice of that unperplexed luxuriating life. I
remember staying to look at it for a long time, as one would
linger within reach of a consoling whisper. The sky was
pearly grey. It was one of those overcast days so rare in the
tropics, in which memories crowd upon one, memories of
other shores, of other faces.

'I drove back to town the same afternoon, taking
with me Tamb' Itam and the other Malay, in whose
seagoing craft they had escaped in the bewilderment, fear,
and gloom of the disaster. The shock of it seemed to have
changed their natures. It had turned her passion into stone,
and it made the surly taciturn Tamb' Itam almost
loquacious. His surliness, too, was subdued into puzzled
humility, as though he had seen the failure of a potent
charm in a supreme moment. The Bugis trader, a
shy hesitating man, was very clear in the little he had to
say. Both were evidently overawed by a sense of deep
inexpressible wonder, by the touch of an inscrutable
mystery.

There with Marlow's signature the letter proper ended.
The privileged reader screwed up his lamp, and solitary

above the billowy roofs of the town, like a lighthouse-
keeper above the sea, he turned to the pages of the
story.

# CHAPTER THIRTY-EIGHT

'It all begins, as I've told you, with the man called Brown,' ran the opening sentence of Marlow's narrative. 'You who have knocked about the Western Pacific must have heard of him. He was the show ruffian on the Australian coast – not that he was often to be seen there, but because he was always trotted out in the stories of lawless life a visitor from home is treated to; and the mildest of these stories which were told about him from Cape York to Eden Bay was more than enough to hang a man if told in the right place. They never failed to let you know, too, that he was supposed to be the son of a baronet. Be it as it may, it is certain he had deserted from a home ship in the early gold-digging days, and in a few years became talked about as the terror of this or that group of islands in Polynesia. He would kidnap natives, he would strip some lonely white trader to the very pyjamas he stood in, and after he had robbed the poor devil, he would as likely as not invite him to fight a duel with shot-guns on the beach – which would have been fair enough as these things go, if the other man hadn't been by that time already half-dead with fright. Brown was a latter-day buccaneer, sorry enough, like his more celebrated prototypes; but what distinguished him from his contemporary brother ruffians, like Bully Hayes or the mellifluous Pease, or that perfumed, Dundreary-whiskered, dandified scoundrel known as Dirty Dick, was the arrogant temper of his misdeeds and a vehement scorn for mankind at large and for his victims in particular. The others were merely vulgar and greedy brutes, but he seemed moved by some complex intention. He would rob a man as if only to demonstrate his

317

poor opinion of the creature, and he would bring to the shooting or maiming of some quiet, unoffending stranger a savage and vengeful earnestness fit to terrify the most reckless of desperadoes. In the days of his greatest glory he owned an armed barque, manned by a mixed crew of Kanakas and runaway whalers, and boasted, I don't know with what truth, of being financed on the quiet by a most respectable firm of copra merchants. Later on he ran off – it was reported – with the wife of a missionary, a very young girl from Clapham way, who had married the mild, flat-footed fellow in a moment of enthusiasm, and suddenly transplanted to Melanesia, lost her bearings somehow. It was a dark story. She was ill at the time he carried her off, and died on board his ship. It is said – as the most wonder-ful part of the tale – that over her body he gave way to an outburst of sombre and violent grief. His luck left him, too, very soon after. He lost his ship on some rocks off Malaita, and disappeared for a time as though he had gone down with her. He is heard of next at Nuka-Hiva, where he bought an old French schooner out of Government service. What creditable enterprise he might have had in view when he made that purchase I can't say, but it is evident that what with High Commissioners, consuls, men-of-war, and international control, the South Seas were getting too hot to hold gentlemen of his kidney. Clearly he must have shifted the scene of his operations farther west, because a year later he plays an incredibly audacious, but not a very profitable part, in a serio-comic business in Manila Bay, in which a peculating governor and an absconding treasurer are the principal figures; thereafter he seems to have hung around the Philippines in his rotten schooner, battling with an adverse fortune, till at last, running his appointed course, he sails into Jim's history, a blind accomplice of the Dark Powers.

'His tale goes that when a Spanish patrol cutter captured him he was simply trying to run a few guns for the insur-gents. If so, then I can't understand what he was doing off the south coast of Mindanao. My belief, however, is that he was blackmailing the native villages along the coast. The principal thing is that the cutter, throwing a guard on board, made him sail in company towards Zamboanga. On the way, for some reason or other, both vessels had to call at one of these new Spanish settlements – which never came to anything in the end – where there was not only a civil official in charge on shore, but a good stout coasting schooner lying at anchor in the little bay; and this craft, in every way much better than his own, Brown made up his mind to steal.

'He was down on his luck – as he told me himself. The world he had bullied for twenty years with fierce, aggressive disdain, had yielded him nothing in the way of material advantage except a small bag of silver dollars, which was concealed in his cabin so that "the devil himself couldn't smell it out." And that was all – absolutely all. He was tired of his life, and not afraid of death. But this man, who would stake his existence on a whim with a bitter and jeering recklessness, stood in mortal fear of imprisonment. He had an unreasoning cold-sweat, nerve-shaking, blood-to-water-turning sort of horror at the bare possibility of being locked up – the sort of terror a superstitious man would feel at the thought of being embraced by a spectre. Therefore the civil official who came on board to make a preliminary investigation into the capture, investigated arduously all day long, and only went ashore after dark, muffled up in a cloak, and taking great care not to let Brown's little all clink in its bag. Afterwards, being a man of his word, he contrived (the very next evening, I believe) to send off the Government cutter on some urgent bit of special service. As her commander could not spare a prize crew, he contented himself by taking away before he left all the sails of Brown's schooner to the very last rag, and took good care to tow his two boats on to the beach a couple of miles off.

'But in Brown's crew there was a Solomon Islander, kidnapped in his youth and devoted to Brown, who was the best man of the whole gang. That fellow swam off to the coaster – five hundred yards or so – with the end of a warp made up of all the running gear unrove for the purpose. The water was smooth, and the bay dark, "like the inside of a cow," as Brown described it. The Solomon Islander clambered over the bulwarks with the end of the rope in his teeth. The crew of the coaster – all Tagals – were ashore having a jollification in the native village. The two shipkeepers left on board woke up suddenly and saw the devil. It had glittering eyes and leaped quick as lightning about the deck. They fell on their knees, paralysed with fear, crossing themselves and mumbling prayers. With a long knife he found in the caboose the Solomon Islander, without interrupting their orisons, stabbed first one, then the other; with the same knife he set to sawing patiently at the coir cable till suddenly it parted under the blade with a splash. Then in the silence of the bay he let out a cautious shout, and Brown's gang, who meantime had been peering and straining their hopeful ears in the darkness, began to pull gently at their end of the warp. In less than five minutes the two schooners came together with a slight shock and a creak of spars.

'Brown's crowd transferred themselves without losing an instant, taking with them their firearms and a large supply of ammunition. They were sixteen in all: two runaway blue-jackets, a lanky deserter from a Yankee man-of-war, a couple of simple, blond Scandinavians, a mulatto of sorts, one bland Chinaman who cooked – and the rest of the nondescript spawn of the South Seas. None of them cared; Brown bent them to his will, and Brown, indifferent to gallows, was running away from the spectre of a Spanish prison. He didn't give them the time to trans-ship enough provisions; the weather was calm, the air was charged with dew, and when they cast off the ropes and set sail to a faint offshore draught there was no flutter in the damp canvas; their old schooner seemed to detach itself gently from the stolen craft and slip away silently, together with the black mass of the coast, into the night.

'They got clear away. Brown related to me in detail their passage down the Straits of Macassar. It is a harrowing and desperate story. They were short of food and water; they boarded several native craft and got a little from each. With a stolen ship Brown did not dare to put into any port, of course. He had no money to buy anything, no papers to show, and no lie plausible enough to get him out again. An Arab barque, under the Dutch flag, surprised one night at anchor off Poulo Laut, yielded a little dirty rice, a bunch of bananas, and a cask of water; three days of squally misty weather from the north-east shot the schooner across the Java Sea. The yellow muddy waves drenched that collection of hungry ruffians. They sighted mailboats moving on their appointed routes; passed well-found home ships with rusty iron sides anchored in the shallow sea waiting for a change of weather or the turn of the tide; an English gunboat, white and trim, with two slim masts, crossed their bows one day in the distance; and on another occasion a Dutch corvette, black and heavily sparred, loomed upon their quarter, steaming dead slow in the mist. They slipped through unseen or disregarded, a wan, sallow-faced band of utter outcasts, enraged with hunger and hunted by fear. Brown's idea was to make for Madagascar, where he expected, on grounds not altogether illusory, to sell the schooner in Tamatave, and no questions asked, or perhaps obtain some more or less forged papers for her. Yet before he could face the long passage across the Indian Ocean food was wanted – water, too.

'Perhaps he had heard of Patusan – or perhaps he just only happened to see the name written in small letters on the chart – probably that of a largish village up a river in a native state, perfectly defenceless, far from the beaten tracks of the sea and from the ends of submarine cables. He had done that kind of thing before – in the way of business; and this now was an absolute necessity, a question of life and death – or rather of liberty. Of liberty! He was sure to get provisions – bullocks – rice – sweet-potatoes.

The sorry gang licked their chops. A cargo of produce for the schooner perhaps could be extorted – and, who knows? – some real ringing coined money! Some of these chiefs and village headmen can be made to part freely. He told me he would have roasted their toes rather than be baulked. I believe him. His men believed him too. They didn't cheer aloud, being a dumb pack, but made ready wolfishly.

'Luck served him as to weather. A few days of calm would have brought unmentionable horrors on board that schooner, but with the help of land and sea breezes, in less than a week after clearing the Sunda Straits, he anchored off the Batu Kring mouth within a pistol-shot of the fishing village.

'Fourteen of them packed into the schooner's long-boat (which was big, having been used for cargo-work) and started up the river, while two remained in charge of the schooner with food enough to keep starvation off for ten days. The tide and wind helped, and early one afternoon the big white boat under a ragged sail shouldered its way before the sea breeze into Patusan Reach, manned by fourteen assorted scarecrows glaring hungrily ahead, and fingering the breech-blocks of cheap rifles. Brown calculated upon the terrifying surprise of his appearance. They sailed in with the last of the flood; the Rajah's stockade gave no sign; the first houses on both sides of the stream seemed deserted. A few canoes were seen up the reach in full flight. Brown was astonished at the size of the place. A profound silence reigned. The wind dropped between the houses; two oars were got out and the boat held on upstream, the idea being to effect a lodgment in the centre of the town before the inhabitants could think of resistance.

'It seems, however, that the headman of the fishing village at Batu Kring had managed to send off a timely warning. When the long-boat came abreast of the mosque (which Doramin had built: a structure with gables and roof finials of carved coral) the open space before it was full of people. A shout went up, and was followed by a clash of gongs all up the river. From a point above two little brass six-pounders were discharged, and the round-shot came skipping down the empty reach, spirting glittering jets of water in the sunshine. In front of the mosque a shouting lot of men began firing in volleys that whipped athwart the current of the river; an irregular, rolling fusillade was opened on the boat from both banks, and Brown's men replied with a wild, rapid fire. The oars had been got in.

'The turn of the tide at high water comes on very quick in that river, and the boat in midstream, nearly hidden in smoke, began to drift back stern foremost. Along both shores the smoke thickened also, lying below the roofs in a level streak as you may see a long cloud cutting the slope of a mountain. A tumult of war-cries, the vibrating clang of gongs, the deep snoring of drums, yells of rage, crashes of volley-firing, made an awful din, in which Brown sat confounded but steady at the tiller, working himself into a fury of hate and rage against those people who dared to defend themselves. Two of his men had been wounded, and he saw his retreat cut off below the town by some boats that had put off from Tunku Allang's stockade. There were six of them full of men. While he was thus beset he perceived the entrance of the narrow creek (the same which Jim had jumped at low water). It was then brim full. Steering the long-boat in, they landed, and, to make a long story short, they established themselves on a little knoll about 900 yards from the stockade, which, in fact, they commanded from that position. The slopes of the knoll were bare, but there were a few trees on the summit. They went to work cutting these down for a breastwork, and were fairly intrenched before dark; meantime the Rajah's boats remained in the river with curious neutrality. When the sun set the glare of many brushwood blazes lighted on the river-front, and between the double line of houses on the land side threw into black relief the roofs, the groups of slender palms, the heavy clumps of fruit-trees. Brown ordered the grass round his position to be fired; a low ring of thin flames under the slow, ascending smoke wriggled rapidly down the slopes of the knoll; here and there a dry bush caught with a tall, vicious roar. The conflagration made a clear zone of fire for the rifles of the small party, and expired smouldering on the edge of the forests and along the muddy bank of the creek. A strip of jungle luxuriating in a damp hollow between the knoll and the Rajah's stockade stopped it on that side with a great crackling and detonations of bursting bamboo stems. The sky was sombre, velvety, and swarming with stars. The blackened ground smoked quietly with low creeping wisps, till a little breeze came on and blew everything away. Brown expected an attack to be delivered as soon as the tide had flowed enough again to enable the war-boats which had cut off his retreat to enter the creek. At any rate he was sure there would be an attempt to carry off his long-boat, which lay below the hill, a dark high lump on the feeble sheen of a wet mud-flat. But no move of any sort was made by the boats in the river. Over the stockade and the Rajah's buildings Brown saw their lights on the water. They seemed to be anchored across the stream. Other lights afloat were moving in the reach, crossing and recrossing from side to side. There were also lights twinkling motionless upon the long walls of houses up the reach, as far as the bend, and more still beyond, others isolated inland. The loom of the big fires disclosed buildings, roofs, black piles as far as he could see. It was an immense place. The fourteen desperate invaders lying flat behind the felled trees raised their chins to look over at the stir of that town that seemed to extend up-river for miles and swarm with thousands of angry men. They did not speak to each other. Now and then they would hear a loud yell, or a single shot rang out, fired very far somewhere. But round their position everything was still, dark, silent. They seemed to be forgotten, as if the excitement keeping awake all the population had nothing to do with them, as if they had been dead already.'

# CHAPTER THIRTY-NINE

'ALL the events of that night have a great importance, since they brought about a situation which remained unchanged till Jim's return. Jim had been away in the interior for more than a week, and it was Dain Waris who had directed the first repulse. That brave and intelligent youth ("who knew how to fight after the manner of white men") wished to settle the business off-hand, but his people were too much for him. He had not Jim's racial prestige and the reputation of invincible, supernatural power. He was not the visible, tangible incarnation of unfailing truth and of unfailing victory. Beloved, trusted, and admired as he was, he was still one of *them*, while Jim was one of *us*. Moreover, the white man, a tower of strength in himself, was invulnerable, while Dain Waris could be killed. Those unexpressed thoughts guided the opinions of the chief men of the town, who elected to assemble in Jim's fort for deliberation upon the emergency, as if expecting to find wisdom and courage in the dwelling of the absent white man. The shooting of Brown's ruffians was so far good, or lucky, that there had been half-a-dozen casualties amongst the defenders. The wounded were lying on the verandah tended by their women-folk. The women and children from the lower part of the town had been sent into the fort at the first alarm. There Jewel was in command, very efficient and high-spirited, obeyed by Jim's "own people," who, quitting in a body their little settlement under the stockade, had gone in to form the garrison. The refugees crowded round her; and through the whole affair, to the very disastrous last, she showed an extraordinary martial ardour. It was to her that Dain Waris had gone at once at the first intelligence of danger, for you must know that Jim was the only one in Patusan who possessed a store of gunpowder. Stein, with whom he had kept up intimate relations by letters, had obtained from the Dutch Government a special authorisation to export five hundred kegs of it to Patusan. The powder-magazine was a small hut of rough logs covered entirely with earth, and in Jim's absence the girl had the key. In the council, held at eleven o'clock in the evening in Jim's dining-room, she backed up Waris's advice for immediate and vigorous action. I am told that she stood up by the side of Jim's empty chair at the head of the long table and made a warlike impassioned speech, which for the moment extorted murmurs of approbation from the assembled headmen. Old Doramin, who had not showed himself outside his own gate for more than a year, had been brought across with great difficulty. He was, of course, the chief man there. The temper of the council was very unforgiving, and the old man's word would have been decisive; but it is my opinion that, well aware of his son's fiery courage, he dared not pronounce the word. More dilatory counsels prevailed. A certain Haji Saman pointed out at great length that "these tyrannical and ferocious men had delivered themselves to a certain death in any case. They would stand fast on their hill and starve, or they would try to regain their boat and be shot from ambushes across the creek, or they would break and fly into the forest and perish singly there." He argued that by the use of proper stratagems these evil-minded strangers could be destroyed without the risk of a battle, and his words had a great weight, especially with the Patusan men proper. What unsettled the minds of the townsfolk was the failure of the Rajah's boats to act at the decisive moment. It was the diplomatic Kassim who represented the Rajah at the council. He spoke very little, listened smilingly, very friendly and impenetrable. During the sitting messengers kept arriving every few minutes almost, with reports of the invaders' proceedings. Wild and exaggerated rumours were flying: there was a large ship at the mouth of the river with big guns and many more men – some white, others with black skins and of bloodthirsty appearance. They were coming with many more boats to exterminate every living thing. A sense of near, incomprehensible danger affected the common people. At one moment there was a panic in the courtyard amongst the women; shrieking; a rush; children crying – Haji Saman went out to quiet them. Then a fort sentry fired at something moving on the river, and nearly killed a villager bringing in his women-folk in a canoe together with the best of his domestic utensils and a dozen fowls. This caused more confusion. Meantime the palaver inside Jim's house went on in the presence of the girl. Doramin sat fierce-faced, heavy, looking at the speakers in turn, and breathing slow like a bull. He didn't speak till the last, after Kassim had declared that the Rajah's boats would be called in because the men were required to defend his master's stockade. Dain Waris in his father's presence would offer no opinion, though the girl entreated him in Jim's name to speak out. She offered him Jim's own men in her anxiety to have these intruders driven out at once. He only shook his head, after a glance or two at Doramin. Finally, when the council broke up it had been decided that the houses nearest the creek should be strongly occupied to obtain the command of the enemy's boat. The boat itself was not to be interfered with openly, so that the robbers on the hill should be tempted to embark, when a well-directed fire would kill most of them, no doubt. To cut the escape of those who might survive, and to prevent more of them coming up, Dain Waris was ordered by Doramin to take an armed party of Bugis down the river to a certain spot ten miles below Patusan, and there form a camp on the shore and blockade the stream with the canoes. I don't believe for a moment that Doramin feared the arrival of fresh forces. My opinion is, that his conduct was guided solely by his wish to keep his son out of harm's way. To prevent a rush being made into the town the construction of a stockade

was to be commenced at daylight at the end of the street on
the left bank. The old *nakhoda* declared his intention to
command there himself. A distribution of powder, bullets,
and percussion caps was made immediately under the girl's
supervision. Several messengers were to be despatched in
different directions after Jim, whose exact whereabouts
were unknown. These men started at dawn, but before
that time Kassim had managed to open communications
with the besieged Brown.

'That accomplished diplomatist and confidant of the
Rajah, on leaving the fort to go back to his master, took
into his boat Cornelius, whom he found slinking mutely
amongst the people in the courtyard. Kassim had a little
plan of his own and wanted him for an interpreter. Thus it
came about that towards morning Brown, reflecting upon
the desperate nature of his position, heard from the marshy
overgrown hollow an amicable, quavering, strained voice
crying – in English – for permission to come up, under a
promise of personal safety and on a very important errand.
He was overjoyed. If he was spoken to he was no longer a
hunted wild beast. These friendly sounds took off at once
the awful stress of vigilant watchfulness as of so many blind
men not knowing whence the deathblow might come. He
pretended a great reluctance. The voice declared itself "a
white man. A poor, ruined, old man who had been living
here for years." A mist, wet and chilly, lay on the slopes of
the hill, and after some more shouting from one to the
other, Brown called out, "Come on, then, but alone, mind!"
As a matter of fact – he told me, writhing with rage at the
recollection of his helplessness – it made no difference.
They couldn't see more than a few yards before them, and
no treachery could make their position worse. By-and-by
Cornelius, in his week-day attire of a ragged dirty shirt and
pants, barefooted, with a broken-rimmed pith hat on his
head, was made out vaguely, sidling up to the defences,
hesitating, stopping to listen in a peering posture. "Come
along! You are safe," yelled Brown, while his men stared.

All their hopes of life became suddenly centred in that dilapidated, mean new-comer, who in profound silence clambered clumsily over a felled tree-trunk, and shivering, with his sour mistrustful face, looked about at the knot of bearded, anxious, sleepless desperadoes.

'Half an hour's confidential talk with Cornelius opened Brown's eyes as to the home affairs of Patusan. He was on the alert at once. There were possibilities, immense possibilities; but before he would talk over Cornelius's proposals he demanded that some food should be sent up as a guarantee of good faith. Cornelius went off, creeping sluggishly down the hill on the side of the Rajah's palace, and after some delay a few of Tunku Allang's men came up, bringing a scanty supply of rice, chillies, and dried fish. This was immeasurably better than nothing. Later on Cornelius returned accompanying Kassim, who stepped out with an air of perfect good-humoured trustfulness, in sandals, and muffled up from neck to ankles in dark-blue sheeting. He shook hands with Brown discreetly, and the three drew aside for a conference. Brown's men, recovering their confidence, were slapping each other on the back, and cast knowing glances at their captain while they busied themselves with preparations for cooking.

'Kassim disliked Doramin and his Bugis very much, but he hated the new order of things still more. It had occurred to him that these whites, together with the Rajah's followers, could attack and defeat the Bugis before Jim's return. Then, he reasoned, general defection of the townsfolk was sure to follow, and the reign of the white man who protected poor people would be over. Afterwards the new allies could be dealt with. They would have no friends. The fellow was perfectly able to perceive the difference of character, and had seen enough of white men to know that these new-comers were outcasts, men without country. Brown preserved a stern and inscrutable demeanour. When he first heard Cornelius's voice demanding admittance, it brought merely the hope of a loophole for escape.

In less than an hour other thoughts were seething in his head. Urged by an extreme necessity, he had come there to steal food, a few tons of rubber or gum maybe, perhaps a handful of dollars, and had found himself enmeshed by deadly dangers. Now in consequence of these overtures from Kassim he began to think of stealing the whole country. Some confounded fellow had apparently accomplished something of the kind – single-handed at that. Couldn't have done it very well though. Perhaps they could work together – squeeze everything dry and then go out quietly. In the course of his negotiations with Kassim he became aware that he was supposed to have a big ship with plenty of men outside. Kassim begged him earnestly to have this big ship with his many guns and men brought up the river without delay for the Rajah's service. Brown professed himself willing, and on this basis the negotiation was carried on with mutual distrust. Three times in the course of the morning the courteous and active Kassim went down to consult the Rajah and came up busily with his long stride. Brown, while bargaining, had a sort of grim enjoyment in thinking of his wretched schooner, with nothing but a heap of dirt in her hold, that stood for an armed ship, and a Chinaman and a lame ex-beachcomber of Levuka on board, who represented all his many men. In the afternoon he obtained further doles of food, a promise of some money, and a supply of mats for his men to make shelters for themselves. They lay down and snored, protected from the burning sunshine; but Brown, sitting fully exposed on one of the felled trees, feasted his eyes upon the view of the town and the river. There was much loot here. Cornelius, who had made himself at home in the camp, talked at his elbow, pointing out the localities, imparting advice, giving his own version of Jim's character, and commenting in his own fashion upon the events of the last three years. Brown, who, apparently indifferent and gazing away, listened with attention to every word, could not make out clearly what sort of man this Jim could be. "What's his

name? Jim! Jim! That's not enough for a man's name."
"They call him," said Cornelius, scornfully, "Tuan Jim
here. As you may say Lord Jim." "What is he? Where
does he come from?" inquired Brown. "What sort of man
is he? Is he an Englishman?" "Yes, yes, he's an Englishman.
I am an Englishman, too. From Malacca. He is a fool. All
you have to do is to kill him and then you are king here.
Everything belongs to him," explained Cornelius. "It
strikes me he may be made to share with somebody before
very long," commented Brown half aloud. "No, no. The
proper way is to kill him the first chance you get, and then
you can do what you like," Cornelius would insist earnestly.
"I have lived for many years here, and I am giving you a
friend's advice."

'In such converse and in gloating over the view of
Patusan, which he had determined in his mind should
become his prey, Brown whiled away most of the afternoon, his men, meantime, resting. On that day Dain
Waris's fleet of canoes stole one by one under the shore
farthest from the creek, and went down to close the river
against his retreat. Of this Brown was not aware, and
Kassim, who came up the knoll an hour before sunset,
took good care not to enlighten him. He wanted the
white man's ship to come up the river, and this news, he
feared, would be discouraging. He was very pressing with
Brown to send the "order," offering at the same time a
trusty messenger, who for greater secrecy (as he explained)
would make his way by land to the mouth of the river and
deliver the "order" on board. After some reflection Brown
judged it expedient to tear a page out of his pocket-book,
on which he simply wrote, "We are getting on. Big job.
Detain the man." The stolid youth selected by Kassim for
that service performed it faithfully, and was rewarded by
being suddenly tipped, head first, into the schooner's
empty hold by the ex-beachcomber and the Chinaman,
who thereupon hastened to put on the hatches. What
become of him afterwards Brown did not say.'

# CHAPTER FORTY

'Brown's object was to gain time by fooling with Kassim's diplomacy. For doing a real stroke of business he could not help thinking the white man was the person to work with. He could not imagine such a chap (who must be confoundedly clever after all to get hold of the natives like that) refusing a help that would do away with the necessity for slow, cautious, risky cheating, that imposed itself as the only possible line of conduct for a single-handed man. He, Brown, would offer him the power. No man could hesitate. Everything was in coming to a clear understanding. Of course they would share. The idea of there being a fort – all ready to his hand – a real fort, with artillery (he knew this from Cornelius), excited him. Let him only once get in and... He would impose modest conditions. Not too low, though. The man was no fool, it seemed. They would work like brothers till... till the time came for a quarrel and a shot that would settle all accounts. With grim impatience of plunder he wished himself to be talking with the man now. The land already seemed to be his to tear to pieces, squeeze, and throw away. Meantime Kassim had to be fooled for the sake of food first – and for a second string. But the principal thing was to get something to eat from day to day. Besides, he was not averse to begin fighting on that Rajah's account, and teach a lesson to those people who had received him with shots. The lust of battle was upon him.

'I am sorry that I can't give you this part of the story, which of course I have mainly from Brown, in Brown's own words. There was in the broken, violent speech of that man, unveiling before me his thoughts with the very hand of Death upon his throat, an undisguised ruthlessness of purpose, a strange vengeful attitude towards his own past, and a blind belief in the righteousness of his will against all mankind, something of that feeling which could induce the leader of a horde of wandering cut-throats to call himself proudly the Scourge of God. No doubt the natural senseless ferocity which is the basis of such a character was exasperated by failure, ill-luck, and the recent privations, as well as by the desperate position in which he found himself; but what was most remarkable of all was this, that while he planned treacherous alliances, had already settled in his own mind the fate of the white man, and intrigued in an overbearing, offhand manner with Kassim, one could perceive that what he had really desired, almost in spite of himself, was to play havoc with that jungle town which had defied him, to see it strewn over with corpses and enveloped in flames. Listening to his pitiless, panting voice, I could imagine how he must have looked at it from the hillock, peopling it with images of murder and rapine. The part nearest to the creek wore an abandoned aspect, though as a matter of fact every house concealed a few armed men on the alert. Suddenly beyond the stretch of waste ground, interspersed with small patches of low dense bush, excavations, heaps of rubbish, with trodden paths between, a man, solitary and looking very small, strolled out into the deserted opening of the street between the shut-up, dark, lifeless buildings at the end. Perhaps one of the inhabitants, who had fled to the other bank of the river, coming back for some object of domestic use. Evidently he supposed himself quite safe at that distance from the hill on the other side of the creek. A light stockade, set up hastily, was just round the turn of the street, full of his friends. He moved leisurely. Brown saw him, and instantly called to his side the Yankee deserter, who acted as a sort of second in command. This lanky, loose-jointed fellow came forward, wooden-faced, trailing his rifle lazily. When he understood what was wanted from him a homicidal and conceited

smile uncovered his teeth, making two deep folds down his
sallow, leathery cheeks. He prided himself on being a
dead shot. He dropped on one knee, and taking aim from
a steady rest through the unlopped branches of a felled tree,
fired, and at once stood up to look. The man, far away,
turned his head to the report, made another step forward,
seemed to hesitate, and abruptly got down on his hands and
knees. In the silence that fell upon the sharp crack of the
rifle, the dead shot, keeping his eyes fixed upon the quarry,
guessed that "this there coon's health would never be a
source of anxiety to his friends any more." The man's
limbs were seen to move rapidly under his body in an
endeavour to run on all-fours. In that empty space arose a
multitudinous shout of dismay and surprise. The man sank
flat, face down, and moved no more. "That showed them
what we could do," said Brown to me. "Struck the fear of
sudden death into them. That was what we wanted. They
were two hundred to one, and this gave them something to
think over for the night. Not one of them had an idea of
such a long shot before. That beggar belonging to the
Rajah scouted down-hill with his eyes hanging out of his
head."

'As he was telling me this he tried with a shaking hand to
wipe the thin foam on his blue lips. "Two hundred to one.
Two hundred to one . . . strike terror . . . terror, terror, I tell
you. . . ." His own eyes were starting out of their sockets.
He fell back, clawing the air with skinny fingers, sat up
again, bowed and hairy, glared at me sideways like some
man-beast of folklore, with open mouth in his miserable
and awful agony before he got his speech back after that fit.
There are sights one never forgets.

'Furthermore, to draw the enemy's fire and locate such
parties as might have been hiding in the bushes along the
creek, Brown ordered the Solomon Islander to go down to
the boat and bring an oar, as you send a spaniel after a stick
into the water. This failed, and the fellow came back without a single shot having been fired at him from anywhere.

"There's nobody," opined some of the men. It is "onnatural," remarked the Yankee. Kassim had gone, by that time, very much impressed, pleased, too, and also uneasy. Pursuing his tortuous policy, he had despatched a message to Dain Waris warning him to look out for the white men's ship, which, he had had information, was about to come up the river. He minimised its strength and exhorted him to oppose its passage. This double-dealing answered his purpose, which was to keep the Bugis forces divided and to weaken them by fighting. On the other hand, he had in the course of that day sent word to the assembled Bugis chiefs in town, assuring them that he was trying to induce the invaders to retire; his messages to the fort asked earnestly for powder for the Rajah's men. It was a long time since Tunku Allang had had ammunition for the score or so of old muskets rusting in their arm-racks in the audience-hall. The open intercourse between the hill and the palace unsettled all the minds. It was already time for men to take sides, it began to be said. There would soon be much bloodshed, and thereafter great trouble for many people. The social fabric of orderly, peaceful life, when every man was sure of to-morrow, the edifice raised by Jim's hands, seemed on that evening ready to collapse into a ruin reeking with blood. The poorer folk were already taking to the bush or flying up the river. A good many of the upper class judged it necessary to go and pay their court to the Rajah. The Rajah's youths jostled them rudely. Old Tunku Allang, almost out of his mind with fear and indecision, either kept a sullen silence or abused them violently for daring to come with empty hands: they departed very much frightened; only old Doramin kept his countrymen together and pursued his tactics inflexibly. Enthroned in a big chair behind the improvised stockade, he issued his orders in a deep veiled rumble, unmoved, like a deaf man, in the flying rumours.

'Dusk fell, hiding first the body of the dead man, which had been left lying with arms outstretched as if nailed to the ground, and then the revolving sphere of the night rolled smoothly over Patusan and came to a rest, showering the glitter of countless worlds upon the earth. Again, in the exposed part of the town big fires blazed along the only street, revealing from distance to distance upon their glares the falling straight lines of roofs, the fragments of wattled walls jumbled in confusion, here and there a whole hut elevated in the glow upon the vertical black stripes of a group of high piles; and all this line of dwellings, revealed in patches by the swaying flames, seemed to flicker tortuously away up-river into the gloom at the heart of the land. A great silence, in which the looms of successive fires played without noise, extended into the darkness at the foot of the hill; but the other bank of the river, all dark save for a solitary bonfire at the river-front before the fort, sent out into the air an increasing tremor that might have been the stamping of a multitude of feet, the hum of many voices, or the fall of an immensely distant waterfall. It was then, Brown confessed to me, while, turning his back on his men, he sat looking at it all, that notwithstanding his disdain, his ruthless faith in himself, a feeling came over him that at last he had run his head against a stone wall. Had his boat been afloat at the time, he believed he would have tried to steal away, taking his chances of a long chase down the river and of starvation at sea. It was very doubtful whether he would have succeeded in getting away. However, he didn't try this. For another moment he had a passing thought of trying to rush the town, but he perceived very well that in the end he would find himself in the lighted street, where they would be shot down like dogs from the houses. They were two hundred to one – he thought, while his men, huddling round two heaps of smouldering embers, munched the last of the bananas and roasted the few yams they owed to Kassim's diplomacy. Cornelius sat amongst them dozing sulkily.

'Then one of the whites remembered that some tobacco had been left in the boat, and, encouraged by the impunity

of the Solomon Islander, said he would go to fetch it. At
this all the others shook off their despondency. Brown
applied to, said, "Go, and be d—d to you," scornfully. He
didn't think there was any danger in going to the creek in
the dark. The man threw a leg over the tree-trunk and
disappeared. A moment later he was heard clambering into
the boat and then clambering out. "I've got it," he cried. A
flash and a report at the very foot of the hill followed. "I am
hit," yelled the man. "Look out, look out – I am hit," and
instantly all the rifles went off. The hill squirted fire and
noise into the night like a little volcano, and when Brown
and the Yankee with curses and cuffs stopped the panic-
stricken firing, a profound, weary groan floated up from
the creek, succeeded by a plaint whose heart-rending sadness was like some poison turning the blood cold in the
veins. Then a strong voice pronounced several distinct
incomprehensible words somewhere beyond the creek.
"Let no one fire," shouted Brown. "What does it
mean?" . . . "Do you hear on the hill? Do you hear? Do
you hear?" repeated the voice three times. Cornelius trans-
lated, and then prompted the answer. "Speak," cried
Brown, "we hear." Then the voice, declaiming in the sonor-
ous inflated tone of a herald, and shifting continually on
the edge of the vague waste-land, proclaimed that between
the men of the Bugis nation living in Patusan and the white
men on the hill and those with them, there would be no
faith, no compassion, no speech, no peace. A bush rustled;
a haphazard volley rang out. "Dam' foolishness," muttered
the Yankee, vexedly grounding the butt. Cornelius trans-
lated. The wounded man below the hill, after crying out
twice, "Take me up! take me up!" went on complaining in
moans. While he had kept on the blackened earth of the
slope and afterwards crouching in the boat, he had been
safe enough. It seems that in his joy at finding tobacco he
forgot himself and jumped out on her off-side, as it were.
The white boat, lying high and dry, showed him up; the
creek was no more than seven yards wide in that place, and

there happened to be a man crouching in the bush on the other bank.

'He was a Bugis of Tondano only lately come to Patusan, and a relation of the man shot in the afternoon. That famous long shot had indeed appalled the beholders. The man in utter security had been struck down, in full view of his friends, dropping with a joke on his lips, and they seemed to see in the act an atrocity which had stirred a bitter rage. That relation of his, Si-Lapa by name, was then with Doramin in the stockade only a few feet away. You who know these chaps must admit that the fellow showed an unusual pluck by volunteering to carry the message, alone, in the dark. Creeping across the open ground, he had deviated to the left and found himself opposite the boat. He was startled when Brown's man shouted. He came to a sitting position with his gun to his shoulder, and when the other jumped out, exposing himself, he pulled the trigger and lodged three jagged slugs point-blank into the poor wretch's stomach. Then, lying flat on his face, he gave himself up for dead, while a thin hail of lead chopped and swished the bushes close on his right hand; afterwards he delivered his speech shouting, bent double, dodging all the time in cover. With the last word he leaped sideways, lay close for a while, and afterwards got back to the houses unharmed, having achieved on that night such a renown as his children will not willingly allow to die.

'And on the hill the forlorn band let the two little heaps of embers go out under their bowed heads. They sat dejected on the ground with compressed lips and downcast eyes, listening to their comrade below. He was a strong man and died hard, with moans now loud, now sinking to a strange confidential note of pain. Sometimes he shrieked, and again, after a period of silence, he could be heard muttering deliriously a long and unintelligible complaint. Never for a moment did he cease.

'"What's the good?" Brown had said unmoved once, seeing the Yankee, who had been swearing under his

breath, prepare to go down. "That's so," assented the
deserter, reluctantly desisting. "There's no encouragement
for wounded men here. Only his noise is calculated to make
all the others think too much of the hereafter, cap'n."
"Water!" cried the wounded man in an extraordinarily
clear vigorous voice, and then went off moaning feebly.
"Ay, water. Water will do it," muttered the other to himself,
resignedly. "Plenty by-and-by. The tide is flowing."

'At last the tide flowed, silencing the plaint and the cries
of pain, and the dawn was near when Brown, sitting with
his chin in the palm of his hand before Patusan, as one
might stare at the unscalable side of a mountain, heard the
brief ringing bark of a brass six-pounder far away in town
somewhere. "What's this?" he asked of Cornelius, who
hung about him. Cornelius listened. A muffled roaring
shout rolled down-river over the town; a big drum began
to throb, and others responded, pulsating and droning.
Tiny scattered lights began to twinkle in the dark half of
the town, while the part lighted by the loom of fires
hummed with a deep and prolonged murmur. "He has
come," said Cornelius. "What? Already? Are you sure?"
Brown asked. "Yes! yes! Sure. Listen to the noise." "What
are they making that row about?" pursued Brown. "For joy,"
snorted Cornelius; "he is a very great man, but all the same,
he knows no more than a child, and so they make a great
noise to please him, because they know no better." "Look
here," said Brown, "how is one to get at him?" "He shall
come to talk to you," Cornelius declared. "What do you
mean? Come down here strolling as it were?" Cornelius
nodded vigorously in the dark. "Yes. He will come straight
here and talk to you. He is just like a fool. You shall see
what a fool he is." Brown was incredulous. "You shall see;
you shall see," repeated Cornelius. "He is not afraid – not
afraid of anything. He will come and order you to leave his
people alone. Everybody must leave his people alone. He is
like a little child. He will come to you straight." Alas! he
knew Jim well – that "mean little skunk," as Brown called

him to me. "Yes, certainly," he pursued with ardour, "and then, captain, you tell that tall man with a gun to shoot him. Just you kill him, and you shall frighten everybody so much that you can do anything you like with them afterwards – get what you like – go away when you like. Ha! ha! ha! Fine...." He almost danced with impatience and eagerness; and Brown, looking over his shoulder at him, could see, shown up by the pitiless dawn, his men drenched with dew, sitting amongst the cold ashes and the litter of the camp, haggard, cowed, and in rags.'

# CHAPTER FORTY-ONE

'To THE very last moment, till the full day came upon them with a spring, the fires on the west bank blazed bright and clear; and then Brown saw in a knot of coloured figures motionless between the advanced houses a man in European clothes, in a helmet, all white. "That's him; look! look!" Cornelius said excitedly. All Brown's men had sprung up and crowded at his back with lustreless eyes. The group of vivid colours and dark faces with the white figure in the midst were observing the knoll. Brown could see naked arms being raised to shade the eyes and other brown arms pointing. What should he do? He looked around, and the forests that faced him on all sides walled the cock-pit of an unequal contest. He looked once more at his men. A contempt, a weariness, the desire of life, the wish to try for one more chance – for some other grave – struggled in his breast. From the outline the figure presented it seemed to him that the white man there, backed up by all the power of the land, was examining his position through binoculars. Brown jumped up on the log, throwing his arms up, the palms outwards. The coloured group closed round the white man, and fell back twice before he got clear of them, walking slowly alone. Brown remained standing on the log till Jim, appearing and disappearing between the patches of thorny scrub, had nearly reached the creek; then Brown jumped off and went down to meet him on his side.

'They met, I should think, not very far from the place, perhaps on the very spot, where Jim took the second desperate leap of his life – the leap that landed him into the life of Patusan, into the trust, the love, the confidence of the people. They faced each other across the creek, and with steady eyes tried to understand each other before they opened their lips. Their antagonism must have been expressed in their glances; I know that Brown hated Jim at first sight. Whatever hopes he might have had vanished at once. This was not the man he had expected to see. He hated him for this – and in a checked flannel shirt with sleeves cut off at the elbows, grey bearded, with a sunken, sun-blackened face – he cursed in his heart the other's youth and assurance, his clear eyes and his untroubled bearing. That fellow had got in a long way before him! He did not look like a man who would be willing to give anything for assistance. He had all the advantages on his side – possession, security, power; he was on the side of an overwhelming force! He was not hungry and desperate, and he did not seem in the least afraid. And there was something in the very neatness of Jim's clothes, from the white helmet to the canvas leggings and the pipe-clayed shoes, which in Brown's sombre irritated eyes seemed to belong to things he had in the very shaping of his life contemned and flouted.

'"Who are you?" asked Jim at last, speaking in his usual voice. "My name's Brown," answered the other, loudly; "Captain Brown. What's yours?" and Jim after a little pause went on quietly, as if he had not heard: "What made you come here?" "You want to know," said Brown, bitterly. "It's easy to tell. Hunger. And what made you?"

'"The fellow started at this," said Brown, relating to me the opening of this strange conversation between those two men, separated only by the muddy bed of a creek, but standing on the opposite poles of that conception of life which includes all mankind – "The fellow started at this and got very red in the face. Too big to be questioned, I suppose. I told him that if he looked upon me as a dead man with whom you may take liberties, he himself was not a whit better off really. I had a fellow up there who had a bead drawn on him all the time, and only waited for a sign

from me. There was nothing to be shocked at in this. He
had come down of his own freewill. 'Let us agree,' said I,
'that we are both dead men, and let us talk on that basis, as
equals. We are all equal before death,' I said. I admitted I
was there like a rat in a trap, but we had been driven to it,
and even a trapped rat can give a bite. He caught me up in a
moment. 'Not if you don't go near the trap till the rat is
dead.' I told him that sort of game was good enough for
these native friends of his, but I would have thought him
too white to serve even a rat so. Yes, I had wanted to talk
with him. Not to beg for my life, though. My fellows were
– well – what they were – men like himself, anyhow. All we
wanted from him was to come on in the devil's name and
have it out. 'God d—n it,' said I, while he stood there as still
as a wooden post, 'you don't want to come out here every
day with your glasses to count how many of us are left on
our feet. Come. Either bring your infernal crowd along or
let us go out and starve in the open sea, by God! You have
been white once, for all your tall talk of this being your own
people and you being one with them. Are you? And what
the devil do you get for it; what is it you've found here that
is so d—d precious? Hey? You don't want us to come down
here perhaps – do you? You are two hundred to one. You
don't want us to come down into the open. Ah! I promise
you we shall give you some sport before you've done. You
talk about me making a cowardly set upon unoffending
people. What's that to me that they are unoffending when I
am starving for next to no offence? But I am not a coward.
Don't you be one. Bring them along or, by all the fiends, we
shall yet manage to send half your unoffending town to
heaven with us in smoke!' "

'He was terrible – relating this to me – this tortured
skeleton of a man drawn up together with his face over his
knees, upon a miserable bed in that wretched hovel, and
lifting his head to look at me with malignant triumph.

'"That's what I told him – I knew what to say," he
began again, feebly at first, but working himself up with

incredible speed into a fiery utterance of his scorn. "We aren't going into the forest to wander like a string of living skeletons dropping one after another for ants to go to work upon us before we are fairly dead. Oh, no!... 'You don't deserve a better fate,' he said. 'And what do you deserve,' I shouted at him, 'you that I find skulking here with your mouth full of your responsibility, of innocent lives, of your infernal duty? What do you know more of me than I know of you? I came here for food. D'ye hear? – food to fill our bellies. And what did *you* come for? What did you ask for when you came here? We don't ask you for anything but to give us a fight or a clear road to go back whence we came....' 'I would fight with you now,' says he, pulling at his little moustache. 'And I would let you shoot me, and welcome,' I said. 'This is as good a jumping-off place for me as another. I am sick of my infernal luck. But it would be too easy. There are my men in the same boat – and, by God, I am not the sort to jump out of trouble and leave them in a d—d lurch,' I said. He stood thinking for a while and then wanted to know what I had done ('out there,' he says, tossing his head down-stream) to be hazed about so. 'Have we met to tell each other the story of our lives?' I asked him. 'Suppose you begin. No? Well, I am sure I don't want to hear. Keep it to yourself. I know it is no better than mine. I've lived – and so did you though you talk as if you were one of those people that should have wings so as to go about without touching the dirty earth. Well – it is dirty. I haven't got any wings. I am here because I was afraid once in my life. Want to know what of? Of a prison. That scares me, and you may know it – if it's any good to you. I won't ask you what scared you into this infernal hole, where you seem to have found pretty pickings. That's your luck and this is mine – the privilege to beg for the favour of being shot quickly, or else kicked out to go free and starve in my own way.'"...

'His debilitated body shook with an exultation so vehement, so assured, and so malicious that it seemed to have driven off the death waiting for him in that hut. The corpse of his mad self-love uprose from rags and destitution as from the dark horrors of a tomb. It is impossible to say how much he lied to Jim then, how much he lied to me now – and to himself always. Vanity plays lurid tricks with our memory, and the truth of every passion wants some pretence to make it live. Standing at the gate of the other world in the guise of a beggar, he had slapped this world's face, he had spat on it, he had thrown upon it an immensity of scorn and revolt at the bottom of his misdeeds. He had overcome them all – men, women, savages, traders, ruffians, missionaries – and Jim – that beefy-faced beggar. I did not begrudge him this triumph *in articulo mortis*, this almost posthumous illusion of having trampled all the earth under his feet. While he was boasting to me, in his sordid and repulsive agony, I couldn't help thinking of the chuckling talk relating to the time of his greatest splendour when, during a year or more, Gentleman Brown's ship was to be seen, for many days on end, hovering off an islet befringed with green upon azure, with the dark dot of the mission-house on a white beach; while Gentleman Brown, ashore, was casting his spells over a romantic girl for whom Melanesia had been too much, and giving hopes of a remarkable conversion to her husband. The poor man, some time or other, had been heard to express the intention of winning "Captain Brown to a better way of life." ... "Bag Gentleman Brown for Glory" – as a leery-eyed loafer expressed it once – "just to let them see up above what a Western Pacific trading skipper looks like." And this was the man, too, who had run off with a dying woman, and had shed tears over her body. "Carried on like a big baby," his then mate was never tired of telling, "and where the fun came in may I be kicked to death by diseased Kanakas if *I* know. Why, gents! she was too far gone when he brought her aboard to know him; she just lay there on her back in his bunk staring at the beam with awful shining eyes – and then she died. Dam' bad sort of fever, I guess...."

I remembered all these stories while, wiping his matted lump of a beard with a livid hand, he was telling me from his noisome couch how he got round, got in, got home, on that confounded, immaculate, don't-you-touch-me sort of fellow. He admitted that he couldn't be scared, but there was a way, "as broad as a turnpike, to get in and shake his twopenny soul around and inside out and upside down – by God!"'

# CHAPTER FORTY-TWO

'I DON'T think he could do more than perhaps look upon that straight path. He seemed to have been puzzled by what he saw, for he interrupted himself in his narrative more than once to exclaim, "He nearly slipped from me there. I could not make him out. Who was he?" And after glaring at me wildly he would go on, jubilating and sneering. To me the conversation of these two across the creek appears now as the deadliest kind of duel on which Fate looked on with her cold-eyed knowledge of the end. No, he didn't turn Jim's soul inside out, but I am much mistaken if the spirit so utterly out of his reach had not been made to taste to the full the bitterness of that contest. These were the emissaries with whom the world he had renounced was pursuing him in his retreat. White men from "out there" where he did not think himself good enough to live. This was all that came to him – a menace, a shock, a danger to his work. I suppose it is this sad, half-resentful, half-resigned feeling, piercing through the few words Jim said now and then, that puzzled Brown so much in the reading of his character. Some great men owe most of their greatness to the ability of detecting in those they destine for their tools the exact quality of strength that matters for their work, and Brown, as though he had been really great, had a satanic gift of finding out the best and the weakest spot in his victims. He admitted to me that Jim wasn't of the sort that can be got over by truckling, and accordingly he took care to show himself as a man confronting without dismay ill-luck, censure, and disaster. The smuggling of a few guns was no great crime, he pointed out. As to coming to Patusan, who had the right to say he hadn't come to beg?

The infernal people here let loose at him from both banks without staying to ask questions. He made the point brazenly, for, in truth, Dain Waris's energetic action had prevented the greatest calamities; because Brown told me distinctly that, perceiving the size of the place, he had resolved instantly in his mind that as soon as he had gained a footing he would set fire right and left, and begin by shooting down everything living in sight, in order to cow and terrify the population. The disproportion of forces was so great that this was the only way giving him the slightest chance of attaining his ends – he argued in a fit of coughing. But he didn't tell Jim this. As to the hardships and starvation they had gone through, these had been very real; it was enough to look at his band. He made, at the sound of a shrill whistle, all his men appear standing in a row on the logs in full view, so that Jim could see them. For the killing of the man, it had been done – well, it had – but was not this war, bloody war – in a corner? and the fellow had been killed cleanly, shot through the chest, not like that poor devil of his lying now in the creek. They had to listen to him dying for six hours, with his entrails torn with slugs. At any rate this was a life for a life.... And all this was said with the weariness, with the recklessness of a man spurred on and on by ill-luck till he cares not where he runs. When he asked Jim, with a sort of brusque despairing frankness, whether he himself – straight now – didn't understand that when "it came to saving one's life in the dark, one didn't care who else went – three, thirty, three hundred people" – it was as if a demon had been whispering advice in his ear. "I made him wince," boasted Brown to me. "He very soon left off coming the righteous over me. He just stood there with nothing to say, and looking as black as thunder – not at me – on the ground." He asked Jim whether he had nothing fishy in his life to remember that he was so damnedly hard upon a man trying to get out of a deadly hole by the first means that came to hand – and so on, and so on. And there ran through the rough talk a vein of subtle reference to their common blood, an assumption of common experience; a sickening suggestion of common guilt, of secret knowledge that was like a bond of their minds and of their hearts.

'At last Brown threw himself down full length and watched Jim out of the corners of his eyes. Jim on his side of the creek stood thinking and switching his leg. The houses in view were silent, as if a pestilence had swept them clean of every breath of life; but many invisible eyes were turned, from within, upon the two men with the creek between them, a stranded white boat, and the body of the third man half sunk in the mud. On the river canoes were moving again, for Patusan was recovering its belief in the stability of earthly institutions since the return of the white lord. The right bank, the platforms of the houses, the rafts moored along the shores, even the roofs of bathing-huts, were covered with people that, far away out of earshot and almost out of sight, were straining their eyes towards the knoll beyond the Rajah's stockade. Within the wide irregular ring of forests broken in two places by the sheen of the river there was a silence. "Will you promise to leave the coast?" Jim asked. Brown lifted and let fall his hand, giving everything up as it were – accepting the inevitable. "And surrender your arms?" Jim went on. Brown sat up and glared across. "Surrender our arms! Not till you come to take them out of our stiff hands. You think I am gone crazy with funk? Oh, no! That and the rags I stand in is all I have got in the world, besides a few more breechloaders on board; and I expect to sell the lot in Madagascar, if I ever get so far – begging my way from ship to ship."

'Jim said nothing to this. At last, throwing away the switch he held in his hand, he said, as if speaking to himself, "I don't know whether I have the power."...."You don't know! And you wanted me just now to give up my arms! That's good, too," cried Brown. "Suppose they say one thing to you, and do the other thing to me." He calmed down markedly. "I daresay you have the power, or what's the meaning of all this talk?" he continued. "What did you come down here for? To pass the time of day?"

'"Very well," said Jim, lifting his head suddenly after a long silence. "You shall have a clear road or else a clear fight." He turned on his heel and walked away.

'Brown got up at once, but he did not go up the hill till he had seen Jim disappear between the first houses. He never set his eyes on him again. On his way back he met Cornelius slouching down with his head between his shoulders. He stopped before Brown. "Why didn't you kill him?" he demanded in a sour, discontented voice. "Because I could do better than that," Brown said with an amused smile. "Never! never!" protested Cornelius with energy. "Couldn't. I have lived here for many years." Brown looked up at him curiously. There were many sides to the life of that place in arms against him; things he would never find out. Cornelius slunk past dejectedly in the direction of the river. He was now leaving his new friends; he accepted the disappointing course of events with a sulky obstinacy which seemed to draw more together his little yellow old face; and as he went down he glanced askant here and there, never giving up his fixed idea.

'Henceforth events move fast without a check, flowing from the very hearts of men like a stream from a dark source, and we see Jim amongst them, mostly through Tamb' Itam's eyes. The girl's eyes had watched him, too, but her life is too much entwined with his: there is her passion, her wonder, her anger, and, above all, her fear and her unforgiving love. Of the faithful servant, uncomprehending as the rest of them, it is the fidelity alone that comes into play; a fidelity and a belief in his lord so strong that even amazement is subdued to a sort of saddened acceptance of a mysterious failure. He has eyes only for one figure, and through all the mazes of bewilderment he preserves his air of guardianship, of obedience, of care.

'His master came back from his talk with the white men, walking slowly towards the stockade in the street. Everybody was rejoiced to see him return, for while he was away every man had been afraid not only of him being killed, but also of what would come after. Jim went into one of the houses, where old Doramin had retired, and remained alone for a long time with the head of the Bugis settlers. No doubt he discussed the course to follow with him then, but no man was present at the conversation. Only Tamb' Itam, keeping as close to the door as he could, heard his master say, "Yes. I shall let all the people know that such is my wish; but I spoke to you, O Doramin, before all the others, and alone; for you know my heart as well as I know yours and its greatest desire. And you know well also that I have no thought but for the people's good." Then his master, lifting the sheeting in the doorway, went out, and he, Tamb' Itam, had a glimpse of old Doramin within, sitting in the chair with his hands on his knees, and looking between his feet. Afterwards he followed his master to the fort, where all the principal Bugis and Patusan inhabitants had been summoned for a talk. Tamb' Itam himself hoped there would be some fighting. "What was it but the taking of another hill?" he exclaimed regretfully. However, in the town many hoped that the rapacious strangers would be induced, by the sight of so many brave men making ready to fight, to go away. It would be a good thing if they went away. Since Jim's arrival had been made known before daylight by the gun fired from the fort and the beating of the big drum there, the fear that had hung over Patusan had broken and subsided like a wave on a rock, leaving the seething foam of excitement, curiosity, and endless speculation. Half of the population had been ousted out of their homes for purposes of defence, and were living in the street on the left side of the river, crowding round the fort, and in momentary expectation of seeing their abandoned dwellings on the threatened bank burst into flames. The general anxiety was to see the matter settled quickly. Food, through

Jewel's care, had been served out to the refugees. Nobody knew what their white man would do. Some remarked that it was worse than in Sherif Ali's war. Then many people did not care; now everybody had something to lose. The movements of canoes passing to and fro between the two parts of the town were watched with interest. A couple of Bugis war-boats lay anchored in the middle of the stream to protect the river, and a thread of smoke stood at the bow of each; the men in them were cooking their midday rice when Jim, after his interviews with Brown and Doramin, crossed the river and entered by the water-gate of his fort. The people inside crowded round him so that he could hardly make his way to the house. They had not seen him before, because on his arrival during the night he had only exchanged a few words with the girl, who had come down to the landing-stage for the purpose, and had then gone on at once to join the chiefs and the fighting men on the other bank. People shouted greetings after him. One old woman raised a laugh by pushing her way to the front madly and enjoining him in a scolding voice to see to it that her two sons, who were with Doramin, did not come to harm at the hands of the robbers. Several of the bystanders tried to pull her away, but she struggled and cried, "Let me go. What is this, O Muslims? This laughter is unseemly. Are they not cruel, bloodthirsty robbers bent on killing?" "Let her be," said Jim, and as a silence fell suddenly, he said slowly, "Everybody shall be safe." He entered the house before the great sigh, and the loud murmurs of satisfaction, had died out.

'There's no doubt his mind was made up that Brown should have his way clear back to the sea. His fate, revolted, was forcing his hand. He had for the first time to affirm his will in the face of out-spoken opposition. "There was much talk, and at first my master was silent," Tamb' Itam said. "Darkness came, and then I lit the candles on the long table. The chiefs sat on each side, and the lady remained by my master's right hand."

'When he began to speak the unaccustomed difficulty seemed only to fix his resolve more immovably. The white men were now waiting for his answer on the hill. Their chief had spoken to him in the language of his own people, making clear many things difficult to explain in any other speech. They were erring men whom suffering had made blind to right and wrong. It is true that lives had been lost already, but why lose more? He declared to his hearers, the assembled heads of the people, that their welfare was his welfare, their losses his losses, their mourning his mourning. He looked round at the grave listening faces and told them to remember that they had fought and worked side by side. They knew his courage ... Here a murmur interrupted him ... And that he had never deceived them. For many years they had dwelt together. He loved the land and the people living in it with a very great love. He was ready to answer with his life for any harm that should come to them if the white men with beards were allowed to retire. They were evil-doers, but their destiny had been evil, too. Had he ever advised them ill? Had his words ever brought suffering to the people? he asked. He believed that it would be best to let these whites and their followers go with their lives. It would be a small gift. "I whom you have tried and found always true ask you to let them go." He turned to Doramin. The old *nakhoda* made no movement. "Then," said Jim. "call in Dain Waris, your son, my friend, for in this business I shall not lead."

# CHAPTER FORTY-THREE

'TAMB' ITAM behind his chair was thunderstruck. The declaration produced an immense sensation. "Let them go because this is best in my knowledge which has never deceived you," Jim insisted. There was a silence. In the darkness of the courtyard could be heard the subdued whispering, shuffling noise of many people. Doramin raised his heavy head and said that there was no more reading of hearts than touching the sky with the hand, but – he consented. The others gave their opinion in turn. "It is best," "Let them go," and so on. But most of them simply said that they "believed Tuan Jim."

'In this simple form of assent to his will lies the whole gist of the situation; their creed, his truth; and the testimony to that faithfulness which made him in his own eyes the equal of the impeccable men who never fall out of the ranks. Stein's words, "Romantic! – Romantic!" seem to ring over those distances that will never give him up now to a world indifferent to his failing and his virtues, and to that ardent and clinging affection that refuses him the dole of tears in the bewilderment of a great grief and of eternal separation. From the moment the sheer truthfulness of his last three years of life carries the day against the ignorance, the fear, and the anger of men, he appears no longer to me as I saw him last – a white speck catching all the dim light left upon a sombre coast and the darkened sea – but greater and more pitiful in the loneliness of his soul, that remains even for her who loved him best a cruel and insoluble mystery.

'It is evident that he did not mistrust Brown; there was no reason to doubt the story, whose truth seemed

354

warranted by the rough frankness, by a sort of virile sincerity in accepting the morality and the consequences of his acts. But Jim did not know the almost inconceivable egotism of the man which made him, when resisted and foiled in his will, mad with the indignant and revengeful rage of a thwarted autocrat. But if Jim did not mistrust Brown, he was evidently anxious that some misunderstanding should not occur, ending perhaps in collision and bloodshed. It was for this reason that directly the Malay chiefs had gone he asked Jewel to get him something to eat, as he was going out of the fort to take command in the town. On her remonstrating against this on the score of his fatigue, he said that something might happen for which he would never forgive himself. "I am responsible for every life in the land," he said. He was moody at first; she served him with her own hands, taking the plates and dishes (of the dinner-service presented him by Stein) from Tamb' Itam. He brightened up after a while; told her she would be again in command of the fort for another night. "There's no sleep for us, old girl," he said, "while our people are in danger." Later on he said jokingly that she was the best man of them all. "If you and Dain Waris had done what you wanted, not one of these poor devils would be alive to-day." "Are they very bad?" she asked, leaning over his chair. "Men act badly sometimes without being much worse than others," he said after some hesitation.

'Tamb' Itam followed his master to the landing-stage outside the fort. The night was clear, but without a moon, and the middle of the river was dark, while the water under each bank reflected the light of many fires "as on a night of Ramadan," Tamb' Itam said. War-boats drifted silently in the dark lane or, anchored, floated motionless with a loud ripple. That night there was much paddling in a canoe and walking at his master's heels for Tamb' Itam: up and down the street they tramped, where the fires were burning, inland on the outskirts of the town where small parties of men kept guard in the fields. Tuan Jim gave his orders and was obeyed. Last of all they went to the Rajah's stockade, which a detachment of Jim's people manned on that night. The old Rajah had fled early in the morning with most of his women to a small house he had near a jungle village on a tributary stream. Kassim, left behind, had attended the council with his air of diligent activity to explain away the diplomacy of the day before. He was considerably cold-shouldered, but managed to preserve his smiling, quiet alertness, and professed himself highly delighted when Jim told him sternly that he proposed to occupy the stockade on that night with his own men. After the council broke up he was heard outside accosting this and that departing chief, and speaking in a loud, gratified tone of the Rajah's property being protected in the Rajah's absence.

'About ten or so Jim's men marched in. The stockade commanded the mouth of the creek, and Jim meant to remain there till Brown had passed below. A small fire was lit on the flat, grassy point outside the wall of stakes, and Tamb' Itam placed a little folding-stool for his master. Jim told him to try and sleep. Tamb' Itam got a mat and lay down a little way off; but he could not sleep, though he knew he had to go on an important journey before the night was out. His master walked to and fro before the fire with bowed head and with his hands behind his back. His face was sad. Whenever his master approached him Tamb' Itam pretended to sleep, not wishing his master to know he had been watched. At last his master stood still, looking down on him as he lay, and said softly, "It is time."

'Tamb' Itam arose directly and made his preparations. His mission was to go down the river, preceding Brown's boat by an hour or more, to tell Dain Waris finally and formally that the whites were to be allowed to pass out unmolested. Jim would not trust anybody else with that service. Before starting Tamb' Itam, more as a matter of form (since his position about Jim made him perfectly known), asked for a token. "Because, Tuan," he said, "the

message is important, and these are thy very words I carry."
His master first put his hand into one pocket, then into
another, and finally took off his forefinger Stein's silver
ring, which he habitually wore, and gave it to Tamb'
Itam. When Tamb' Itam left on his mission, Brown's
camp on the knoll was dark but for a single small glow
shining through the branches of one of the trees the white
men had cut down.

'Early in the evening Brown had received from Jim a
folded piece of paper on which was written, "You get the
clear road. Start as soon as your boat floats on the morning
tide. Let your men be careful. The bushes on both sides of
the creek and the stockade at the mouth are full of well-
armed men. You would have no chance, but I don't believe
you want bloodshed." Brown read it, tore the paper into
small pieces, and, turning to Cornelius, who had brought
it, said jeeringly, "Good-bye, my excellent friend."
Cornelius had been in the fort, and had been sneaking
around Jim's house during the afternoon. Jim chose him
to carry the note because he could speak English, was
known to Brown, and was not likely to be shot by some
nervous mistake of one of the men as a Malay, approaching
in the dusk, perhaps might have been.

'Cornelius didn't go away after delivering the paper.
Brown was sitting up over a tiny fire; all the others were
lying down. "I could tell you something you would like to
know," Cornelius mumbled crossly. Brown paid no attention. "You did not kill him," went on the other, "and what
do you get for it? You might have had money from the
Rajah, besides the loot of all the Bugis houses, and now you
get nothing." "You had better clear out from here," growled
Brown, without even looking at him. But Cornelius let
himself drop by his side and began to whisper very fast,
touching his elbow from time to time. What he had to say
made Brown sit up at first, with a curse. He had simply
informed him of Dain Waris's armed party down the river.
At first Brown saw himself completely sold and betrayed,

but a moment's reflection convinced him that there could be no treachery intended. He said nothing, and after a while Cornelius remarked, in a tone of complete indifference, that there was another way out of the river which he knew very well. "A good thing to know, too," said Brown, pricking up his ears; and Cornelius began to talk of what went on in town and repeated all that had been said in council, gossiping in an even undertone at Brown's ear as you talk amongst sleeping men you do not wish to wake. "He thinks he has made me harmless, does he?" mumbled Brown very low.... "Yes. He is a fool. A little child. He came here and robbed me," droned on Cornelius, "and he made all the people believe him. But if something happened that they did not believe him any more, where would he be? And the Bugis Dain who is waiting for you down the river there, captain, is the very man who chased you up here when you first came." Brown observed nonchalantly that it would be just as well to avoid him, and with the same detached, musing air Cornelius declared himself acquainted with a backwater broad enough to take Brown's boat past Waris's camp. "You will have to be quiet," he said as an afterthought, "for in one place we pass close behind his camp. Very close. They are camped ashore with their boat hauled up." "Oh, we know how to be as quiet as mice; never fear," said Brown. Cornelius stipulated that in case he were to pilot Brown out, his canoe should be towed. "I'll have to get back quick," he explained.

'It was two hours before the dawn when word was passed to the stockade from outlying watchers that the white robbers were coming down to their boat. In a very short time every armed man from one end of Patusan to the other was on the alert, yet the banks of the river remained so silent that but for the fires burning with sudden blurred flares the town might have been asleep as if in peace-time. A heavy mist lay very low on the water, making a sort of illusive grey light that showed nothing. When Brown's long-boat glided out of the creek into the river, Jim was

standing on the low point of land before the Rajah's stockade – on the very spot where for the first time he put his
foot on Patusan shore. A shadow loomed up, moving in
the greyness, solitary, very bulky, and yet constantly
eluding the eye. A murmur of low talking came out of it.
Brown at the tiller heard Jim speak calmly: "A clear road.
You had better trust to the current while the fog lasts; but
this will lift presently." "Yes, presently we shall see clear,"
replied Brown.

'The thirty or forty men standing with muskets at ready
outside the stockade held their breath. The Bugis owner of
the prau, whom I saw on Stein's verandah, and who was
amongst them, told me that the boat, shaving the low point
close, seemed for a moment to grow big and hang over it
like a mountain. "If you think it worth your while to wait a
day outside," called out Jim, "I'll try to send you down
something – bullock, some yams – what I can." The shadow went on moving. "Yes. Do," said a voice, blank and
muffled out of the fog. Not one of the many attentive
listeners understood what the words meant; and then
Brown and his men in their boat floated away, fading
spectrally without the slightest sound.

'Thus Brown, invisible in the mist, goes out of Patusan
elbow to elbow with Cornelius in the stern-sheets of the
long-boat. "Perhaps you shall get a small bullock," said
Cornelius. "Oh, yes. Bullock. Yam. You'll get it if *he* said
so. He always speaks the truth. He stole everything I had.
I suppose you like a small bullock better than the loot of
many houses." "I would advise you to hold your tongue, or
somebody here may fling you overboard into this damned
fog," said Brown. The boat seemed to be standing still;
nothing could be seen, not even the river alongside, only
the water-dust flew and trickled, condensed, down their
beards and faces. It was weird, Brown told me. Every
individual man of them felt as though he were adrift
alone in a boat, haunted by an almost imperceptible suspicion of sighing, muttering ghosts. "Throw me out, would

you? But I would know where I was," mumbled Cornelius, surlily. "I've lived many years here." "Not long enough to see through a fog like this," Brown said, lolling back with his arm swinging to and fro on the useless tiller. "Yes. Long enough for that," snarled Cornelius. "That's very useful," commented Brown. "Am I to believe you could find that backway you spoke of blindfold, like this?" Cornelius grunted. "Are you too tired to row?" he asked after a silence. "No, by God!" shouted Brown suddenly. "Out with your oars there." There was a great knocking in the fog, which after a while settled into a regular grind of invisible sweeps against invisible thole-pins. Otherwise nothing was changed, and but for the slight splash of a dipped blade it was like rowing a balloon car in a cloud, said Brown. Thereafter Cornelius did not open his lips except to ask querulously for somebody to bale out his canoe, which was towing behind the long-boat. Gradually the fog whitened and became luminous ahead. To the left Brown saw a darkness as though he had been looking at the back of the departing night. All at once a big bough covered with leaves appeared above his head, and ends of twigs, dripping and still, curved slenderly close alongside. Cornelius, without a word, took the tiller from his hand.'

# CHAPTER FORTY-FOUR

'I DON'T think they spoke together again. The boat entered a narrow by-channel, where it was pushed by the oar-blades set into crumbling banks, and there was a gloom as if enormous black wings had been outspread above the mist that filled its depth to the summits of the trees. The branches overhead showered big drops through the gloomy fog. At a mutter from Cornelius, Brown ordered his men to load. "I'll give you a chance to get even with them before we're done, you dismal cripples, you," he said to his gang. "Mind you don't throw it away – you hounds." Low growls answered that speech. Cornelius showed much fussy concern for the safety of his canoe.

'Meantime Tamb' Itam had reached the end of his journey. The fog had delayed him a little, but he had paddled steadily, keeping in touch with the south bank. By-and-by daylight came like a glow in a ground glass globe. The shores made on each side of the river a dark smudge, in which one could detect hints of columnar forms and shadows of twisted branches high up. The mist was still thick on the water, but a good watch was being kept, for as Tamb' Itam approached the camp the figures of two men emerged out of the white vapour, and voices spoke to him boisterously. He answered, and presently a canoe lay alongside, and he exchanged news with the paddlers. All was well. The trouble was over. Then the men in the canoe let go their grip on the side of his dug-out and incontinently fell out of sight. He pursued his way till he heard voices coming to him quietly over the water, and saw, under the now lifting, swirling mist, the glow of many little fires burning on a sandy stretch, backed by lofty thin timber and bushes. There again a look-out was kept, for he was challenged. He shouted his name as the two last sweeps of his paddle ran his canoe up on the strand. It was a big camp. Men crouched in many knots under a subdued murmur of early morning talk. Many thin threads of smoke curled slowly on the white mist. Little shelters, elevated above the ground, had been built for the chiefs. Muskets were stacked in small pyramids, and long spears were stuck singly into the sand near the fires.

'Tamb' Itam, assuming an air of importance, demanded to be led to Dain Waris. He found the friend of his white lord lying on a raised couch made of bamboo, and sheltered by a sort of shed of sticks covered with mats. Dain Waris was awake, and a bright fire was burning before his sleeping-place, which resembled a rude shrine. The only son of Nakhoda Doramin answered his greeting kindly. Tamb' Itam began by handing him the ring which vouched for the truth of the messenger's words. Dain Waris, reclining on his elbow, bade him speak and tell all the news. Beginning with the consecrated formula, "The news is good," Tamb' Itam delivered Jim's own words. The white men, departing with the consent of all the chiefs, were to be allowed to pass down the river. In answer to a question or two Tamb' Itam then reported the proceedings of the last council. Dain Waris listened attentively to the end, toying with the ring which ultimately he slipped on the forefinger of his right hand. After hearing all he had to say he dismissed Tamb' Itam to have food and rest. Orders for the return in the afternoon were given immediately. Afterwards Dain Waris lay down again, open-eyed, while his personal attendants were preparing his food at the fire, by which Tamb' Itam also sat talking to the men who lounged up to hear the latest intelligence from the town. The sun was eating up the mist. A good watch was kept upon the reach of the main stream where the boat of the whites was expected to appear every moment.

'It was then that Brown took his revenge upon the world which, after twenty years of contemptuous and reckless bullying, refused him the tribute of a common robber's success. It was an act of cold-blooded ferocity, and it consoled him on his deathbed like a memory of an indomitable defiance. Stealthily he landed his men on the other side of the island opposite to the Bugis camp, and led them across. After a short but quite silent scuffle, Cornelius, who had tried to slink away at the moment of landing, resigned himself to show the way where the undergrowth was most sparse. Brown held both his skinny hands together behind his back in the grip of one vast fist, and now and then impelled him forward with a fierce push. Cornelius remained as mute as a fish, abject but faithful to his purpose, whose accomplishment loomed before him dimly. At the edge of the patch of forest Brown's men spread themselves out in cover and waited. The camp was plain from end to end before their eyes, and no one looked their way. Nobody even dreamed that the white men could have any knowledge of the narrow channel at the back of the island. When he judged the moment come, Brown yelled, "Let them have it," and fourteen shots rang out like one.

'Tamb' Itam told me the surprise was so great that, except for those who fell dead or wounded, not a soul of them moved for quite an appreciable time after the first discharge. Then a man screamed, and after that scream a great yell of amazement and fear went up from all the throats. A blind panic drove these men in a surging swaying mob to and fro along the shore like a herd of cattle afraid of the water. Some few jumped into the river then, but most of them did so only after the last discharge. Three times Brown's men fired into the ruck, Brown, the only one in view, cursing and yelling, "Aim low! aim low!"

'Tamb' Itam says that, as for him, he understood at the first volley what had happened. Though untouched he fell down and lay as if dead, but with his eyes open. At the sound of the first shots Dain Waris, reclining on the couch, jumped up and ran out upon the open shore, just in time to receive a bullet in his forehead at the second discharge. Tamb' Itam saw him fling his arms wide open before he fell. Then, he says, a great fear came upon him – not before. The white men retired as they had come – unseen.

'Thus Brown balanced his account with the evil fortune. Notice that even in this awful outbreak there is a superiority as of a man who carries right – the abstract thing – within the envelope of his common desires. It was not a vulgar and treacherous massacre; it was a lesson, a retribution – a demonstration of some obscure and awful attribute of our nature which, I am afraid, is not so very far under the surface as we like to think.

'Afterwards the whites depart unseen by Tamb' Itam, and seem to vanish from before men's eyes altogether; and the schooner, too, vanishes after the manner of stolen goods. But a story is told of a white long-boat picked up a month later in the Indian Ocean by a cargo-steamer. Two parched, yellow, glassy-eyed, whispering skeletons in her recognised the authority of a third, who declared that his name was Brown. His schooner, he reported, bound south with a cargo of Java sugar, had sprung a bad leak and sank under his feet. He and his companions were the survivors of a crew of six. The two died on board the steamer which rescued them. Brown lived to be seen by me, and I can testify that he had played his part to the last.

'It seems, however, that in going away they had neglected to cast off Cornelius's canoe. Cornelius himself Brown had let go at the beginning of the shooting, with a kick for a parting benediction. Tamb' Itam, after arising from amongst the dead, saw the Nazarene running up and down the shore amongst the corpses and the expiring fires. He uttered little cries. Suddenly he rushed to the water, and made frantic efforts to get one of the Bugis boats into the water. "Afterwards, till he had seen me," related Tamb' Itam, "he stood looking at the heavy canoe and scratching his head." "What became of him?" I asked. Tamb' Itam, staring at me, made an expressive gesture with his right arm. "Twice I struck, Tuan," he said. "When he beheld me approaching he cast himself violently on the ground and made a great outcry, kicking. He screeched like a frightened hen till he felt the point; then he was still, and lay staring at me while his life went out of his eyes."

'This done, Tamb' Itam did not tarry. He understood the importance of being the first with the awful news at the fort. There were, of course, many survivors of Dain Waris's party; but in the extremity of panic some had swum across the river, others had bolted into the bush. The fact is that they did not know really who struck that blow – whether more white robbers were not coming, whether they had not already got hold of the whole land. They imagined themselves to be the victims of a vast treachery, and utterly doomed to destruction. It is said that some small parties did not come in till three days afterwards. However, a few tried to make their way back to Patusan at once, and one of the canoes that were patrolling the river that morning was in sight of the camp at the very moment of the attack. It is true that at first the men in her leaped overboard and swam to the opposite bank, but afterwards they returned to their boat and started fearfully upstream. Of these Tamb' Itam had an hour's advance.

# CHAPTER FORTY-FIVE

'WHEN Tamb' Itam, paddling madly, came into the town-reach, the women, thronging the platforms before the houses, were looking out for the return of Dain Waris's little fleet of boats. The town had a festive air; here and there men, still with spears or guns in their hands, could be seen moving or standing on the shore in groups. Chinamen's shops had been opened early; but the market-place was empty, and a sentry, still posted at the corner of the fort, made out Tamb' Itam, and shouted to those within. The gate was wide open. Tamb' Itam jumped ashore and ran in headlong. The first person he met was the girl coming down from the house.

'Tamb' Itam, disordered, panting, with trembling lips and wild eyes, stood for a time before her as if a sudden spell had been laid on him. Then he broke out very quickly: "They have killed Dain Waris and many more." She clapped her hands, and her first words were, "Shut the gates." Most of the fortmen had gone back to their houses, but Tamb' Itam hurried on the few who remained for their turn of duty within. The girl stood in the middle of the courtyard while the others ran about. "Doramin," she cried despairingly, as Tamb' Itam passed her. Next time he went by he answered her thought rapidly, "Yes. But we have all the powder in Patusan." She caught him by the arm, and, pointing at the house, "Call him out," she whispered, trembling.

'Tamb' Itam ran up the steps. His master was sleeping. "It is I, Tamb' Itam," he cried at the door, "with tidings that cannot wait." He saw Jim turn over on the pillow and open his eyes, and he burst out at once. "This, Tuan, is a day of

366

evil, an accursed day." His master raised himself on his
elbow to listen – just as Dain Waris had done. And then
Tamb' Itam began his tale, trying to relate the story in
order, calling Dain Waris Panglima, and saying: "The
Panglima then called out to the chief of his own boatmen,
'Give Tamb' Itam something to eat'" – when his master put
his feet to the ground and looked at him with such a
discomposed face that the words remained in his throat.

'"Speak out," said Jim. "Is he dead?" "May you live long,"
cried Tamb' Itam. "It was a most cruel treachery. He ran out
at the first shots and fell...." His master walked to the
window and with his fist struck at the shutter. The room
was made light; and then in a steady voice, but speaking
fast, he began to give him orders to assemble a fleet of boats
for immediate pursuit, go to this man, to the other – send
messengers; and as he talked he sat down on the bed,
stooping to lace his boots hurriedly, and suddenly looked
up. "Why do you stand here?" he asked very red-faced.
"Waste no time." Tamb' Itam did not move. "Forgive me,
Tuan, but... but," he began to stammer. "What?" cried his
master aloud, looking terrible, leaning forward with his
hands gripping the edge of the bed. "It is not safe for thy
servant to go out amongst the people," said Tamb' Itam,
after hesitating a moment.

'Then Jim understood. He had retreated from one
world, for a small matter of an impulsive jump, and now
the other, the work of his own hands, had fallen in ruins
upon his head. It was not safe for his servant to go out
amongst his own people! I believe that in that very moment
he had decided to defy the disaster in the only way it
occurred to him such a disaster could be defied; but all I
know is that, without a word, he came out of his room and
sat before the long table, at the head of which he was
accustomed to regulate the affairs of his world, proclaiming
daily the truth that surely lived in his heart. The dark
powers should not rob him twice of his peace. He sat
like a stone figure. Tamb' Itam, deferential, hinted at

preparations for defence. The girl he loved came in and spoke to him, but he made a sign with his hand, and she was awed by the dumb appeal for silence in it. She went out on the verandah and sat on the threshold, as if to guard him with her body from dangers outside.

'What thoughts passed through his head – what memories? Who can tell? Everything was gone, and he who had been once unfaithful to his trust had lost again all men's confidence. It was then, I believe, he tried to write – to somebody – and gave it up. Loneliness was closing on him. People had trusted him with their lives – only for that; and yet they could never, as he had said, never be made to understand him. Those without did not hear him make a sound. Later, towards the evening, he came to the door and called for Tamb' Itam. "Well?" he asked. "There is much weeping. Much anger, too," said Tamb' Itam. Jim looked up at him. "You know," he murmured. "Yes, Tuan," said Tamb' Itam. "Thy servant does know, and the gates are closed. We shall have to fight." "Fight! What for?" he asked. "For our lives." "I have no life," he said. Tamb' Itam heard a cry from the girl at the door. "Who knows?" said Tamb' Itam. "By audacity and cunning we may even escape. There is much fear in men's hearts, too." He went out, thinking vaguely of boats and of open sea, leaving Jim and the girl together.

'I haven't the heart to set down here such glimpses as she had given me of the hour or more she had passed in there wrestling with him for the possession of her happiness. Whether he had any hope – what he expected, what he imagined – it is impossible to say. He was inflexible, and with the growing loneliness of his obstinacy his spirit seemed to rise above the ruins of his existence. She cried "Fight!" into his ear. She could not understand. There was nothing to fight for. He was going to prove his power in another way and conquer the fatal destiny itself. He came out into the courtyard, and behind him, with streaming hair, wild of face, breathless, she staggered out and leaned on the side of the doorway. "Open the gates," he ordered. Afterwards, turning to those of his men who were inside, he gave them leave to depart to their homes. "For how long, Tuan?" asked one of them timidly. "For all life," he said, in a sombre tone.

'A hush had fallen upon the town after the outburst of wailing and lamentation that had swept over the river, like a gust of wind from the opened abode of sorrow. But rumours flew in whispers, filling the hearts with consternation and horrible doubts. The robbers were coming back, bringing many others with them, in a great ship, and there would be no refuge in the land for any one. A sense of utter insecurity as during an earthquake pervaded the minds of men, who whispered their suspicions, looking at each other as if in the presence of some awful portent.

'The sun was sinking towards the forests when Dain Waris's body was brought into Doramin's *campong*. Four men carried it in, covered decently with a white sheet which the old mother had sent out down to the gate to meet her son on his return. They laid him at Doramin's feet, and the old man sat still for a long time, one hand on each knee, looking down. The fronds of palms swayed gently, and the foliage of fruit-trees stirred above his head. Every single man of his people was there, fully armed, when the old *nakhoda* at last raised his eyes. He moved them slowly over the crowd, as if seeking for a missing face. Again his chin sank on his breast. The whispers of many men mingled with the slight rustling of the leaves.

'The Malay who had brought Tamb' Itam and the girl to Samarang was there, too. "Not so angry as many," he said to me, but struck with a great awe and wonder at the "suddenness of men's fate, which hangs over their heads like a cloud charged with thunder." He told me that when Dain Waris's body was uncovered at a sign of Doramin's, he whom they often called the white lord's friend was disclosed lying unchanged with his eyelids a little open as if about to wake. Doramin leaned forward a little more, like one looking for something fallen on the ground. His eyes searched the body from its feet to its head, for the wound maybe. It was in the forehead and small; and there was no word spoken while one of the bystanders, stooping, took off the silver ring from the cold stiff hand. In silence he held it up before Doramin. A murmur of dismay and horror ran through the crowd at the sight of that familiar token. The old *nakhoda* stared at it, and suddenly let out one great fierce cry, deep from the chest, a roar of pain and fury, as mighty as the bellow of a wounded bull, bringing great fear into men's hearts, by the magnitude of his anger and his sorrow that could be plainly discerned without words. There was a great stillness afterwards for a space, while the body was being borne aside by four men. They laid it down under a tree, and on the instant, with one long shriek, all the women of the household began to wail together; they mourned with shrill cries; the sun was setting, and in the intervals of screamed lamentations the high sing-song voices of two old men intoning the Koran chanted alone.

'About this time Jim, leaning on a gun-carriage, looked at the river, and turned his back on the house; and the girl, in the doorway, panting as if she had run herself to a standstill, was looking at him across the yard. Tamb' Itam stood not far from his master, waiting patiently for what might happen. All at once Jim, who seemed to be lost in quiet thought, turned to him and said, "Time to finish this."

'"Tuan?" said Tamb' Itam, advancing with alacrity. He did not know what his master meant, but as soon as Jim made a movement the girl started, too, and walked down into the open space. It seems that no one else of the people of the house was in sight. She tottered slightly, and about half-way down called out to Jim, who had apparently resumed his peaceful contemplation of the river. He turned round, setting his back against the gun. "Will you fight?"

she cried. "There is nothing to fight for," he said; "nothing is lost." Saying this he made a step towards her. "Will you fly?" she cried again. "There is no escape," he said, stopping short, and she stood still also, silent, devouring him with her eyes. "And you shall go?" she said, slowly. He bent his head. "Ah!" she exclaimed, peering at him as it were, "you are mad or false. Do you remember the night I prayed you to leave me, and you said that you could not? That it was impossible! Impossible! Do you remember you said you would never leave me? Why? I asked you for no promise. You promised unasked – remember." "Enough, poor girl," he said. "I should not be worth having."

'Tamb' Itam said that while they were talking she would laugh loud and senselessly like one under the visitation of God. His master put his hands to his head. He was fully dressed as for every day, but without a hat. She stopped laughing suddenly, "For the last time," she cried, men-acingly, "will you defend yourself?" "Nothing can touch me," he said in a last flicker of superb egoism. Tamb' Itam saw her lean forward where she stood, open her arms, and run at him swiftly. She flung herself upon his breast and clasped him round the neck.

'"Ah! but I shall hold thee thus," she cried. . . . "Thou art mine!"

'She sobbed on his shoulder. The sky over Patusan was blood-red, immense, streaming like an open vein. An enormous sun nestled crimson amongst the tree-tops, and the forest below had a black and forbidding face.

'Tamb' Itam tells me that on that evening the aspect of the heavens was angry and frightful. I may well believe it, for I know that on that very day a cyclone passed within sixty miles of the coast, though there was hardly more than a languid stir of air in the place.

'Suddenly Tamb' Itam saw Jim catch her arms, trying to unclasp her hands. She hung on them with her head fallen back; her hair touched the ground. "Come here!" his master called, and Tamb' Itam helped to ease her down. It was difficult to separate her fingers. Jim, bending over her, looked earnestly upon her face, and all at once ran to the landing-stage. Tamb' Itam followed him, but turning his head, he saw that she had struggled up to her feet. She ran after them a few steps, then fell down heavily on her knees. "Tuan! Tuan!" called Tamb' Itam, "look back;" but Jim was already in a canoe, standing up paddle in hand. He did not look back. Tamb' Itam had just time to scramble in after him when the canoe floated clear. The girl was then on her knees, with clasped hands, at the water-gate. She remained thus for a time in a supplicating attitude before she sprang up. "You are false!" she screamed out after Jim. "Forgive me," he cried. "Never! Never!" she called back.

'Tamb' Itam took the paddle from Jim's hands, it being unseemly that he should sit while his lord paddled. When they reached the other shore his master forbade him to come any farther; but Tamb' Itam did follow him at a distance, walking up the slope to Doramin's *campong*.

'It was beginning to grow dark. Torches twinkled here and there. Those they met seemed awestruck, and stood aside hastily to let Jim pass. The wailing of women came from above. The courtyard was full of armed Bugis with their followers, and of Patusan people.

'I do not know what this gathering really meant. Were these preparations for war, or for vengeance, or to repulse a threatened invasion? Many days elapsed before the people had ceased to look out, quaking, for the return of the white men with long beards and in rags, whose exact relation to their own white man they could never understand. Even for those simple minds poor Jim remains under a cloud.

'Doramin, alone, immense and desolate, sat in his arm-chair with the pair of flintlock pistols on his knees, faced by an armed throng. When Jim appeared, at somebody's exclamation, all the heads turned round together, and then the mass opened right and left, and he walked up a lane of averted glances. Whispers followed him; murmurs:

"He has worked all the evil." "He hath a charm." ... He heard them – perhaps!

'When he came up into the light of torches the wailing of the women ceased suddenly. Doramin did not lift his head, and Jim stood silent before him for a time. Then he looked to the left, and moved in that direction with measured steps. Dain Waris's mother crouched at the head of the body, and the grey dishevelled hair concealed her face. Jim came up slowly, looked at his dead friend, lifting the sheet, then dropped it without a word. Slowly he walked back.

'"He came! He came!" was running from lip to lip, making a murmur to which he moved. "He hath taken it upon his own head," a voice said aloud. He heard this and turned to the crowd. "Yes. Upon my head." A few people recoiled. Jim waited awhile before Doramin, and then said gently, "I am come in sorrow." He waited again. "I am come ready and unarmed," he repeated.

'The unwieldy old man, lowering his big forehead like an ox under a yoke, made an effort to rise, clutching at the flintlock pistols on his knees. From his throat came gurgling, choking, inhuman sounds, and his two attendants helped him from behind. People remarked that the ring which he had dropped on his lap fell and rolled against the foot of the white man, and that poor Jim glanced down at the talisman that had opened for him the door of fame, love, and success within the wall of forests fringed with white foam, within the coast that under the western sun looks like the very stronghold of the night. Doramin, struggling to keep his feet, made with his two supporters a swaying, tottering group; his little eyes stared with an expression of mad pain, of rage, with a ferocious glitter, which the bystanders noticed; and then, while Jim stood stiffened and with bared head in the light of torches, looking him straight in the face, he clung heavily with his left arm round the neck of a bowed youth, and lifting deliberately his right, shot his son's friend through the chest.

'The crowd, which had fallen apart behind Jim as soon as Doramin had raised his hand, rushed tumultuously forward after the shot. They say that the white man sent right and left at all those faces a proud and unflinching glance. Then with his hand over his lips he fell forward, dead.

'And that's the end. He passes away under a cloud, inscrutable at heart, forgotten, unforgiven, and excessively romantic. Not in the wildest days of his boyish visions could he have seen the alluring shape of such an extraordinary success! For it may very well be that in the short moment of his last proud and unflinching glance, he had beheld the face of that opportunity which, like an Eastern bride, had come veiled to his side.

'But we can see him, an obscure conqueror of fame, tearing himself out of the arms of a jealous love at the sign, at the call of his exalted egoism. He goes away from a living woman to celebrate his pitiless wedding with a shadowy ideal of conduct. Is he satisfied – quite, now, I wonder? We ought to know. He is one of us – and have I not stood up once, like an evoked ghost, to answer for his eternal constancy? Was I so very wrong after all? Now he is no more, there are days when the reality of his existence comes to me with an immense, with an overwhelming force; and yet upon my honour there are moments, too, when he passes from my eyes like a disembodied spirit astray amongst the passions of this earth, ready to surrender himself faithfully to the claim of his own world of shades.

'Who knows? He is gone, inscrutable at heart, and the poor girl is leading a sort of soundless, inert life in Stein's house. Stein has aged greatly of late. He feels it himself, and says often that he is "preparing to leave all this; preparing to leave..." while he waves his hand sadly at his butterflies.

*September 1899 – July 1900.*

# NOTES

## SOURCES

*Lord Jim* demonstrates Conrad's use of the four major sources of material for his fiction: personal experience, observation, the experience of others and reading.

Personal Experience
Much in the novel derives from Conrad's experiences as a merchant seaman during the three voyages that he made in the Eastern seas. On 14th March 1883 the captain and crew of the barque *Palestine*, in which Conrad was second mate, abandoned her in the Bangka Strait in the south-east Asian archipelago when her cargo of coal caught fire. After a thirteen-and-a-half-hour journey in an open boat, Conrad first saw the East when he reached Muntok, on the island of Bangka, off the coast of Sumatra (cf. 'Youth'). He went on to Singapore where an inquiry into the loss of the *Palestine* was held and he was discharged. Conrad stayed one month in the city that was to become the 'great Eastern port' of *Lord Jim*, *The Shadow-Line* and 'The End of the Tether', and his descriptions in these novels accurately mirror the parts of the city he knew: the area round the sea-front where the Post Office, Harbour Office, Cathedral, Hotel de l'Europe, Sailors' Home and padang were situated.

On 22nd September 1885 he arrived in Singapore for the second time on the *Tilkhurst* departing again on 19th October 1885, but it was his third visit that was to be most significant for his later novels. In 1887 he sailed from Amsterdam as first mate in the sailing ship *Highland Forest*. His back was injured by a flying spar during the voyage, he was discharged at Samarang and, on the advice of a doctor, went into hospital in Singapore – as did *Lord Jim* – and, again like his hero, on being discharged from hospital did not return to England but took a berth on a local ship. This was the steamship *Vidar*, which traded among the islands of the south-east Asian archipelago. Conrad was with her from 22nd August 1887 to 4th January 1888, making four journeys in her. During these voyages he came to know the Berau River in Borneo and the settlement of Tandjong Redeb on its banks. Here he made the acquaintance, at a trading post, of Charles Olmeijer (the inspiration for Almayer of *Almayer's Folly*) and, presumably, of Jim Lingard, nephew of Captain William Lingard who had established the trading post and was to be the inspiration for the Captain Tom Lingard of Conrad's Malayan novels. It was these voyages to Berau that provided the setting for the second part of *Lord Jim*, and Jim Lingard is the source for Jim in that he was a white man living alone of his kind in an isolated Malay village.

Observation
This source of information is, of course, closely linked with personal experience and the experience of others, but Conrad's presentation of Singapore, Bangkok and the Berau River in this novel demonstrates the accuracy of his observation during a brief experience of the area. Geographically and topographically, he is very exact. And during his first visit to Singapore he must have seen in port the pilgrim ship *Jeddah*, and have seen her again on her second visit when her name had been changed to the *Diamond* and she was up for sale. He must have heard then the story of the *Jeddah*, and probably recalled reading, in the London papers in August 1880, of the scandal that surrounded her. It was the story of the *Jeddah* and the experiences of some of her crew that were to provide the major incident for *Lord Jim*.

The Experience of Others
The *Jeddah*, owned by the Singapore Steamship Company, carried Muslim pilgrims bound for Mecca from Singapore to Jeddah, an Arabian port on the Red Sea. On 17th July 1880 she left Singapore with about 1,000 pilgrims on board, crossing the Straits of Malacca, calling at Penang, continuing through the Bay of Bengal and passing Cape Guardafui.

On the 10th August the steamship *Scindia* arrived in Aden with the Captain, Clark, and the European officers of the *Jeddah* on board, and they reported that the *Jeddah* had foundered with all pilgrims on board. Syed Muhammad bin Alsagoff, Managing Director of the Singapore Steamship Company, received the following telegram (printed in the local press) on 12th August:

> Aden, 10th August 8.20 p.m.
> Jeddah foundered. Self, wife, Syed Omar,
> 18 others saved.
> > Clark.

Then on 11th August another ship, the *Antenor*, towed the *Jeddah* into Aden with all the pilgrims safe on board, and Syed Muhammed received the following cable:

> Aden, 11th August 9.15 p.m.
> *Antenor* towed down here *Jeddah* full of water,
> All life saved, now in charge of Government.
> Telegraph further particulars tomorrow. Omar
> gone Jeddah last night.

This was 'that scandal of the eastern seas that would not die out', that had the whole water-front of Singapore talking. The incident made headlines in London and Singapore, and was the subject of two inquiries, one in Aden and one in Singapore, a debate in the Singapore Legislative Assembly, and a question in the British House of Commons. The following quotations from London newspapers give some indication of the reaction to the event in Britain: '... There was something very unpleasant in the facts thus stated; for, to the honour of sailors, nothing is more rare than that, in a disaster at sea, the Captain and the principal officers of the vessel should be the chief or sole survivors...' (*The Times*); 'The relief which is felt at the safety of the pilgrims will be modified by a feeling of indignation and horror at what seems the cowardly desertion of their post and trust by the master and seamen of the ship.' (*Daily News*.)

Investigation showed that during heavy weather the *Jeddah* began to leak and her boilers broke loose. The captain ordered the ship's boats to be swung out, although there were not enough boats for the number of passengers; the pilgrims thought they were being abandoned and in the disturbances that followed, Captain Clark and his officers abandoned the ship.

After the inquiry at Aden, Captain Clark had his certificate of competency as a master suspended for three years. 'Public excitement has risen to fever heat here,' commented the *Straits Times Overland Journal*, 'in surveying the conduct of Captain Clark, who is well known here [in Singapore], and his officers and engineers in deserting the S.S. *Jeddah*.'

It is clear that the *Patna* incident in the novel is based on the *Jeddah* and her story and that Conrad learnt of it through many sources – personal observation, gossip among seamen, newspaper reports. And it was from the *Jeddah* incident that he found the source for his hero *Lord Jim*. Jim is mate of the *Patna*, the son of a vicar, and after the abandonment of the pilgrims becomes a ship-chandler's water-clerk in the Eastern port. The first mate of the *Jeddah* was A. P. Williams, who was reprimanded by the court of inquiry for his part in the desertion of the ship. His father was vicar of Porthleven, Cornwall, and like Jim he was one of five sons. He was twenty-eight when he joined the *Jeddah* in Singapore (Jim was not yet four and twenty). Like Jim, he returned to the Eastern port that was buzzing with news of the desertion and faced it out, even to the extent of writing to the *Straits Times Overland Journal* a letter justifying his actions in which he stated: 'I am the Chief Officer of the *Jeddah*. . . .' He remained in Singapore, sticking it out as a water-clerk for the firm of McAlisters, ship-chandlers. He prospered, married a beautiful Eurasian girl, as Jim lived with his Jewel, and celebrated his silver wedding at the Hotel de l'Europe in 1908, the hotel Conrad describes as the Malabar Hotel in the novel. He ran his own ship-chandler's business at one time, but went bankrupt. He died in 1916 and was buried in the Bidadari Cemetery, Singapore, his obituary in the newspaper still referring to his part in the *Jeddah* disaster, and his tombstone having a carving of an anchor on it.

Conrad says in his Author's Note that he saw the original of Jim pass by 'in the commonplace surroundings of an Eastern roadstead', but he was more familiar with A. P. Williams and his story than this suggests. He must have heard of Williams when he served in the *Vidar*, for Williams was also first mate of the *Vidar* some years earlier, and he may also have met him in Singapore, and perhaps seen him at work as a ship-chandler's water-clerk there.

The experience of another seaman was used by Conrad in the story of Captain Brierly's suicide. This was based on the suicide of Captain Wallace, of the famous clipper *Cutty Sark*, in 1880. Like Brierly, Wallace was a young and very successful skipper, being master of the *Cutty Sark* at the age of twenty-seven and, in the same year, for no apparent reason, he committed suicide by walking over the side of his ship. The reason put forward was that he feared an inquiry into the escape of his chief officer who had killed a seaman. (For further information see Sherry: *Conrad's Eastern World*, Chapter 14.) Conrad did not himself give away the origin of Brierly but a Miss Dickson, who met Conrad in Ajaccio, Corsica, in 1920, recalled to me in 1966 that Conrad had admitted that he only met Brierly once: 'a tall, handsome man, with a neatly clipped golden beard – wearing a blue serge suit and a bowler hat – that was in a shipping office in London'.

Reading
Conrad appears to have drawn upon a number of books about the Far East to provide additional information, names, incidents and suggestions for settings and characters. Richard Curle recalled: 'He [Conrad] loved old memoirs and travels – and I think Wallace's *Malay Archipelago* was his favourite bedside book.' Wallace, a naturalist who travelled in the Malay archipelago, is in part the source for Stein; his book suggested the imprisonment of Jim by Rajah Allang, and the characters of Doramin and his wife and their home. It would seem most likely also that the life and adventures of Rajah Brooke of Sarawak influenced the second part of *Lord Jim*. Conrad's use of such sources can best be demonstrated by some quotations.

Alfred Russel Wallace, *The Malay Archipelago* (London, 1894): ... we reached our destination ... and entered the outer court of a house belonging to one of the chiefs ... Here we were requested to seat ourselves under an open shed with a raised floor of bamboo, a place used to receive visitors and hold audiences. Turning our horses to graze on the luxuriant grass of the courtyard, we waited ... As we had not yet breakfasted, we begged he (the Malay interpreter) would get us something to eat, which he promised to do as soon as possible. It was however about two hours before anything appeared, when a small tray was brought containing two saucers of rice, four small fried fish, and a few vegetables ... At length, about four o'clock the Pumbuckle (chief) [presumably 'Penghulu': a headman] made his appearance ... [and] he seemed somewhat disturbed, and asked if we had brought a letter from the Anak Agong (Son of

Heaven), which is the title of the Rajah of Lombock. This we had
not done, thinking it quite unnecessary; and he then abruptly told us
that he must go and speak to his Rajah, to see if we could stay. Hours
passed away, night came and he did not return. I began to think we
were suspected of some evil designs . . . The sun set, and it soon
became dark, and we got rather hungry as we sat wearily under the
shed and no one came. Still hour after hour we waited, till about
nine o'clock, the Pumbuckle, the Rajah, some priests, and a number
of their followers arrived . . . Then the Rajah asked what we wanted
. . . questions were asked about my guns, and what powder I had,
and whether I used shot or bullets; also what the birds were for, and
how I preserved them, and what was done with them in England.
Each of my answers and explanations was followed by a low and
serious conversation which we could not understand, but the pur-
port of which we could guess. They were evidently quite puzzled,
and did not believe a word we had told them. They then inquired if
we were really English, and not Dutch; and although we strongly
asserted our nationality, they did not seem to believe us. (pp. 127–8.)

   At length, about one in the morning, the whole party rose to
depart . . . We now begged the interpreter . . . to show us a place to
sleep in, at which he seemed very much surprised, saying he thought
we were very well accommodated where we were . . . all we could get
after another hour's talk was a native mat and pillow, and a few old
curtains to hang round three sides of the open shed and protect us a
little from the cold breeze. (pp. 128–9.) Cf. *Lord Jim*, pp. 224–6.

Wallace, *The Malay Archipelago:*

As soon as I was well, I again went to Goa, accompanied by Mr
Mesman, to beg the Rajah's assistance in getting a small house built
for me near the forest. We found him at a cock-fight in a shed near
his palace, which however he immediately left to receive us, and
walked with us up an inclined plane of boards which served for stairs
to his house. This was large, well built, and lofty, with bamboo floor
and glass windows. The greater part of it seemed to be one large hall
divided by the supporting posts. Near a window sat the Queen
squatting on a rough wooden armchair, chewing the everlasting

sirih and betel-nut, while a brass spittoon by her side and a sirih-box in front were ready to administer to her wants. The Rajah seated himself opposite to her in a similar chair, and a similar spittoon and sirih-box were held by a little boy squatting at his side.... Several young women, some the Rajah's daughters, others slaves, were standing about; a few were working at frames making sarongs, but most of them were idle.... Everything had a dingy and faded appearance.... The only thing that excited some degree of admiration was the quiet and dignified manner of the Rajah, and the great respect always paid to him. (pp. 167–8) Cf. *Lord Jim*, pp. 230–1.

Major Fred McNair, *Perak and the Malays: 'Sarong' and 'Kris'* (London, 1878), gives the account of a British Admiral's interview with the Sultan of Selangor who

> was surrounded by his chiefs and people...The Admiral, in referring to the barbarity of the Jungra piracy, advised and urged upon the Sultan to caution his people against being guilty of such acts in future, pointing out how it was impossible that they could be left unpunished...The Sultan listened very attentively, and then turning quickly round to his people, he exclaimed: *Dungar lah, jangan kitah main main lagi!* – 'Hear now, my people! Don't let us have any more of this little game!' (p. 289).

Cf. *Lord Jim*, pp 224–5.

## THE TEXT AND ITS GROWTH

*Lord Jim* was begun, as Conrad records in his Author's Note, as a short story concerned only with the pilgrim ship episode. It was written between May 1898 (on 3rd June he sent Meldrum, the literary adviser to Blackwood's, 'the first 18 pages of *Jim: A sketch*') and 14th July 1900 when it was completed 'with a steady drag of twenty-one hours':

> I sent wife and child out of the house (to London) and sat down at 9 a.m. with a desperate resolve to be done with it. Now and then I took a walk round the house, out at one door in at the other. Ten-minute meals. A great hush. Cigarette ends growing

into a mound similar to a cairn over a dead hero. Moon rose over the barn, looked in at the window and climbed out of sight. Dawn broke, brightened. I put the lamp out and went on, with the morning breeze blowing the sheets of MS. all over the room. Sun rose. I wrote the last word and went into the dining-room. Six o'clock I shared a piece of cold chicken with Escamillo (who was very miserable and in want of sympathy, having missed the child dreadfully all day). Felt very well, only sleepy; had a bath at seven and at 8.30 was on my way to London.

(*Letter to Galsworthy, 20th July 1900.*)

It was a very disturbed period of his life, but also a fruitful one. He was especially plagued by financial difficulties and was particularly distressed by the need to finish *The Rescue* (not completed until 1919) for which he had received an advance of £250. He was making strong efforts to return to the sea but by November 1898 had given up hopes of obtaining a command: 'This confounded literature has ruined me entirely,' he wrote to Cunninghame Graham on 9th November 1898. In September he met Ford Madox Hueffer and in October the Conrads moved to Pent Farm which they rented from him, and a productive period of writing began which included collaboration with Hueffer.

Conrad was ill in January 1900, and in May went to Dover to see Stephen Crane, his close friend, who was moving to the Black Forest in an attempt to save his life. Crane died at Badenweiler on 5th June.

Although Conrad says that he began *Lord Jim* as a short story, dealing with the incident of the pilgrim ship, which he thought might make up a volume of 'short tales' which would include 'Youth', the manuscript suggests that as early as May 1898, when he first drafted the story of Jim, he had in mind the idea of Jim's being driven from civilization to a Malay village. And a further indication of his plans when he began writing is given in his inscription in Curle's copy of the novel: 'When I began this story, which some people think my best – personally I don't – I formed the resolve to cram as much character and episode into it as it could hold. This explains its length which the story itself does not justify.'

Even so, while in May 1898 he contemplated a story of twenty to twenty-five thousand words which would run to two or three instalments in *Blackwood's Magazine*, by 6th July 1899 he saw it running to forty thousand words, and the story ultimately covered fourteen instalments and was 120,000 words long.

Having sent 'the first 18 pages' to Meldrum in June 1898, by 14th February 1899 Conrad was writing to William Blackwood: 'I have a story *Jim* half-written or one-third written (10,000 words),' but the real pressure of writing the novel seems to have begun in about July 1899 when he began sending copy regularly to Meldrum. Through his letters one can trace the ups and downs of his confidence: 'I am going straight ahead with Jim and am rather pleased with him so far' (to David S. Meldrum, 22nd August 1899); 'I also send you 2d inst of Jim – which is too wretched for words' (to Edward Garnett, 19th November 1899); 'I am old and sick and in debt – but lately I've found I can still write – *it* comes! *it* comes! – and I am young and healthy and rich' (to Edward Garnett, 26th March 1900). One can trace also the way in which the story grows and grows under his hands, and his constant attempts to bring it to an end: 'Jim is approaching his climax' (to David S. Meldrum, 18th October 1899); 'Jan and Febr... instalments without being unduly long will contain the end of the story' (to David S. Meldrum, 24th October 1899); 'I still think I shall finish the story this year (to David S. Meldrum, 17th December 1899); 'the end... seems well in view now' (to William Blackwood, 26th December 1899); 'The next batch should be the last' (to David S. Meldrum, 3rd January 1900); 'I am still at Jim' (to Edward Garnett, 26th March 1900); 'I feel the need...to assure you that *Lord Jim* has an end' (to William Blackwood, 12th April 1900); 'The last word of Lord Jim is written' (to William Blackwood, 14th July 1900). On 14th July 1900 Meldrum wrote to Blackwood: 'Fortunately, I was in the office this morning when Conrad called with the conclusion of *Jim*, which went off to the type-writer *instanter*. He was, of course, in great spirits at being finished, and goes to Bruges on Wednesday, I think.'

The serialization was from October 1899 to November 1900 in *Blackwood's Magazine*. This was carefully revised for book publication in the first English edition by William Blackwood & Son, 1900, revisions mainly taking the form of cutting in the first half, particularly to make less explicit his dealing with Jim's psychology. Conrad made two interesting statements about the later English and American editions. Of the first American edition, published by Doubleday and McClure in 1900, he wrote in Richard Curle's copy that it was 'neither revised nor in any other way corrected by me. It is probably much nearer the text of *B'Wood's Maga.* than the first English Ed. of book form.' And in 1917 he wrote: 'The only edition in which I take interest is the Collected edition (limited to 1,000 sets in England and the U.S.) which Doubleday, Page in New York and Wm. Heinemann here are going to publish after the war... the text... will be exactly the text of the English first editions freed from misprints and with, perhaps, a few (very few) verbal alterations.

The 'Author's Note' was first published in the second English edition by J. M. Dent & Sons, in 1917.

## THE MANUSCRIPT

The manuscript of the novel has its own interest. One part, probably written in May 1898, is in a brown leather album inlaid with metal and mother-of-pearl, which belonged to Conrad's grandmother, Teofila Bobrowska. In it are copied twenty-five pages of Polish poetry in his grandmother's handwriting. On the remaining twenty-eight pages Conrad has written *Tuan Jim: A Sketch*, the first draft of *Lord Jim*, and some other fragments. This is in the Houghton Library, Harvard. It corresponds more or less to the first two chapters of the novel. In the Rosenbach Collection is a second fragment of manuscript of 356 pages, incomplete at both ends and with considerable gaps. There are also seven typewritten pages, covering the first four and a half pages of Chapter 14, in the Rosenbach museum, and a corrected copy of chapters 31 to 35 of the serial publication.